TERRY EICHER was for many years Assistant Director
of Yale University's Institute for Social and Policy Studies,
and he is currently completing his Ph.D. in clinical
psychology at Yale. The father of two daughters, he also
writes fiction, some of which has appeared recently in
the *North American Review.* **JESSE D. GELLER** is Associate Clinical Professor of Psychology at Yale University
School of Medicine, as well as Director of the Yale
Psychological Services Clinic. He recently co-edited
another anthology entitled *Psychotherapy: Portraits in
Fiction.* He also has two daughters.

FATHERS AND DAUGHTERS

Portraits in Fiction

◇ ◇ ◇

EDITED BY

TERRY EICHER

AND **JESSE D. GELLER**

A PLUME BOOK

PLUME
Published by the Penguin Group
Penguin Books USA Inc., 375 Hudson Street, New York, New York 10014, U.S.A.
Penguin Books Ltd, 27 Wrights Lane, London W8 5TZ, England
Penguin Books Australia Ltd, Ringwood, Victoria, Australia
Penguin Books Canada Ltd, 2801 John Street, Markham, Ontario, Canada L3R 1B4
Penguin Books (N.Z.) Ltd, 182–190 Wairau Road, Auckland 10, New Zealand

Penguin Books Ltd, Registered Offices: Harmondsworth, Middlesex, England

Published by Plume, an imprint of New American Library, a division of Penguin Books USA Inc.
Previously published in an NAL Books edition

First Printing, May, 1991
10 9 8 7 6 5 4 3 2 1

 REGISTERED TRADEMARK—MARCA REGISTRADA

Acknowledgments

(For permissions to use these stories please turn to page 303.)

Library of Congress Cataloging-in-Publication Data

Fathers and daughters : portraits in fiction / edited by Terry Eicher and Jesse D. Geller.
   p.   cm.
   Reprint. Originally published: New York : NAL Books, 1990.
   ISBN 0-452-26618-1
   1. Fathers and daughters—Fiction. 2. Short stories, American. 3. Short stories, English.
I. Eicher, Terry. II. Geller, Jesse D.
[PS648.F36F3   1991]
813'.01083520431—dc20   91-7890
                                                                         CIP

PRINTED IN THE UNITED STATES OF AMERICA
Original hardcover design by Leonard Telesca

For our parents, wives, and daughters

Eichers	*Gellers*
Don	William
Yvonne	Thelma
Ginny	Ruth
Jessica	Elizabeth
Caitlin	Jennifer

◇ ◇ ◇

Contents

◇ ◇ ◇

Introduction

This book contains twenty-three short stories by celebrated writers about fathers of daughters. Both of us have two daughters. The stories in this volume have helped us think more clearly about their profound influences on our lives. The stories have also brought us into the company of other fathers of daughters. They are welcome company, for like other men, we have rarely given full voice to what our daughters mean to us.

The stories we have chosen focus attention on the ways in which the continuing process of learning to be a father influences a man's life. The writers of these stories pose basic questions: What pleasures and fears are aroused in a father by his love for his daughter? How do fathers and daughters cope with inevitable disappointments in one another? How does a daughter affect a man's marriage, his work, and his relationship to his own parents? How does a father let go of his daughter? How would a man answer these questions if he were raising a son rather than a daughter?

We are accustomed to being curious about the effects that parents have on their children. For most people, though, a radical shift of perspective is required to think instead about children's effects on their parents and on the way their parents' personalities continue to develop throughout adulthood. Social scientists have rarely asked men to speak candidly about what it means to be a father, of either sons or daughters. There is, in fact, not one single study in the psychological literature that examines the relationship between fathers and daughters from the father's perspective. Consequently psychologists do not know whether the changes in a man's life that are set in motion by the birth of a daughter are different, in nature and extent, from those initiated by the birth of a son. But we suspect—as the stories suggest—that daughters and sons exert their influences in distinctive ways.

We read hundreds of stories before making our final selections. What we discovered is that the unfolding internal dramas of fatherhood represent a relatively unexplored terrain in literature, as well as in psychology. Many more stories are about fathers and sons than fathers and daughters; and most stories about fathers and daughters concentrate on the (often disappointed) daughter's views of her father. Many fewer stories take the *father's* perspective that we wished to explore in this volume. This imbalance is not too surprising. Literature, like psychology, is often about a child's struggle to create an identity separate from his or her parents. Even so, of course, there *are* great representations of fathers of daughters in Shakespeare, Hawthorne, Balzac, James, and others—and we were able to assemble this array of arresting short fiction by recent and contemporary masters.

Obviously there is no one, all-encompassing truth about what it means to be a father, nor is there a single "type" of father. We believe that at one and the same time fathers and children influence each other's development. We believe that being a father plays a vital role in defining the ways men think about themselves, their relationships, values, and priorities. We have come to this view as a result of our experiences as psychotherapists, as research psychologists concerned with adult development, and as fathers of daughters. The stories in this volume reveal that fatherhood can exert as powerful an influence on a man as work and marriage. The way raising a daughter directs a man's striving for meaning, maturity, and virtue reverberates through this volume. These stories illuminate what daughters mean to their fathers and how fathers interact with their daughters over the course of their lives together.

The men brought together in this volume span the twentieth century and illustrate a range of life circumstances familiar to our time. Some of their dilemmas and uncertainties follow from the fact that the ways in which fathers and daughters interact are evolving as social and work roles for men and women change. Some of the challenges they face are timeless, as are the satisfactions they derive from giving love to and receiving love from their daughters.

The stories are arranged in a roughly chronological order that carries the reader from the father of a three-week-old daughter in Raymond Carver's "Distance," the first story, to the elderly fathers of middle-aged daughters in the final stories, E. M. Forster's "The Road from Colonus" and Muriel Spark's "The Fathers' Daughters." Similar scenes recur and resonate throughout this volume and throughout the life cycles of these fathers and daughters. Taken together, in order, the stories coalesce and can be read as chapters of a novel that carries *one* man—a single character of many faces and circumstances—forward through his life with his daughter, from her infancy in the full strength of his youth to his decline and dependence on her in his old or middle age. For its richest yield, therefore, we recommend reading this volume from start to finish.

Carver's "Distance" shows us that the responsibilities of fatherhood—even more powerfully than marriage itself—can catapult a man into adulthood. In Carver's story a father reminisces with his daughter about his decision to forgo a hunting trip in order to care for her when she was three weeks old. Renouncing the easy companionship of male friends is one of the sacrifices fathers may be asked to make on behalf of their daughters. In the poem "Home Burial," Robert Frost wrote that "a man must partly give up being a man/with women-folk." Some men come to welcome this predicament as much as they fear it.

These stories indicate that the most compelling responsibility that fathers feel toward their daughters is to protect them. A father may find that his wish to protect his daughter brings him into conflict with other men. In F. Scott Fitzgerald's "The Baby Party," a father does battle with a neighbor to defend the honor of his two-and-a-half-year-old daughter. Throughout this volume fathers struggle mightily to protect their daughters, as we see in S. Y. Agnon's "Outset of the Day," Andre Dubus's "A Father's Story," and in Joyce Carol Oates's "Wednesday's Child," in which a father takes his young autistic daughter on a rare and threatening outing. In Dubus's "A Father's Story," a father's desire to protect his daughter conflicts with his religious faith. Dubus's father insists that fathers are less equipped to endure the suffering of a daughter than a son. Sometimes fathers must reckon painfully with their inevitable failures to protect their daughters adequately. In Budd Schulberg's "A Short Digest of a Long Novel," for example, a father impotently watches his three-year-old daughter betrayed by a little boy and struggles with his own complicated reaction to her disillusionment.

Schulberg's is the first of many fathers in this collection who have misgivings about the men with whom their daughters are involved. These misgivings typically arise most intensely during their daughters' adolescence. The breakthrough into puberty is problematic for the men in these stories, not least because they sometimes become dimly aware of unsettling erotic undercurrents in their homes. As their daughters become sexually involved with men for the first time, they may also feel the loss of a more innocent love. Those themes are taken up in John Updike's "Man and Daughter in the Cold," Dubus's "A Father's Story," and Joyce Cary's "Growing Up," a surrealistic story about the primitive fears evoked in a father while he roughhouses with his pubescent daughters.

In William Trevor's "Autumn Sunshine," an elderly Irish clergyman with four adult daughters receives a visit from his estranged youngest daughter and her boyfriend. The visit prompts a reconsideration of his life with daughters and a rich and subtle elaboration of the folk wisdom that fathers always contend with mixed feelings toward their daughters' boyfriends, lovers, fiancés, and husbands.

It is not only with other men that these fathers find their relationships altered. Most fathers are also husbands. The birth of a child may enhance or undermine the quality of their marriages. Again, this theme is introduced in the very first story, for it is the wife in Carver's story who sharply outlines for her young husband the new configuration of his life and persuades him to honor it and to remain with them. Fathers also find themselves torn between loyalties to wives and daughters in Fitzgerald's "The Baby Party" and in Updike's "Should Wizard Hit Mommy?" in which father and daughter dispute mother's fate as they make up a bedtime story together.

And yet, almost nothing struck us more forcefully than how frequently mothers are absent in the stories we considered for this volume. Among the stories we have included, mothers are (or appear to be) *killed off* in Max Apple's "Bridging," Stephen Minot's "The Tide and Isaac Bates," Trevor's "Autumn Sunshine," Forster's "The Road from Colonus," and Spark's "The Fathers' Daughters"; *divorced* in Carver's "Distance," Harold Brodkey's "On the Waves," Herbert Gold's "I Want a Sunday Kind of Love," Alice Adams's "Snow," Mavis Gallant's "The Prodigal Parent," and Dubus's "A Father's Story," *elsewhere* in Oates's "Wednesday's Child," Minot's "Crossing," Cary's "Growing Up," and Updike's "Man and Daughter in the Cold"; mysteriously *missing* in Agnon's "At the Outset of the Day"; and *unmentioned* in Schulberg's "A Short Digest of a Long Novel." Must the mother be absent in order to permit fathers and daughters the opportunity for intimacy? At the very least, this seems to be a narrative device that throws into bold relief fathers' and daughters' mutual dependencies, with their attendant rewards and hardships.

Daughters sometimes provide their fathers with opportunities to reflect on the unfinished business of their own childhood, including their relationships with their own parents. The feelings that come to light may be either painful or imbued with the playfulness of childhood. In Minot's "Crossings," for example, a ten-year-old daughter's conversion to Catholicism prompts an evening conversation in which a father is moved to remember his childhood and the origins of his own atheism.

The wrenching dilemma faced by mothers who work outside their homes and at the same time yearn to be with their children is now commonplace in discussions about contemporary American families. These stories point to the complex interplay of work and family among fathers too. In both Fitzgerald's "The Baby Party" and Cary's "Growing Up," we see a father's troubling reentry into domestic life at the end of a day at work. In Peter Taylor's "Je Suis Perdu," an American scholar in Paris considers the sources of satisfaction in his life and is surprised by the way his fervent desire for productive solitude is mysteriously challenged by the claims of his daughter and the rest of his family. And in R. K. Narayan's "Forty-Five a Month," a bookkeeper in India feels trapped at his office while his daughter waits excitedly for him to return home and fulfill a promise. It is an O'Henry-like story of a man's poignant failure to balance the reciprocally antagonistic demands of family and work.

Our work as psychotherapists has made us aware of the often tragic consequences of failures of communication between fathers and daughters. Happily, long conversations between fathers and daughters abound in these stories. In Brodkey's "On the Waves," the conversation takes place aboard a gondola in Venice. The story is a romance of sorts, as a divorced American father surrenders to his love for his seven-year-old daughter. Their conversation captures the swift, unexpected, and sometimes unspoken shifts in emotion that a man can feel toward his daughter in a single afternoon—boredom, irritation, respect, wonder, jealousy, guilt, protectiveness, delight, impatience, weariness, and adoration. This range of feeling is evident in the conversations we overhear between fathers and young daughters in Updike's "Should Wizard Hit Mommy?" Gold's " 'I Want a Sunday Kind of Love,' " Apple's "Bridging," and Minot's "Crossings," as well as between fathers and adult daughters in Trevor's "Autumn Sunshine," Spark's "The Fathers' Daughters"; John O'Hara's "Appearances," in which a father and daughter have a conversation that tests the limits of intimacy as they dance around a family secret; and Adams's "Snow," in which a father goes on a picnic with his lesbian daughter and her lover.

Even the most eloquent men find it difficult to define and express their love for their daughters. Note how often a similiar scene appears in these stories: A man looks at his daughter, as Agnon puts it, "the way a father glances at his little daughter"; he gestures silently; he is unable to find words adequate to his love. These silent gestures recur most prominently in Agnon's "At the Outset of the Day," Brodkey's "On the Waves," Taylor's "Je Suis Perdu," and Dubus's "A Father's Story." The love fathers feel toward their daughters often appears to exist on the frontiers of the expressible.

As their daughters proceed from childhood to adulthood in these stories, the fathers find that they must repeatedly reckon with renunciations and separations, and what seems to them a painful impending loss. This specter of loss is haunting in the stories about divorced fathers, such as Gold's " 'I Want a Sunday Kind of Love,' " in which a father aching with guilt and hope travels to Cleveland for a Christmas visit with his young daughters. In Apple's "Bridging," a widower in Houston becomes an assistant Girl Scout leader of a troop that his isolated nine-year-old daughter refuses to join; instead she remains home and clings to their shared interest in sports. Apple's father is determined to facilitate the myriad separations and renunciations required of fathers and daughters. In the face of impending loss, these men sometimes seem to yearn to stop time and hold on to a moment with their daughters. Updike's "Man and Daughter in the Cold" captures such an instant as a father and his daughter, in "a conspiracy of love," are companions in a hazardous adventure on the ski slopes. Her adroitness and concern for his health bring him to the piercing realization that the innocent intimacies of her childhood are fleeting.

The father in "Man and Daughter in the Cold" realizes, too, that he is aging. Oedipus was led old and blind by Antigone; Milton was read to in his blindness by his daughters. What is it like for fathers to depend on their daughters for care? Usually this happens in old age, as we discover in Spark's "The Fathers' Daughters," in which we see father and daughter "shrewd in their love for each other," or in Forster's "The Road from Colonus," in which an aged and confused father traveling in Oedipus' territory is both led and thwarted by his daughter. But we also see fathers dependent upon their daughters at earlier ages, too, for example, in Larry Woiwode's "Blindness," with its own echoes of Oedipus and Antigone, in which a drunken father is led in the dark by his four-year-old daughter.

Disillusionment and disappointment appear and reappear in these stories. Daughters are disappointing to their fathers in Minot's "Crossings," Cary's "Growing Up," Trevor's "Autumn Sunshine," and Forster's "The Road from Colonus." In Gallant's "The Prodigal Parent," an older father returns to his daughter, yearning for her love and care, yet still cannot restrain himself from alienating and disappointing her, as he has done all his life. Fathers reckon with disappointing their daughters in Brodkey's "On the Waves," Apple's "Bridging," Narayan's "Forty-five a Month," Gold's " 'I Want a Sunday Kind of Love,' " and, most shatteringly, in Minot's "The Tide and Isaac Bates," which begins "He'd wrecked her" then reaches an incestuous crescendo.

If Freud taught us about the conflict between love and hate underlying children's relationships with their fathers, these stories teach us something of the same about fathers' powerful and sometimes ambivalent feelings for their daughters. There is plenty of evidence in these stories for the tragic and darker sides of father-daughter relationships, including those driven by the misuses of love. Yet on the whole, these stories suggest without false sentimentality that the love fathers and daughters give to and receive from one another can also be less conflicted—less ambivalent—than any other in their lives.

RAYMOND CARVER

◇ ◇ ◇

Distance

She's in Milan for Christmas and wants to know what it was like when she was a kid. Always that on the rare occasions when he sees her.

Tell me, she says. Tell me what it was like then. She sips Strega, waits, eyes him closely.

She is a cool, slim, attractive girl, a survivor from top to bottom.

That was a long time ago. That was twenty years ago, he says. They're in his apartment on the Via Fabroni near the Cascina Gardens.

You can remember, she says. Go on, tell me.

What do you want to hear? he asks. What can I tell you? I could tell you about something that happened when you were a baby. It involves you, he says. But only in a minor way.

Tell me, she says. But first get us another drink, so you won't have to interrupt half way through.

He comes back from the kitchen with drinks, settles into his chair, begins.

They were kids themselves, but they were crazy in love,

this eighteen-year-old boy and his seventeen-year-old girl friend when they married. Not all that long afterwards they had a daughter.

The baby came along in late November during a severe cold spell that just happened to coincide with the peak of the water-fowl season in that part of the country. The boy loved to hunt, you see, that's part of it.

The boy and girl, husband and wife now, father and mother, lived in a three-room apartment under a dentist's office. Each night they cleaned the upstairs office in exchange for their rent and utilities. In the summer they were expected to maintain the lawn and the flowers, and in winter the boy shoveled snow from the walks and spread rock salt on the pavement. The two kids, I'm telling you, were very much in love. On top of this they had great ambitions and they were wild dreamers. They were always talking about the things they were going to do and the places they were going to go.

He gets up from his chair and looks out the window for a minute over the tile rooftops at the snow that falls steadily through the late afternoon light.

Tell the story, she says.

The boy and girl slept in the bedroom, and the baby slept in a crib in the living room. You see, the baby was about three weeks old at this time and had only just begun to sleep through the night.

One Saturday night, after finishing his work upstairs, the boy went into the dentist's private office, put his feet up on the desk, and called Carl Sutherland, an old hunting and fishing friend of his father's.

Carl, he said when the man picked up the receiver. I'm a father. We had a baby girl.

Congratulations, boy, Carl said. How is the wife?

She's fine, Carl. The baby's fine, too, the boy said. Everybody's fine.

That's good, Carl said. I'm glad to hear it. Well, you give my regards to the wife. If you called about going hunting,

I'll tell you something. The geese are flying down there to beat the band. I don't think I've ever seen so many of them and I've been going for years. I shot five today. Two this morning and three this afternoon. I'm going back in the morning and you come along if you want to.

I want to, the boy said. That's why I called.

You be here at five-thirty sharp then and we'll go, Carl said. Bring lots of shells. We'll get some shooting in all right. I'll see you in the morning.

The boy liked Carl Sutherland. He'd been a friend of the boy's father, who was dead now. After the father's death, maybe trying to replace a loss they both felt, the boy and Sutherland had started hunting together. Sutherland was a heavy-set, balding man who lived alone and was not given to casual talk. Once in a while, when they were together, the boy felt uncomfortable, wondered if he had said or done something wrong because he was not used to being around people who kept still for long periods of time. But when he did talk the older man was often opinionated, and frequently the boy didn't agree with the opinions. Yet the man had a toughness and woods-savvy about him that the boy liked and admired.

The boy hung up the telephone and went downstairs to tell the girl. She watched while he laid out his things. Hunting coat, shell bag, boots, socks, hunting cap, long underwear, pump gun.

What time will you be back? the girl asked.

Probably around noon, he said. But maybe not until after five or six o'clock. Is that too late?

It's fine, she said. We'll get along just fine. You go and have some fun. You deserve it. Maybe tomorrow evening we'll dress Catherine up and go visit Sally.

Sure, that sounds like a good idea, he said. Let's plan on that.

Sally was the girl's sister. She was ten years older. The boy was a little in love with her, just as he was a little in love with Betsy, who was another sister the girl had. He'd said to the girl, If we weren't married I could go for Sally.

What about Betsy? the girl had said. I hate to admit it but I truly feel she's better looking than Sally or me. What about her?

Betsy too, the boy said and laughed. But not in the same way I could go for Sally. There's something about Sally you could fall for. No, I believe I'd prefer Sally over Betsy, if I had to make a choice.

But who do you really love? the girl asked. Who do you love most in all the world? Who's your wife?

You're my wife, the boy said.

And will we always love each other? the girl asked, enormously enjoying this conversation he could tell.

Always, the boy said. And we'll always be together. We're like the Canada geese, he said, taking the first comparison that came to mind, for they were often on his mind in those days. They only marry once. They choose a mate early in life, and they stay together always. If one of them dies or something, the other one will never remarry. It will live off by itself somewhere, or even continue to live with the flock, but it will stay single and alone amongst all the other geese.

That's sad, the girl said. It's sadder for it to live that way, I think, alone but with all the others, than just to live off by itself somewhere.

It is sad, the boy said. But it's Nature.

Have you ever killed one of those marriages? she asked. You know what I mean.

He nodded. He said, Two or three times I've shot a goose, then a minute or two later I'd see another goose turn back from the rest and begin to circle and call over the goose that lay on the ground.

Did you shoot it too? she asked with concern.

If I could, he answered. Sometimes I missed.

And it didn't bother you? she said.

Never, he said. You can't think about it when you're

doing it. You see, I love everything there is about geese. I love to just watch them even when I'm not hunting them. But there are all kinds of contradictions in life. You can't think about the contradictions.

After dinner he turned up the furnace and helped her bathe the baby. He marveled again at the infant who had half his features, the eyes and mouth, and half the girl's, the chin and the nose. He powdered the tiny body and then powdered in between the fingers and toes. He watched the girl put the baby into its diaper and pajamas.

He emptied the bath into the shower basin and then he went upstairs. It was cold and overcast outside. His breath streamed in the air. The grass, what there was of it, looked like canvas, stiff and gray under the street light. Snow lay in piles beside the walk. A car went by and he heard sand grinding under the tires. He let himself imagine what it might be like tomorrow, geese milling in the air over his head, the gun plunging against his shoulder.

Then he locked the door and went downstairs.

In bed they tried to read but both of them fell asleep, she first, letting the magazine sink to the quilt. His eyes closed, but he roused himself, checked the alarm, and turned off the lamp.

He woke to the baby's cries. The light was on out in the living room. He could see the girl standing beside the crib rocking the baby in her arms. In a minute she put the baby down, turned out the light and came back to bed.

It was two o'clock in the morning and the boy fell asleep once more.

The baby's cries woke him again. This time the girl continued to sleep. The baby cried fitfully for a few minutes and stopped. The boy listened, then began to doze.

He opened his eyes. The living room light was burning. He sat up and turned on the lamp.

I don't know what's wrong, the girl said, walking back and forth with the baby. I've changed her and given her something more to eat. But she keeps crying. She won't stop crying. I'm so tired I'm afraid I might drop her.

You come back to bed, the boy said. I'll hold her for a while.

He got up and took the baby while the girl went to lie down.

Just rock her for a few minutes, the girl said from the bedroom. Maybe she'll go back to sleep.

The boy sat on the sofa and held the baby. He jiggled it in his lap until its eyes closed. His own eyes were near closing. He rose carefully and put the baby back in the crib.

It was fifteen minutes to four and he still had forty-five minutes that he could sleep. He crawled into bed.

But a few minutes later the baby began to cry once more. This time they both got up, and the boy swore.

For God's sake what's the matter with you? the girl said to him. Maybe she's sick or something. Maybe we shouldn't have given her the bath.

The boy picked up the baby. The baby kicked its feet and was quiet. Look, the boy said, I really don't think there's anything wrong with her.

How do you know that? the girl said. Here, let me have her. I know that I ought to give her something, but I don't know what I should give her.

After a few minutes had passed and the baby had not cried, the girl put the baby down again. The boy and the girl looked at the baby, and then they looked at each other as the baby opened its eyes and began to cry.

The girl took the baby. Baby, baby, she said with tears in her eyes.

Probably it's something on her stomach, the boy said.

The girl didn't answer. She went on rocking the baby in her arms, paying no attention now to the boy.

The boy waited a minute longer then went to the kitchen and put on water for coffee. He drew on his woolen underwear and buttoned up. Then he got into his clothes.

What are you doing? the girl said to him.

Going hunting, he said.

I don't think you should, she said. Maybe you could go later on in the day if the baby is all right then. But I don't think you should go hunting this morning. I don't want to be left alone with the baby crying like this.

Carl's planning on me going, the boy said. We've planned it.

I don't give a damn about what you and Carl have planned, she said. And I don't give a damn about Carl, either. I don't even know the man. I don't want you to go is all. I don't think you should even consider wanting to go under the circumstances.

You've met Carl before, you know him, the boy said. What do you mean you don't know him?

That's not the point and you know it, the girl said. The point is I don't intend to be left alone with a sick baby.

Wait a minute, the boy said. You don't understand.

No, you don't understand, she said. I'm your wife. This is your baby. She's sick or something. Look at her. Why is she crying? You can't leave us to go hunting.

Don't get hysterical, he said.

I'm saying you can go hunting any time, she said. Something's wrong with this baby and you want to leave us to go hunting.

She began to cry. She put the baby back in the crib, but the baby started up again. The girl dried her eyes hastily on the sleeve of her nightgown and picked the baby up once more.

The boy laced his boots slowly, put on his shirt, sweater, and his coat. The kettle whistled on the stove in the kitchen.

You're going to have to choose, the girl said. Carl or us. I mean it, you've got to choose.

What do you mean? the boy said.

You heard what I said, the girl answered. If you want a family you're going to have to choose.

They stared at each other. Then the boy took his hunting

gear and went upstairs. He started the car, went around to the windows and, making a job of it, scraped away the ice.

The temperature had dropped during the night, but the weather had cleared so that stars had come out. The stars gleamed in the sky over his head. Driving, the boy looked out at the stars and was moved when he considered their distance.

Carl's porchlight was on, his station wagon parked in the drive with the motor idling. Carl came outside as the boy pulled to the curb. The boy had decided.

You might want to park off the street, Carl said as the boy came up the walk. I'm ready, just let me hit the lights. I feel like hell, I really do, he went on. I thought maybe you had overslept so I just this minute called your place. Your wife said you had left. I feel like hell.

It's okay, the boy said, trying to pick his words. He leaned his weight on one leg and turned up his collar. He put his hands in his coat pockets. She was already up, Carl. We've both been up for a while. I guess there's something wrong with the baby. I don't know. The baby keeps crying, I mean. The thing is, I guess I can't go this time, Carl.

You should have just stepped to the phone and called me, boy, Carl said. It's okay. You know you didn't have to come over here to tell me. What the hell, this hunting business you can take it or leave it. It's not important. You want a cup of coffee?

I'd better get back, the boy said.

Well, I expect I'll go ahead then, Carl said. He looked at the boy.

The boy kept standing on the porch, not saying anything.

It's cleared up, Carl said. I don't look for much action this morning. Probably you won't have missed anything anyway.

The boy nodded. I'll see you, Carl, he said.

So long, Carl said. Hey, don't let anybody ever tell you otherwise, Carl said. You're a lucky boy and I mean that.

The boy started his car and waited. He watched Carl go

through the house and turn off all the lights. Then the boy put the car in gear and pulled away from the curb.

The living room light was on, but the girl was asleep on the bed and the baby was asleep beside her.

The boy took off his boots, pants and shirt. He was quiet about it. In his socks and woolen underwear, he sat on the sofa and read the morning paper.

Soon it began to turn light outside. The girl and the baby slept on. After a while the boy went to the kitchen and began to fry bacon.

The girl came out in her robe a few minutes later and put her arms around him without saying anything.

Hey, don't catch your robe on fire, the boy said. She was leaning against him but touching the stove, too.

I'm sorry about earlier, she said. I don't know what got into me. I don't know why I said those things.

It's all right, he said. Here, let me get this bacon.

I didn't mean to snap like that, she said. It was awful.

It was my fault, he said. How's Catherine?

She's fine now. I don't know what was the matter with her earlier. I changed her again after you left, and then she was fine. She was just fine and she went right off to sleep. I don't know what it was. Don't be mad with us.

The boy laughed. I'm not mad with you. Don't be silly, he said. Here, let me do something with this pan.

You sit down, the girl said. I'll fix this breakfast. How does a waffle sound with this bacon?

Sounds great, he said. I'm starved.

She took the bacon out of the pan and then she made waffle batter. He sat at the table, relaxed now, and watched her move around the kitchen.

She left to close their bedroom door. In the living room she put on a record that they both liked.

We don't want to wake that one up again, the girl said.

That's for sure, the boy said and laughed.

She put a plate in front of him with bacon, a fried egg, and a waffle. She put another plate on the table for herself. It's ready, she said.

It looks swell, he said. He spread butter and poured syrup over the waffle. But as he started to cut into the waffle, he turned the plate into his lap.

I don't believe it, he said, jumping up from the table.

The girl looked at him and then at the expression on his face. She began to laugh.

If you could see yourself in the mirror, she said. She kept laughing.

He looked down at the syrup that covered the front of his woolen underwear, at the pieces of waffle, bacon, and egg that clung to the syrup. He began to laugh.

I was starved, he said, shaking his head.

You were starved, she said, laughing.

He peeled off the woolen underwear and threw it at the bathroom door. Then he opened his arms and she moved into them.

We won't fight any more, she said. It's not worth it, is it?

That's right, he said.

We won't fight any more, she said.

The boy said, We won't. Then he kissed her.

He gets up from his chair and refills their glasses.

That's it, he says. End of story. I admit it's not much of one.

I was interested, she says. It was very interesting if you want to know. But what happened? she says. I mean later.

He shrugs and carries his drink over to the window. It's dark now but still snowing.

Things change, he says. I don't know how they do. But they do without your realizing it or wanting them to.

Yes, that's true, only—but she does not finish what she started.

She drops the subject then. In the window's reflection he sees her study her nails. Then she raises her head. Speaking brightly, she asks if he is going to show her the city, after all.

He says, Put your boots on and let's go.

But he stays by the window, remembering that life. They had laughed. They had leaned on each other and laughed until the tears had come, while everything else—the cold and where he'd go in it—was outside, for a while anyway.

F. SCOTT FITZGERALD

◇ ◇ ◇

The Baby Party

When John Andros felt old he found solace in the thought of life continuing through his child. The dark trumpets of oblivion were less loud at the patter of his child's feet or at the sound of his child's voice babbling mad non sequiturs to him over the telephone. The latter incident occurred every afternoon at three when his wife called the office from the country, and he came to look forward to it as one of the vivid minutes of his day.

He was not physically old, but his life had been a series of struggles up a series of rugged hills, and here at thirty-eight having won his battles against ill-health and poverty he cherished less than the usual number of illusions. Even his feeling about his little girl was qualified. She had interrupted his rather intense love-affair with his wife, and she was the reason for their living in a suburban town, where they paid for country air with endless servant troubles and the weary merry-go-round of the commuting train.

It was little Ede as a definite piece of youth that chiefly interested him. He liked to take her on his lap and examine minutely her fragrant, downy scalp and her eyes with their irises of morning blue. Having paid this homage John was content that the nurse should take her away. After ten minutes the very vitality of the child irritated him; he was inclined to lose his temper when things were broken, and one Sunday afternoon when she had disrupted a bridge game by permanently hiding up the ace of spades, he had made a scene that had reduced his wife to tears.

This was absurd and John was ashamed of himself. It was inevitable that such things would happen, and it was impossible that little Ede should spend all her indoor hours in the nursery up-stairs when she was becoming, as her mother said, more nearly a "real person" every day.

She was two and a half, and this afternoon, for instance, she was going to a baby party. Grown-up Edith, her mother, had telephoned the information to the office, and little Ede had confirmed the business by shouting "I yam going to a *pantry*!" into John's unsuspecting left ear.

"Drop in at the Markeys' when you get home, won't you, dear?" resumed her mother. "It'll be funny. Ede's going to be all dressed up in her new pink dress——"

The conversation terminated abruptly with a squawk which indicated that the telephone had been pulled violently to the floor. John laughed and decided to get an early train out; the prospect of a baby party in some one else's house amused him.

"What a peach of a mess!" he thought humorously. "A dozen mothers, and each one looking at nothing but her own child. All the babies breaking things and grabbing at the cake, and each mama going home thinking about the subtle superiority of her own child to every other child there."

He was in a good humor to-day—all things in his life were going better than they had ever gone before. When he got off the train at his station he shook his head at an importunate taxi man, and began to walk up the long hill toward his house through the crisp December twilight. It was only six o'clock but the moon was out, shining with proud brilliance on the thin sugary snow that lay over the lawns.

As he walked along drawing his lungs full of cold air his happiness increased, and the idea of a baby party appealed to him more and more. He began to wonder how Ede compared to other children of her own age, and if the pink dress she was to wear was something radical and mature. Increasing his gait he came in sight of his own house, where the lights of a defunct Christmas-tree still blossomed in the window, but he continued on past the walk. The party was at the Markeys' next door.

As he mounted the brick step and rang the bell he became aware of voices inside, and he was glad he was not too late. Then he raised his head and listened—the voices were not children's voices, but they were loud and pitched high with anger; there were at least three of them and one, which rose as he listened to a hysterical sob, he recognized immediately as his wife's.

"There's been some trouble," he thought quickly.

Trying the door, he found it unlocked and pushed it open.

The baby party began at half past four, but Edith Andros, calculating shrewdly that the new dress would stand out more sensationally against vestments already rumpled, planned the arrival of herself and little Ede for five. When they appeared it was already a flourishing affair. Four baby girls and nine baby boys, each one curled and washed and dressed with all the care of a proud and jealous heart, were dancing to the music of a phonograph. Never more than two or three were dancing at once, but as all were continually in motion running to and from their mothers for encouragement, the general effect was the same.

As Edith and her daughter entered, the music was temporarily drowned out by a sustained chorus, consisting largely of the word *cute* and directed toward little Ede, who stood looking timidly about and fingering the edges of her pink dress. She was not kissed—this is the sanitary age—but she was passed along a row of mamas each one of whom said "cu-u-ute" to her and held her pink little hand before passing her on to the next. After some encouragement and a few mild pushes she was absorbed into the dance, and became an active member of the party.

Edith stood near the door talking to Mrs. Markey, and keeping one eye on the tiny figure in the pink dress. She did not care for Mrs. Markey; she considered her both snippy and common, but John and Joe Markey were congenial and went in together on the commuting train every morning, so the two women kept up an elaborate pretense of warm amity. They were always reproaching each other for "not coming to see me," and they were always planning the kind of parties that began with "You'll have to come to dinner with us soon, and we'll go in to the theatre," but never matured further.

"Little Ede looks perfectly darling," said Mrs. Markey, smiling and moistening her lips in a way that Edith found particularly repulsive. "So *grown-up*—I can't *believe* it!"

Edith wondered if "little Ede" referred to the fact that Billy Markey, though several months younger, weighed almost five pounds more. Accepting a cup of tea she took a seat with two other ladies on a divan and launched into the real business of the afternoon which of course lay in relating the recent accomplishments and insouciances of her child.

An hour passed. Dancing palled and the babies took to sterner sport. They ran into the dining-room, rounded the big table, and essayed the kitchen door, from which they were rescued by an expeditionary force of mothers. Having been rounded up they immediately broke loose, and rushing back to the dining-room tried the familiar swinging door again. The word *overheated* began to be used, and small white brows were dried with small white handkerchiefs. A general attempt to make the babies sit down began, but the babies squirmed off laps with peremptory cries of "Down! Down!" and the rush into the fascinating dining-room began anew.

This phase of the party came to an end with the arrival of refreshments, a large cake with two candles, and saucers of vanilla ice-cream. Billy Markey, a stout laughing baby with red hair and legs somewhat bowed, blew out the candles, and placed an experimental thumb on the white frosting. The refreshments were distributed, and the children ate, greedily but without confusion—they had behaved remarkably well all afternoon. They were modern babies who ate and slept at regular hours, so their dispositions were good, and their faces healthy and pink—such a peaceful party would not have been possible thirty years ago.

After the refreshments a gradual exodus began. Edith glanced anxiously at her watch—it was almost six, and John had not arrived. She wanted him to see Ede with the other children—to see how dignified and polite and intelligent she was, and how the only ice-cream spot on her dress was some that had dropped from her chin when she was joggled from behind.

"You're a darling," she whispered to her child, drawing her suddenly against her knee. "Do you know you're a darling? Do you *know* you're a darling?"

Ede laughed. "Bow-wow," she said suddenly.

"Bow-wow?" Edith looked around. "There isn't any bow-wow."

"Bow-wow," repeated Ede. "I want a bow-wow."

Edith followed the small pointed finger.

"That isn't a bow-wow, dearest, that's a teddy-bear."

"Bear?"

"Yes, that's a teddy-bear, and it belongs to Billy Markey. You don't want Billy Markey's teddy-bear, do you?"

Ede did want it.

She broke away from her mother and approached Billy Markey, who held the toy closely in his arms. Ede stood regarding him with inscrutable eyes, and Billy laughed.

Grown-up Edith looked at her watch again, this time impatiently.

The party had dwindled until, besides Ede and Billy, there were only two babies remaining—and one of the two remained only by virtue of having hidden himself under the dining-room table. It was selfish of John not to come. It showed so little pride in the child. Other fathers had come, half a dozen of them, to call for their wives, and they had stayed for a while and looked on.

There was a sudden wail. Ede had obtained Billy's teddy-bear by pulling it forcibly from his arms, and on Billy's attempt to recover it, she had pushed him casually to the floor.

"Why, Ede!" cried her mother, repressing an inclination to laugh.

Joe Markey, a handsome, broad-shouldered man of thirty-five, picked up his son and set him on his feet. "You're a fine fellow," he said jovially. "Let a girl knock you over! You're a fine fellow."

"Did he bump his head?" Mrs. Markey returned anxiously from bowing the next to last remaining mother out the door.

"No-o-o-o," exclaimed Markey. "He bumped something else, didn't you, Billy? He bumped something else."

Billy had so far forgotten the bump that he was already making an attempt to recover his property. He seized a leg of the bear which projected from Ede's enveloping arms and tugged at it but without success.

"No," said Ede emphatically.

Suddenly, encouraged by the success of her former half-accidental manœuvre, Ede dropped the teddy-bear, placed her hands on Billy's shoulders and pushed him backward off his feet.

This time he landed less harmlessly; his head hit the bare floor just off the rug with a dull hollow sound, whereupon he drew in his breath and delivered an agonized yell.

Immediately the room was in confusion. With an exclamation Markey hurried to his son, but his wife was first to reach the injured baby and catch him up into her arms.

"Oh, *Billy*," she cried, "what a terrible bump! She ought to be spanked."

Edith, who had rushed immediately to her daughter, heard this remark, and her lips came sharply together.

"Why, Ede," she whispered perfunctorily, "you bad girl!"

Ede put back her little head suddenly and laughed. It was a loud laugh, a triumphant laugh with victory in it and challenge and contempt. Unfortunately it was also an infectious laugh. Before her mother realized the delicacy of the situation, she too had laughed, an audible, distinct laugh not unlike the baby's, and partaking of the same overtones.

Then, as suddenly, she stopped.

Mrs. Markey's face had grown red with anger, and Markey, who had been feeling the back of the baby's head with one finger, looked at her, frowning.

"It's swollen already," he said with a note of reproof in his voice. "I'll get some witch-hazel."

But Mrs. Markey had lost her temper. "I don't see anything funny about a child being hurt!" she said in a trembling voice.

Little Ede meanwhile had been looking at her mother curiously. She noted that her own laugh had produced her mother's and she wondered if the same cause would always produce the same effect. So she chose this moment to throw back her head and laugh again.

To her mother the additional mirth added the final touch of hysteria to the situation. Pressing her handkerchief to her mouth she giggled irrepressibly. It was more than nervousness —she felt that in a peculiar way she was laughing with her child—they were laughing together.

It was in a way a defiance—those two against the world.

While Markey rushed up-stairs to the bathroom for ointment, his wife was walking up and down rocking the yelling boy in her arms.

"Please go home!" she broke out suddenly. "The child's badly hurt, and if you haven't the decency to be quiet, you'd better go home."

"Very well," said Edith, her own temper rising. "I've never seen any one make such a mountain out of——"

"Get out!" cried Mrs. Markey frantically. "There's the door, get out—I never want to see you in our house again. You or your brat either!"

Edith had taken her daughter's hand and was moving quickly toward the door, but at this remark she stopped and turned around, her face contracting with indignation.

"Don't you dare call her that!"

Mrs. Markey did not answer but continued walking up and down, muttering to herself and to Billy in an inaudible voice.

Edith began to cry.

"I will get out!" she sobbed, "I've never heard anybody so rude and c-common in my life. I'm glad your baby did get pushed down—he's nothing but a f-fat little fool anyhow."

Joe Markey reached the foot of the stairs just in time to hear this remark.

"Why, Mrs. Andros," he said sharply, "can't you see the child's hurt? You really ought to control yourself."

"Control m-myself!" exclaimed Edith brokenly. "You better ask her to c-control herself. I've never heard anybody so c-common in my life."

"She's insulting me!" Mrs. Markey was now livid with rage. "Did you hear what she said, Joe? I wish you'd put her out. If she won't go, just take her by the shoulders and put her out!"

"Don't you dare touch me!" cried Edith. "I'm going just as quick as I can find my c-coat!"

Blind with tears she took a step toward the hall. It was just at this moment that the door opened and John Andros walked anxiously in.

"John!" cried Edith, and fled to him wildly.

"What's the matter? Why, what's the matter?"

"They're—they're putting me out!" she wailed, collapsing against him. "He'd just started to take me by the shoulders and put me out I want my coat!"

"That's not true," objected Markey hurriedly. "Nobody's

going to put you out." He turned to John. "Nobody's going to put her out," he repeated. "She's——"

"What do you mean 'put her out'?" demanded John abruptly. "What's all this talk, anyhow?"

"Oh, let's go!" cried Edith. "I want to go. They're so *common*, John!"

"Look here!" Markey's face darkened. "You've said that about enough. You're acting sort of crazy."

"They called Ede a brat!"

For the second time that afternoon little Ede expressed emotion at an inopportune moment. Confused and frightened at the shouting voices, she began to cry, and her tears had the effect of conveying that she felt the insult in her heart.

"What's the idea of this?" broke out John. "Do you insult your guests in your own house?"

"It seems to me it's your wife that's done the insulting!" answered Markey crisply. "In fact, your baby there started all the trouble."

John gave a contemptuous snort. "Are you calling names at a little baby?" he inquired. "That's a fine manly business!"

"Don't talk to him, John," insisted Edith. "Find my coat!"

"You must be in a bad way," went on John angrily, "if you have to take out your temper on a helpless little baby."

"I never heard anything so damn twisted in my life," shouted Markey. "If that wife of yours would shut her mouth for a minute——"

"Wait a minute! You're not talking to a woman and child now——"

There was an incidental interruption. Edith had been fumbling on a chair for her coat, and Mrs. Markey had been watching her with hot, angry eyes. Suddenly she laid Billy down on the sofa, where he immediately stopped crying and pulled himself upright, and coming into the hall she quickly found Edith's coat and handed it to her without a word. Then she went back to the sofa, picked up Billy, and rocking him in her arms looked again at Edith with hot, angry eyes. The interruption had taken less than half a minute.

"Your wife comes in here and begins shouting around about how common we are!" burst out Markey violently. "Well, if we're so damn common, you'd better stay away! And, what's more, you'd better get out now!"

Again John gave a short, contemptuous laugh.

"You're not only common," he returned, "you're evidently an awful bully—when there's any helpless women and children around." He felt for the knob and swung the door open. "Come on, Edith."

Taking up her daughter in her arms, his wife stepped outside and John, still looking contemptuously at Markey, started to follow.

"Wait a minute!" Markey took a step forward; he was trembling slightly, and two large veins on his temple were suddenly full of blood. "You don't think you can get away with that, do you? With me?"

Without a word John walked out the door, leaving it open.

Edith, still weeping, had started for home. After following her with his eyes until she reached her own walk, John turned back toward the lighted doorway where Markey was slowly coming down the slippery steps. He took off his overcoat and hat, tossed them off the path onto the snow. Then, sliding a little on the iced walk, he took a step forward.

At the first blow, they both slipped and fell heavily to the sidewalk, half rising then, and again pulling each other to the ground. They found a better foothold in the thin snow to the side of the walk and rushed at each other, both swinging wildly and pressing out the snow into a pasty mud underfoot.

The street was deserted, and except for their short tired gasps and the padded sound as one or the other slipped down into the slushy mud, they fought in silence, clearly defined to each other by the full moonlight as well as by the amber glow that shone out of the open door. Several times they both slipped down together, and then for a while the conflict threshed about wildly on the lawn.

For ten, fifteen, twenty minutes they fought there sense-lessly in the moonlight. They had both taken off coats and vests at some silently agreed upon interval and now their shirts dripped from their backs in wet pulpy shreds. Both were torn and bleeding and so exhausted that they could stand only when by their position they mutually supported each other—the impact, the mere effort of a blow, would send them both to their hands and knees.

But it was not weariness that ended the business, and the very meaninglessness of the fight was a reason for not stop-ping. They stopped because once when they were straining at each other on the ground, they heard a man's footsteps coming along the sidewalk. They had rolled somehow into the shadow, and when they heard these footsteps they stopped fighting, stopped moving, stopped breathing, lay huddled together like two boys playing Indian until the footsteps had passed. Then, staggering to their feet, they looked at each other like two drunken men.

"I'll be damned if I'm going on with this thing any more," cried Markey thickly.

"I'm not going on any more either," said John Andros. "I've had enough of this thing."

Again they looked at each other, sulkily this time, as if each suspected the other of urging him to a renewal of the fight. Markey spat out a mouthful of blood from a cut lip; then he cursed softly, and picking up his coat and vest, shook off the snow from them in a surprised way, as if their comparative dampness was his only worry in the world.

"Want to come in and wash up?" he asked suddenly.

"No, thanks," said John. "I ought to be going home—my wife'll be worried."

He too picked up his coat and vest and then his overcoat and hat. Soaking wet and dripping with perspiration, it seemed absurd that less than half an hour ago he had been wearing all these clothes.

"Well—good night," he said hesitantly.

Suddenly they both walked toward each other and shook hands. It was no perfunctory hand-shake: John Andros's arm went around Markey's shoulder, and he patted him softly on the back for a little while.

"No harm done," he said brokenly.

"No—you?"

"No, no harm done.

"Well," said John Andros after a minute, "I guess I'll say good night."

Limping slightly and with his clothes over his arm, John Andros turned away. The moonlight was still bright as he left the dark patch of trampled ground and walked over the intervening lawn. Down at the station, half a mile away, he could hear the rumble of the seven o'clock train.

"But you must have been crazy," cried Edith brokenly. "I thought you were going to fix it all up there and shake hands. That's why I went away."

"Did you want us to fix it up?"

"Of course not, I never want to see them again. But I thought of course that was what you were going to do." She was touching the bruises on his neck and back with iodine as he sat placidly in a hot bath. "I'm going to get the doctor," she said insistently. "You may be hurt internally."

He shook his head. "Not a chance," he answered. "I don't want this to get all over town."

"I don't understand yet how it all happened."

"Neither do I." He smiled grimly. "I guess these baby parties are pretty rough affairs."

"Well, one thing—" suggested Edith hopefully, "I'm certainly glad we have beefsteak in the house for to-morrow's dinner."

"Why?"

"For your eye, of course. Do you know I came within an ace of ordering veal? Wasn't that the luckiest thing?"

Half an hour later, dressed except that his neck would accommodate no collar, John moved his limbs experimentally before the glass. "I believe I'll get myself in better shape," he said thoughtfully. "I must be getting old."

"You mean so that next time you can beat him?"

"I did beat him," he announced. "At least, I beat him as much as he beat me. And there isn't going to be any next time. Don't you go calling people common any more. If you get in any trouble, you just take your coat and go home. Understand?"

"Yes, dear," she said meekly. "I was very foolish and now I understand."

Out in the hall, he paused abruptly by the baby's door.

"Is she asleep?"

"Sound asleep. But you can go in and peek at her—just to say good night."

They tiptoed in and bent together over the bed. Little Ede, her cheeks flushed with health, her pink hands clasped tight together, was sleeping soundly in the cool, dark room. John reached over the railing of the bed and passed his hand lightly over the silken hair.

"She's asleep," he murmured in a puzzled way.

"Naturally, after such an afternoon."

"Miz Andros," the colored maid's stage whisper floated in from the hall, "Mr. and Miz Markey downstairs an' want to see you. Mr. Markey he's all cut up in pieces, mam'n. His face look like a roast beef. An' Miz Markey she 'pear mighty mad."

"Why, what incomparable nerve!" exclaimed Edith. "Just tell them we're not home. I wouldn't go down for anything in the world."

"You most certainly will." John's voice was hard and set.

"What?"

"You'll go down right now, and what's more, whatever that other woman does, you'll apologize for what you said this afternoon. After that you don't ever have to see her again."

"Why—John, I can't."

"You've got to. And just remember that she probably hated to come over here just twice as much as you hate to go downstairs."

"Aren't you coming? Do I have to go alone?"

"I'll be down—in just a minute."

John Andros waited until she had closed the door behind her; then he reached over into the bed, and picking up his daughter, blankets and all, sat down in the rocking-chair holding her tightly in his arms. She moved a little, and he held his breath, but she was sleeping soundly, and in a moment she was resting quietly in the hollow of his elbow. Slowly he bent his head until his cheek was against her bright hair. "Dear little girl," he whispered. "Dear little girl, dear little girl."

John Andros knew at length what it was he had fought for so savagely that evening. He had it now, he possessed it forever, and for some time he sat there rocking very slowly to and fro in the darkness.

BUDD SCHULBERG

◇ ◇ ◇

A Short Digest of a Long Novel

Her legs were shapely and firm and when she crossed them and smiled with the self-assurance that always delighted him, he thought she was the only person he knew in the world who was unblemished. Not lifelike but an improvement on life, as a work of art, her delicate features were chiseled from a solid block. The wood-sculpture image came easy to him because her particular shade of blonde always suggested maple polished to a golden grain. As it had been from the moment he stood in awe and amazement in front of the glass window where she was first exhibited, the sight of her made him philosophical. Some of us appear in beautiful colors, too, or with beautiful grains, but we develop imperfections. Inspect us very closely and you find we're damaged by the elements. Sometimes we're only nicked with cynicism. Sometimes we're cracked with disillusionment. Or we're split with fear.

When she began to speak, he leaned forward, eager for the words that were like good music, profundity expressed in terms that pleased the ear while challenging the mind.

"Everybody likes me," she said. "Absolutely everybody."

It was not that she was conceited. It was simply that she

was only three. No one had ever taken her with sweet and whispered promises that turned into morning-after lies, ugly and cold as unwashed dishes from last night's dinner lying in the sink. She had never heard a dictator rock her country to sleep with peaceful lullabies one day and rock it with bombs the next. She was undeceived. Her father ran his hands reverently through her soft yellow hair. She is virgin, he thought, for this is the true virginity, that brief moment in the time of your life before your mind or your body has been defiled by acts of treachery.

It was just before Christmas and she was sitting on her little chair, her lips pressed together in concentration, writing a last-minute letter to Santa Claus. The words were written in some language of her own invention but she obligingly translated as she went along.

Dear Santa, I am a very good girl and everybody likes me. So please don't forget to bring me a set of dishes, a doll that goes to sleep and wakes up again, and a washing machine. I need the washing machine because Raggedy Ann's dress is so dirty.

After she had finished her letter, folded it, and asked him to address it, he tossed her up in the air, caught her and tossed her again, to hear her giggle. "Higher, Daddy, higher," she instructed. His mind embraced her sentimentally: She is a virgin island in a lewd world. She is a winged seed of innocence blown through the wasteland. If only she could root somewhere. If only she could grow like this.

"Let me down, Daddy," she said when she decided that she had indulged him long enough, "I have to mail my letter to Santa."

"But didn't you see him this afternoon?" he asked. "Didn't you ask for everything you wanted? Mommy said she took you up to meet him and you sat on his lap."

"I just wanted to remind him," she said. "There were so many other children."

He fought down the impulse to laugh, because she was not something to laugh at. And he was obsessed with the idea that to hurt her feelings with laughter was to nick her, to blemish the perfection.

"Daddy can't catch me-ee," she sang out, and the old chase was on, following the pattern that had become so familiar to them, the same wild shrieks and the same scream of pretended anguish at the inevitable result. Two laps around the dining-room table was the established course before he caught her in the kitchen. He swung her up from the floor and set her down on the kitchen table. She stood on the edge, poised confidently for another of their games. But this was no panting, giggling game like tag or hide-and-seek. This game was ceremonial. The table was several feet higher than she was. "Jump, jump, and Daddy will catch you," he would challenge. They would count together, *one, two* and on *three* she would leap out into the air. He would not even hold out his arms to her until the last possible moment. But he would always catch her. They had played the game for more than a year and the experience never failed to exhilarate them. You see, I am always here to catch you when you are falling, it said to them, and each time she jumped, her confidence increased and their bond deepened.

They were going through the ceremony when the woman next door came in with her five-year-old son, Billy. "Hello, Mr. Steevers," she said. "Would you mind if I left Bill with you for an hour while I go do my marketing?"

"No, of course not, glad to have him," he said and he mussed Billy's hair playfully. "How's the boy, Billy?"

But his heart wasn't in it. This was his only afternoon of the week with her and he resented the intrusion. And then too, he was convinced that Billy was going to grow up into the type of man for whom he had a particular resentment. A sturdy, good-looking boy, big for his age, aggressively unchildlike, a malicious, arrogant, insensitive extrovert. I can just see him drunk and red-faced and pulling up girls' dresses at Legion Conventions, Mr. Steevers would think.

And the worst of it was, his daughter seemed blind to Billy's faults. The moment she saw him she forgot about their game.

"Hello, Billy-Boy," she called and ran over to hug him.

"I want a cookie," said Billy.

"Oh, yes, a cookie; some animal crackers, Daddy."

She had her hostess face on and as he went into the pantry, he could hear the treble of her musical laughter against the premature baritone of Billy's guffaws.

He swung open the pantry door with the animal crackers in his hand just in time to see it. She was poised on the edge of the table. Billy was standing below her, as he had seen her father do. "Jump and I'll catch you," he was saying.

Smiling, confident and unblemished, she jumped. But no hands reached out to break her flight. With a cynical grin on his face, Billy stepped back and watched her fall.

Watching from the doorway, her father felt the horror that possessed him the time he saw a parachutist smashed like a bug on a windshield when his chute failed to open. She was lying there, crying, not so much in pain as in disillusionment. He ran forward to pick her up and he would never forget the expression on her face, the *new* expression, unchildlike, unvirginal, embittered.

"I hate you, I hate you," she was screaming at Billy through hysterical sobs.

Well, now she knows, thought her father, the facts of life. Now she's one of us. Now she knows treachery and fear. Now she must learn to replace innocence with courage.

She was still bawling. He knew these tears were as natural and as necessary as those she shed at birth, but that could not overcome entirely the heavy sadness that enveloped him. Finally, when he spoke, he said, a little more harshly than he had intended, "Now, now, stop crying. Stand up and act like a big girl. A little fall like that can't hurt you."

JOHN UPDIKE

◇ ◇ ◇

Should Wizard Hit Mommy?

In the evenings and for Saturday naps like today's, Jack told his daughter Jo a story out of his head. This custom, begun when she was two, was itself now nearly two years old, and his head felt empty. Each new story was a slight variation of a basic tale: a small creature, usually named Roger (Roger Fish, Roger Squirrel, Roger Chipmunk), had some problem and went with it to the wise old owl. The owl told him to go to the wizard, and the wizard performed a magic spell that solved the problem, demanding in payment a number of pennies greater than the number Roger Creature had but in the same breath directing the animal to a place where the extra pennies could be found. Then Roger was so happy he played many games with other creatures, and went home to his mother just in time to hear the train whistle that brought his daddy home from Boston. Jack described their supper, and the story was over. Working his way through this scheme was especially fatiguing on Saturday, because Jo never fell asleep in naps any more, and knowing this made the rite seem futile.

The little girl (not so little any more; the bumps her feet made under the covers were halfway down the bed, their big double bed that they let her be in for naps and when she was sick) had at last arranged herself, and from the way her fat face deep in the pillow shone in the sunlight sifting through the drawn shades, it did not seem fantastic that something magic would occur, and she would take her nap like an infant of two. Her brother, Bobby, was two, and already asleep with his bottle. Jack asked, "Who shall the story be about today?"

"Roger . . ." Jo squeezed her eyes shut and smiled to be thinking she was thinking. Her eyes opened, her mother's blue. "Skunk," she said firmly.

A new animal; they must talk about skunks at nursery school. Having a fresh hero momentarily stirred Jack to creative enthusiasm. "All right," he said. "Once upon a time, in the deep dark woods, there was a tiny little creature name of Roger Skunk. And he smelled very bad—"

"Yes," Jo said.

"He smelled so bad none of the other little wood-land creatures would play with him." Jo looked at him solemnly; she hadn't foreseen this. "Whenever he would go out to play," Jack continued with zest, remembering certain humiliations of his own childhood, "all of the other tiny animals would cry, 'Uh-oh, here comes Roger Stinky Skunk,' and they would run away, and Roger Skunk would stand there all alone, and two little round tears would fall from his eyes." The corners of Jo's mouth drooped down and her lower lip bent forward as he traced with a forefinger along the side of her nose the course of one of Roger Skunk's tears.

"Won't he see the owl?" she asked in a high and faintly roughened voice.

Sitting on the bed beside her, Jack felt the covers tug as her legs switched tensely. He was pleased with this moment —he was telling her something true, something she must know—and had no wish to hurry on. But downstairs a chair scraped, and he realized he must get down to help Clare paint the living-room woodwork.

"Well, he walked along very sadly and came to a very big tree, and in the tiptop of the tree was an enormous wise old owl."

"Good."

" 'Mr. Owl,' Roger Skunk said, 'all the other little animals run away from me because I smell so bad.' 'So you do,' the owl said. 'Very, very bad.' 'What can I do?' Roger Skunk said, and he cried very hard."

"The wizard, the wizard," Jo shouted, and sat right up, and a Little Golden Book spilled from the bed.

"Now, Jo. Daddy's telling the story. Do you want to tell Daddy the story?"

"No. You me."

"Then lie down and be sleepy."

Her head relapsed onto the pillow and she said, "Out of your head."

"Well. The owl thought and thought. At last he said, 'Why don't you go see the wizard?' "

"Daddy?"

"What?"

"Are magic spells *real?*" This was a new phase, just this last month, a reality phase. When he told her spiders eat bugs, she turned to her mother and asked, "Do they *really?*" and when Clare told her God was in the sky and all around them, she turned to her father and insisted, with a sly yet eager smile, "Is He *really?*"

"They're real in stories," Jack answered curtly. She had made him miss a beat in the narrative. "The owl said, 'Go through the dark woods, under the apple trees, into the swamp, over the crick—' "

"What's a crick?"

"A little river. 'Over the crick, and there will be the wizard's house.' And that's the way Roger Skunk went, and pretty soon he came to a little white house, and he rapped on the door." Jack rapped on the window sill, and under the covers Jo's tall figure clenched in an infantile thrill. "And then a tiny little old man came out, with a long white beard and a pointed blue hat, and said, 'Eh? Whatzis? Whatcher want? You smell awful.' " The wizard's voice was one of Jack's own favorite effects; he did it by scrunching up his face and somehow whining through his eyes, which felt for the interval rheumy. He felt being an old man suited him.

" 'I know it,' Roger Skunk said, 'and all the little animals run away from me. The enormous wise owl said you could help me.'

" 'Eh? Well, maybe. Come on in. Don't git too close.' Now, inside, Jo, there were all these magic things, all jumbled together in a big dusty heap, because the wizard did not have any cleaning lady."

"Why?"

"Why? Because he was a wizard, and a very old man."

"Will he die?"

"No. Wizards don't die. Well, he rummaged around and found an old stick called a magic wand and asked Roger Skunk what he wanted to smell like. Roger thought and thought and said, 'Roses.' "

"Yes. Good," Jo said smugly.

Jack fixed her with a trancelike gaze and chanted in the wizard's elderly irritable voice:

> " 'Abracadabry, hocus-poo,
> Roger Skunk, how do you do,
> Roses, boses, pull an ear,
> Roger Skunk, you never fear:
> *Bingo!* ' "

He paused as a rapt expression widened out from his daughter's nostrils, forcing her eyebrows up and her lower lip down in a wide noiseless grin, an expression in which Jack was startled to recognize his wife feigning pleasure at cocktail parties. "And all of a sudden," he whispered, "the whole inside of the wizard's house was full of the smell of —*roses!* 'Roses!' Roger Fish cried. And the wizard said, very cranky, 'That'll be seven pennies.' "

"Daddy."

"What?"

"Roger *Skunk*." You said Roger Fish."

"Yes. Skunk."

"You said Roger *Fish*. Wasn't that silly?"

"Very silly of your stupid old daddy. Where was I? Well, you know about the pennies."

"Say it."

"O.K. Roger Skunk said, 'But all I have is four pennies,' and he began to cry." Jo made the crying face again, but this time without a trace of sincerity. This annoyed Jack. Downstairs some more furniture rumbled. Clare shouldn't move heavy things; she was six months pregnant. It would be their third.

"So the wizard said, 'Oh, very well. Go to the end of the lane and turn around three times and look down the magic well and there you will find three pennies. Hurry up.' So Roger Skunk went to the end of the lane and turned around three times and there in the magic well were *three pennies!* So he took them back to the wizard and was very happy and ran out into the woods and all the other little animals gathered around him because he smelled so good. And they played tag, baseball, football, basketball, lacrosse, hockey, soccer, and pick-up-sticks."

"What's pick-up-sticks?"

"It's a game you play with sticks."

"Like the wizard's magic wand?"

"Kind of. And they played games and laughed all afternoon and then it began to get dark and they all ran home to their mommies."

Jo was starting to fuss with her hands and look out of the window, at the crack of day that showed under the shade. She thought the story was all over. Jack didn't like women when they took anything for granted; he liked them apprehensive, hanging on his words. "Now, Jo, are you listening?"

"Yes."

"Because this is very interesting. Roger Skunk's mommy said, 'What's that awful smell?' "

"Wha-at?"

"And Roger Skunk said, 'It's me, Mommy. I smell like roses.' And she said, 'Who made you smell like that?' And he said, 'The wizard,' and she said, 'Well, of all the nerve. You come with me and we're going right back to that very awful wizard.' "

Jo sat up, her hands dabbling in the air with genuine fright. "But Daddy, then he said about the other little animals run *away!*" Her hands skittered off, into the underbrush.

"All right. He said, 'But Mommy, all the other little animals run away,' and she said, 'I don't care. You smelled the way a little skunk should have and I'm going to take you right back to that wizard,' and she took an umbrella and went back with Roger Skunk and hit that wizard right over the head."

"No," Jo said, and put her hand out to touch his lips, yet even in her agitation did not quite dare to stop the source of truth. Inspiration came to her. "Then the wizard hit *her* on the head and did not change that little skunk back."

"No," he said. "The wizard said 'O.K.' and Roger Skunk did not smell of roses any more. He smelled very bad again."

"But the other little amum—*oh!*—amum—"

"Joanne. It's Daddy's story. Shall Daddy not tell you any more stories?" Her broad face looked at him through sifted light, astounded. "This is what happened, then. Roger Skunk and his mommy went home and they heard *Woo-oo, woooo-oo* and it was the choo-choo train bringing Daddy Skunk home from Boston. And they had lima beans, pork chops, celery, liver, mashed potatoes, and Pie-Oh-My for dessert. And when Roger Skunk was in bed Mommy Skunk came up and hugged him and said he smelled like her little baby skunk again and she loved him very much. And that's the end of the story."

"But Daddy."

"What?"

"Then did the other little ani-mals run away?"

"No, because eventually they got used to the way he was and did not mind it at all."

"What's evenshiladee?"

"In a little while."

"That was a stupid mommy."

"It was *not,*" he said with rare emphasis, and believed, from her expression, that she realized he was defending his own mother to her, or something as odd. "Now I want you to put your big heavy head in the pillow and have a good long nap." He adjusted the shade so not even a crack of day showed, and tiptoed to the door, in the pretense that she was already asleep. But when he turned, she was crouching on top of the covers and staring at him. "Hey. Get under the covers and fall faaast asleep. Bobby's asleep."

She stood up and bounced gingerly on the springs. "Daddy."

"What?"

"Tomorrow, I want you to tell me the story that that wizard took that magic wand and hit that mommy"—her plump arms chopped fiercely—"right over the head."

"No. That's not the story. The point is that the little skunk loved his mommy more than he loved aaall the other little animals and she knew what was right."

"No. Tomorrow you say he hit that mommy. Do it." She kicked her legs up and sat down on the bed with a great heave and complaint of springs, as she had done hundreds of times before, except that this time she did not laugh. "Say it, Daddy."

"Well, we'll see. Now at least have a rest. Stay on the bed. You're a good girl."

He closed the door and went downstairs. Clare had spread the newspapers and opened the paint can and, wearing an old shirt of his on top of her maternity smock, was stroking the chair rail with a dipped brush. Above him footsteps vibrated and he called, "*Joanne*. Shall I come up there and spank you?" The footsteps hesitated.

"That was a long story," Clare said.

"The poor kid," he answered, and with utter weariness watched his wife labor. The woodwork, a cage of moldings and rails and baseboards all around them, was half old tan and half new ivory and he felt caught in an ugly middle position, and though he as well felt his wife's presence in the cage with him, he did not want to speak with her, work with her, touch her, anything.

LARRY WOIWODE

◇ ◇ ◇

Blindness

"This can't be happening," Mel whispered, and felt his breath drift up over his face in the cold. Once he and his daughter had walked out of the range of the yard light at their house, the landmarks that he generally negotiated by had become dimmer and dimmer until the ground itself felt strange underfoot, and he had to stop in the lane and stand as he did now, with his head back and a hand out, unable to see at all. Or only enough to guess that the layered shapes to his left were the branches of trees overhanging this part of the lane, and to assume that the moving place of sheen, lower and farther on, was his daughter continuing ahead in her self-absorbed strides of a four-year-old. Then a crowd of silvery, fluttering particles, like a flock of startled birds, went out of his vision in a molecular release, and he wasn't sure he was seeing anything, or anything real.

"Evelyn."

"Yes, Dad." She turned to him, from the tone and angle of her voice—a responsive, obedient, easygoing child—and he thought he could distinguish, across the blank darkness between them, a lighter outline around an area that must be her face: her silver-blonde hair, inherited from her mother.

He shivered. It was early spring, cold enough for winter coats (although he had on only a jacket), and over the last few nights the crescent of the moon had turned all the way under to new. Was some faint illumination from behind, perhaps the yard light, falling over her hair? He craned his head toward the house, resettling his feet for balance, and saw a faint blur or smudge which seemed to rock as he watched, in the way that the yard light sometimes rocked in a high wind. But there was no wind tonight. He turned in the direction of his daughter. Blankness. He was afraid to tell her he couldn't see.

"Can you make out things all right, Evelyn?"

"Sure, Dad. What do you mean?" She might have moved a step or two closer, from her voice.

"You can see the road okay?"

"Sure, Dad. Why?"

"I wondered." He looked down and felt he might as well be on a black carpet in a pitch-dark room. He squinted his eyes and couldn't even locate the tracks of the lane, which usually showed up gray, no matter how dark it was. In his confusion, he'd stepped out of the track he'd been walking in and now wasn't sure if he was off in the grass at one side of the lane, or in the grass down its center. Leaf fringe, ferns, thistles—pictures of these flowed past him, although he wasn't taking them in with his eyes. A springing rush of his mind to fill the emptiness. This had happened before. When he was in college and had worked two days and two nights on his senior project, the design for a theater, and had gone out early the second morning for coffee, the buildings he walked along suddenly looked cellular, as if composed of particles that began to vibrate as he watched, and then every shade of color left them; it left the street and the automobiles and trees until they were only bleached shapes. Gray. Gray-white. Then these began to waver as if to go, and it was only by main force of his will, it seemed—he was about to call out for his parents—that their colors began to return, slowly, and he leaned against a car, trembling, until everything was itself again.

Now he tested with his feet for one of the worn tracks. The lane led from here to a shallow river that he usually drove their Jeep across, and then drove on back to the clearing where they lived. But lately he'd been leaving the Jeep on the other side of the river and walking, because if he started it up late at night (as he'd been doing for the past couple of weeks, to go out for beer), it woke Evelyn, and she called out to ask where he was going, or started crying because he'd left them at home. His wife had told him this, and had suggested that he park the Jeep where it was, and then tonight had asked him to take Evelyn along, as if to insure his prompt return. He'd been drinking too much.

"Are you upset, Dad?"

"No," he said, but heard his voice go up and leave an opening—tentative and questioning—between them in the night. His wife had been favoring that word, as in "Are you upset again?" or "Well, now I'm upset" or "Evelyn is getting upset about all this." He'd been working on a set of plans for a city library over the last week and a half, while trying to finish up, at the same time, the plans for their own house; they were living in a trailer house until the new place was built. Chaos. The worst situation in which to work. They'd never been able to afford a house and he thought the finished plans might give him and his wife some head-room, so they could bear the trailer another year. He was free-lancing for a firm of architectural associates in Minneapolis; he'd worked several years for the firm full-time, and then decided to move off on his own, and hadn't been as successful as he and his wife had hoped. Or so far hadn't. Which was an understatement. This week he'd had to admit to himself (though not to her, yet), that if his plans for this library weren't accepted, they'd soon be back in the Twin Cities. It was his wife who had wanted to move here, to this Wisconsin countryside an hour from St. Paul—for their daughter's sake, she said, although he was the one who had always talked of them as a self-sufficient family, off in the woods somewhere, alone.

"No," he said again. "I guess it's just that your dad's getting old."

He meant to be light-hearted about this sensitive issue between him and his wife; he was older than she, in his early thirties. Lately, whenever he began filling out a personal check, he found himself thinking, November? January? April?—although he was usually fairly close about the date. The geometric clarity of numbers. He would glance up from the checkbook and find he couldn't focus on anything, always distracted, as his wife said; a new inwardness of age, he assumed. "November ninth," a store clerk would say (or whatever the date was), apparently familiar with his type. A certain personal music, as he sensed it, had seeped out of his bones at about twenty-nine; he no longer took the time to fashion the sort of speeches he once had, to put an edge on every turn of conversation—that edge that's the badge of all ambitious, educated youth. He'd begun to mumble a lot, his wife complained. When they made love, he always seemed to wrench a muscle, or pull something loose in his rib cage; or he'd lie beside her, listening to her sleep, feeling an arm or leg trembling from the strain.

"Old, Dad?"

"I guess."

"Did you say 'old,' Dad?"

"Yes." Did she think he'd said "owed"? That, too, had come up a lot, with his wife's worries about land payments, Jeep payments, and all their other obligations. Which was how it had to be, he thought, shaking his head to clear it, or perhaps bring his vision back, since he ignored their finances, now that he wasn't receiving a salary, and tried to bury every consideration of the sort in his work.

"I don't think you're old, Dad."

"Good."

"I think you look nice."

"Thank you, honey."

He had done more historical research for the library than for any other project, which had left him feeling less spontaneous, less original, less young, and then for the past three nights he'd been working over his table-sized drafting board, with its adjustable fluorescents reflecting light up into the backs of his eyes, or turning to the other fluorescent-lit drafting board behind him, where the expanding plans for their new house lay taped—always keeping a bottle of beer in reach, and sipping at it enough to maintain the displacing warmth within at a constant, and discovered he was finishing a case a day. "An expensive job," his wife said, "if you figure the beer. You should realize why I'm upset. You haven't been eating like you should, either." Now a metallic chill penetrated his body, drawing his tongue up against a dry metallic taste, as if some cushioning element had been stripped from him by the beer, and he was sure it was a combination of all this that had affected his eyesight.

"Good Lord," he whispered, and his breath over his blind face seemed to outline a sharpened form: a wedge.

"What, Dad?"

It wasn't his work, or the quality of it, that had caused this. His work always moved in its own direction, never derivative after the first year or two, toward unexampled clarity. He had a gift, like Frank Lloyd Wright in the best of his work, for abstracting classical lines, as if the complexity of a building's structure only led him further inward to its indisputable form. Yet a curious division of feeling invaded him lately when he worked, as if he'd reached a level of objectivity that obliterated his real self; he felt that he'd traveled into a realm so far removed from his father, a common laborer, that he no longer had a generational shield between himself and his work. Or the world. While on the other hand it seemed inconceivable that he should receive the fees he did for drawing pictures—his single love since childhood—or for teasing the shapes of daily life into an artwork, which is what it seemed to him, now, his mother had done all the time; her structure of every day and event rendered the room for him and his father to maneuver through life. The lines he put down on paper, which became spaces for people to live and work within, returned that structure to her and filled him with the same pleasure he felt when he sat at her feet and played as a child, or drew on a tablet to satisfy her, while she moved around the kitchen or the living room, always at work. Her towering legs, the buttresses of her shoulders, the arch of her hair—that perfect form he could never capture. It seemed paradoxical that people should pay him for this, especially when he looked up from his work and found he was still a child of five.

"What did you say, Dad?" his daughter asked, and now she was so close her voice startled him. Perhaps it wasn't her hair he'd seen earlier. He couldn't see it at all now. He felt her hands, fine-boned but firm, grasp and tug at his right hand, and then he let her take it in hers, and thought for a moment he was falling forward as he made some blind passes with his other hand for her head. He found it, finally, and placed his hand over her crown, gripping the heat that rose from her thick hair, and imagined he could smell his wife's blonde and oily, outdoor health.

"Can't you see, Dad?" she asked, her head lifting under his palm as if to look up at him, and he was so relieved he had to laugh. He sometimes said to his wife, "We're raising a mind-reader. She always knows exactly what I'm up to." And his wife would look levelly at him out of her large green eyes, and say, "That's your fault."

"Well, to tell you the truth," he said to his daughter, "not really." And then, to soften the possible effect of this on her: "I mean, with it so dark, like it is tonight, it doesn't seem I can see well at all."

"That's okay, Dad," she said, and gave his fingers a confirming shake. "I'll keep hold of your hand like this and you can follow me."

His wife often intimated that he and his daughter were too close. "What kind of expression is it you get," she would ask, "when you sit there holding her like that?" He couldn't judge his expression, of course, but was aware that his wife's voice had called him back from so far, into such alien surroundings, it was as if he'd fully entered the five-year-old he sometimes sat staring out of. He would look down at his daughter in his lap, cradled in his arms, below him at a great distance, it seemed, blinking sleepily up at him, and sense a stripped ache from the center of his groin to the cords of his arches, as if she'd just poured out of his interior into existence, as she once had, but now full blown, with her flesh entirely formed.

"Here," she said, and gave a pull. "You just walk real slow, like you do when you hold my hand."

He took some hesitating steps and felt his fear, filtering through the alcohol, start up a wild amusement.

"You really can't see, can you, Dad? You're not kidding!"

"No," he said, struggling for control over the amusement. "No! Can you?"

"I can see almost like it's day out, but not as good."

"Oh, that's funny!" he said, trying to explain away his laughter, which sounded close to hysteria. "You're funny!"

"Yes, Dad," she said.

And with the directness of her answer Mel pictured his own father turning up to him from a floor where he was crouched, laying asphalt tile, and heard the astonished exclamation, as of ribald glee, that came from his father at the moment he wrenched one knee—a response that was usual with his father, along with a grinning shame, whenever his father found a new physical limitation in himself, or an ache caused by age, as if his father were saying by this, "I'm on my way out! Good!" Mel felt a sympathetic pain in his own knee, still trying not to laugh, and realized that his daughter was the only person he would ever give himself over to in this way, in such complete trust. Then he glimpsed silver-toned trunks and limbs of trees, as if he were seeing out through his blindness to a negative-image of the wooded countryside. For whatever reasons the blindness had struck him, it was leaving, he knew, seeing for a second the negative-image of his daughter's hair moving blackly below. He was walking—he was being led by her out of that blindness into an entirely different world, and although that world was in its essentials the same as the world that he had always known—now branches sprang into sight, unfurling leaves, saplings—it was also a larger world, as he felt with his first tentative footsteps over its surface, and was the world of his daughter now.

JOYCE CAROL OATES

◇ ◇ ◇

Wednesday's Child

Around the high handsome roof of the house birds flew in the first hours of daylight, calling out, so that their small shadows fell against the bedroom curtains harmless as flowers thrown by anonymous admirers. Squirrels ran along the gutters. At some distance the horns of river freighters sounded, melancholy and exciting. Today he was not going to work; today he woke slowly, with a sense of luxury, aware of these sounds and their lovely softness, thinking that sound itself seemed a kind of touch.

His wife lay sleeping beside him. She was a dark-haired woman of thirty-five, attractive, exhausted even in sleep, wounded by small impatient lines in her forehead; he did not quite believe in those lines. He always expected them to be gone. Even in sleep his wife seemed to him thoughtful, thinking, sensitive to his feeling of luxury—so she lay perfectly still, not waking. She would not join him in it.

Several shadows fell against the curtains—the weightless shadows of birds. He watched. Everything was still. This house, thirty years old, had stood firm and wonderfully solid among its more contemporary neighbors, a high brick colonial home with white shutters, quite perfect. It was not his

63

idea of a final home. It was his idea of a home for himself and his wife and daughter in this decade, just as this famous suburb was his idea of a way of preparing for a distant, delightful, aristocratic life in another part of the country. He was an architect and worked for an excellent firm. Only thirty-seven, he was successful in the eyes of his parents and even in the eyes of his friends, who were themselves scampering like squirrels with their tiny shrewd toe-nails pulling them, pulling them up, always up, their cheeks rosy with the exhilaration of success. He was one of them. He was not his parents' son any longer; his father had been a high-school teacher, a good, deferential, exploited man.

So he woke on Wednesday morning, very early. The day would be a long one. His wife was evidently not going to wake, but lay frowning and severe in sleep, as if giving up to him the burden of this day. Already he could hear his daughter. Coming out of her room . . . in the hall . . . now on her way downstairs. He listened closely. He could hear, or could imagine, her pulling the piano bench away from the piano, down in the living room. Yes, she must be there. The bench was white—a white grand piano, very beautiful—and she sat at it, seriously, frowning like her mother, staring down at the keys. White and black keys. Even the cracks arrested her attention. He lay in bed on the second floor of his house, imagining his daughter almost directly below him, sitting at the piano. He heard the first note. His face went rigid.

He got dressed quickly. He put on a tie his mother had given him, a very conservative tie, dark green. His secret was a dark, serious, grimly green soul—he liked to hide it behind smiles, enthusiasm for football, hearty compliments to his wife. . . . She had turned over in bed, she was still asleep or pretending to sleep. The other day she had told him she would not remain herself much longer. "I can't live like this much longer," she had said. It was not a threat or a warning, only a curious, exploratory remark. They had come in late from a dinner party, from a marvelous evening, and she had told him suddenly that she was failing, giving up, being conquered, defeated . . . all she had accomplished as a mother was failure. Failure.

Why should she wake up to see him off?

Downstairs he saw with a slight shock Brenda at the piano, seated just as he had imagined her. She was running her fingers gently over the keyboard. The sound was gentle, soft. It would not shatter any crystal; there was no power behind it. Down at the far end of the living room the wide French windows were seared with light, the filmy curtains glowing. He appreciated that; he appreciated beauty. The living room had been decorated in white and gold. His daughter's face was pale, not quite white, and her legs pale, limp, motionless. She had put her little white socks on perfectly. She wore a yellow dress, perfectly ironed by the laundry that did her father's shirts so meticulously, and her hair was a fine, dull gold, very neat. Everything matched. He appreciated that.

She was playing the "Moonlight Sonata" with a numb, feverish, heavy rhythm, leaning too hard on the more emphatic passages, too breathy and rushed with the delicate ones. She played like a sixteen-year-old girl who had taken lessons dutifully for years, mediocre and competent, with a firm failure of imagination underlying every note. Brenda was only six and had never had any music lessons, did not even listen in any evident way to music, and yet she could play for hours with this mysterious sub-competence—why? He stood staring at her. She was oblivious to him. Why, if his daughter must be insane, why not brilliantly insane? Why not a genius?

Instead, she was extraordinary but not astonishing. She might be written up in someone's textbook someday, but the case history would not be important; there wasn't enough to her. "Good morning, honey," he said. He came to her and put his arms gently around her. She stopped playing the piano but did not seem to notice him. Instead, as if paralyzed by a thought that had nothing to do with him, she sat rigid, intense, staring at her fingers on the keyboard.

"You're all ready, are you? Scrubbed and clean and ready for the trip?"

She did not appear to have heard him. She did hear him, of course, every word, and some words hardly audible—they had discovered that when she was hardly a year old, her uncanny animallike omnipotence. She heard what was breathed into his ear by his wife, up in their secret bed, she heard the secret date of her next appointment with the Dreaded Doctor, she knew instinctively when an innocent drive would take her to the dentist, she knew everything. . . . Today, Wednesday, was not a fearful day. She was not afraid of school. She gave no indication of liking it, or of anticipating it, but she was not afraid and she would not go limp, forcing them to carry her out to the car.

"I'll have some coffee, then we'll leave. Mommy's staying home today and I'm taking you. I thought we'd have a nice drive to school, then come back through the park. . . . I took the whole day off today. I hope the sun stays out."

He was aware of the paragraphs of his speech. Talking to his silent, frowning daughter, a child of six with an ageless look, he understood how silence mocks words; her blocks of silence, like terrible monstrous blocks of stone, fell heavily on either side of his words. What he said was never quite accurate. He was speaking to a child when, perhaps, he should have been speaking to an adult. Brenda's intelligence had never been measured. She might be ten years old, or eighteen, or two. It was a mystery, an abyss. As soon as he entered the kitchen he heard her begin to play where she had left off, the "Moonlight Sonata" in that sun-filled living room. . . .

He made instant coffee. His hands had begun to tremble. The harmonic green and brown of the kitchen did not soothe him, he could not sit down. When he came home from the office each day he always came out to the kitchen to talk to his wife, and he talked energetically about his work. His wife always appeared to listen with sympathy. His paragraphs of words, tossed against her appreciative silence, were attempts to keep her quiet; he realized that now. She made dinner and listened to him, flattering him with her complete attention. He hinted of trouble at work, maybe a union threatening to strike, or the federal government again raising mortgage interest rates . . . tricks to keep his wife from talking about Brenda. He realized that now.

When he returned to the living room Brenda slid dutifully off the bench. She never resisted physically; her body was not really her own. She was quite small for her age, with knobby white knees. He loved her knees. Her hair was thin and straight, cut off to show her delicate ears. Her face was a pretty face, though too thin, unnaturally pale; her eyes were a light green. Seeing her was always a shock; you expected to see a dull, squat child, a kind of dwarf. Not at all. Everyone, especially the two sets of grandparents, remarked on her beauty. "She's so pretty! It will all work itself out!" both grandmothers said constantly. They were anxious to share in her mythical progress and contributed toward the tuition charged by the private, expensive school she went to, though Arthur resented this. He made enough money to send his own child to school. But the grandparents wanted to get as close as possible, nudging their beautiful prodigy into life, breathing the mysterious breath of normal life into her. Why, why was she not normal, when it was so obviously easier to be normal than to be Brenda? Perfectly stupid children were normal, ugly children were normal, and this golden-haired little lady, with her perfect face and ears and limbs, was somehow not . . . not "normal." It was an abyss, the fact of her.

Drawing slightly away from him, with a woman's coolness, she put on her own coat. He knelt to check her, to see if the buttons were lined up correctly. Of course. It had been years since she'd buttoned them wrong. "All set? Great! We're on our way!" Arthur said heartily. She did not look at him. She never met his eye, that was part of her strangeness—she would not look anyone in the eye, as if some secret shame or hatred forced her away, like the invisible force of like magnets.

And so . . . they were on their way. No backing out. His wife had driven Brenda to school ever since Brenda had begun, and today he was driving her, a generous act. Minutes flew by. It was a surprise how quickly time had passed, getting him up out of bed and on his way, drawing him to the ride. The minutes had passed as if flying toward an execution. . . . He had tried to think of this day as a gift, a day off from work, but it had been nothing but pretense. He was afraid of the long trip and afraid of his daughter.

Between his wife and himself was the fact of their daughter. They had created her together, somehow they had brought her into the world. It was a mystery that jarred the soul; better not to think of it. His wife had accused him more than once of blaming her for the child. "You hate me unconsciously. You can't control it," she had said. Her wisdom was sour and impregnable. "You hate failure," she said. Didn't he hate, in his cheerful secretive way, his own father because his own father was something of a failure? "Jesus Christ, what are you saying?" he had shouted. He denied everything.

The school was experimental and chancy, very expensive. Was it really quite professional? The several doctors they'd taken Brenda to were not enthusiastic; they expressed their opinion of the school with a neutral shrug of the shoulders. Why not try? And so, desperate, they had driven fifty miles to talk with the director, a long-nosed, urgent female with grimy fingernails and great excitement, and she had agreed to take Brenda on. "But we make no promises. Everything is exploratory," she had said. "Nothing is given a form, no theories are allowed to be hardened into dogma, no theories are rejected without trial, no emotions are stifled. . . ." Why not try? After several months Brenda showed no signs of improvement, and no signs of degeneration. If she showed any "signs" at all, they were private and indecipherable.

But Wednesday had become the center of the week. He and his wife looked to Wednesday, that magic day, as a kind of Sabbath; on that day he drove to work with a sense of anticipation, and his wife drove Brenda fifty miles to school and fifty miles back again, hoping. This was the usual procedure. Then, when he came home, he would always ask, "How do you think it went today?" and she would always reply, "The director is still hopeful . . . I think it's going well . . . yes, I think it's going well."

In the car Brenda seated herself as far from him as possible. No use to urge her to move over. She was not stubborn, not exactly. It was rather as if no one inhabited her body, as if her spirit had abandoned it. "A great day for a ride!" he said. He chatted with her, or toward her. His voice sounded nervous. He disliked silence because of its emptiness, the possibility of anything happening inside it—no warning, no form to it. He was amorous of forms, solid forms. He distrusted shapelessness. In his daydreams he had always wanted to force action into a shape, to freeze explosions into art, into the forms in which beauty is made bearable. He lived in one of those forms. The style of his living was one of them. Why not? The work he did was professional in every way, geared to a market, imagination within certain limiting forms. He was not a genius, he would not revolutionize architecture. Like his daughter, he was extraordinary but not astonishing.

Brenda took a piece of spaghetti out of her coat pocket. It was uncooked, broken in half. She began to chew on it. Except for random, unlikely things—fish sticks, bits of cardboard, cucumber, grapes with seeds—she ate nothing but uncooked spaghetti. She bit pieces off slowly, solemnly, chewing them with precision. Her green eyes were very serious. Every day she stuffed her pockets with pieces of spaghetti, broken in pieces. Bits of spaghetti were all over the house. His wife vacuumed every day, with great patience. It wasn't that Brenda seemed to like spaghetti, or that she had any concept of "liking" food at all. Perhaps she could not taste it. But she would not eat anything else. Arthur had long ago stopped snatching it away from her. He had stopped pleading with her. For what had seemed a decade she had sat at the table with them, listless and stony-eyed, refusing to eat. She did not quite *refuse*—nothing so emphatic. But she would not eat. She had no obvious conception of "eating." What she did was nibble slowly at pieces of spaghetti, all day long, or chew cardboard and shape it into little balls, or suck at grapes and very carefully extract the seeds. She walked around the house or out in the back yard as if in a trance, slow, precise, unhurried, spiritless. Demurely she turned aside when someone approached her. She went dead. The only life she showed was her piano playing, which was monotonous and predictable, the same pieces over and over again for months. . . . Her silence was immense as a mountain neither Arthur nor his wife could climb. And when the silence came to an end—when Brenda cried, which was infrequent—they heard to their horror the sobs of a six-year-old child, breathy and helpless. But how to help her? She could not be embraced, even by a distraught parent. A bump on the head, a bleeding scratch, would not soften her. The jolly mindlessness of Christmas would not give any grandparent the right to hug her. No nonsense. No touching. When his wife took Brenda for her monthly checkup, at which time the doctor gave her vitamin shots, she always asked the doctor how Brenda was "doing"; and the doctor always said, with a special serious smile to show how sorry he was about all this, "She's surprisingly healthy, considering her diet. You should be thankful."

It was a long drive. Arthur began to think longingly of his office—an older associate of his whom he admired and imitated, the naïveté of a secretary he could almost have loved, in another dimension. Elevators, high buildings. Occasional long lunches. He thought of his office, of his working space. He liked to work. He liked problems. They came to him in the shape of lines with three dimensions. It was remarkable how they were then transferred into shapes that were solid, into buildings. He was working on a shopping plaza. A shopping "mall." With love he dreamed of the proper shapes of banks, the proper shapes of supermarkets, of hardware stores—seductive as music! Their lines had to be gentle, seductive, attractive as the face of his secretary, who was only twenty-three. He wanted to love them. Certainly he had enough love in him . . . love for his work, for his wife, his secretary, his parents, his friends, his daughter. . . . Why did he feel so exhausted though it was early morning?

He entered the expressway in silence. Brenda was awake but silent. It was worse than being truly alone, for a swerving of the car would knock her around; if he slammed on the brakes she would fly forward and crack her skull. A limp weight. No true shape to her, because she was so empty. What was she thinking? He glanced sideways at her, smiling in case she noticed him. He and his wife believed that their daughter was thinking constantly. Her silence was not peaceful. It seemed to them nervous, jumpy, alert, but alert to invisible shapes. Something unseen would move in the corner of her eye and she would shiver, almost imperceptibly. What did she see? What did she think? Idiot children who giggle and squirm happily in their mothers' embraces make more sense, being only defective of intelligence. It would be possible to love them.

"Look at the cows!" he said, pointing. "Do you see the cows?"

No response. No cows.

"Look at the big truck up ahead . . . all those new cars on it. . . ." He felt the need to talk. He wanted to keep a sense of terror at some distance; her silence, her terrifying silence! He stared at the carrier with its double row of shining cars, cars of all colors, very handsome. He was preparing to pass the truck. What if, at the crucial moment, the truck wobbled and the cars came loose? They seemed precariously fastened to the carrier. He imagined metal shearing through metal, slicing off the top of his skull. The steering wheel would cut him in two. And his daughter would be crushed in an instant, pressed into her essential silence. The end.

"Like to hear some music, Brenda?" He turned on the radio. Strange, how he felt the need to talk to her in spurts, as if offering her a choice of remarks. Like his wife, he somehow thought that a magic moment would arrive and Brenda would wake up, a fairy princess awakened by the right incantation. . . . If only she would let them kiss her, perhaps the perfect kiss would awaken her. But she did not hear the words, did not hear the love and yearning behind them, would not suffer the kiss, nothing. She did not need them. She was a delicate weight in the corner of his eye, not a threat, not really a burden because she wanted nothing— unlike other children, she wanted nothing. And so there was nothing to give her.

She ate uncooked spaghetti for the rest of the drive.

The school was housed in a one-story building, previously a small-parts shop. On the walk he noticed a bit of drool about Brenda's mouth—should he wipe it off? He wanted to wipe it off, not because he was anxious for her to look neat for school but because he was her father and had the right to touch her.

"Do you have a handkerchief, honey?"

This was too mild. She sensed his weakness. She wiped her own mouth with her hand, blankly and efficiently. A college-age girl with a suntanned face took Brenda from him, all popeyed charm and enthusiasm. He watched Brenda walk away. It pained him to see how easily she left him, how unconnected they were. There was nothing between them. She did not glance back, did not notice that he was remaining behind. Nothing.

He drove around for a while, feeling sorry for himself, then stopped to have some coffee. Then he walked around the university, browsing in bookstores, wondering if he could remain sane—he had several hours to get through. What did his wife do on these holy Wednesdays? At noon he went to a good restaurant for lunch. Two cocktails first, then a steak sandwich. Women shoppers surrounded him. He admired their leisure, their rings, their gloves; women who had the air of being successes. They seemed happy. Once at a party he had noticed his wife in deep conversation with a stranger, and something in his wife's strained, rapt face had frightened him. When he asked her about it later she had said, "With him I felt anonymous, I could have begun everything again. He doesn't know about me. About Brenda." Like those bizarre unshaped pieces of sculpture that are placed around new buildings to suggest their important ties with the future, he and his wife had lost their ability to maintain a permanent shape; they were always being distorted. Too many false smiles, false enthusiasm and fear covered over. . . . The very passage of days had tugged at their faces and bodies, aging them. They were no longer able to touch each other and to recognize a human form. But he had seen her touch that man's arm, unconsciously, wanting from him the gift of a sane perspective, an anonymous freedom, that Arthur could no longer give her.

He wandered into another bookstore. In a mirror he caught sight of himself and was surprised, though pleasantly —so much worry and yet he was a fairly young man, still handsome, with light hair and light, friendly eyes, a good face. The necktie looked good. He wandered along the aisles, looking at textbooks. These manuals for beginning lives, for starting out fresh. . . . Engineering texts, medical texts. French dictionaries. A crunching sound at the back of the store put him in mind of his daughter eating. Spaghetti being bitten, snapped, crunched, chewed . . . an eternity of spaghetti. . . . He wandered to another part of the store and picked up a paperback book, *Forbidden Classics*. An Egyptian woman, heavily made up, beckoned to him from the cover. He picked up another book, *Bizarre Customs of the World*; on this cover a child beckoned to him, dressed in an outlandish outfit of feathers and furs. . . . He leafed through the book, paused at a few pages, then let the book fall.

Garbage. He was insulted. A sense of disorder threatened. Better for him to leave.

He strolled through the campus but its buildings had no interest for him. They were dead, they were tombs. The sidewalks were newer, wide, functional. The university's landscaping was impressive. Students sat on the grass, reading. A girl caught his attention—she wore soiled white slacks, sat with her legs apart, her head flung back so that the sun might shine flatly onto her face. Her long brown hair hung down behind her. She was immobile, alone. Distracted, he nearly collided with someone. He stared at the girl and wondered why she frowned so, why her face was lined though she could not have been more than twenty—what strange intensity was in her?

He walked in another direction. There were too many young girls, all in a hurry. Their faces were impatient. Their hair swung around their eyes impatiently, irritably. His blood seemed to return to his heart alert and jumpy, as if infected by their intensity, by the mystery of their secret selves. He felt panic. A metallic taste rose to his mouth, as if staining his mouth. He felt that something was coming loose in him, something dangerous.

What did his wife do on these long hateful days?

He went to the periodical room of the university's undergraduate library. He leafed through magazines. World affairs; nothing of interest. Domestic affairs: no, nothing. What about medicine, what new miracles? What about architecture? He could not concentrate. He tried to daydream about his work, his problems, about the proper shapes of banks and stores. . . . Nothing. He thought of his salary, his impressive salary, and tried to feel satisfaction; but nothing. His brain was dazzled as if with sparks. Suddenly he saw the girl on the grass, in a blaze of light, her white slacks glowing. An anonymous girl. Beginning again with an anonymous girl. The girl shivered in his brain, wanting more from the sun than the sun could give her.

He wanted to leave the library and find her, but he did

not move. He remained with the magazines on his lap. He waited. After a while, when he thought it was safe, he went to a campus bar and had a drink. Two drinks. Around him were music, noise; young people who were not youthful. People jostled his chair all the time, as if seeking him out, contemptuous of his age. A slight fever had begun in his veins. Around him the boys and girls hung over one another, arguing, stabbing the air with their fingers, scraping their chairs angrily on the floor. "I am not defensive!" a girl cried. Now and then a girl passed by him who was striking as a poster—lovely face, lovely eyes. Why didn't she glance at Arthur? It was as if she sensed the failure of his genes, the quiet catastrophe of his chromosomes. He heard beneath the noise in the bar a terrible silence, violent as the withheld violence of great boulders.

When he picked Brenda up he felt a sense of levity rising in him, as if he had survived an ordeal. "How was it today, honey? What is that you've got—a paper flower?" He took it from her buttonhole, the buttonhole indifferent as her face. Yes, a paper flower. A red rose. "It's great. Did you make it yourself, honey?" He put it in his own buttonhole, as if his daughter had made it for him. She did not glance up. In the car she sat as far from him as possible, while he chattered wildly, feeling his grin slip out of control. Around him boulders precarious on mountainsides were beginning their long fall, soundlessly.

"We'll stop in the park for a few minutes. You should get out in the sun." He tried to sound festive. Parks meant fun; children knew that. The park was large, mostly trees, with a few swings and tennis courts. It was nearly empty. He walked alongside her on one of the paths, not touching her, the two of them together but wonderfully independent. "Look at the birds. Blue jays," he said. He wanted to take her hand but feared her rejection. Only by force could anyone take her hand. She took a stick of spaghetti out of her pocket and bit into it, munching slowly and solemnly. "Look at the squirrels, aren't they cute? There's a chipmunk," he said. He felt that he was in charge of all these animals and that he must point them out to his daughter, as if he had to inform her of their names. What terror, not to know the names of animals, of objects, of the world! What if his daughter woke someday to a world of total blankness, terror? He was responsible for her. He had created her.

"Stay nearby, honey. Stay on the path," he said. He was suddenly exhausted; he sat on a bench. Brenda walked along the path in her precise, spiritless baby steps, munching spaghetti. She seemed not to have noticed that he was sitting, weary. He put his hands to his head and heard the notes of the "Moonlight Sonata." Brenda walked on slowly, not looking around. She could walk like this for hours in the back yard of their house, circling the yard in a certain space of time. A safe child, predictable. She might have been walking on a ledge, high above a street. She might have been stepping through poisonous foam on a shore. . . . The shadows of leaves moved about her and on her, silently. Birds flew overhead. She saw nothing. Arthur thought suddenly of his father sitting on the steps of the back porch of their old house, his head in his hands, weeping. Why had his father wept?

It seemed suddenly important for him to know why his father had wept, and why Brenda so rarely wept.

And then something happened—afterward Arthur was never able to remember it clearly. Brenda was on the path not far from him, no one was in sight, the park was ordinary and unsurprising, and yet out of nowhere a man appeared, running. He was middle-aged. In spite of the mild September day he wore an overcoat that flapped around his knees; his face was very red; his hair was gray and spiky; he ran bent over, stooped as if about to snatch up something from the ground. Arthur was watching Brenda and then, in the next instant, this outlandish running figure appeared, colliding with her, knocking her down. The man began to scream. He seized Brenda's arm and shook her, screaming down into her face in a high, waspish, womanish voice, screaming

words Arthur could not make out. "What are you doing—
what are you doing?" Arthur cried. He ran to Brenda and
the man jumped back. His mouth worked. He was crouching, foolishly alert, his face very red—he began to back up
slowly, cunningly. Arthur picked Brenda up. "Are you all
right? Are you hurt?" He stared into her face and saw the
same face, unchanged. He wondered if he was going out of
his mind. Now, as if released, the man in the overcoat
turned and began walking quickly away. He was headed
back into the woods. "You'd better get out of here before I
call the police!" Arthur yelled. His voice was shrill. He was
terribly agitated, he could not control the sickening fear in
his body.

The man was nearly gone. He was escaping. Arthur's
heart pounded, he looked down at Brenda and back up, at
the woods, and suddenly decided to run after the man.
"You, hey wait! You'd better wait!" he yelled. He left
Brenda behind and ran after the man. "Come back here,
you dirty bastard, dirty filthy pervert bastard!" The man
crashed into something. He stumbled in a thicket. Arthur
caught up with him and could hear his panicked breathing.
The back of the man's neck was dirty and reddened, blush-
ing fiercely. He turned away from the thicket and tried to
run in another direction, but his knees seemed broken. He
was sobbing. Panicked, defeated, stumbling, he turned suddenly toward Arthur as if to push past him—Arthur swung
his fist around and struck the man on the side of the neck.
One hard blow. The man cried out sharply, nearly fell.
Arthur struck him again. "Dirty bastard! Filth!" Arthur
cried. His third blow knocked the man down, and then he
found himself standing over him, kicking him—his heel into
the jawbone, into the nose, crunching the nose, splattering
blood onto the grass, onto his shoe. He could actually feel
the nose break! Something gave way, he felt even the vibra-
tions of the man's screams, his stifled screams. Arthur bent
over him, pounding with his fists. *I'll kill you, I'll tear you
into pieces!* The man rolled over wildly onto his stomach,

hiding his face in his hands. Arthur kicked viciously at his back. He kicked the back of his head. "I'm going to call the police—throw you in jail—you can rot—you dirty pervert, dirty bastard—" Arthur kicked at the body until he could not recall what he was doing; the paper rose fell out of his buttonhole and onto the man's back, and onto the ground. "You'd better get the hell out of here because I'm going to call the police. You'd better not be here when I come back," he said, backing away.

And he had forgotten . . . about Brenda. . . . What was wrong with him? He ran back to her and there she was, safe. Only her leg was a little dirty. A small scratch, small dots of blood. Nothing serious! Greatly relieved, panting with relief, Arthur bent to dab at her knee with a Kleenex. She stepped away. "There, there, it's just a tiny scratch . . " he said. He was very hot, sweating. He could feel sweat everywhere on his body. Hardly able to bear the pounding of his heart, he made another attempt to blot the blood, but Brenda side-stepped him. He looked sharply up at her and saw her look away from him. Just in that instant she had been looking at him . . . and then she looked away, at once. Their eyes had almost met.

He took her back to the car. They were safe, nothing had happened. Safe. No one had seen. His clothes were rumpled, his breathing hoarse, but still they were safe. He was alarmed at the pounding of his heart. Excitement still rose in him in waves, overwhelming his heart. . . . Wait, he should wait for a few minutes. Sit quietly. The two of them sat in the front seat of the car, in silence. Arthur wiped his face. He looked over at his daughter and saw that her coat was perfectly buttoned, her hair was not even mussed, her face was once again composed and secret. His panting alarmed him. Did she notice? Of course she noticed, she noticed everything, understood everything, and yet would never inform on him; what gratitude he felt for her silence!

After a few minutes he felt well enough to drive. He was a little nauseous with excitement. A little lightheaded. He turned on the radio, heard static and loud music, then turned it off again, not knowing what he was doing. He headed for the expressway and saw with burning eyes the signs pointing toward home; everything had been composed in a perfect design, no one could get lost. It was impossible to get lost in this country. Beside him, in the far corner of the seat, his daughter took out a small piece of spaghetti and began to chew on it. They were safe. He glanced at her now and then as if to check her—had that man really collided with her? Knocked her down and shaken her, screamed into her face? Or had he imagined it all—no man, no smashed nose, no blood? There was blood on his shoes. Good. He drove home at a leisurely pace, being in no hurry. Brenda said nothing.

PETER TAYLOR

◇ ◇ ◇

JE SUIS PERDU

L'Allegro

The sound of their laughter came to him along the narrow passage that split the apartment in two. It was the laughter of his wife and his little daughter, and he could tell they were laughing at something the baby had done or had tried to say. Shutting off the water in the washbasin, he cracked the door and listened. There was simply no mistaking a certain note in the little girl's giggles. Her naturally deep little voice could never be brought to such a high pitch except by her baby brother's "being funny." And on such a day as this, the day for packing the last suitcases and for setting the furnished apartment in order, the day before the day when they would really pull up stakes in Paris and take the boat train for Cherbourg—on such a day, only the baby could evoke from its mother that resonant, relaxed, almost abandoned kind of laughter . . . *They* were in the dining room just sitting down to breakfast. *He* had eaten when he got up with the baby an hour before, and was now in the *salle de bain* preparing to shave.

The *salle de bain*, which was at one end of the long central passage, was the only room in the apartment that

always went by its French name. For good reason, too: it
lacked the one all-important convenience that an American
expects of what he will willingly call a bathroom. It possessed a bathtub and a washbasin, and it had a bidet, which
was wonderful for washing the baby in. But the missing
convenience was in a closet close by the entrance to the
apartment, at the very opposite end of the passage from the
salle de bain. Altogether it was a devilish arrangement. But
the separation of conveniences was not itself so devilish as
the particular location of each. For instance just now, with
only a towel wrapped around his middle and with his face
already lathered, he hesitated to throw open the door and
take part in a long-distance conversation with the rest of the
family, because at any moment he expected to hear the
maid's key rattling in the old-fashioned lock of the entry
door down the passage. Instead, he had to remain inside the
salle de bain with his hand on the doorknob and his gaze on
the blank washbasin mirror (still misted over from the hot
bath he had just got out of); had to stand there and be
content merely with hearing the sound of merriment in
yonder, not able—no matter how hard he strained—to de-
termine the precise cause of it.

At last, he could resist no longer. He pushed the door
half open and called out to them, "What is it? What's the
baby up to?"

His daughter's voice piped from the dining room, "Come
see, Daddy! Come see him!" And in the next instant she
had bounced out of the dining room into the passage, and
she continued bouncing up and down there as if she were on
a pogo stick. She was a tall little girl for her seven years,
and she looked positively lanky in her straight white nightgown and with her yellow hair not yet combed this morning
but drawn roughly into a ponytail high on the back of her
head.

And then his wife's voice: "It's incredible, honey! You
really must come! And quick, before he stops! He's a perfect little monkey!"

But already it was too late. The maid's key rattled noisily in the lock. As he quickly stepped backward into the *salle de bain* and pulled the door to, he called to them in a stage whisper, "Bring me my bathrobe."

Through the door he heard his wife's answer: "You know your bathrobe's packed. You said you wouldn't need it again. Put on your clothes."

His trousers and his shirt and underwear hung on one door hook, beside his pajamas on another. His first impulse was to slip into his clothes and go and see what it was the baby was doing. But on second thought there seemed too many arguments against this. His face was already lathered. He much, much preferred shaving as he now was, wearing only his towel. But still more compelling was the argument that it was to be a very special shave this morning. *This morning the mustache was going to go!*

Months back he had made a secret pact with himself to the effect that if the work he came over here to do was really finished when the year was up, then the mustache he had begun growing the day he arrived would *go* the day he left. From the beginning his wife had pretended to loathe it, though he knew she rather favored the idea as long as they were here, and only dreaded, as he did, the prospect of his going home with that brush on his upper lip. But he had not even mentioned the possibility of shaving the mustache. And as he wiped the mist from the mirror and then slipped a fresh blade into his razor, he smiled in anticipation of the carrying on there would be over its removal.

In the passage now there was the clacking sound of the maid's footsteps. He could hear her taking all her usual steps —putting away the milk and bread that she had picked up on her way to work, crossing to the cloak closet, and placing her worn suede jacket and her silk scarf on a hanger—just as though this were not her last day on the job; or rather, last day with *them* in the apartment, because she was coming the following day, faithful and obliging soul, to wax the floors and hang the clean curtains she herself had washed.

Their blessed, hardworking Marie. According to his wife, their having had Marie constituted their greatest luck and their greatest luxury this year. He scarcely ever saw her himself, and sometimes he had passed her down on the boulevard without recognizing her until, belatedly, he realized that it had been her scarf and her jacket, and his baby in the carriage she pushed. But he had gradually assumed his wife's view that their getting hold of Marie had been the real pinnacle of all their good luck about living arrangements. Their apartment was a fourth-floor walkup, overlooking the Boulevard Saint-Michel and just two doors from the rue des Écoles; with its genuine *chauffage central* and its Swedish kitchen, and even a study for him. It was everything they could have wished for. At first they had thought they ought not to afford such an apartment as this one, but because of the children they decided it was worth the price to them. And after his work on the book got off to a good start and he saw that the first draft would almost certainly get finished this year, they decided that it would be a shame not to make the most of the year; that is, not to have some degree of freedom from housekeeping and looking after the children. And so they spoke to the concierge, who recommended Marie to them, saying that she was a mature woman who knew what it was to work but who might have to be forgiven a good deal of ignorance since she had not lived always in Paris. They had found nothing to forgive in Marie. Even her haggard appearance his wife had come to speak of as her "ascetic look." Even her reluctance to try to understand a single word of English represented, as did the noisy rattling of the door key, her extreme consideration for their privacy. Every morning at half-past eight, her key rattled in the lock to their door. She was with them all day, sometimes taking the children to the park, always going out to do more marketing, never off her feet, never idle a moment until she had prepared their evening meal and left them, to ride the Métro across Paris again—almost to Saint-Denis—and prepare another evening meal for her own husband and son.

Yet this maid of theirs was, in his mind, only a symbol of how they had been served this year. It was hard to think of anything that had not worked out in their favor. They had ended by even liking their landlady, who, although she lived but a block away up the Boulevard Saint-Michel, had been no bother to them whatever, and had just yesterday actually returned the full amount of their deposit on the furniture. Their luck had, of course, been phenomenal. After one week in the Hôtel des Saints-Pères, someone there had told them about M. Pavlushkoff, "the honest real-estate agent." They had put their problem in the hands of this splendid White Russian—this amiable, honest, intelligent, efficient man, with his office (to signalize his greatest virtue, his sensibility) in the beautiful Place des Vosges. Once M. Pavlushkoff had found them their apartment they never saw him again, but periodically he would telephone them to inquire if all went well and if he could assist them in any way. And once in a desperate hour—near midnight—they telephoned him, to ask for the name of a doctor. In less than half an hour M. Pavlushkoff had sent dear old Dr. Marceau to them.

And Dr. Marceau himself had been another of their angels. The concierge had fetched round another doctor for them the previous afternoon, and he had made the little girl's ailment out to be something very grave and mysterious. He had prescribed some kind of febrifuge and the burning of eucalyptus leaves in her room. But Dr. Marceau immediately diagnosed measles (which they had believed it to be all along, with half her class at L'École Père Castor already out of school with it). Next day, Dr. Marceau had returned to give the baby an injection that made the little fellow's case a light one; and later on he saw them through the children's siege of chicken pox. Both the children were completely charmed by the old doctor. Even on that first visit, when the little girl had not yet taken possession of the

French language, she found the doctor irresistible. He had bent over her and listened to her heart not through a stethoscope but with only a piece of Kleenex spread out between her bare chest and his big pink ear. As he listened, sticking the top of his bald head directly in her face, he quite unintentionally tickled her nose with the pretty ruffle of white hair that ringed his pate. Instantly the little girl's eyes met her mother's. From her sickbed she burst into giggles and came near to causing her mother to do the same. After that, whenever the doctor came to see her, or to see her little brother, she would insist upon his listening to her heart. It would be hard to say whether Dr. Marceau was ever aware of why the little girl giggled, but he always said in French that she had the heart of a lioness, and he always stopped and kissed her on the forehead when he was leaving.

That's what the whole year had been like. There was *that*, and there had been the project—the work on his book, which was about certain Confederate statesmen and agents who, with their families, were in Paris at the end of the Civil War, and who had to decide whether to go home and live under the new regime or remain permanently in Europe.

As far as his research was concerned, he had soon found that there was nothing to be got hold of at the Bibliothèque Nationale or anywhere else in Paris that was not available at home. And yet how stimulating to his imagination it was just to walk along the rue de l'Université in the late afternoon, or along the rue de Varenne, or over on the other side of the Seine along the rue de Rivoli and the rue Saint-Antoine, hunting out the old addresses of the people he was writing about. And of course how stimulating to his work it was just being in Paris, no matter what his subject. Certain of his cronies back home at the university had accused him of selecting his subject merely as an excuse to come to Paris . . . He couldn't be sure himself what part that had played in it. But it didn't matter. *He had had the idea, and he had done the work.*

*   *   *

With his face smoothly shaven, and dressed in his clean clothes, he was in such gay spirits that he was tempted to go into the dining room and announce that he was dedicating this book to M. Pavlushkoff, to Dr. Marceau, to Marie, to all his French collaborators.

He found the family in the dining room, still lingering over breakfast, the little girl still in her nightgown, his wife in her nylon housecoat. At sight of his naked upper lips his wife's face lit up. Without rising from her chair, she threw out her arms, saying, "*I* must have the first kiss! How beautiful you are!"

The little girl burst into laughter again. "Mama!" she exclaimed. "Don't *say* that! *Men* aren't beautiful, *are* they, Daddy?" She still had not noticed that the mustache was gone.

It was only a token kiss he got from his wife. She was afraid that Marie might come in at any moment to take their breakfast dishes. Keeping her eyes on the door to the passage, she began pushing him away almost before their lips met. And so he turned to his daughter, trying to give her a kiss. Still she hadn't grasped what had brought on her parents' foolishness, and she wriggled away from him and out of her chair, laughing and fairly shrieking out, "What's the matter with him, Mama?"

"Just look!" whispered his wife; and at first he thought of course she meant look at him. "Look at the baby, for heaven's sake," she said.

The baby was in his playpen in the corner of the dining room. With his hands clasped on the top of his head and his fat little legs stuck out before him, he was using his heels to turn himself round and round, pivoting on his bottom.

"How remarkable!" the baby's daddy now heard himself saying.

"Watch his eyes," said the mother. "Watch how he rolls them."

"Why he *is* rolling them! How really remarkable!" He glanced joyfully at his wife.

"That's only the half of it," she said. "In a minute he'll begin going around the other way and rolling his eyes in the other direction."

"It's amazing," he said, speaking very earnestly and staring at the baby. "He already has better coordination than I've *ever* had or ever *hope* to have. I've noticed it in other things he's done recently. What a lucky break!"

And presently the baby, having made three complete turns to the right, did begin revolving the other way round and rolling his eyes in the other direction. The two parents and the little girl were laughing together now and exchanging intermittent glances in order to share the moment fully. The most comical aspect of it was the serious expression on the baby's face, particularly at the moment when, facing them and stopping quite still, he shifted the direction of his eye rolling. At this moment the little girl's voice moved up at least one octave. She never showed any natural jealousy of her baby brother, but at such times as this she often seemed to be determined to outdo her parents in their amusement and in their admiration of the baby. Just now she was so convulsed with laughter that she staggered back to her chair and threw herself into it and leaned against the table. As she did so, one of her flailing hands struck her milk glass, which was still half full. The milk poured out over the placemat and then traced little white rivulets over the dark surface of the table.

Both parents pounced upon the child at once: "Honey! Honey! Watch out! Watch what you're doing!"

The little girl crimsoned. Her lips trembled as she said under her breath, *"Je regrette."*

"If you had drunk your milk this wouldn't have happened," said the mother, dabbing at the milk with a paper napkin.

"Regardless of that," said the father with unusual severity in his voice, "she has no business throwing herself about so and going into such paroxysms over nothing." But he knew, really, that it was not the threshing about that irritated him so much as it was the lapse into French. And it was almost as though his wife understood this and wished to point it out. For, discovering that a few drops of milk had trickled down one table leg and onto the carpet, she turned and herself called out in French to the maid to come and bring a cloth. His own mastery of French speech, he reflected, was the thing that *hadn't* gone well this year. After all, as he was in the habit of telling himself, *he* hadn't had the opportunity to converse with Marie a large part of each day, or to attend a primary school where the teacher and the other pupils spoke no English, and he hadn't—with his responsibilities to his work and his family—been able to hang about the cafés like some student. It was a consoling thought. Righteously, he put aside his irritation.

But now his little daughter, sitting erect in her chair, repeated aloud: *"Je regrette. Je regrette."* This time it affected him differently. It was impossible to tell whether she was using the French phrase deliberately or whether she wasn't even aware of doing so. But whether deliberate or not, it had its effect on her father. For a time it caused him to stare at his daughter with the same kind of interest that he had watched his son with a few moments before. And all the while his mind was busily tying the present incident to one that had occurred several weeks before. He had taken the little girl to see an old Charlie Chaplin film one afternoon at a little movie theater around the corner from them on the rue des Écoles. They had stayed on after the feature to see the newsreel, and then after the newsreel, along with a fairly large proportion of the audience, they had risen in the dark to make their way out. The ushers at the rear of the theater were not able to restrain the crowd that was waiting for seats; and so there was the inevitable melee in the aisles. When finally he came out into the lighted lobby he assumed that his little girl was still sticking close behind him, and he began getting into his mackinaw without even looking back to see that she was there. Yes, it was thoughtless of him, all right; but it was what he had done. As he tugged at the belt of the bulky mackinaw, he became aware of a small voice crying out above the noise of the canned music back in the theater. What interested him first was merely the fact that he did understand the cry: *"Je suis perdu! Je suis perdu!"* Actually he didn't recognize it as his daughter's voice until rather casually and quite by chance he glanced behind him and saw that she was not there. He threw himself against the crowd that was still emerging from the exit, all the while mumbling apologies to them in his Tennessee French which he was sure they would not understand (though himself understanding perfectly their oaths and expletives) and still hearing from the darkness ahead her repeated cry: *"Je suis perdu!"* When he found her she was standing against the side wall of the theater, perfectly rigid. Reaching down in the darkness to take her hand he found her hand made into a tight little fist. By the time he got her out into the light of the lobby her hand in his felt quite relaxed. Along the way she had begun to cry a little, but already she was smiling at him through her tears. "I thought I was lost, Daddy," she said to him. He had been so relieved at finding her and at seeing her smiling so soon that he had not even tried to explain how it had happened, much less describe the chilling sensations that had been his at that moment when he realized it was the voice of his own child calling out to him, in French, that she was lost.

Now, in the dining room of their apartment, he was looking into the same flushed little face and suddenly he saw that the eyelashes were wet with tears. He was overcome with shame.

His wife must have discovered the tears at the same moment. He glanced at her and saw that she, too, was now filled with pity for the child and was probably thinking, as he was, that they were all of them keyed up this morning of their last day before starting home.

"Oh, it's all right, sweetie," said his wife, putting her hand on the top of the blond little head and pointing out the milk to Marie. "Accidents will happen."

Squatting down beside his daughter, he said, "Don't you notice anything different?" And he stuck his forefinger across his upper lip.

"Oh, Mama, it's gone!" she squealed. Placing her two little hands on his shoulders, she bent forward and kissed him on the mouth. "Mama, you're right," she exclaimed. "He *is* beautiful!"

After that, the spilled milk and the baby's gyrations were events of ancient history—dismissed and utterly forgotten.

A few minutes later, the little girl and Marie were beside the playpen chattering to the baby in French. His wife had wandered off into the bedroom, where she would dress and then throw herself into a final fury of packing. She had already asked him to make himself scarce this day, to keep out of the way of women's work. *His* duties, she had said, would begin when it came time to leave for the boat train tomorrow morning. Now he followed her into the bedroom to put on a tie and a jacket before setting out on his day's expedition.

She had taken off her housecoat and was standing in her slip before the big armoire, searching there among the few dresses that hadn't already been packed for something she might wear today. He stopped in front of the mirror above the chest of drawers and began slipping a tie into his collar. He was thinking of just how he would spend his last day. Not, certainly, with any of his acquaintances. He had said goodbye to everyone he wanted to say goodbye to. No, he would enjoy the luxury of being by himself, of buying a paper and reading it over coffee somewhere, of wandering perhaps one more time through the Luxembourg Gardens—the wonderful luxury of walking in Paris on a June day without purpose or direction.

When he had finished with his tie, he discovered that his wife was now watching his face in the mirror. She was smiling, and as their eyes met she said, "I'm glad you shaved it but I shall miss it a little, along with everything

else." And before she began pulling her dress over her head
she blew him a kiss.

Il Penseroso

The feeling came over him in the Luxembourg Gardens at
the very moment he was passing the Medici Grotto at the
end of its little lagoon. He simply could not imagine what it
was that had been able to depress his spirits so devastatingly
on a day that had begun so well. Looking back at the grotto,
he wanted to think that his depression had been induced by
the ugliness and the triteness of the sculpture about the
fountain there, but he knew that the fountain had nothing to
do with it. He was so eager to dispel this sudden gloom and
return to his earlier mood, however, that he turned to walk
back to the spot and see what else might have struck his
eye. Above all, it was important for it to be something
outside himself that had crushed his fine spirits this way,
and that was thus threatening to spoil his day.

He didn't actually return to the spot, but he did linger a
moment by the corner of the palace, beside a flower bed
where two workmen—surreptitiously, it seemed to him—were
sinking little clay pots of already blooming geranium plants
into the black soil, trying to make it look as though the
plants honestly grew and bloomed there. From here he eyed
other strollers along the path and beside the lagoon, hoping
to discover in one of them something tragic or pathetic
which he might hold responsible for the change he had felt
come over him. He would have much preferred finding an
object, something not human, to pin it on, but, that failing,
he was now willing to settle for any unhappy or unpleasant-
looking person—a stranger, of course, someone who had no
claim of any kind on him. But every child and its nurse,
each shabby student with satchel and notebooks, every old
gentleman or old lady waiting for his terrier or her poodle to
perform in the center of the footpath appeared relatively

happy (in their limited French way, of course, he found himself thinking)—as happy, almost, as he must have appeared not five minutes earlier. He even tried looking farther back on the path toward the gate into the rue de Vaugirard, but it availed him nothing. Then his thoughts took him beyond the gate, and he remembered the miserable twenty minutes he had just been forced to spend trying to read his paper and enjoy his coffee in the Café Tournon, while a bearded fellow American explained to him what was wrong with their country and why Americans were "universally unpopular" abroad.

But even this wouldn't do. For he was as used to the ubiquitous bearded American and his café explanations of everything as he was to the ugly Italian grotto; and he disliked them to just the same degree and found them equally incapable of disturbing him in this way. He gave up the search now, and as he strode out into the brightness of the big sunken garden he quietly conceded the truth of the matter: the feeling was not evoked by his surroundings at all but had sprung from something inside himself. Further, it was not worth all this searching; it wasn't important; it would pass soon. Why, as soon as it had run its course with him he would not even remember the feeling again until . . . until it would come upon him again in the same unreasonable way, perhaps in six months, or in a few days, or in a year. When the mood was not on him, he could never believe in it. For instance, while he had been shaving this morning he truly did not know or, rather, he *knew not* that he was ever in his life subject to such fits of melancholy and gloom . . . But still the mood *was* on him now. And actually he understood the source well enough.

It sprang from the same thing his earlier cheerful mood had come from—his own consciousness of how well everything had gone for him this year, and last year, and always, really. It was precisely this, he told himself, that depressed him. At the present moment he could almost wish that he hadn't finished the work on his book. He was able to wish this (or almost wish it) because he knew it was so typical of him to have accomplished just precisely what he had come to accomplish—and so American of him. Generally speaking, he didn't dislike being himself or being American, but to recognize that he was so definitely the man he was, so definitely the combination he was, and that certain experiences and accomplishments were now typical of him was to recognize how he was getting along in the world and how the time was moving by. He was only thirty-eight. But the bad thought was that he was no longer *going to be* this or that. He *was*. It was a matter of *be*ing. And to *be* meant, or seemed to mean at such a moment, to *be over with*. Yet this, too, was a tiresome, recurrent thought of his—very literary, he considered it, and a platitude.

He went on with his walk. The Jardin du Luxembourg was perfection this morning, with its own special kind of sky and air and its wall of flat-topped chestnuts with their own delicate shade of green foliage, and he tried to feel guilty about his wife's being stuck back there in the apartment, packing their possessions, trying to fit everything that had not gone into the foot lockers and the duffel-bags into six small pieces of luggage. But the guiltiness he tried for wouldn't materialize. Instead, he had a nasty little feeling of envy at her packing. And so he had to return to his efforts at delighting in the singular charm of the park on a day like this. "There is nothing else like it in Paris," he said, moving his lips, "which is to say there is nothing else like it in the world." And this pleased him just as long as it took for his lips to form the words.

It wasn't yet midmorning, but the little boys—both the ragged and the absurdly over-dressed-up ones—had already formed their circle about the boat basin in the center, and, balancing themselves on the masonry there, were sending their sailboats out over the bright water. This was almost a cheering sight to him. But not quite. For it was, after all, a regular seasonal feature of the place, like the puppet shows and the potted palm trees, and it was hardly less artificial in its effect.

He was rounding the lower garden of the park now; had passed the steps that led up toward the Boulevard Saint-Michel entrance and toward that overpowering monster the Panthéon. (There were monsters and monstrous things everywhere he turned now.) He was walking just below the clumsy balustrade of the upper garden; and now, across the boat basin, across the potted flower beds and the potted palms, above the heads of the fun-loving, freedom-loving, stiff-necked, and pallid-faced Parisians, he saw the façade of the old palace itself. It also loomed large and menacing. There was no look of fun or freedom about it. It did not smile down upon the garden. Rather, out of that pile of ponderous, dirty stone, all speckled with pigeon droppings, twenty eyes glared at him over the iron fencing, which seemed surely to have been put there to protect the people from the monster—not the monster from the people. It was those vast, terrible, blank windows, like the whitened eyes of a blind horse, that made the building hideous. How could anyone ever have found it a thing of beauty? How could . . . Then suddenly: "Oh, do stop it!" he said to himself. But he couldn't stop it. Wasn't it from one of those awful windows that the great David, as a prisoner of the Revolution, had painted his only landscape? That unpleasant man David, that future emperor of art, that personification of the final dead end to a long-dying tradition! "Oh, do stop it!" he said again to himself. "Can't you stop it?"

But still he couldn't. The palace *was* a tomb. The park was a formal cemetery. He was where everything was finished and over with. Too much had already happened here, and whatever else might come would be only anticlimactic. And nothing could be so anticlimactic as an American living on the left bank of the Seine and taking a morning walk in the Jardin du Luxembourg. He remembered two novels whose first chapters took for their setting this very spot. Nothing was so deadening to a place as literature! And wasn't it true, after all, that their year in that fourth-floor walkup had been a dismal, lonely one? Regardless of his having got his work done, of his having had his afternoons free to wander not only through the streets where his heroes had once lived but also through the Louvre and the Musée Cluny and through the old crumbling *hôtels* of the Marais? Regardless of the friends they had made and even of the occasional gay evening on the town. Wasn't it really so that he had just not been willing to admit this truth until this moment? Wasn't it so, really, that he had come to Paris too late? That this was a city for the very young and the very rich, and that he, being neither, might as well not have come? What was he but a poor plodding fellow approaching middle age, doing all right, getting along with his work well enough, providing for his family; and the years were moving by . . .

Suddenly he turned his back on the boat basin and the palace, and started at a brisk pace up the ramp that leads toward the great gilded south gate. And immediately he saw his daughter in the crowd! She was moving toward him, walking under the trees.

He saw her before she saw him. This gave him time to gather his wits, and to recall his wife, as soon as she got *him* out of the apartment, was determined to get *them* out, too, so that there would be no one to interfere with her packing. And now, during the moment that *she* did not see him, he managed to find something that he could be cross with her about. She was ambling along, absent-mindedly leaning on the baby's carriage—that *awful* habit of hers—and making it all but impossible for Marie to push the carriage. She had come out from under the trees now, and as she skipped and danced along, her two bouncing blond ponytails, which Marie had fixed, one directly above each ear, were literally dazzling in the sunlight. "Daddy," she said, as she came within his shadow on the gravel path. Her eyes were just exactly the color of the park's own blue heaven. His wife's mother had said it didn't seem quite normal for a girl to have such "positive blue" eyes. And her long little face with the chin just a tiny bit crooked, like his own!

He took her hand, and they went down the ramp toward the row of chairs on their left. "If we sit down, you'll have to pay," she warned him.

"That's all right," he said.

"I'll sit on your lap if you'll give me the ten francs for the extra chair."

"And if I won't?"

"Oh, I'll sit on your lap anyway, since you've shaved that mustache."

The old woman who collected for chairs was hot on their heels. He paid for the single chair and tipped her the price of another.

"I saw how much you gave her," his daughter said reproachfully. "But it's all right. She's one of the nice ones."

"Oh, they're all nice when you get to know them," he said, laughing.

She nodded. "And isn't it a lovely park, Daddy? I think it is."

"It's too bad we're going home so soon, isn't it?" he said.

"Daddy, we just *got* here!" she protested.

"I mean going back to America, silly," he said.

"I thought you meant to the apartment . . . But we're *not* going back to America *today*."

"No, but tomorrow."

"Well, what difference does *that* make?"

He saw Marie approaching with the carriage. "Let's give our chair to Marie, since I have to be on my way," he said.

"Then you have to leave now?" she asked forlornly.

He gave her a big squeeze with his arms and held her a moment longer on his knee. He was wondering where his dark mood had gone. It was not just gone. He felt it had never been. And why had he lied to himself about this year? It *had* been a fine year. But still he kept thinking also of how she had interrupted his mood. And as soon as she was off his knee, he began to feel resentful again of the interruption and of the mysterious power she had over him He found that he wanted the mood of despondency to return, and he knew it wouldn't for a long while. It was something she had taken from him, something she had taken from him before and would take from him again and again—she and the little fellow in the carriage there, and their mother, too, even before they were born. They would never allow him to have it for days and days at a time, as he once did. He felt he had been cheated. But this was not a mood, it was only a thought. He felt a great loss—except he didn't really feel it, he only thought of it. And he felt, he *knew* that he had after all gotten to Paris too late . . . after he had already established steady habits of work . . . after he had acknowledged claims that others had on him . . . after there were ideas and truths and work and people that he loved better even than himself.

HAROLD BRODKEY

◇ ◇ ◇

On the Waves

In the churning wake of a motorboat from one of the luxury hotels, the gondola bobbed with graceful disequilibrium. The tall, thin, handsome man sitting in the gondola gripped the sides of the small wooden craft and said to his seven-year-old daughter, "Hold on." He thought, Gondolas are atavistic.

He wore a white polo shirt. Once he had been the sixth-ranking tennis player in the United States, and had married a rich girl; his days on the tennis circuit were five years past, and the marriage had ended in divorce twelve months before. Now he taught American history in an American school in Rome and played tennis with various members of the diplomatic set. He still kept to the course of reading he had drawn up and that he hoped would give him intelligence, or, failing that, education. Gifted with a strong body and good nerves, he had never felt so harassed by ignorance that a sense of his own worth could not come to his rescue; then in the fourth year of his marriage, his tennis game and marriage deteriorating, he had begun wanting desperately to know more about everything. He had settled down to read the philosophers, the psychologists, the historians, the poets,

98

the critics. He had had no clear idea what he would do as an educated man, a self-made intellectual, and so he decided to teach. He had left his wife, unwilling to quarrel with her, unable to bear her restlessness at the change in him. He had gone to Europe. The divorce had depressed him. He had missed his daughter unconscionably. He wrote his former wife and asked if the child Melinda could visit him. He would pay her plane passage to Europe. His former wife agreed to permit the journey. Melinda had sent him a note in block capitals: "CAN WE SEE VENICE DADDY?"

She sat beside him in the gondola, white-skinned, thin-boned, with straight eyebrows like his and green eyes like her mother's. Her reddish-blond hair was her own. So was the dull stubbornness with which she maintained a polite and lifeless manner toward Henry. This was the fourth day of her visit, their second day in Venice.

He had a headache. He sat slouching, hands between his knees. He wondered irritably how the Venetians managed to live day after day with the illusive and watery haze, the heat, the mind-scattering profusion of reflections, of smells, of playful architectural details, with the unsettling mixture of squalor and ostentation, with the silent, silvery air, the decay, the history, and the atmosphere of vice. But he felt constrained to be honest. The truth was, he thought ashamedly, he was bored. It was dull as hell to spend so many hours in the company of a child.

They had been to the Ca' d'Oro that morning. Henry had said, "Isn't it pretty? It's supposed to be one of the prettiest houses in Europe."

"It's pretty," the child said.

She had grown restless when he'd dawdled in front of the Mantegna. "Tell me the story of that picture, Daddy," she'd said.

"The man being shot with arrows is a saint," he'd said.

So much in Venice was unsuitable for a child.

It had been perhaps a mistake, this trip: movement was half a child's charm. Children stilled—on a train, at a dinner table, in a gondola—were reduced: one was chafed by the limitations of their intellects and the hardness of their voices.

When they'd left the Ca' d'Oro, they'd hired a gondola and embarked on the Grand Canal. Noticing the child's lackluster eyes, the loose setting of her lips, Henry had asked her, "You're not seasick or anything?" He suggested, "Some people don't like gondolas. If the gondola bothers you, we can go ashore."

"Could we have lunch?"

"I forgot," Henry had said. "It's your lunchtime. Can you hold out until we get to San Marco? I know the restaurants there."

As the gondolier resumed his steady stroke, Melinda turned to Henry—the angle of her head upon her shoulders indicated melancholy—and asked in a weak voice, "Why did they build Venice on the water?"

Henry replied without thought, "To be safe."

"It's safe on the water?"

Henry, whose eleventh-grade history students adored him and trusted his opinions, said, "Well, children might fall in. But the people here wanted to be safe from armies."

The child waited questioningly.

Henry was thinking that a gondola was an inefficient watercraft, keelless (a bent demiquaver, a notation of the music of the water). He woke from his reverie with a start. "Armies can't fight and swim at the same time."

"They could come in little boats," the child said.

Henry dusted off the knees of his trousers. "The Venetians could swim out and overturn little boats, they could do all sorts of things to little boats. The Venetians had no trouble with armies for a thousand years." He smiled to cover any deficiencies in his explanation—he had always been extraordinarily confident of his physical charm.

"A thousand years?" the child asked.

"Yes," he said reassuringly, "a thousand years."

The child closed one eye, looked at him through the other. "Is that a long time, Daddy?"

Henry swallowed a sigh. "I'll tell you," he said. "let's take Grandmother Beecher. You think she's old, don't you?" Henry's eyes held the child's attention. "Now imagine *her* grandmother. And keep going back for *twenty* grandmothers. Isn't that a lot of grandmothers?"

His and the child's eyes seemed hopelessly locked. Then, as he watched, the child's eyes slowly went out of focus.

Slowly, she extended her arm over the water; she observed the shadow of her hand change shape on the sun-gilt waves. She was as lifeless as a mosaic, yet she spoke: "Are the palaces so wibbly-wobbly because they're so old?"

Henry said, "Well, yes and no." He paused, then went on heartily, "The buildings are old, yes, but that's not the entire story. The islands they are built on were mudbanks—they just barely stuck out of the water, and the Venetians made them bigger by throwing stones and logs and garbage—"

"Garbage—eeugh!" The child held her nose.

"Well," her father said, "they made the islands bigger. But as the years pass, the water licks away at them. Waves are like little tongues," he said with sudden poetry. "They eat out little pieces of the islands, the islands sink, and the buildings wobble." It was sad she was too young, Henry thought, for him to tell her that suns, stars, people, intelligence, and every other bit of created matter began by law in chaos and aged into chaos.

Melinda, squinting, peered up into Henry's face. "Is Venice falling apart, Daddy?" she asked.

"Well—yes and no," Henry said. "It's *sinking*, but very slowly."

"Gee, Daddy, you know an awful lot," she said with despairing enthusiasm.

Henry felt his face heating into a blush. He said, "Any guidebook would tell you . . ." He did not finish. He gazed at the Baroque palaces along this newer stretch of the Grand Canal, palaces spotted with noon shadows, draped in cornices, pilasters, and balustrades, sad.

"It won't fall down while we're here?" the child asked. She laughed faintly.

Did she want Venice to fall? Henry said, "No. It won't fall." It was disappointment he saw in her face. He said, "You know that big tower in the Piazza—the red tower? It fell down once. . . . In Henry James's time. About sixty years ago." Melinda was watching him, he thought, expectantly. She wanted to hear more about the collapse of Venice. Good God, why did the child wish harm to this fanciful city built on mud and garbage? Was it that, betrayed, she resented the world of adults, hoped for its destruction? Henry's heart trembled: the child was a betrayed idealist. Achingly, he looked at her.

She wore the dim frown that suggested she might be grappling with a half-formulated female thought.

"What is it?" Henry asked. "Are you thinking something? What are you thinking?"

The child, startled, shook her head and drew her shoulders up.

"You can tell me," Henry said encouragingly.

"You'll get angry," she said.

"Me?" He stopped. He said slowly, "It doesn't matter if I get angry. Fathers and daughters can get mad at each other if they want. It doesn't mean a thing. We can't go through life being afraid of each other." Melinda studied her thumb. "Why, if I got angry, I might shout and wave my arms and fall into the Grand Canal—wouldn't that be funny?"

Melinda was silent.

"Go ahead," Henry said. He leaned closer. "Try to make me angry. See what happens."

"I'm too scared."

"Of me?"

"I don't know," she said tactfully. She stuck her forefinger into the water. Henry could see only the back of her head.

He felt the rush of innocence that accompanies a sense of being misunderstood. "The water's dirty!" he exclaimed.

Melinda raised her finger and held it in her other hand on her lap; drops of water darkened her pale-blue skirt.

Henry said, "I don't see that anything you can tell me would make me any angrier than I am at your *not* telling me."

Melinda whispered, "All right. . . ." The gondola rocked. A lifeboat-shaped motor vessel was chugging by, stacked with Coca-Cola cartons. "I don't really like Venice."

He had expected her to say—his hopes had grown so from the moment when he realized she wanted Venice to fall— something more illuminating, something like an admission that it saddened her, the distance that had come between her and Henry since the divorce, something like "I hate it that you and Mommy don't live together anymore," something honest like that.

He said, "You wanted to come to Venice! It was your idea!"

"It's not the way I thought it would be," she said. "Nothing here is sincere except the water."

Henry's mouth opened, then emitted laughter. He laughed rather a long time. He sobered: Would Melinda care that a city was *insincere* if Henry's leaving home had not taught her that insincerity was everywhere? He blinked at her pityingly, tenderly.

"Why did you laugh?" Her face was pink with hurt.

"Because I thought what you said was witty." He watched her. "Do you know what 'witty' means?"

"No."

"Something true—more or less—that comes as a surprise makes people laugh. That's witty."

"I did?" she said.

"Yes. You did. . . . But, Melinda, Venice is supposed to be nice, even though it's insincere," Henry said.

The child's face caved in, as if she took what he'd said for an expression of disapproval.

Henry, with that sensation of clumsiness that came to him whenever she asked him to help with one of her small buttons, tried to put things right. "But you like the water?"

"And the pigeons," the child said, anxious to please.

"Why? Are they sincere?"

"Yes," the child said, and nodded vigorously.

Why did she look so expectant? *I give up*, Henry thought, and laughed with exasperation and weariness. Melinda's face pinkened again, slowly. She smoothed her skirt. She seemed to have come into possession of a gentle incandescence. He said, "We certainly won't stay here if you don't like it. We can go to Paris."

"Paris?" The incandescence grew, then dimmed. "If you want to," she said, staring into her lap.

Henry had come to hate her pale good manners. The first days of her visit, he had thought she was still shocked that Mother-and-Daddy were no longer a single, hyphenated warm beast; he had told himself, "She will have to get used to me as an individual." He had not expected her to go on so long being mannerly and frightened with that individual. He began to rattle off words like a salesman trying to confuse a customer. "We'll go swimming—at the Lido—this afternoon. We'll take the launch over. We'll swim in the 'sincere' water, and tonight we'll eat and pack and have some ice cream, and tomorrow we'll fly to Paris. We'll fly over the Alps. You'll see the Alps—you've never seen the Alps before. We'll get to Paris in time for lunch. We'll have lunch outside on the street—"

"I know. I saw it on television."

"But you'll like it?"

The child said worriedly, "Do you have enough money?"

Oh, my God, Henry thought, *she did overhear those quarrels*. "No," he said, "I can't afford it. But we're going to do it anyway."

Melinda's eyes grew large. Her face seemed distended with pleasure. She put her hand to her mouth and laughed in the shelter of her hand.

Henry said, "What's so funny?"

"You're funny, Daddy. You're so bad." She inserted her hand inside his and gripped his fingers with an industrious and rubbery pressure—an active possession. Light dipped and danced along the swan's neck of the gondola's fantastic prow. She sighed. "Daddy," she said after a while. "You know that boy who lives across the hall?" From the apartment in the States where she lived with her mother, she meant. "Well, he likes to play dirty games."

Henry's tongue moved over his lower lip. He thought, How strangely moving it is that the child trusts me. "He does?" he said.

"Yes," she said.

"What do you mean by dirty games?" His eyes probed a corner of the Venetian sky; his voice was as calm as a psychiatrist's.

"You know."

"Give me an example."

"Oh, he wants me to go into the closet with him and take my clothes off."

The gondola slid under the Ponte dell'Accademia. Henry said, "Is that so?"

Melinda said, "Yes," nodding.

Henry switched his eyes to a different corner of the sky. "Is that all?" he asked.

"He's really silly," she said, noncommittal. ". . . He likes to push stomachs."

Henry heard the muted rumble of footsteps on the wooden bridge. "Do you like to push stomachs?"

Melinda said, "Sometimes." She drew the end of a strand of hair back from her cheek. "But I don't really like playing those games with *him*." She looked up at her father, her brows knit. "He gets angry if I won't play those games."

"Why does that bother you? What do you care if he gets angry?"

"Well, I don't like him to get too angry. I like having him to play with when I get bored."

"Is boredom so awful?" Henry said in a louder tone.

"It depends."

Henry thought, *She wants to punish me for abandoning her. My God.* He made a mental note to do some reading about disturbed children. He said, shielding his eyes with his hand, "You stay out of that closet!"

A startled, single peal of involuntary laughter popped out of Melinda. She stared at him with pink astonishment.

"What's funny?" Henry asked.

"You are!" the child shouted. "What you're thinking! You want to kiss me!" Strands of hair bounced on her forehead in the silvery light. She spread her fingers over her mouth and cheeks, hiding them from him.

The sunlit panorama was squeezed into a rich oval in the center of which his daughter's face floated, partly veiled by her fingers. "You're right,' Henry said, with amazement.

A flutter passed across the child's shoulders; a sound halfway between a choked shout and a laugh came from behind her fingers.

Along the canals, at the edge of his vision, Venice trembled on its uncertain islands, assailed by the devouring and protective and odorous wash of the sea. He kissed Melinda's hands, and as she moved them he kissed her cheek, her nose, her chin.

The Gondola floated toward the seaward rim of the Piazzetta. Melinda's head lay on Henry's chest in the exhaustion following laughter. Her arm was thrown across his stomach. "We're at the Piazza," Henry said.

Melinda sat up, touched a hand to her hair. Groggily, she surveyed the approaching landfall, the stone folds of the perspective opening past the winged lion, the lozenge-patterned palace, the benign litter of Byzantine oddments, bronze horses, golden domes, pinnacles, flagpoles, and pigeons. Amiably, the child said, "*Ciao, piazza. Ciao*, lunch. *Ciao*, pigeons."

S. Y. AGNON

◇ ◇ ◇

At the Outset of the Day

After the enemy destroyed my home I took my little daughter in my arms and fled with her to the city. Gripped with terror, I fled in frenzied haste a night and a day until I arrived at the courtyard of the Great Synagogue one hour before nightfall on the eve of the Day of Atonement. The hills and mountains that had accompanied us departed, and I and the child entered into the courtyard. From out of the depths rose the Great Synagogue, on its left the old House of Study and directly opposite that, one doorway facing the other, the new House of Study.

This was the House of Prayer and these the Houses of Torah that I had kept in my mind's eye all my life. If I chanced to forget them during the day, they would stir themselves and come to me at night in my dreams, even as during my waking hours. Now that the enemy had destroyed my home I and my little daughter sought refuge in these places; it seemed that my child recognized them, so often had she heard about them.

An aura of peace and rest suffused the courtyard. The Children of Israel had already finished the afternoon prayer and, having gone home, were sitting down to the last meal before the fast to prepare themselves for the morrow, that they might have strength and health enough to return in repentance.

A cool breeze swept through the courtyard, caressing the last of the heat in the thick walls, and a whitish mist spiraled up the steps of the house, the kind children call angels' breath.

I rid my mind of all that the enemy had done to us and reflected upon the Day of Atonement drawing ever closer, that holy festival comprised of love and affection, mercy and prayer, a day whereon men's supplications are dearer, more desired, more acceptable than at all other times. Would that they might appoint a reader of prayers worthy to stand before the Ark, for recent generations have seen the decline of emissaries of the congregation who know how to pray; and cantors who reverence their throats with their trilling, but bore the heart, have increased. And I, I needed strengthening—and, needless to say, my little daughter, a babe torn away from her home.

I glanced at her, at my little girl standing all atremble by the memorial candle in the courtyard, warming her little hands over the flame. Growing aware of my eyes, she looked at me like a frightened child who finds her father standing behind her and sees that his thoughts are muddled and his heart humbled.

Grasping her hand in mine, I said, "Good men will come at once and give me a prayer shawl with an adornment of silver just like the one the enemy tore. You remember the lovely prayer shawl that I used to spread over your head when the priests would rise up to bless the people. They will give me a large festival prayerbook filled with prayers, too, and I will wrap myself in the prayer shawl and take the book and pray to God, who saved us from the hand of the enemy who sought to destroy us.

"And what will they bring you, my dearest daughter? You, my darling, they will bring a little prayerbook full of letters, full of all of the letters of the alphabet and the vowel-marks, too. And now, dearest daughter, tell me, an *alef* and a *bet* that come together with a *kametz* beneath the *alef*—how do you say them?"

"*Av*," my daughter answered.

"And what does it mean?" I asked.

"Father," my daughter answered, "like you're my father."

"Very nice, that's right, an *alef* with a *kametz* beneath and a *bet* with no dot in it make '*Av*.'

"And now, my daughter," I continued, "what father is greater than all other fathers? Our Father in Heaven, who is my father and your father and the father of the whole world. You see, my daughter, two little letters stand there in the prayerbook as if they were all alone, then they come together and lo and behold they are '*Av*.' And not only these letters but all letters, all of them join together to make words and words make prayers and the prayers rise up before our Father in Heaven who listens very, very carefully, to all that we pray, if only our hearts cling to the upper light like a flame clings to a candle."

Even as I stood there speaking of the power of the letters a breeze swept through the courtyard and pushed the memorial candle against my daughter. Fire seized hold of her dress. I ripped off the flaming garment, leaving the child naked, for what she was wearing was all that remained of her lovely clothes. We had fled in panic, destruction at our heels, and had taken nothing with us. Now that fire had consumed her dress I had nothing with which to cover my daughter.

I turned this way and that, seeking anything my daughter could clothe herself with. I sought, but found nothing. Wherever I directed my eyes, I met emptiness. I'll go to the corner of the storeroom, I said to myself, where torn sacred books are hidden away, perhaps there I will find something. Many a time when I was a lad I had rummaged about there and found all sorts of things, sometimes the conclusion of a matter and sometimes its beginning or its middle. But now I turned there and found nothing with which to cover my little girl. Do not be surprised that I found nothing. When books were read, they were rent; but now that books are not read, they are not rent.

I stood there worried and distraught. What could I do for my daughter, what could I cover her nakedness with? Night was drawing on and with it the chill of the night, and I had no garment, nothing to wrap my daughter in. I recalled the home of Reb Alter, who had gone up to the Land of Israel. I'll go to his sons and daughters, I decided, and ask clothing of them. I left my daughter as she was and headed for the household of Reb Alter.

How pleasant to walk without being pursued. The earth is light and comfortable and does not burn beneath one's feet, nor do the Heavens fling thorns into one's eyes. But I ran rather than walked, for even if no man was pursuing me, time was: the sun was about to set and the hour to gather for the evening prayer was nigh. I hurried lest the members of Reb Alter's household might already be getting up to leave for the House of Prayer.

It is comforting to remember the home of a dear friend in time of distress. Reb Alter, peace be with him, had circumcised me, and a covenant of love bound us together. As long as Reb Alter lived in his home I was a frequent visitor there, the more so in the early days when I was a classmate of his grandson Gad. Reb Alter's house was small, so small that one wondered how such a large man could live there. But Reb Alter was wise and made himself so little that his house seemed large.

The house, built on one of the low hills surrounding the Great Synagogue, had a stucco platform protruding from it. Reb Alter, peace be with him, had been in the habit of sitting on that platform with his long pipe in his mouth, sending wreaths of smoke gliding into space. Many a time I stood waiting for the pipe to go out so I could bring him a light. My grandfather, peace be with him, had given Reb

Alter that pipe at my circumcision feast. "Your grandfather knows pipes very well," Reb Alter told me once, "and knows how to pick just the right pipe for every mouth."

Reb Alter stroked his beard as he spoke, like one well aware that he deserved that pipe, even though he was a modest man. His modesty showed itself one Friday afternoon before sunset. As he put out the pipe, and the Sabbath was approaching, he said, "Your grandfather never has to put out his pipe; he knows how to smoke more or less as time necessitates."

Well, then, I entered the home of Reb Alter and found his daughter, together with a small group of old men and old women, sitting near a window while an old man with a face like a wrinkled pear stood reading them a letter. All of them listened attentively, wiping their eyes. Because so many years had passed I mistook Reb Alter's daughter for her mother. What's going on? I asked myself. On the eve of the Day of Atonement darkness is falling, and these people have not lit a "candle of life." And what sort of letter is this? If from Reb Alter, he is already dead. Perhaps it was from his grandson, my friend Gad, perhaps news had come from Reb Alter's grandson Gad, who had frequented the House of Study early and late. One day he left early and did not return.

It is said that two nights prior to his disappearance his wetnurse had seen him in a dream sprouting the plume of a peculiar bird from his head, a plume that shrieked, "A, B, C, D!" Reb Alter's daughter folded the letter and put it between the mirror and the wall. Her face, peeking out of the mirror, was the face of an aged woman bearing the burden of her years. And alongside her face appeared my own, green as a wound that has not formed a scab.

I turned away from the mirror and looked at the rest of the old people in Reb Alter's home and tried to say something to them. My lips flipped against each other like a man who wishes to say something but, upon seeing something bizarre, is seized with fright.

One of the old men noticed the state of panic I was in. Tapping one finger against his spectacles, he said, "You are looking at our torn clothing. Enough that creatures like ourselves still have skin on our flesh." The rest of the old men and old women heard and nodded their heads in agreement. As they did so their skin quivered. I took hold of myself, walked backwards, and left.

I left in despair and, empty-handed, with no clothing, with nothing at all, returned to my daughter. I found her standing in a corner of the courtyard pressed against the wall next to the purification board on which the dead are washed. Her hair was loose and wrapped about her. How great is Thy goodness, O God, in putting wisdom into the heart of such a little girl to enable her to wrap herself in her hair after her dress was burned off, for as long as she had not been given a garment it was good that she covered herself with her hair. But how great was the sadness that enveloped me at that moment, the outset of this holy festival whose joy has no parallel all the year. But now there was no joy and no sign of joy, only pain and anguish.

The stone steps sounded beneath feet clad in felt slippers and long stockings, as Jews bearing prayer shawls and ritual gowns streamed to the House of Prayer. With my body I covered my little girl, trembling from the cold, and I stroked her hair. Again I looked in the storeroom where the torn pages from sacred books were kept, the room where in my youth I would find, among the fragments, wondrous and amazing things. I remember one of the sayings, it went approximately like this: "At times she takes the form of an old woman and at times the form of a little girl. And when she takes the form of a little girl, don't imagine that your soul is as pure as a little girl; this is but an indication that she passionately yearns to recapture the purity of her infancy when she was free of sin. The fool substitutes the *form* for the *need*; the wise man substitutes *will* for *need*."

A tall man with a red beard came along, picking from his

teeth the last remnants of the final meal, pushing his wide belly out to make room for himself. He stood about like a man who knew that God would not run away and there was no need to hurry. He regarded us for a moment, ran his eyes over us, then said something with a double meaning.

My anger flowed into my hand, and I caught him by the beard and began yanking at his hair. Utterly astonished, he did not move. He had good cause to be astonished too: a small fellow like me lifting my hand against a brawny fellow like him. Even I was astonished: had he laid hold of me, he would not have let me go whole.

Another tall, husky fellow came along, one who boasted of being my dearest friend. I looked up at him, hoping that he would come between us. He took his spectacles, wiped them, and placed them on his nose. The whites of his eyes turned green and his spectacles shone like moist scales. He stood looking at us as though we were characters in an amusing play.

I raised my voice and shouted, "A fire has sprung up and has burned my daughter's dress, and here she stands shivering from the cold!" He nodded his head in my direction and once more wiped his spectacles. Again they shone like moist scales and flashed like green scum on water. Once more I shouted, "It's not enough that no one gives her any clothing, but they must abuse us, too!" The fellow nodded his head and repeated my words as though pleased by them. As he spoke he turned his eyes away from me so that they might not see me, and that he might imagine he had made up the story on his own. I was no longer angry with my enemy, being so gripped with fury at this man: though he had prided himself on being my friend, he was repeating all that had befallen me as though it were a tale of his own invention.

My daughter began crying. "Let's run away from here."

"What are you saying?" I answered. "Don't you see that night has fallen and that we have entered the holy day? And if we were to flee, where would we flee and where could we hide?"

Where could we hide? Our home lay in ruins and the enemies covered all the roads. And if by some miracle we escaped, could we depend upon miracles? And here were the two Houses of Study and the Great Synagogue in which I studied Torah and in which I prayed and here was the corner where they had hidden away sacred books worn with age. As a little boy I rummaged about here frequently, finding all sorts of things. I do not know why, on this particular day, we found nothing, but I remember that I once found something important about *need* and *form* and *will*. Were it not for the urgency of the day I would explain this matter to you thoroughly, and you would see that it is by no means allegorical but a simple and straightforward affair.

I glanced at my little girl who stood trembling from the cold, for she had been stripped of her clothing, she didn't even have a shirt, the night was chill and the song of winter birds resounded from the mountains. I glanced at my daughter, the darling of my heart, like a father who glances at his little daughter, and a loving smile formed on my lips. This was a very timely smile, for it rid her of her fear completely. I stood then with my daughter in the open courtyard of the Great Synagogue and the two Houses of Study which all my life stirred themselves and came to me in my dreams and now stood before me, fully real. The gates of the Houses of Prayer were open, and from all three issued the voices of the readers of prayer. In which direction should we look and whither should we bend our ears?

He who gives eyes to see with and ears to hear with directed my eyes and ears to the old House of Study. The House of Study was full of Jews, the doors of the Ark were open and the Ark was full of old Torah scrolls, and among them gleamed a new scroll clothed in a red mantle with silver points. This was the scroll that I had written in memory of the souls of days that had departed. A silver plate was hung over the scroll, with letters engraved upon it, shining letters. And even though I stood far off I saw what they were. A thick rope was stretched in front of the scroll that it might not slip and fall.

My soul fainted within me, and I stood and prayed as those wrapped in prayer shawls and ritual gowns. And even my little girl, who had dozed off, repeated in her sleep each and every prayer in sweet melodies no ear has ever heard.

I do not enlarge. I do not exaggerate.

Translated by DAVID S. SEGAL

R . K . NARAYAN

◇ ◇ ◇

Forty-five a Month

Shanta could not stay in her class any longer. She had done clay-modelling, music, drill, a bit of alphabets and numbers, and was now cutting coloured paper. She would have to cut till the bell rang and the teacher said, "Now you may all go home," or "Put away the scissors and take up your alphabets—" Shanta was impatient to know the time. She asked her friend sitting next to her, "It is five now?"

"Maybe," she replied.

"Or is it six?"

"I don't think so," her friend replied, "because night comes at six."

"Do you think it is five?"

"Yes."

"Oh, I must go. My father will be back at home now. He has asked me to be ready at five. He is taking me to the cinema this evening. I must go home." She threw down her scissors and ran up to the teacher. "Madam, I must go home."

"Why, Shanta Bai?"

"Because it is five o'clock now."

"Who told you it was five?"

"Kamala."

"It is not five now. It is—do you see the clock there? Tell me what the time is. I taught you to read the clock the other day." Shanta stood gazing at the clock in the hall, counted the figures laboriously and declared, "It is nine o'clock."

The teacher called the other girls and said, "Who will tell me the time from that clock?" Several of them concurred with Shanta and said it was nine o'clock, till the teacher said, "You are seeing only the long hand. See the short one, where is it?"

"Two and a half."

"So what is the time?"

"Two and a half."

"It is two forty-five, understand? Now you may all go to your seats—" Shanta returned to the teacher in about ten minutes and asked, "Is it five, madam, because I have to be ready at five. Otherwise my father will be very angry with me. He asked me to return home early."

"At what time?"

"Now." The teacher gave her permission to leave, and Shanta picked up her books and dashed out of the class with a cry of joy. She ran home, threw her books on the floor and shouted, "Mother, Mother," and Mother came running from the next house, where she had gone to chat with her friends.

Mother asked, "Why are you back so early?"

"Has Father come home?" Shanta asked. She would not take her coffee or tiffin but insisted on being dressed first. She opened the trunk and insisted on wearing the thinnest frock and knickers, while her mother wanted to dress her in a long skirt and thick coat for the evening. Shanta picked out a gorgeous ribbon from a cardboard soap box in which she kept pencils, ribbons and chalk bits. There was a heated argument between mother and daughter over the dress, and finally mother had to give in. Shanta put on her favourite pink frock, braided her hair and flaunted a green ribbon on her pigtail. She powdered her face and pressed a vermilion mark on her forehead. She said, "Now Father will say what a nice girl I am because I'm ready. Aren't you also coming, Mother?"

"Not today."

Shanta stood at the little gate looking down the street.

Mother said, "Father will come only after five; don't stand in the sun. It is only four o'clock."

The sun was disappearing behind the house on the opposite row, and Shanta knew that presently it would be dark. She ran in to her mother and asked, "Why hasn't Father come home yet, Mother?"

"How can I know? He is perhaps held up in the office."

Shanta made a wry face. "I don't like these people in the office. They are bad people—"

She went back to the gate and stood looking out. Her mother shouted from inside, "Come in, Shanta. It is getting dark, don't stand there." But Shanta would not go in. She stood at the gate and a wild idea came into her head. Why should she not go to the office and call out Father and then go to the cinema? She wondered where his office might be. She had no notion. She had seen her father take the turn at the end of the street every day. If one went there, perhaps one went automatically to Father's office. She threw a glance about to see if Mother was anywhere and moved down the street.

It was twilight. Everyone going about looked gigantic, walls of houses appeared very high and cycles and carriages looked as though they would bear down on her. She walked on the very edge of the road. Soon the lamps were twinkling, and the passers-by looked like shadows. She had taken two turns and did not know where she was. She sat down on the edge of the road biting her nails. She wondered how she was to reach home. A servant employed in the next house was passing along, and she picked herself up and stood before him.

"Oh, what are you doing here all alone?" he asked. She replied, "I don't know. I came here. Will you take me to our house?" She followed him and was soon back in her house.

Venkat Rao, Shanta's father, was about to start for his office that morning when a *jutka* passed along the street distributing cinema handbills. Shanta dashed to the street and picked up a handbill. She held it up and asked, "Father, will you take me to the cinema today?" He felt unhappy at the question. Here was the child growing up without having any of the amenities and the simple pleasures of life. He had hardly taken her twice to the cinema. He had no time for the child. While children of her age in other houses had all the dolls, dresses and outings that they wanted, this child was growing up all alone and like a barbarian more or less. He felt furious with his office. For forty rupees a month they seemed to have purchased him outright.

He reproached himself for neglecting his wife and child— even the wife could have her own circle of friends and so on: she was after all a grown-up, but what about the child? What a drab, colourless existence was hers! Every day they kept him at the office till seven or eight in the evening, and when he came home the child was asleep. Even on Sundays they wanted him at the office. Why did they think he had no personal life, a life of his own? They gave him hardly any time to take the child to the park or the pictures. He was going to show them that they weren't to toy with him. Yes, he was prepared even to quarrel with his manager if necessary.

He said with resolve, "I will take you to the cinema this evening. Be ready at five."

"Really! Mother!" Shanta shouted. Mother came out of the kitchen.

"Father is taking me to a cinema in the evening."

Shanta's mother smiled cynically. "Don't make false promises to the child—" Venkat Rao glared at her. "Don't talk nonsense. You think you are the only person who keeps promises—"

He told Shanta, "Be ready at five, and I will come and

take you positively. If you are not ready, I will be very angry with you."

He walked to his office full of resolve. He would do his normal work and get out at five. If they started any old tricks of theirs, he was going to tell the boss, "Here is my resignation. My child's happiness is more important to me than these horrible papers of yours."

All day the usual stream of papers flowed onto his table and off it. He scrutinized, signed and drafted. He was corrected, admonished and insulted. He had a break of only five minutes in the afternoon for his coffee.

When the office clock struck five and the other clerks were leaving, he went to the manager and said, "May I go, sir?" The manager looked up from his paper. "You!" It was unthinkable that the cash and account section should be closing at five. "How can you go?"

"I have some urgent private business, sir," he said, smothering the lines he had been rehearsing since the morning. "Herewith my resignation." He visualized Shanta standing at the door, dressed and palpitating with eagerness.

"There shouldn't be anything more urgent than the office work; go back to your seat. You know how many hours I work?" asked the manager. The manager came to the office three hours before opening time and stayed nearly three hours after closing, even on Sundays. The clerks commented among themselves, "His wife must be whipping him whenever he is seen at home; that is why the old owl seems so fond of his office."

"Did you trace the source of that ten-eight difference?" asked the manager.

"I shall have to examine two hundred vouchers. I thought we might do it tomorrow."

"No, no, this won't do. You must rectify it immediately."

Venkat Rao mumbled, "Yes, sir," and slunk back to his seat.

The clock showed 5:30. Now it meant two hours of excruciating search among vouchers. All the rest of the office had gone. Only he and another clerk in his section were working, and of course, the manager was there. Venkat Rao was furious. His mind was made up. He wasn't a slave who had sold himself for forty rupees outright. He could make that money easily; and if he couldn't, it would be more honourable to die of starvation.

He took a sheet of paper and wrote: "Herewith my resignation. If you people think you have bought me body and soul for forty rupees, you are mistaken. I think it would be far better for me and my family to die of starvation than slave for this petty forty rupees on which you have kept me for years and years. I suppose you have not the slightest notion of giving me an increment. You give yourselves heavy slices frequently, and I don't see why you shouldn't think of us occasionally. In any case it doesn't interest me now, since this is my resignation. If I and my family perish of starvation, may our ghosts come and haunt you all your life—" He folded the letter, put it in an envelope, sealed the flap and addressed it to the manager. He left his seat and stood before the manager. The manager mechanically received the letter and put it on his pad.

"Venkat Rao," said the manager, "I'm sure you will be glad to hear this news. Our officer discussed the question of increments today, and I've recommended you for an increment of five rupees. Orders are not yet passed, so keep this to yourself for the present." Venkat Rao put out his hand, snatched the envelope from the pad and hastily slipped it in his pocket.

"What is that letter?"

"I have applied for a little casual leave, sir, but I think . . ."

"You can't get any leave for at least a fortnight to come."

"Yes, sir. I realize that. That is why I am withdrawing my application, sir."

"Very well. Have you traced that mistake?"

"I'm scrutinizing the vouchers, sir. I will find it out within an hour. . . ."

It was nine o'clock when he went home. Shanta was already asleep. Her mother said, "She wouldn't even change her frock, thinking that any moment you might be coming and taking her out. She hardly ate any food; and wouldn't lie down for fear of crumpling her dress. . . ."

Venkat Rao's heart bled when he saw his child sleeping in her pink frock, hair combed and face powdered, dressed and ready to be taken out. "Why should I not take her to the night show?" He shook her gently and called, "Shanta, Shanta." Shanta kicked her legs and cried, irritated at being disturbed. Mother whispered, "Don't wake her," and patted her back to sleep.

Venkat Rao watched the child for a moment. "I don't know if it is going to be possible for me to take her out at all—you see, they are giving me an increment—" he wailed.

HERBERT GOLD

◇ ◇ ◇

"I Want a Sunday Kind of Love"

Dan Shaper had the court-given right to spend Christmas vacation with his children. He drove in this midwinter weather from New York to Cleveland through the wintry length of turnpike—slush and flats of New Jersey, sudden black mountains of Pennsylvania with their marred white tunnels, then slithering down through Ohio foothills—and not a stoplight after Manhattan until he approached Cleveland, his arm still embracing the wheel. He stopped for coffee at a Howard Johnson's, the coffee given by a pimply waitress, and then in the men's room studied the machine which, for an investment of eleven cents, cranked forth the Lord's Prayer engraved on a penny. A dime for labor, one cent for material.

He drove on until, again shaking with fatigue, he stopped at an identical Howard Johnson's, was offered coffee by a girl who had pimples in the same place, and retreated to possibilities for stamping the Lord's Prayer on the same or a similar penny. "Lest We Forget," the placard advised.

Like the famous drowning man, he thought of the ten years of his marriage, but with this difference: the marriage was the drowning, and afterward came the gasping and choking recovery. (Was that an unmarked patrol car behind him? Sometimes they used Edsels.)

Then he thought of Paula and Cynthia, love like lust eating at his belly, and his daughters saying, "Why do you have to stay away so long?" He bit hard into memory as if it were a plum. It was a black rock and his teeth hurt. And then he thought: "I need a wife of my own, wife and children with me every day. I need someone standing with me in the mirror." And thought: no other children could replace Paula and Cynthia, who were born of his first youth when he was a skinny boy, amazed that he could create plump living flesh.

And then thought: another coffee, another doughnut to keep him going. At least his stomach could take it. If the limits of love had been defined by pride and lust, left and right, his stomach could not still have taken doughnuts; but it still could. There was a new rock 'n' roll version of "Jingle Bells" on the radio. Fathers like him all over the world were flying, driving, training in to claim their visiting rights with their children—their stomachs jerking with excitement, hope and strain in their eyes, love and guilt and pride and an aching foot on the accelerator. Merry Christmas. God rest ye, merry gentlemen. "And now the Chipmunk Song, that newest Christmas classic . . ."

Shaper switched stations. He was near enough to Cleveland so that the pushbuttons now brought him the stations for which they had been set.

> For he shall reign for ever and ever
> He shall,
>   He shall,
> He shall reign for ever and ev-ev-ver.

All over America the fathers were returning to the scene of their defeat, their abdication, their flight. Some of them were thinking, like Dan Shaper: "Thank God I escaped! Thank God! I might have been caught forever!" Some of them were thinking, like Dan Shaper: "Regret, I should have tried once more, regret forever."

It was the late evening rush hour when he slid into the frayed edges of Cleveland. Neon and colored lights and sudden frosty forests of ripped-up evergreens beckoned to Christmas shoppers, while the men in vacant lots pounded their mitts together and promised "a nice tree, missus." Under a shelter marked in great letters $2.98! a woman sold teddy bears as large as teddy bears ever grow, and she had a portable coal stove to give her good cheer. The light changed; traffic urged him forward, down the outskirt slopes of the Alleghenies which lead into the flattened industrial town. Through the front vents of his car Shaper breathed the chilled exhaust from the tailpipe ahead of him.

If he could arrive at his friend's apartment before eight, he could call Paula and Cynthia. Or he could stop and call from a gas station. But he liked to talk with them, even by telephone, only when he was clean and shaved and combed, and the shaking fatigue of the five-hundred-mile drive eased by a drink. Then he could lounge at his ease through the first breathless words.

Cynthia, who was eight, would say, "I can say more things in Spanish now! *Buenos días,* Señor Daddy!"

"Señor Daddy too! Señor Daddy too!" would come Paula's protesting wail, twenty desperate squirming inches from the telephone.

"Shh, I'll let you talk. Wait till I'm finished, Paula. Daddy?"

"Yes, honeybear."

"We'll be ready tomorrow morning. You pick us up at nine. We'll be out on the front porch." She was very experienced at these arrangements, busy and bustling to get herself and her sister ready, experienced buffer state between her mother and her father.

"Now it's my turn!" came the distant wail.

"Now do you want to talk to Paula?"

"Yes," he would say.

"All right, Paula, now you talk."

And as Paula wrestled for the telephone, Cynthia's voice receded, becoming childish once again, all arrangements done, repeating merely: "Daddy. Daddy. Daddy?"

He sighed, emitting frost. He was not yet on the telephone with them. He was four blocks farther into the traffic; he had shifted gears four times; he had dreamed again, but it had only gotten him a few hundred yards deeper into Cleveland. There was another lot, festooned with lights, selling rootless and truncated, sap-frozen Christmas trees.

Driving through Cleveland on one of the many nights before Christmas, under fouled industrial skies seen through his greasy windshield, Shaper felt slush under his wheels, a flying soup of snow and dirt and salt, corroding the metal underbodies of automobiles; salt in the greasy air splashed up at nightfall into the traffic, wiping its film across the windshield, rhythmic swish of salt and glass; on the radio, one more God rested his merry gentlemen, followed by the Chipmunk Song. There were snowed-in, secretly salted sheep in the used-car lots. Hunched against the weather and the hurrying shoppers, the 1952 Studebakers and the older Fraziers ($100, nothing down) waited, and the sharp later models waited, too. GIRLS! ARE YOU HARD TO FIT? (A shoe store.) THRILL TO THE GLORY OF THE OPEN ROAD! (A driving school.) And THE ELBOW BAR, THE KNICK-KNACK-KNOOK, STEVE'S PLACE, STEAKS AND TEXAS-BURGERS!

DON'T ASK THE PRICE—YOU NAME IT! EVERYTHING GOES!

CHILI! STARLITE FOOD! DAY-OLD BAKED GOODS! (Slightly used apple pies? Shaper asked. Outgrown marshmallow cookies?) RED HOTS!

Where was that chicken store he remembered? CAPONS FOR SALE! "What's a capon, Daddy?" Cynthia had once asked him.

Answer: "A capon is a very tender chicken, given special treatment, nice and soft, honey."

At last he reached the apartment of his friend, Martie Grant. Warmth and greetings; this friend always saved his

life. There was an amiable steam on the windows. His visits
were special occasions; hot buttered rum and how are we
doing? In answer to the question, Dan answered, "I dunno,
chappie. Maybe I'm making out."

He had already called and the arrangements were fixed
about seeing Cynthia and Paula on their front porch in
the morning. He talked with his friend until they both
grew drowsy, and then one more hot rum and a couple
of salty crackers, and then to the sack. He made out: he
fell asleep. That was all right, chappie, when what you need
is sleep.

The children, thick in mufflers, were waiting on the porch
when he drove up. They had been playing, waiting, talking;
cocking their heads, they watched him turn into the driveway as if interested in his style as a driver.

"Hello, Daddy," said Cynthia very shyly.

"Hello, Daddy," said Paula.

He understood and said with shyness equal to theirs,
"Hello, children. Let's get into the car."

Then out the driveway, down the street and around the
corner; and then he had to pull over to the side of the curb,
crunching frozen snow, when they flung their arms about
him: "Oh Daddy, Daddy, Daddy!" It was as if they had
feared that their mother could see through the walls. But
they did not believe, as he sometimes did, that she could
follow him around corners with an angry eye. There was
now a swarming mass of daughters greeting father, and
then, tousled, flushed, he patted them both and felt pleased
by the happy tears all around.

"Okay. Now, what should we do?" he asked.

"Plans!"

"That's right, I have plans. Now listen—"

"What? What? What are we going to do?"

"A trip to the moon for lunch. Then Bermuda. Then a
snack. Then quickly across two or three oceans for dinner,
and then we'll— "

With relieved howls of laughter at so much eating, so much travel, they said, like happy little girls everywhere, "Oh, Daddy! I don't believe you."

"All right, then I'll have to show you."

And he would show them, would, *would*. If he had to take them to both the moon and Bermuda. Focused on his daughters, he believed that he could infuse them with his energy of feeling for them—right through the snow and ice and his yearning thrust across turnpikes.

"Why are you looking at me, Daddy?"

"I want to look at you, Paula."

"I outgrew the dress you gave me for my birthday already. Mommy says you never buy the right size."

"Tough shit."

"What's that?"

"That's the word for failure to calculate how fast a little girl can grow."

Slowly a smile appeared on her face. She had learned words on the playgrounds already. "Daddy, you're teasing. But when are we going to the television?"

He had promised them a tour at a local television station. It was part of the prolonged animal act of his "visitations"— legal poetry—where he challenged himself to amuse them without going to the movies. He had arranged to watch a local television show, a teen-age "dance party" with genuine rock 'n' roll celebrities and night-club performers doing a spot of afternoon propaganda with the Saturday kids. Two days later it was time and they were having a little meal, their version of oysters, soupe printanière, turbot, sauce Beaumarchais, poulard à l'estragon, macédoine de fruits—in other words, cheeseburgers with malted milk. "Oh, good, good!" said Cynthia, her dewy eyes shining.

"You like my cooking?"

"I like your *ordering*, Daddy," Paula said with great interest in precision. "*Gracias*, Pops!" and she flew up in an infestation of the giggles.

"Tell me about your Spanish class. Do you want some double bubble?"

"Bubble gum is for babies. We're too big," Cynthia said. "Now give us Chiclets."

"That's what we always have," Paula said. "Sometimes we have sugarless for our teeth."

"Sugarless and chlorophyll," said Cynthia.

Dan nodded solemnly. Paula's malted milk repeated warmly and she grinned. Cynthia was frowning with a sudden thought. "Mommy says you only buy us junk," she said.

"But," said Paula, "but I like your junk."

"Daddy, we like your junk." And Cynthia's smile for him, radiant up toward him. The word *junk* would always be a mystery for her, a beautiful and complicated word, like *serendipity* or *communion.* "Now tell us a story."

"Yes, Daddy. A once-upon-a-time story . . ."

The story concerned a prince who wanted more than anything else to be loved. Naturally, a magic potion came into the matter, and thus everyone loved him. But the once-upon-a-time prince remained unhappy because the potion had no effect on *him*, since for happiness to come of a love potion, it must above all make the once-upon-a-time prince love those who drink of his potion.

From that dreamy oblivion of the child which is so much like indifference and contains so much caring, Cynthia looked up at her father and said, "I know you do, Daddy."

"Know I do what?"

"What you said."

"What did I say?"

She laughed, thrilled because he had forgotten—he had not heard himself—the words had slipped out like his breath. But now he heard, he felt, he even saw himself repeating, "I love you, honeybear."

The waitress in the diner came up and said, "Mister, you must be a teacher to tell stories like that. My brat won't listen to any goddamn thing I tell her."

"My father's a lifesaver," Paula said. "He lives in New York. He knows how to save people's lives."

She had been much impressed by his efforts that summer to teach her to swim; she had overcome her fear of the water. Dan smiled because she remembered so well that he had been a junior lifesaver at the age of thirteen.

"Daddy," said Cynthia, "that magic potion made me hungry."

"*Thirsty*," her sister corrected her.

"Hungry *and* thirsty, Paula! Can we have, can we have . . . something?"

"Something! Something!" cried Paula.

They ate again, and this time Dan told a magic story that had no love and food in it. It was a poor magic story, of course, but the children did not object, scattering material ketchup and actual rootbeer on Formica. They liked his poor magic stories, too, and found food therein.

"You promised to take us to the TV station."

"Wait till he finishes the story, Paula."

Pout. Reproach.

"I know. I did. I will," he said.

Reversal of pout and reproach. They blinked at so many intentions. "Let's go," he said, and that was easy to understand.

Snowsuits, rubbers, hats, mittens, and a farewell to the nice and nosy waitress who thought it swell that a father took his daughters adventuring on a Saturday afternoon. Then salty slush, feet and wheels, and Shaper put his hand in his pockets to tip the boy who parked his car.

"You give everybody money," Cynthia observed.

"I sure do." But her face was bland. She was not kidding. She had noticed, was all.

"Can I have a penny?" said Paula. "For Chiclets? A nickel?"

The Saturday-afternoon dance party was a teen-age program which featured night-club stars visiting in town, and kids sucking from bottles of pop and dancing the Chicken or the Fish to records which were put on between the performances, interviews, and commercials. The disc jockey who ran this stew of "live entertainment" was called Fat Ed because he weighed nearly two hundred and fifty long and loose pounds and liked the sound of "Ed." He also wore heavy horn-rimmed glasses with a straight, wide flange of black plastic on each side pressing against his ears; pointed shoes, which made his fat little feet look like frog's flippers; and a smile like a frog's, separating his wide expanse of jowl from an equally generous slab of nose. He was an old acquaintance of Dan's, which in show biz means a lifelong friend or enemy. Since they were not in competition, it was friend and friendly-like. Thanks to this, Dan, Paula, and Cynthia could huddle together beneath the lights just out of camera range and watch the party doings. A shuffling band of stage personnel mystified the girls with their rushing of cameras up, their hustling of people to and fro, their muscular chaos of co-ordinated indecision. "This gets sent into the box at home," Dan elaborately whispered. "You mustn't talk. You can whisper back when I whisper to you. It's what you see in the box."

With florid elegance the deejay introduced Hennery Ford, middle-aged girl singer now appearing at that famous nightspot—"What's the name of that place, doll?"

She told him.

"Reet, Hennery doll. Say, you been in Miami Beach?"

She nodded.

"That's great, Hennery, soaking up all those sun vitamins—Poor old Fat Ed, I have so many heartfelt responsibilities of live entertainment, I just don't have time—But now this here chick, she is—man, I mean the greatest. You know it, dontcha, kids?"

"We know it," screamed the studio visitors, heated by coke and awe.

The hot, stuck deejay wiped the acres of black plastic on his glasses, leaving the lenses fogged. He returned the folded handkerchief to his breast pocket. "Do you *know* it?"

"We *know* it!"

Busily Cynthia whispered to her father something which he did not hear. He answered, "Don't worry, they don't know anything." She smiled quickly, relieved.

"All right!" shouted the deejay. "So now she has chosen to sing for us one of her favorite hit tunes, a religious type love number with a rock 'n' roll beat—it'll live forever, and here's 'I Want a Sunday Kind of Love.' Hennery?"

Microphone, spots, SILENCE, hushed approval, and the sweaty operators rushing cameras in and out. Miss Ford, a wizened, peeling girl of about forty, stood smiling in the light, swaying slightly as her chapped and oiled lips opened over the words:

> I want a Sunday kind of love
> Like the kind I feel Above
> I want a Sunday kind of love
> From that One I'm thinking of—

Her mouth stretched over the sounds, her body swayed, the music shrilled forth; but she did not sing. The voice of Hennery Ford came from a record while the body of Hennery Ford mimed the gestures of singing.

"What did you say?" Dan whispered to Cynthia.

"But she isn't singing!" Cynthia whispered in shock and horror, discovering another instance of the world's corruption.

"She's very foolish," Paula said primly.

Later Dan would explain to them about idealism—how everybody wanted the song to be perfect, the way Hennery had recorded it originally; about pragmatism—how art is the politics of the possible; about mass media and the way of the world—that's how things are. In the meantime, this eight-year-old daughter had found public corruption condoned, and some of her disdain was directed against her father. "I want to go *right now!*" she said.

On the way out, Dan explained, "She has chapped lips

like that from so much traveling. Maybe she has a cold, besides the change of climate." *Kachoo,* he said sympathetically.

"God bless you," said Paula, sure that her wish was His command. "I don't like that song. I like 'I'm itchy lak a man on a fuzzy tree, I'm all shook up.' "

"Paula, that's not right. It's 'Ah'm itchy *lak* a man on a *fuzzy* tree, Ah'm all—shook *up.*' Daddy, let's go someplace else and you tell us a story about magic potions."

"Magic potions!" cried Paula.

"Again?"

"Tell it," said Cynthia, grinning, "just by moving your lips and we'll say the words, okay? Paula, what word am I saying?" And her lips squirmed over the enormous adult teeth that always surprised Dan, since it was still baby-teeth time when he stopped living with their mother. Her lips, glistening and pink, formed and re-formed over the teeth.

Paula watched, peered into her mouth, pulled back, solemnly imitated the gesture, and at last said loud and clear, "Fake! Fake! You were saying 'Fake'!"

"That's what my lips were saying," Cynthia said. "But that's what I think of 'I Want a Sunday Kind of Love' and Miss Hilary Ford."

"I guess you're right," said their father, obscurely troubled, as if somehow the children were judging him and putting him on the same side as poor Hennery-Hilary. Adults move their lips to music offstage; silently they pretend to sing; and what about Dan's willed gaiety with his girls? And did they not sense how terribly he sometimes flagged, their real father in town for a spree with them? Was he really so enthusiastic about milk shakes (magic potions) and the art museum (fairy tales)?

"It's the way of the world," he said.

"Singing like that?"

"Everything." But Cynthia patted his hand with one of her peculiarly adult, maternal gestures. It was like her salt-

ing his eggs. She wanted to be good to him for no purpose
but that she was his daughter, and so she imitated the
anxious gestures of her mother with that second husband
whom she hoped to please and be pleased by. Logic, thought
Shaper. (She had dumped a gagging amount of salt over the
flattened yolk.) My daughter learns the gestures of love by
monkeying around. She broods over my stepwife's gestures
with the man who replaced me.

He ate egg. He wiped his mouth. He drank water and
took toast. Another snack.

He would have liked a son, he suddenly thought—why?
He asked himself why it came to him with such wrenching
despair now, when Cynthia was so ter ier, Paula so sweet
with their ideal, often absent, *real* father. All that rose to
his mind was an image of the Square Deal Club football
team, when at age twelve he had tackled a full-grown boy
and, it turned out, broken his collarbone. Glory and shame
and sudden hot tears making him sneeze. Well, why not
have another child, more children? Why not have a wife
again? He called for coffee; the girls called for milk, and
dimes for the jukebox. Outside, the sky had turned black
for these last days of the year. It could snow and snow and
snow. He held Paula's hand and remembered his own grandfather shaking his hand, holding it, holding to life by an
arthritic claw. The way ancient aunts kiss and uncles clutch,
he thought, is how I hold my daughters.

It was time to take the children home after this last
afternoon of his visit. The sky had clouded over again and
there would be fresh snow as he aimed himself toward the
highway. "What's the matter, Daddy?" Cynthia asked.

"I dunno, chappie. The weather. I'm sorry I won't be
seeing you for another month."

"But you'll write to us," Paula said cheerfully.

"Yes. Yes."

A look of faint disdain and resentment crossed Paula's
face, and her eye just passed to her thumb. No, she would

not suck. She was too old for that. She would speak instead. "You don't come to see us often enough, Daddy. Mommy says we should call you 'Dan,' and we should call Mike 'Daddy.' "

"So," said Cynthia, statesmanlike, "we call you 'Daddy' when we're talking to you, because you're our *real* daddy—"

"And 'Dan,' " continued Paula like Mister Bones, "when we ask Mommy when you're coming to see us. She don't like us to ask."

"Doesn't," her sister corrected her. "You should say: 'Mike and Mommy *don't*,' but 'Mommy *doesn't*.' " She finished this moral and grammatical lesson by putting her finger in her mouth and ferociously pulling at the cuticle with her teeth.

He talked, sang, made rhymes, joked. Paula smiled, but Cynthia huddled against him as he drove. She stared with sleepy cunning at the panel showing gas, mileage, speed. Dan parked before their house and told them he had his suitcase all ready in the trunk. He was spending his last minutes with them, and then he would hurry again toward New York. Then there was silence. Somehow he had asked a question and Cynthia must answer.

She closed her eyes briefly, a gesture of restraint like a much older girl accused. She had a wide, unmarked forehead over the struggling lashes. She closed her eyes, planning. Her mother was training her excellently, but she still loved her father, she cared. Her *real* father, as she explained. And since she cared, really cared, this prematurely adult, scheming gesture of closing the eyes did not mean all that it seemed to mean. But still it meant something. She was angry because he was leaving so soon again; she was hurt, she wanted to touch and hurt him; she cared and was confused; she had something important to say and did not know how to say it. There was an item of information which would have to stand for all this. She opened and closed her eyes once more before she spoke; she squeezed something back into her brain behind the wide, hot, childish forehead. "Daddy," she said, "I didn't get your last letter."

"What do you mean? I'm afraid you don't get all my letters. How do you know about it at all?"

"I just know."

"What do you mean?"

"Rosalie"—the maid—"she said there was a letter. She said to go get it when I came home from school."

Cynthia shut her eyes again. "It must have got lost," she said.

Paula said, "I want to go inside." Dan said good-bye to his younger daughter, carried her across the snow to the door, kissed her. The wintry door opened for her; his invisible former wife took her back. Dan climbed back into the car with Cynthia. They sat awhile in thickening silence. "The letters I sent to you are supposed to be given to you," he said.

"I know, Daddy."

And they looked at each other like grownup lovers fleeing parents and family. Child, he thought; child of mine.

"I really love you awfully much, honey."

Impatient and a child again, she said, "I know. Why don't you ever wear black shoes, Daddy?"

"I like brown ones."

"Brown ones?"

Muffled in coats, they sat together in the front seat of the car as if there were more to say. It began to snow in little flakes colored yellow by industrial smoke, ragged-edged, yellow and faded. The fog of coal and steel and the fog of humid winter held the snow suspended in air, and then let it fall. He ran the motor to keep warm. The snow came down all over the city of Cleveland, and when the wiper of his car worked it left a smear, wiping the glass back and forth. He sat with his daughter before the house in which his former wife, her mother, lived, and explained to her why he wore brown shoes; why he did not wear rubbers; why some singers are fake ard don't really sing; why the snow melted faster on the street than on the grass.

"Write to me anyway," she said.

"We'll figure something out, Cynthia."

"Will you?" she asked.

Fresh snow had shadowed his earlier footsteps by the time he took her to the door; evening had come. Half an hour later he was on the highway leading into the turnpike, which falls with hardly a pause through three states back to Manhattan. There in the new year he would like to find a wife and have children again.

MAX APPLE

◇ ◇ ◇

Bridging

I

At the Astrodome, Nolan Ryan is shaving the corners. He's going through the Giants in order. The radio announcer is not even mentioning that by the sixth the Giants haven't had a hit. The K's mount on the scoreboard. Tonight Nolan passes the Big Train and is now the all-time strikeout king. He's almost as old as I am and he still throws nothing but smoke. His fastball is an aspirin; batters tear their tendons lunging for his curve. Jessica and I have season tickets, but tonight she's home listening and I'm in the basement of St. Anne's Church watching Kay Randall's fingertips. Kay is holding her hands out from her chest, her fingertips on each other. Her fingers move a little as she talks and I can hear her nails click when they meet. That's how close I'm sitting.

Kay is talking about "bridging"; that's what her arched fingers represent.

"Bridging," she says, "is the way Brownies become Girl Scouts. It's a slow steady process. It's not easy, but we allow a whole year for bridging."

138

Eleven girls in brown shirts with red bandannas at their neck are imitating Kay as she talks. They hold their stumpy chewed fingertips out and bridge them. So do I.

I brought the paste tonight and the stick-on gold stars and the thread for sewing buttonholes.

"I feel a little awkward," Kay Randall said on the phone, "asking a man to do these errands . . . but that's my problem, not yours. Just bring the supplies and try to be at the church meeting room a few minutes before seven."

I arrive a half hour early.

"You're off your rocker," Jessica says. She begs me to drop her at the Astrodome on my way to the Girl Scout meeting. "After the game, I'll meet you at the main souvenir stand on the first level. They stay open an hour after the game. I'll be all right. There are cops and ushers every five yards."

She can't believe that I am missing this game to perform my functions as an assistant Girl Scout leader. Our Girl Scout battle has been going on for two months.

"Girl Scouts is stupid," Jessica says. "Who wants to sell cookies and sew buttons and walk around wearing stupid old badges?"

When she agreed to go to the first meeting, I was so happy I volunteered to become an assistant leader. After the meeting, Jessica went directly to the car the way she does after school, after a birthday party, after a ball game, after anything. A straight line to the car. No jabbering with girlfriends, no smiles, no dallying, just right to the car. She slides into the back seat, belts in, and braces herself for destruction. It has already happened once.

I swoop past five thousand years of stereotypes and accept my assistant leader's packet and credentials.

"I'm sure there have been other men in the movement," Kay says, "we just haven't had any in our district. It will be good for the girls."

Not for my Jessica. She won't bridge, she won't budge.

"I know why you're doing this," she says. "You think

that because I don't have a mother, Kay Randall and the Girl Scouts will help me. That's crazy. And I know that Sharon is supposed to be like a mother too. Why don't you just leave me alone."

Sharon is Jessica's therapist. Jessica sees her twice a week. Sharon and I have a meeting once a month.

"We have a lot of shy girls," Kay Randall tells me. "Scouting brings them out. Believe me, it's hard to stay shy when you're nine years old and you're sharing a tent with six other girls. You have to count on each other, you have to communicate."

I imagine Jessica zipping up in her sleeping bag, mumbling good night to anyone who first says it to her, then closing her eyes and hating me for sending her out among the happy.

"She likes all sports, especially baseball," I tell my leader.

"There's room for baseball in scouting," Kay says. "Once a year the whole district goes to a game. They mention us on the big scoreboard."

"Jessica and I go to all the home games. We're real fans." Kay smiles.

"That's why I want her in Girl Scouts. You know, I want her to go to things with her girlfriends instead of always hanging around with me at ball games."

"I understand," Kay says. "It's part of bridging."

With Sharon the term is "separation anxiety." That's the fastball, "bridging" is the curve. Amid all their magic words I feel as if Jessica and I are standing at home plate blindfolded.

While I await Kay and the members of Troop 111, District 6, I eye St. Anne in her grotto and St. Gregory and St. Thomas. Their hands are folded as if they started out bridging, ended up praying.

In October the principal sent Jessica home from school because Mrs. Simmons caught her in spelling class listening to the World Series through an earphone.

"It's against the school policy," Mrs. Simmons said. "Jessica understands school policy. We confiscate radios and send the child home."

"I'm glad," Jessica said. "It was a cheap-o radio. Now I can watch the TV with you."

They sent her home in the middle of the sixth game. I let her stay home for the seventh too.

The Brewers are her favorite American League team. She likes Rollie Fingers, and especially Robin Yount.

"Does Yount go in the hole better than Harvey Kuenn used to?"

"You bet," I tell her. "Kuenn was never a great fielder but he could hit three hundred with his eyes closed."

Kuenn is the Brewers' manager. He has an artificial leg and can barely make it up the dugout steps, but when I was Jessica's age and the Tigers were my team, Kuenn used to stand at the plate, tap the corners with his bat, spit some tobacco juice, and knock liners up the alley.

She took the Brewers' loss hard.

"If Fingers wasn't hurt they would have squashed the Cards, wouldn't they?"

I agreed.

"But I'm glad for Andujar."

We had Andujar's autograph. Once we met him at a McDonald's. He was a relief pitcher then, an erratic right-hander. In St. Louis he improved. I was happy to get his name on a napkin. Jessica shook his hand.

One night after I read her a story, she said, "Daddy, if we were rich could we go to the away games too? I mean, if you didn't have to be at work every day."

"Probably we could," I said, "but wouldn't it get boring? We'd have to stay at hotels and eat in restaurants. Even the players get sick of it."

"Are you kidding?" she said. "I'd never get sick of it."

"Jessica has fantasies of being with you forever, following baseball or whatever," Sharon says. "All she's trying to do is please you. Since she lost her mother she feels that you and she are alone in the world. She doesn't want to let anyone or anything else into that unit, the two of you. She's afraid of any more losses. And, of course, her greatest worry is about losing you."

"You know," I tell Sharon, "that's pretty much how I feel too."

"Of course it is," she says. "I'm glad to hear you say it."

Sharon is glad to hear me say almost anything. When I complain that her $100-a-week fee would buy a lot of peanut butter sandwiches, she says she is "glad to hear me expressing my anger."

"Sharon's not fooling me," Jessica says. "I know that she thinks drawing those pictures is supposed to make me feel better or something. You're just wasting your money. There's nothing wrong with me."

"It's a long, difficult, expensive process," Sharon says. "You and Jessica have lost a lot. Jessica is going to have to learn to trust the world again. It would help if you could do it too."

So I decide to trust Girl Scouts. First Girl Scouts, then the world. I make my stand at the meeting of Kay Randall's fingertips. While Nolan Ryan breaks Walter Johnson's strikeout record and pitches a two-hit shutout, I pass out paste and thread to nine-year-olds who are sticking and sewing their lives together in ways Jessica and I can't.

II

Scouting is not altogether new to me. I was a Cub Scout. I owned a blue beanie and I remember very well my den mother, Mrs. Clark. A den mother made perfect sense to me then and still does. Maybe that's why I don't feel uncomfortable being a Girl Scout assistant leader.

We had no den father. Mr. Clark was only a photograph on the living room wall, the tiny living room where we held our monthly meetings. Mr. Clark was killed in the Korean War. His son John was in the troop. John was stocky but

Mrs. Clark was huge. She couldn't sit on a regular chair, only on a couch or a stool without sides. She was the cashier in the convenience store beneath their apartment. The story we heard was that Walt, the old man who owned the store, felt sorry for her and gave her the job. He was her landlord too. She sat on a swivel stool and rang up the purchases.

We met at the store and watched while she locked the door; then we followed her up the steep staircase to her three-room apartment. She carried two wet glass bottles of milk. Her body took up the entire width of the staircase. She passed the banisters the way semi trucks pass each other on a narrow highway.

We were ten years old, a time when everything is funny, especially fat people. But I don't remember anyone ever laughing about Mrs. Clark. She had great dignity and character. So did John. I didn't know what to call it then, but I knew John was someone you could always trust.

She passed out milk and cookies, then John collected the cups and washed them. They didn't even have a television set. The only decoration in the room that barely held all of us was Mr. Clark's picture on the wall. We saw him in his uniform and we knew he died in Korea defending his country. We were little boys in blue beanies drinking milk in the apartment of a hero. Through that aura I came to scouting. I wanted Kay Randall to have all of Mrs. Clark's dignity.

When she took a deep breath and then bridged, Kay Randall had noticeable armpits. Her wide shoulders slithered into a tiny rib cage. Her armpits were like bridges. She said "bridging" like a mantra, holding her hands before her for about thirty seconds at the start of each meeting.

"A promise is a promise," I told Jessica. "I signed up to be a leader, and I'm going to do it with you or without you."

"But you didn't even ask me if I liked it. You just signed up without talking it over."

"That's true; that's why I'm not going to force you to go along. It was my choice."

"What can you like about it? I hate Melissa Randall. She always has a cold."

"Her mother is a good leader."

"How do you know?"

"She's my boss. I've got to like her, don't I?" I hugged Jessica. "C'mon, honey, give it a chance. What do you have to lose?"

"If you make me go I'll do it, but if I have a choice I won't."

Every other Tuesday, Karen, the fifteen-year-old Greek girl who lives on the corner, babysits Jessica while I go to the Scout meetings. We talk about field trips and how to earn merit badges. The girls giggle when Kay pins a promptness badge on me, my first.

Jessica thinks it's hilarious. She tells me to wear it to work.

Sometimes when I watch Jessica brush her hair and tie her ponytail and make up her lunch kit I start to think that maybe I should just relax and stop the therapy and the scouting and all my not-so-subtle attempts to get her to invite friends over. I start to think that, in spite of everything, she's a good student and she's got a sense of humor. She's barely nine years old. She'll grow up like everyone else does. John Clark did it without a father; she'll do it without a mother. I start to wonder if Jessica seems to the girls in her class the way John Clark seemed to me: dignified, serious, almost an adult even while we were playing. I admired him. Maybe the girls in her class admire her. But John had that hero on the wall, his father in a uniform, dead for reasons John and all the rest of us understood.

My Jessica had to explain a neurologic disease she couldn't even pronounce. "I hate it when people ask me about Mom," she says. "I just tell them she fell off the Empire State Building."

III

Before our first field trip I go to Kay's house for a planning session. We're going to collect wildflowers in East Texas. It's a one-day trip. I arranged to rent the school bus.

I told Jessica that she could go on the trip even though she wasn't a troop member, but she refused.

We sit on colonial furniture in Kay's den. She brings in coffee and we go over the supply list. Another troop is joining ours so there will be twenty-two girls, three women, and me, a busload among the bluebonnets.

"We have to be sure the girls understand that the bluebonnets they pick are on private land and that we have permission to pick them. Otherwise they might pick them along the roadside, which is against the law."

I imagine all twenty-two of them behind bars for picking bluebonnets and Jessica laughing while I scramble for bail money.

I keep noticing Kay's hands. I notice them as she pours coffee, as she checks off the items on the list, as she gestures. I keep expecting her to bridge. She has large, solid, confident hands. When she finishes bridging I sometimes feel like clapping the way people do after the national anthem.

"I admire you," she tells me. "I admire you for going ahead with Scouts even though your daughter rejects it. She'll get a lot out of it indirectly from you."

Kay Randall is thirty-three, divorced, and has a Bluebird too. Her older daughter is one of the stubby-fingered girls, Melissa. Jessica is right; Melissa always has a cold.

Kay teaches fifth grade and has been divorced for three years. I am the first assistant she's ever had.

"My husband, Bill, never helped with Scouts," Kay says. "He was pretty much turned off to everything except his business and drinking. When we separated I can't honestly say I missed him; he'd never been there. I don't think the girls miss him either. He only sees them about once a month. He has girlfriends, and his business is doing very well. I guess he has what he wants."

"And you?"

She uses one of those wonderful hands to move the hair away from her eyes, a gesture that makes her seem very young.

"I guess I do too. I've got the girls and my job. I'm lonesome, though. It's not exactly what I wanted."

We both think about what might have been as we sit beside her glass coffeepot with our lists of sachet supplies. If she was Barbra Streisand and I Robert Redford and the music started playing in the background to give us a clue and there was a long close-up of our lips, we might just fade into middle age together. But Melissa called for Mom because her mosquito bite was bleeding where she scratched it. And I had an angry daughter waiting for me. And all Kay and I had in common was Girl Scouts. We were both smart enough to know it. When Kay looked at me before going to put alcohol on the mosquito bite, our mutual sadness dripped from us like the last drops of coffee through the grinds.

"You really missed something tonight," Jessica tells me. "The Astros did a double steal. I've never seen one before. In the fourth they sent Thon and Moreno together, and Moreno stole home."

She knows batting averages and won-lost percentages too, just like the older boys, only they go out to play. Jessica stays in and waits for me.

During the field trip, while the girls pick flowers to dry and then manufacture into sachets, I think about Jessica at home, probably beside the radio. Juana, our once-a-week cleaning lady, agreed to work on Saturday so she could stay with Jessica while I took the all-day field trip.

It was no small event. In the eight months since Vicki died I had not gone away for an entire day.

I made waffles in the waffle iron for her before I left, but she hardly ate.

"If you want anything, just ask Juana."

"Juana doesn't speak English."

"She understands, that's enough."

"Maybe for you it's enough."

"Honey, I told you, you can come; there's plenty of room on the bus. It's not too late for you to change your mind."

"It's not too late for you either. There's going to be plenty of other leaders there. You don't have to go. You're just doing this to be mean to me."

I'm ready for this. I spent an hour with Sharon steeling myself. "Before she can leave you," Sharon said, "you'll have to show her that you can leave. Nothing's going to happen to her. And don't let her be sick that day either."

Jessica is too smart to pull the "I don't feel good" routine. Instead she becomes more silent, more unhappy looking than usual. She stays in her pajamas while I wash the dishes and get ready to leave.

I didn't notice the sadness as it was coming upon Jessica. It must have happened gradually in the years of Vicki's decline, the years in which I paid so little attention to my daughter. There were times when Jessica seemed to recognize the truth more than I did.

As my Scouts picked their wildflowers, I remembered the last outing I had planned for us. It was going to be a Fourth of July picnic with some friends in Austin. I stopped at the bank and got $200 in cash for the long weekend. But when I came home Vicki was too sick to move and the air conditioner had broken. I called our friends to cancel the picnic; then I took Jessica to the mall with me to buy a fan. I bought the biggest one they had, a 58-inch oscillating model that sounded like a hurricane. It could cool 10,000 square feet, but it wasn't enough.

Vicki was home sitting blankly in front of the TV set. The fan could move eight tons of air an hour, but I wanted it to save my wife. I wanted a fan that would blow the whole earth out of its orbit.

I had $50 left. I gave it to Jessica and told her to buy anything she wanted.

"Whenever you're sad, Daddy, you want to buy me things." She put the money back in my pocket. "It won't help." She was seven years old, holding my hand tightly in the appliance department at J. C. Penney's.

I watched Melissa sniffle even more among the wildflowers, and I pointed out the names of various flowers to Carol and JoAnne and Sue and Linda and Rebecca, who were by now used to me and treated me pretty much as they treated Kay. I noticed that the Girl Scout flower book had very accurate photographs that made it easy to identify the bluebonnets and buttercups and poppies. There were also several varieties of wild grasses.

We were only 70 miles from home on some land a wealthy rancher long ago donated to the Girl Scouts. The girls bending among the flowers seemed to have been quickly transformed by the colorful meadow. The gigglers and monotonous singers on the bus were now, like the bees, sucking strength from the beauty around them. Kay was in the midst of them and so, I realized, was I, not watching and keeping score and admiring from the distance but a participant, a player.

JoAnne and Carol sneaked up from behind me and dropped some dandelions down my back. I chased them; then I helped the other leaders pour the Kool-Aid and distribute the Baggies and the name tags for each girl's flowers.

My daughter is home listening to a ball game, I thought, and I'm out here having fun with nine-year-olds. It's upside down.

When I came home with dandelion fragments still on my back, Juana had cleaned the house and I could smell the taco sauce in the kitchen. Jessica was in her room. I suspected that she had spent the day listless and tearful, although I had asked her to invite a friend over.

"I had a lot of fun, honey, but I missed you."

She hugged me and cried against my shoulder. I felt like

holding her the way I used to when she was an infant, the way I rocked her to sleep. But she was a big girl now and needed not sleep but wakefulness.

"I heard on the news that the Rockets signed Ralph Sampson," she sobbed, "and you hardly ever take me to any pro basketball games."

"But if they have a new center things will be different. With Sampson we'll be contenders. Sure I'll take you."

"Promise?"

"Promise." I promise to take you everywhere, my lovely child, and then to leave you. I'm learning to be a leader.

STEPHEN MINOT

◇ ◇ ◇

Crossings

What do you do with a young daughter who has just gone over to Roman Catholicism? Me at thirty-six and her at ten—that's quite a span. And me an atheist. There's another span.

I'm sitting on the edge of her bed with a copy of H. G. Wells' *Outline of History* in my hand, feeling rather pious because of my attention to parental duty at the end of a very tiring and monotonous day spent revising plans for a new school in Bronxville, and she asks me straight out if it will be all right to dispense with our reading that night so she can say her prayers. It is, of course, news to me that she knows what a prayer is.

For just a moment we look at each other, mutually startled but playing it very cool, and we listen to the hiss of snow against the apartment window and it seems as if there is a hush over all Manhattan.

Now, I'm not the shouting kind of atheist. I don't write pamphlets called "The Bible Exposed" or alarmist articles about the power of Rome and I don't picket against school prayers or anything like that. I really don't feel much stronger about my nonbelief than most of my friends do about their

150

beliefs. I never proselytize, and I've always sent my daughter to Unitarian Sunday school to keep her from feeling different.

I suppose I could be accused of being a backsliding atheist. I'm a far cry from my father. Now, *there* was a man of dynamic nonfaith.

People sometimes ask me what it was like to be brought up an atheist, and I have to stop and think. As in good religious homes, the faith of the family was so intermeshed with daily life that we could hardly separate the two. Take, for example, the grace my father said before every meal. He had a black beard like a Greek Orthodox priest, and a very low, rumbling voice that comes to me with great clarity when I recall his recitation: "We take this food remembering those who are less fortunate, humble before fate, yet proud of our labor." It never consciously occurred to me that perhaps other fathers said it differently.

On a less subtle level there were the Wednesday evenings of instruction—resurrection explained, Genesis compared with Ovid's account, Abraham set against *The Golden Bough*, and all that. But as with most religions, what stays with you is not the direct teaching but the ritual, and particularly the familiarity of feast days. Like Easter Sunday. We all looked forward to that. My younger sister and older brother and I would hurry through breakfast and then present ourselves for inspection. Our clothes had to be neither too dressy nor too sloppy. We would be sent back if we wore party shoes "like a damned Lutheran," but we couldn't look as if we were begging, either.

Then, inspection passed, we children would head for Manhattan. Since we lived on Staten Island, the trip was made via trolley, ferry and subway, in that order. The selection of exactly which corner on Fifth Avenue to station ourselves was up to us, and sometimes we would argue a good deal about this, since we all were well trained in debate. But once we had settled on a spot (sometimes by a two-thirds vote), we were rigidly bound by ritual. My brother timed us, my sister recorded, and I called out the finds. For every silk hat we spotted in the next sixty minutes we later would receive twenty-five cents. These, you see, were the Christian hypocrites off to worship a prophet who himself wore rags and preached against pomp. The fact that our totals— recorded on the pantry wall beside our annual heights— declined each year like the population of whooping cranes was convincing proof that the number of Christians was declining and that social progress was indeed a demonstrable fact. But I must admit that for somewhat less than altruistic reasons, there was a sinful portion of us that secretly hoped for a dramatic religious revival.

Exciting as Easter was, the high point of the year was Christmas. Like our Lutheran neighbors, we counted the days of December. Our own celebration, however, came on the twenty-fourth. Again there was a ferry ride to Manhattan, with all the excitement and wonder that one can experience at that age; but this time the destination was F.A.O. Schwarz. We had been given just a half-hour to cover that entire store and find the three most expensive toys on exhibit. We moved rapidly up and down the aisles, solemn-faced and tense, muttering, "You take that counter," and "Skip that kiddy stuff," and "I'll check the trains," all the time being watched by slit-eyed clerks who could sense only that something darkly subversive was going on.

Our finds, honestly reported, netted each of us a fifty-fifty split; half the figure was deposited in our college fund and the other half went to the charity of our choice—mine, I believe, being the Perkins Institute for the Blind, at one point, and later a local cat hospital.

But none of this, I realize now, has really prepared me to deal with a daughter who wants to recite prayers right here in my presence. And mine alone—her mother is off attending a school committee meeting again.

"What prayer do you have in mind?" I ask with splendid

control, picking an imaginary flake of lint from my pants leg.

"The Rosary prayer," she says to me, as if I should have known.

"And where, Susan, did you learn the Rosary prayer?" I ask.

"From Sister Theresa."

"And who is Sister Theresa?"

"At the convent." I know what she means by this because we live on Fourteenth Street and there is a small convent smack in the middle of our block. "I go with Marie," she adds. Marie is a prematurely haughty little girl whose father is with the French embassy and who lives in the new apartment building that also is on our block.

"Regularly?" I ask.

"Afternoons. After school."

"You've talked this over with your mother?"

"I didn't think she'd understand. She used to be a Congregationalist."

This exchange has been going on straight-faced, low-voiced and almost breathlessly—like two poker players who have discovered with some alarm that they have staked most of their life savings on a single hand.

"Marie's Catholic," she says pointlessly. "Also," she adds.

I stiffen.

"Being French," I say, "I suppose she was *born* a Catholic." It is my first cautious step into argument, and I realize at once it was poorly conceived. It won't do to treat the revered Marie as a victim of a congenital defect. "People tend to follow the teachings they were brought up with," I say, groping for a retreat.

"And some don't," she says, her voice trembling just a bit. "Like Uncle Hubert." She has me there, since my older brother Hubert went High Episcopalian with a vengeance. I'm only hoping that she won't also recall my sister Tilly.

"And Aunt Tilly," she adds in a consciously offhand manner. "But I won't say prayers if you don't want me to."

"Oh, I don't mind," I say, even more offhandedly. "Not at all. It's your decision. Entirely. But"—and this is absolutely my last card—"I believe for that particular prayer it's customary to have beads." I try smiling.

And then, like those naive cavalry officers on the late show who suddenly realize that they have led their forces into a hopelessly indefensible ravine and can only watch with fatalistic wonder as the redskins pour down from both sides, whooping with glee, I see my daughter's hand dart under the pillow and pull out a rosary—black, plastic and wriggling.

So the next minute my daughter and only child is no longer beside me but on her knees at the edge of the bed, beads in hand, and I hear her voice mumbling. Only certain phrases come through to me: ". . . heaven and earth . . . all things visible and invisible. . . ."

I look down at the top of her head—long hair parted neatly and falling like the lip of a gentle waterfall. Her voice is clearer than an oboe. All grace. The prayer moves on to "Our Father"— which I have heard before—and then to "Hail Mary, full of grace, the Lord is with thee. . . ." And within me there is a most graceless battle—in the white hat is the liberal who votes the reform ticket, and numbers among his friends Protestants, Catholics, Jews, two Moslems, and one Ethical Culturalist, and occasionally attends a reasonable facsimile of the church of his choice, which makes a point of accepting anyone regardless of race, creed, or conviction; and in the black hat is a surly, provincial father who is saying to himself, My God, that prayer is *really* offensive— fruit of womb indeed!

They continue to take shots at each other, these two, but my attention wanders—I have seen the show before—and I'm caught by a sense of excitement that I cannot identify. It has the touch of the illicit without being vulgar, of an escape without being lost. But these abstractions are getting me nowhere. The little, wavering sensation collapses under the weight of analysis, and I am listening to Susan again.

Such shockingly adult language—and that repetition! Yet she is high on it, and lovely in her intoxication.

Drunk with it. This is once again the beginning of something parallel. I reach for it, but the memory is already in fragments and crumbles further. A trip on a ferry. But that is no help. My life is cluttered with crossings and recrossings. Yet I try again, because it is terribly important now to share at least a glimpse of this girl's new environment. She is my daughter, after all.

I am crossing the water now, and it is between night and day. We are flying through mists, and somewhere to the right there is the first glow of a rising sun. I feel the wet of the night air and my legs swing free, not quite touching the car floor. But this makes no sense; when I was too small to touch the floor of a car, I was too young to be up at dawn.

Susan's voice ripples on, repeating the prayer bead by bead, and the words blur. I hear an older woman's voice speaking to me earnestly, and in that car again I see this person's face—round and a little puffy, but earnest and intense too.

Aunt Elnora! Of course! Until now I had thought I had no clear memory of her. But now, miraculously, she has returned to me. She is sitting beside me in the car, one hand on the wood steering wheel and the other on the black leather of the seat, and she is talking about souls within souls and how each drop of mist out there over the bay has a soul that will be born and reborn until it is ready for a richer, more complex body, and how every soul will, in centuries to come, experience the lives of plants, animals, human beings, planets, universes, and on and on—an endless system like an enormous river but without a beginning or an end.

River. That's part of the memory. Not just a metaphor, either—I can really see the water glistening out there. Actually it is New York's Upper Bay, and Aunt Elnora's splendid black touring car is the first one on the ferry—so that from my height the water speeds right under the hood as if we are in some new Jules Verne adventure, our Victorian flying machine skimming over the misty waters, to the amazement of fishermen in their dories. Aunt Elnora is saying in her contralto voice, "More than fifty or eighty or two hundred lives you've led, Peter, my boy, and the memory of them flickers by you twenty times a day, but *they've* taught you to look the other way. Oh, that father of yours! How are you going to evolve if you don't recall what you've learned? Answer me that one, Peter, my boy. Oh, the blinders they've put on you! The lives you'll have to live!"

Her voice has a vibrancy, low but with enormous reserves, like an engine that can do wonders with only half its potential power. I remember once again an aging mechanic who, years later, would ask me, "Do you recall that car of your aunt's?" I would nod, and without fail he would add, "Three rows of seats it had, with the best leather this side of Italy. Well, when I first opened up that there hood and saw *sixteen* spark plugs, I said to myself, 'Holy Christ!' and I'm not one to use the Lord's name in vain."

But now it is Susan who is speaking. I am, she tells me *sotto voce* between beads, listening to the Sorrowful Mysteries; and I'm wondering what right *they*—the sisters at that church—have to inject all this into such a young girl. There are laws against alienation of affection. Kidnapping.

Abduction! That's what my father called it. And that's why we never saw Aunt Elnora again. *He* claimed that she kept me up all night talking religion—she was active in something called the Disciples of Life—and then drove me to Manhattan, leaving before dawn, for some cultists' meeting. It made a good after-dinner story, him pointing his

cigar at his listener and summing it all up with, "My own
sister, mind you, *abducting* my son and spiriting him to New
York and *seducing* him!"

"Figuratively speaking," my mother would add, as firmly
as any woman could in that house.

I suppose I heard the story about forty times during the
course of my later childhood. I always assumed that, like
biblical miracles, it was rooted somewhere in truth and grew
with retelling just to make life more vivid and comprehensi-
ble. With the past flooding up to me as clearly as the
present, I am assured that it is all true. We really are
flying over the waters of the Upper Bay, skimming just
above the misty surface, to the amazement of fishermen in
their dories.

We are landing now, and the great touring car roars out
through the rosy maze of deserted streets; then we park. We
mount the steps of a towering town house and enter a huge,
crowded room. The babble of strangers ruffles me, but
when a bell rings there is calm. A speaker chants and the
many people answer. They have become a group and I am
part of it. Speaker and group take turns, a bell rings, a
chorus recites, and the cycle is repeated again.

All the words are blurred and I make no effort to sort
them out. Whatever it all means is in the rhythm and in the
pressure of others standing on both sides, and this is made
even clearer as my right hand is guided to the left side and
my left hand, crossing, reaches to the right so that each of
my hands is clasped in another's. I am too short to see
anything of the room, but I know that this chain of people
has been made continuous, like a string of beads. We are
one. As we sway, chanting, it seems as if I am even those
drops of water that died against my face and are reborn, just
as I am now being reborn and will die again. The dying and
coming forth glitter equally, almost like dawn light flicker-
ing on ripples of the bay.

Now there are tears forming because I have finally, again,

learned to remember what I had forgotten—and will forget again.

"Daddy, what's the matter?" She is looking up at me with alarm, thinking that she has hurt me. "What is it?"

And for a moment she is a parent, and I know that this is the tone and the expression—perhaps even the phrasing—that she will use again as a mother long after my body has been struck down and has run back into the sea.

I cannot answer her at once. I feel as if I have been wrenched out of a dream I don't want to forget. Yet I must have been listening too, because some of her phrases still turn like water wheels in my head—"blessed art thou among women," "pray for us sinners," "now and at the hour of our death." Having no beads to hold, my eyes rest on her as the phrases turn and turn. I must have been looking very serious to have startled her so.

"Sorry," I say. "I am sorry, Susan." And my words come out stronger, more emotional than I'd intended. "Is that the end of the prayer?"

"No. It goes on and on. But. . . ."

"Well, don't stop," I say. I have the guilty feeling of having accidentally tripped her. "Can't you go on?"

She shook her head. "Not tonight."

"Tomorrow, then?"

I take her hand in mine, but somehow it doesn't seem like a natural gesture. I have long, bony fingers that look better against a drafting table. My confidence as a designer of schools fails me here, and I feel wholly inadequate. I want her to understand that wherever she has been during this episode is an important part of her, that it doesn't matter whether I have been there, that she should have the courage to explore, that—

"Boy!" she says with a sudden grin. "I sure thought you'd be mad!"

I stare at her in amazement as she hops into bed as if this were any other night and snuggles down in the covers, arranging her stuffed kitten on the pillow beside her. The adult in her suddenly dies and I am allowed to be parent again. I've won. I've won!

I go over to open the window, taking pleasure in the old, familiar bedtime ritual. I feel almost like skipping. Nothing has changed. Nothing. And then I tug upward at the small brass inserts that are supposed to serve as handles. Ice has frozen the window.

"Damnation," I mutter, and am surprised at this absurd choice of archaic profanity. No one today uses a word like that seriously. With a jolt it hits me that the word, and even the intonation, come directly from my father. He is long since dead, but I feel suddenly victimized by him—an invasion of privacy on his part.

And now as I strain to open the window I see an imperfect reflection of myself in the dark pane directly before my eyes. Somehow the shadow and the frost make it appear to be a bearded face—like his.

Outrage seizes me, and I pound upward with the heels of my hands against the upper molding, temper lost.

"You listen to me!" I say to her sharply over the pounding. "It doesn't matter whether I'd be mad. Not with that. It doesn't matter what your mother thinks." I go on beating at the window, furious now. "All that's *your* business. No one else's. Your private business!"

And through all this racket I am dimly aware that she has been repeating something. I stop, breathing hard, just long enough to hear her saying, "The lock—Daddy, turn the lock."

It takes a few moments before the tumblers of my mind click into proper position. Then I reach up and turn the silly little brass-plated window lock, which was inches from my nose. After that the window zips wide open with almost no effort.

I stand there without moving, waiting for her laugh. But mercifully it does not come.

"You're queer," she says with sleepy affection. In *my* childhood that word was an insult, but she uses it all the time to mean special, or even wonderful. I remember once she looked up at the stars on a crisp April evening and said, "Hey, that's queer" with a tone almost of reverence.

"You're queer," I say, using her language and her tone, speaking partly to her and partly to the individual snow-flakes that are zig-zagging in crazy patterns through the night like three billion children pouring out of school.

JOHN UPDIKE

◇ ◇ ◇

Man and Daughter in the Cold

Look at that girl ski!" The exclamation arose at Ethan's side as if, in the disconnecting cold, a rib of his had cried out; but it was his friend, friend and fellow-teacher, an inferior teacher but superior skier, Matt Langley, admiring Becky, Ethan's own daughter. It took an effort, in this air like slices of transparent metal interposed everywhere, to make these connections and to relate the young girl, her round face red with windburn as she skimmed down the run-out slope, to himself. She was his daughter, age thirteen. Ethan had twin sons, two years younger, and his attention had always been focussed on their skiing, or the irksome comedy of their double needs—the four boots to lace, the four mittens to find—and then their cute yet grim competition as now one and now the other gained the edge in the expertise of geländesprungs and slalom form. On their trips north into the mountains, Becky had come along for the ride. "Look how solid she is," Matt went on. "She doesn't cheat on it like your boys—those feet are absolutely together." The girl, grinning as if she could hear herself praised, wiggle-waggled to a flashy stop that sprayed snow over the men's ski tips.

161

"Where's Mommy?" she asked.

Ethan answered, "She went with the boys into the lodge. They couldn't take it." Their sinewy little male bodies had no insulation; weeping and shivering, they had begged to go in after a single T-bar run.

"What sissies," Becky said.

Matt said, "This wind is wicked. And it's picking up. You should have been here at nine; Lord, it was lovely. All that fresh powder, and not a stir of wind."

Becky told him, "Dumb Tommy couldn't find his mittens, we spent an *hour* looking, and then Daddy got the Jeep stuck." Ethan, alerted now for signs of the wonderful in his daughter, was struck by the strange fact that she was making conversation. Unafraid, she was talking to Matt without her father's intercession.

"Mr. Langley was saying how nicely you were skiing."

"You're Olympic material, Becky."

The girl perhaps blushed; but her cheeks could get no redder. Her eyes, which, were she a child, she would have instantly averted, remained a second on Matt's face, as if to estimate how much he meant it. "It's easy down here," Becky said. "It's babyish."

Ethan asked, "Do you want to go up to the top?" He was freezing standing still, and the gondola would be sheltered from the wind.

Her eyes shifted to his, with another unconsciously thoughtful hesitation. "Sure. If you want to."

"Come along, Matt?"

"Thanks, no. It's too rough for me; I've had enough runs. This is the trouble with January—once it stops snowing, the wind comes up. I'll keep Elaine company in the lodge." Matt himself had no wife, no children. At thirty-eight, he was as free as his students, as light on his skis and as full of brave know-how. "In case of frostbite," he shouted after them, "rub snow on it."

Becky effortlessly skated ahead to the lift shed. The encumbered motion of walking on skis, not natural to him, made Ethan feel asthmatic: a fish out of water. He touched his parka pocket, to check that the inhalator was there. As a child he had imagined death as something attacking from outside, but now he saw that it was carried within; we nurse it for years, and it grows. The clock on the lodge wall said a quarter to noon. The giant thermometer read two degrees above zero. The racks outside were dense as hedges with idle skis. Crowds, any sensation of crowding or delay, quickened his asthma; as therapy he imagined the emptiness, the blue freedom, at the top of the mountain. The clatter of machinery inside the shed was comforting, and enough teen-age boys were boarding gondolas to make the ascent seem normal and safe. Ethan's breathing eased. Becky proficiently handed her poles to the loader points up; her father was always caught by surprise, and often as not fumbled the little maneuver of letting his skis be taken from him. Until, five years ago, he had become an assistant professor at a New Hampshire college an hour to the south, he had never skied; he had lived in those Middle Atlantic cities where snow, its moment of virgin beauty by, is only an encumbering nuisance, a threat of suffocation. Whereas his children had grown up on skis.

Alone with his daughter in the rumbling isolation of the gondola, he wanted to explore her, and found her strange— strange in her uninquisitive child's silence, her accustomed poise in this ascending egg of metal. A dark figure with spreading legs veered out of control beneath them, fell forward, and vanished. Ethan cried out, astonished, scandalized; he imagined the man had buried himself alive. Becky was barely amused, and looked away before the dark spots struggling in the drift were lost from sight. As if she might know, Ethan asked, "Who was that?"

"Some kid." Kids, her tone suggested, were in plentiful supply; one could be spared.

He offered to dramatize the adventure ahead of them: "Do you think we'll freeze at the top?"

"Not exactly."

"What do you think it'll be like?"

"Miserable."

"Why are we doing this, do you think?"

"Because we paid the money for the all-day lift ticket."

"Becky, you think you're pretty smart, don't you?"

"Not really."

The gondola rumbled and lurched into the shed at the top; an attendant opened the door, and there was a howling mixed of wind and of boys whooping to keep warm. He was roughly handed two pairs of skis, and the handler, muffled to the eyes with a scarf, stared as if amazed that Ethan was so old. All the others struggling into skis in the lee of the shed were adolescent boys. Students: after fifteen years of teaching, Ethan tended to flinch from youth—its harsh noises, its cheerful rapacity, its cruel onward flow as one class replaced another, ate a year of his life, and was replaced by another.

Away from the shelter of the shed, the wind was a high monotonous pitch of pain. His cheeks instantly ached, and the hinges linking the elements of his face seemed exposed. His septum tingled like glass—the rim of a glass being rubbed by a moist finger to produce a note. Drifts ribbed the trail, obscuring Becky's ski tracks seconds after she made them, and at each push through the heaped snow his scope of breathing narrowed. By the time he reached the first steep section, the left half of his back hurt as it did only in the panic of a full asthmatic attack, and his skis, ignored, too heavy to manage, spread and swept him toward a snowbank at the side of the trail. He was bent far forward but kept his balance; the snow kissed his face lightly, instantly, all over; he straightened up, refreshed by the shock, thankful not to have lost a ski. Down the slope Becky had halted and was staring upward at him, worried. A huge blowing feather, a partition of snow, came between them. The cold, unprecedented in his experience, shone through his clothes like furious light, and as he rummaged through his parka for the inhalator he seemed to be searching glass shelves backed by a black wall. He found it, its icy plastic the touch of life, a clumsy key to his insides. Gasping, he exhaled, put it into his mouth, and inhaled; the isoproterenol spray, chilled into drops, opened his lungs enough for him to call to his daughter, "Keep moving! I'll catch up!"

Solid on her skis, she swung down among the moguls and wind-bared ice, and became small, and again waited. The moderate slope seemed a cliff; if he fell and sprained anything, he would freeze. His entire body would become locked tight against air and light and thought. His legs trembled; his breath moved in and out of a narrow slot beneath the pain in his back. The cold and blowing snow all around him constituted an immense crowding, but there was no way out of this white cave but to slide downward toward the dark spot that was his daughter. He had forgotten all his lessons. Leaning backward in an infant's tense snowplow, he floundered through alternating powder and ice.

"You O.K., Daddy?" Her stare was wide, its fright underlined by a pale patch on her cheek.

He used the inhalator again and gave himself breath to tell her, "I'm fine. Let's get down."

In this way, in steps of her leading and waiting, they worked down the mountain, out of the worst wind, into the lower trail that ran between birches and hemlocks. The cold had the quality not of absence but of force: an inverted burning. The last time Becky stopped and waited, the colorless crescent on her scarlet cheek disturbed him, reminded him of some injunction, but he could find in his brain, whittled to a dim determination to persist, only the advice to keep going, toward shelter and warmth. She told him, at a division of trails, "This is the easier way."

"Let's go the quicker way," he said, and in this last descent recovered the rhythm—knees together, shoulders facing the valley, weight forward as if in the moment of release from a diving board—not a resistance but a joyous acceptance of falling. They reached the base lodge, and with unfeeling hands removed their skis. Pushing into the cafeteria, Ethan saw in the momentary mirror of the door window that his face was a spectre's; chin, nose, and eyebrows had retained the snow from that near-fall near the top. "Becky, look," he said, turning in the crowded warmth and clatter inside the door. "I'm a monster."

"I know, your face was absolutely white, I didn't know whether to tell you or not. I thought it might scare you."

He touched the pale patch on her cheek. "Feel anything?"

"No."

"Damn. I should have rubbed snow on it."

Matt and Elaine and the twins, flushed and stripped of their parkas, had eaten lunch; shouting and laughing with a strange guilty shrillness, they said that there had been repeated loud-speaker announcements not to go up to the top without face masks, because of frostbite. They had expected Ethan and Becky to come back down on the gondola, as others had, after tasting the top. "It never occurred to us," Ethan said. He took the blame upon himself by adding, "I wanted to see the girl ski."

Their common adventure, and the guilt of his having given her frostbite, bound Becky and Ethan together in complicity for the rest of the day. They arrived home as sun was leaving even the tips of the hills; Elaine had invited Matt to supper, and while the windows of the house burned golden Ethan shovelled out the Jeep. The house was a typical New Hampshire farmhouse, less than two miles from the college, on the side of a hill, overlooking what had been a pasture, with the usual capacious porch running around three sides, cluttered with cordwood and last summer's lawn furniture. The woodsy sheltered scent of these porches, the sense of rural waste space, never failed to please Ethan, who had been raised in a Newark half-house, then a West Side apartment, and just before college a row house in Baltimore, with his grandparents. The wind had been left behind in the mountains. The air was as still as the stars. Shovelling the light dry snow became a lazy dance. But when he bent suddenly, his knees creaked, and his breathing shortened so that he paused. A sudden rectangle of light was flung from the shadows of the porch. Becky came out into the cold with him. She was carrying a lawn rake.

He asked her, "Should you be out again? How's your frostbite?" Though she was a distance away, there was no need, in the immaculate air, to raise his voice.

"It's O.K. It kind of tingles. And under my chin. Mommy made me put on a scarf."

"What's the lawn rake for?"

"It's a way you can make a path. It really works."

"O.K., you make a path to the garage and after I get my breath I'll see if I can get the Jeep back in."

"Are you having asthma?"

"A little."

"We were reading about it in biology. Dad, see, it's kind of a tree inside you, and every branch has a little ring of muscle around it, and they tighten." From her gestures in the dark she was demonstrating, with mittens on.

What she described, of course, was classic unalloyed asthma, whereas his was shading into emphysema, which could only worsen. But he liked being lectured to—preferred it, indeed, to lecturing—and as the minutes of companionable silence with his daughter passed he took inward notes on the bright quick impressions flowing over him like a continuous voice. The silent cold. The stars. Orion behind an elm. Minute scintillae in the snow at his feet. His daughter's strange black bulk against the white; the solid grace that had stolen upon her. The conspiracy of love. His father and he shovelling the car free from a sudden unwelcome storm in Newark, instantly gray with soot, the undercurrent of desperation, his father a salesman and must get to Camden. Got to get to Camden, boy, get to Camden or bust. Dead of a heart attack at forty-seven. Ethan tossed a shovelful into the air so the scintillae flashed in the steady golden chord from the house windows. Elaine and Matt sitting flushed at the lodge table, parkas off, in deshabille, as if sitting up in bed. Matt's way of turning a half circle on the top of a mogul, light as a diver. The cancerous unwieldiness of Ethan's own skis. His jealousy of his students, the many-headed immortality of their annual renewal. The flawless tall cruelty of the stars. Orion intertwined with the silhouetted elm. A black tree inside him. His daughter, busily sweeping with the rake, childish yet lithe, so curiously demonstrating this preference for his company. Feminine of her to forgive him her frostbite. Perhaps, flattered on skis, felt the cold her element. Her womanhood soon enough to be smothered in warmth. A plow a mile away painstakingly scraped. He was missing the point of the lecture. The point was unstated: an absence. He was looking upon his daughter as a woman but without lust. The music around him was being produced, in the zero air, like a finger on crystal, by this hollowness, this generosity of negation. Without lust, without jealousy. Space seemed love, bestowed to be free in, and coldness the price. He felt joined to the great dead whose words it was his duty to teach.

The Jeep came up unprotestingly from the fluffy snow. It looked happy to be penned in the garage with Elaine's station wagon, and the skis, and the oiled chain saw, and the power mower dreamlessly waiting for spring. Ethan was happy, precariously so, so that rather than break he uttered a sound: "Becky?"

"Yeah?"

"You want to know what else Mr. Langley said?"

"What?" They trudged toward the porch, up the path the gentle rake had cleared.

"He said you ski better than the boys."

"I bet," she said, and raced to the porch, and in the precipitate way, evasive and female and pleased, that she flung herself to the top step he glimpsed something generic and joyous, a pageant that would leave him behind.

JOYCE CARY

◇ ◇ ◇

Growing Up

Robert Quick, coming home after a business trip, found a note from his wife. She would be back at four, but the children were in the garden. He tossed down his hat, and still in his dark business suit, which he disliked very much, made at once for the garden.

He had missed his two small girls and looked forward eagerly to their greeting. He had hoped indeed that they might, as often before, have been waiting at the corner of the road, to flag the car, and drive home with him.

The Quicks' garden was a wilderness. Except for a small vegetable patch near the pond, and one bed where Mrs Quick grew flowers for the house, it had not been touched for years. Old apple trees tottered over seedy laurels, unpruned roses. Tall ruins of dahlias and delphiniums hung from broken sticks.

The original excuse for this neglect was that the garden was for the children. They should do what they liked there. The original truth was that neither of the Quicks cared for gardening. Besides, Mrs Quick was too busy with family, council, and parish affairs, Quick with his office, to give time to a hobby that bored them both.

But the excuse had become true. The garden belonged to the children, and Quick was even proud of it. He would boast of his wild garden, so different from any neighbour's shaved grass and combed beds. It had come to seem, for him, a triumph of imagination; and this afternoon, once more, he found it charming in its wildness, an original masterpiece among gardens.

And, in fact, with the sun just warming up in mid-May, slanting steeply past the trees, and making even old weeds shine red and gold, it had the special beauty of untouched woods, where there is still, even among closely farmed lands, a little piece of free nature left, a suggestion of the frontier, primeval forests.

'A bit of real wild country,' thought Quick, a townsman for whom the country was a place for picnics. And he felt at once released, escaped. He shouted, 'Hullo, hullo, children.'

There was no answer. And he stopped, in surprise. Then he thought, 'They've gone to meet me—I've missed them.' And this gave him both pleasure and dismay. The last time the children had missed him, two years before, having gone a mile down the road and lain in ambush behind a hedge, there had been tears. They had resented being searched for, and brought home; they had hated the humiliating failure of their surprise.

But even as he turned back towards the house, and dodged a tree, he caught sight of Jenny, lying on her stomach by the pond, with a book under her nose. Jenny was twelve and had lately taken furiously to reading.

Quick made for the pond with long steps, calling, 'Hullo, hullo, Jenny, hullo,' waving. But Jenny merely turned her head slightly and peered at him through her hair. Then she dropped her cheek on the book as if to say, 'Excuse me, it's really too hot.'

And now he saw Kate, a year older. She was sitting on the swing, leaning sideways against a rope, with her head down, apparently in deep thought. Her bare legs, blotched with mud, lay along the ground, one foot hooked over the other. Her whole air was one of languor and concentration. To her father's 'Hullo,' she answered only in a faint muffled voice, 'Hullo, Daddy.'

'Hullo, Kate.' But he said no more and did not go near. Quick never asked for affection from his girls. He despised fathers who flirted with their daughters, who encouraged them to love. It would have been especially wrong, he thought, with these two. They were naturally impulsive and affectionate—Jenny had moods of passionate devotion, especially in the last months. She was growing up, he thought, more quickly than Kate and she was going to be an exciting woman, strong in all her feelings, intelligent, reflective. 'Well, Jenny,' he said, 'what are you reading now?' But the child answered only by a slight wriggle of her behind.

Quick was amused at his own disappointment. He said to himself, 'Children have no manners but at least they're honest—they never pretend.' He fetched himself a deck chair and the morning paper, which he had hardly looked at before his early start on the road. He would make the best of things. At fifty-two, having lost most of his illusions, he was good at making the best of things. 'It's a lovely day,' he thought, 'and I'm free till Sunday night.' He looked round him as he opened the paper and felt again the pleasure of the garden. What a joy, at last, to be at peace. And the mere presence of the children was a pleasure. Nothing could deprive him of that. He was home again.

Jenny had got up and wandered away among the trees; her legs too were bare and dirty, and her dress had a large green stain at the side. She had been in the pond. And now Kate allowed herself to collapse slowly out of the swing and lay on her back with her hair tousled in the dirt, her arms thrown apart, her small dirty hands with black nails turned palm upwards to the sky. Her cocker bitch, Snort, came loping and sniffing, uttered one short bark and rooted at her mistress' legs. Kate raised one foot and tickled her stomach, then rolled over and buried her face in her arms. When Snort tried to push her nose under Kate's thigh as if to turn her over, she made a half kick and murmured, 'Go away, Snort.'

'Stop it, Snort,' Jenny echoed in the same meditative tone. The sisters adored each other and one always came to the other's help. But Snort only stopped a moment to gaze at Jenny, then tugged at Kate's dress. Kate made another more energetic kick and said, 'Oh, do go away, Snort.'

Jenny stopped in her languid stroll, snatched a bamboo from the border, and hurled it at Snort like a spear.

The bitch, startled, uttered a loud uncertain bark and approached, wagging her behind so vigorously that she curled her body sideways at each wag. She was not sure if this was a new game, or if she had committed some grave crime. Jenny gave a yell and rushed at her. She fled yelping. At once Kate jumped up, seized another bamboo and threw it, shouting, 'Tiger, tiger.'

The two children dashed after the bitch, laughing, bumping together, falling over each other and snatching up anything they could find to throw at the fugitive, pebbles, dead daffodils, bits of flower-pots, lumps of earth. Snort, horrified, overwhelmed, dodged to and fro, barked hysterically, crazily, wagged her tail in desperate submission; finally put it between her legs and crept whining between a broken shed and the wall.

Robert was shocked. He was fond of the sentimental foolish Snort, and he saw her acute misery. He called to the children urgently, 'Hi, Jenny—don't do that. Don't do that, Kate. She's frightened—you might put her eye out. Hi, stop—stop.'

This last cry expressed real indignation. Jenny had got hold of a rake and was trying to hook Snort by the collar. Robert began to struggle out of his chair. But suddenly Kate turned round, aimed a pea-stick at him and shouted at the top of her voice, 'Yield, Paleface.' Jenny at once turned and cried, 'Yes, yes—Paleface, yield.' She burst into a shout of laughter and could not speak, but rushed at the man with the rake carried like a lance.

The two girls, staggering with laughter, threw themselves upon their father. 'Paleface—Paleface Robbie. Kill him—scalp him. Torture him.'

They tore at the man and suddenly he was frightened. It seemed to him that both the children, usually so gentle, so affectionate, had gone completely mad, vindictive. They were hurting him, and he did not know how to defend himself without hurting them, without breaking their skinny bones, which seemed as fragile as a bird's legs. He dared not even push too hard against the thin ribs which seemed to bend under his hand. Snort, suddenly recovering confidence, rushed barking from cover and seized this new victim by the sleeve, grunting and tugging.

'Hi,' he shouted, trying to catch at the bitch. 'Call her off, Kate. Don't, don't, children.' But they battered at him, Kate was jumping on his stomach, Jenny had seized him by the collar as if to strangle him. Her face, close to his own, was that of a homicidal maniac; her eyes were wide and glaring, her lips were curled back to show all her teeth. And he was really strangling. He made a violent effort to throw the child off, but her hands were firmly twined in his collar. He felt his ears sing. Then suddenly the chair gave way—all three fell with a crash. Snort, startled, and perhaps pinched, gave a yelp, and snapped at the man's face.

Kate was lying across his legs, Jenny on his chest; she still held his collar in both hands. But now, gazing down at him, her expression changed. She cried, 'Oh, she's bitten you. Look, Kate.' Kate, rolling off his legs, came to her knees. 'So she has, bad Snort.'

The girls were still panting, flushed, struggling with laughter. But Jenny reproached her sister, 'It's not a joke. It might be poisoned.'

'I know,' Kate was indignant. But burst out again into helpless giggles.

Robert picked himself up and dusted his coat. He did not utter any reproaches. He avoided even looking at the girls in case they should see his anger and surprise. He was deeply shocked. He could not forget Jenny's face, crazy, murderous; he thought, 'Not much affection there—she wanted to hurt. It was as if she hated me.'

It seemed to him that something new had broken into his old simple and happy relation with his daughters; that they had suddenly receded from him into a world of their own in which he had no standing, a primitive, brutal world.

He straightened his tie. Kate had disappeared; Jenny was gazing at his forehead and trying to suppress her own giggles. But when he turned away, she caught his arm, 'Oh Daddy, where are you going?'

'To meet your mother—she must be on her way.'

'Oh, but you can't go like that—we've got to wash your bite.'

'That's all right, Jenny. It doesn't matter.'

'But Kate is getting the water—and it might be quite bad.'

And now, Kate, coming from the kitchen with a bowl of water, called out indignantly, 'Sit down, Daddy—sit down—how dare you get up.'

She was playing the stern nurse. And in fact, Robert, though still in a mood of disgust, found himself obliged to submit to this new game. At least it was more like a game. It was not murderous. And a man so plump and bald could not allow himself even to appear upset by the roughness of children. Even though the children would not understand why he was upset, why he was shocked.

'Sit down at once, man,' Jenny said. 'Kate, put up the chair.'

Kate put up the chair, the two girls made him sit down, washed the cut, painted it with iodine, stuck a piece of plaster on it. Mrs Quick, handsome, rosy, good-natured, practical, arrived in the middle of this ceremony, with her friend Jane Martin, Chairman of the Welfare Committee. Both were much amused by the scene, and the history of the afternoon. Their air said plainly to Robert, 'All you children— amusing yourselves while we run the world.'

Kate and Jenny were sent to wash and change their dirty

frocks. The committee was coming to tea. And at tea, the two girls, dressed in smart clean frocks, handed round cake and bread and butter with demure and reserved looks. They knew how to behave at tea, at a party. They were enjoying the dignity of their own performance. Their eyes passed over their father as if he did not exist, or rather as if he existed only as another guest, to be waited on.

And now, seeking as it were a new if lower level of security, of resignation, he said to himself, 'Heavens, but what did I expect? In a year or two more I shan't count at all. Young men will come prowling, like the dogs after Snort—I shall be an old buffer, useful only to pay bills.'

The ladies were talking together about a case—the case of a boy of fourteen, a nice respectable boy, most regular at Sunday school, who had suddenly robbed his mother's till and gone off in a stolen car. Jenny, seated at her mother's feet, was listening intently, Kate was feeding chocolate roll to Snort, and tickling her chin.

Quick felt all at once a sense of stuffiness. He wanted urgently to get away, to escape. Yes, he needed some male society. He would go to the club. Probably no one would be there but the card-room crowd, and he could not bear cards. But he might find old Wilkins in the billiard room. Wilkins at seventy was a crashing, a dreary bore, who spent half his life at the club; who was always telling you how he had foreseen the slump, and how clever he was at investing his money. What good was money to old Wilkins? But, Quick thought, he could get up a game with Wilkins, pass an hour or two with him, till dinner-time, even dine with him. He could phone his wife. She would not mind. She rather liked a free evening for her various accounts. And he need not go home till the children were in bed.

And when, after tea, the committee members pulled out their agenda, he stole away. Suddenly, as he turned by the corner house, skirting its front garden wall, he heard running steps and a breathless call. He turned, it was Jenny.

She arrived, panting, holding herself by the chest. 'Oh, I couldn't catch you.'

'What is it now, Jenny?'

'I wanted to look—at the cut.'

Robert began to stoop. But she cried, 'No, I'll get on the wall. Put me up.'

He lifted her on the garden wall which made her about a foot taller than himself. Having reached this superior position, she poked the plaster.

'I just wanted to make sure it was sticking. Yes, it's all right.'

She looked down at him with an expression he did not recognise. What was the game, medical, maternal? Was she going to laugh? But the child frowned. She was also struck by something new and unexpected.

Then she tossed back her hair. 'Good-bye.' She jumped down and ran off. The man walked slowly towards the club. 'No,' he thought, 'not quite a game—not for half a second. She's growing up—and so am I.'

ANDRE DUBUS

◇ ◇ ◇

A Father's Story

My name is Luke Ripley, and here is what I call my life: I own a stable of thirty horses, and I have young people who teach riding, and we board some horses too. This is in northeastern Massachusetts. I have a barn with an indoor ring, and outside I've got two fenced-in rings and a pasture that ends at a woods with trails. I call it my life because it looks like it is, and people I know call it that, but it's a life I can get away from when I hunt and fish, and some nights after dinner when I sit in the dark in the front room and listen to opera. The room faces the lawn and the road, a two-lane country road. When the cars come around the curve northwest of the house, they light up the lawn for an instant, the leaves of the maple out by the road and the hemlock closer to the window. Then I'm alone again, or I'd appear to be if someone crept up to the house and looked through a window: a big-gutted grey-haired guy, drinking tea and smoking cigarettes, staring out at the dark woods across the road, listening to a grieving soprano.

My real life is the one nobody talks about anymore, except Father Paul LeBoeuf, another old buck. He has a decade on me: he's sixty-four, a big man, bald on top with grey at the

177

sides; when he had hair, it was black. His face is ruddy, and he jokes about being a whiskey priest, though he's not. He gets outdoors as much as he can, goes for a long walk every morning, and hunts and fishes with me. But I can't get him on a horse anymore. Ten years ago I could badger him into a trail ride; I had to give him a western saddle, and he'd hold the pommel and bounce through the woods with me, and be sore for days. He's looking at seventy with eyes that are younger than many I've seen in people in their twenties. I do not remember ever feeling the way they seem to; but I was lucky, because even as a child I knew that life would try me, and I must be strong to endure, though in those early days I expected to be tortured and killed for my faith, like the saints I learned about in school.

Father Paul's family came down from Canada, and he grew up speaking more French than English, so he is different from the Irish priests who abound up here. I do not like to make general statements, or even to hold general beliefs, about people's blood, but the Irish do seem happiest when they're dealing with misfortune or guilt, either their own or somebody else's, and if you think you're not a victim of either one, you can count on certain Irish priests to try to change your mind. On Wednesday nights Father Paul comes to dinner. Often he comes on other nights too, and once, in the old days when we couldn't eat meat on Fridays, we bagged our first ducks of the season on a Friday, and as we drove home from the marsh, he said: For the purposes of Holy Mother Church, I believe a duck is more a creature of water than land, and is not rightly meat. Sometimes he teases me about never putting anything in his Sunday collection, which he would not know about if I hadn't told him years ago. I would like to believe I told him so we could have philosophical talk at dinner, but probably the truth is I suspected he knew, and I did not want him to think I so loved money that I would not even give his church a coin on Sunday. Certainly the ushers who pass the baskets know me as a miser.

I don't feel right about giving money for buildings, places. This starts with the Pope, and I cannot respect one of them till he sells his house and everything in it, and that church too, and uses the money to feed the poor. I have rarely, and maybe never, come across saintliness, but I feel certain it cannot exist in such a place. But I admit, also, that I know very little, and maybe the popes live on a different plane and are tried in ways I don't know about. Father Paul says his own church, St. John's, is hardly the Vatican. I like his church: it is made of wood, and has a simple altar and crucifix, and no padding on the kneelers. He does not have to lock its doors at night. Still it is a place. He could say Mass in my barn. I know this is stubborn, but I can find no mention by Christ of maintaining buildings, much less erecting them of stone or brick, and decorating them with pieces of metal and mineral and elements that people still fight over like barbarians. We had a Maltese woman taking riding lessons, she came over on the boat when she was ten, and once she told me how the nuns in Malta used to tell the little girls that if they wore jewelry, rings and bracelets and necklaces, in purgatory snakes would coil around their fingers and wrists and throats. I do not believe in frightening children or telling them lies, but if those nuns saved a few girls from devotion to things, maybe they were right. That Maltese woman laughed about it, but I noticed she wore only a watch, and that with a leather strap.

The money I give to the church goes in people's stomachs, and on their backs, down in New York City. I have no delusions about the worth of what I do, but I feel it's better to feed somebody than not. There's a priest in Times Square giving shelter to runaway kids, and some Franciscans who run a bread line; actually it's a morning line for coffee and a roll, and Father Paul calls it the continental breakfast for winos and bag ladies. He is curious about how much I am sending, and I know why: he guesses I send a lot, he has said probably more than tithing, and he is right; he wants to know how much because he believes I'm generous and good, and he is wrong about that; he has never had much money and does not know how easy it is to write a check when you have every thing you will ever need, and the figures are mere numbers, and represent no sacrifice at all. Being a real Catholic is too hard; if I were one, I would do with my house and barn what I want the Pope to do with his. So I do not want to impress Father Paul, and when he asks me how much, I say I can't let my left hand know what my right is doing.

He came on Wednesday nights when Gloria and I were married, and the kids were young; Gloria was a very good cook (I assume she still is, but it is difficult to think of her in the present), and I liked sitting at the table with a friend who was also a priest. I was proud of my handsome and healthy children. This was long ago, and they were all very young and cheerful and often funny, and the three boys took care of their baby sister, and did not bully or tease her. Of course they did sometimes, with that excited cruelty children are prone to, but not enough so that it was part of her days. On the Wednesday after Gloria left with the kids and a U-Haul trailer, I was sitting on the front steps, it was summer, and I was watching cars go by on the road, when Father Paul drove around the curve and into the driveway. I was ashamed to see him because he is a priest and my family was gone, but I was relieved too. I went to the car to greet him. He got out smiling, with a bottle of wine, and shook my hand, then pulled me to him, gave me a quick hug, and said: 'It's Wednesday, isn't it? Let's open some cans.'

With arms about each other we walked to the house, and it was good to know he was doing his work but coming as a friend too, and I thought what good work he had. I have no calling. It is for me to keep horses.

In that other life, anyway. In my real one I go to bed early and sleep well and wake at four forty-five, for an hour of silence. I never want to get out of bed then, and every morning I know I can sleep for another four hours, and still not fail at any of my duties. But I get up, so have come to believe my life can be seen in miniature in that struggle in the dark of morning. While making the bed and boiling water for coffee, I talk to God: I offer Him my day, every act of my body and spirit, my thoughts and moods, as a prayer of thanksgiving, and for Gloria and my children and my friends and two women I made love with after Gloria left. This morning offertory is a habit from my boyhood in a Catholic school; or then it was a habit, but as I kept it and grew older it became a ritual. Then I say the Lord's Prayer, trying not to recite it, and one morning it occurred to me that a prayer, whether recited or said with concentration, is always an act of faith.

I sit in the kitchen at the rear of the house and drink coffee and smoke and watch the sky growing light before sunrise, the trees of the woods near the barn taking shape, becoming single pines and elms and oaks and maples. Sometimes a rabbit comes out of the treeline, or is already sitting there, invisible till the light finds him. The birds are awake in the trees and feeding on the ground, and the little ones, the purple finches and titmice and chickadees, are at the feeder I rigged outside the kitchen window; it is too small for pigeons to get a purchase. I sit and give myself to coffee and tobacco, that get me brisk again, and I watch and listen. In the first year or so after I lost my family, I played the radio in the mornings. But I overcame that, and now I rarely play it at all. Once in the mail I received a questionnaire asking me to write down everything I watched on television during the week they had chosen. At the end of those seven days I wrote in *The Wizard of Oz* and returned it. That was in winter and was actually a busy week for my television, which normally sits out the cold months without once warming up. Had they sent the questionnaire during baseball season, they would have found me at my set. People at the stables talk about shows and performers I have never heard of, but I cannot get interested; when I am in the mood to watch television, I go to a movie or read a detective novel. There are always good detective novels to be found, and I like remembering them next morning with my coffee.

I also think of baseball and hunting and fishing, and of my children. It is not painful to think about them anymore, because even if we had lived together, they would be gone now, grown into their own lives, except Jennifer. I think of death too, not sadly, or with fear, though something like excitement does run through me, something more quickening than the coffee and tobacco. I suppose it is an intense interest, and an outright distrust: I never feel certain that I'll be here watching birds eating at tomorrow's daylight. Sometimes I try to think of other things, like the rabbit that is warm and breathing but not there till twilight. I feel on the brink of something about the life of the senses, but either am not equipped to go further or am not interested enough to concentrate. I have called all of this thinking, but it is not, because it is unintentional; what I'm really doing is feeling the day, in silence, and that is what Father Paul is doing too on his five-to-ten-mile walks.

When the hour ends I take an apple or carrot and I go to the stable and tack up a horse. We take good care of these horses, and no one rides them but students, instructors, and me, and nobody rides the horses we board unless an owner asks me to. The barn is dark and I turn on lights and take some deep breaths, smelling the hay and horses and their manure, both fresh and dried, a combined odor that you either like or you don't. I walk down the wide space of dirt between stalls, greeting the horses, joking with them about their quirks, and choose one for no reason at all other than the way it looks at me that morning. I get my old English saddle that has smoothed and darkened through the years, and go into the stall, talking to this beautiful creature who'll swerve out of a canter if a piece of paper blows in front of him, and if the barn catches fire and you manage to get him out he will, if he can get away from you, run back into the fire, to his stall. Like the smells that surround them, you either like them or you don't. I love them, so am spared having to try to explain why. I feed one the carrot or apple and tack up and lead him outside, where I mount, and we go down the driveway to the road and cross it and turn northwest and walk then trot then canter to St. John's.

A few cars are on the road, their drivers looking serious about going to work. It is always strange for me to see a woman dressed for work so early in the morning. You know how long it takes them, with the makeup and hair and clothes, and I think of them waking in the dark of winter or early light of other seasons, and dressing as they might for an evening's entertainment. Probably this strikes me because I grew up seeing my father put on those suits he never wore on weekends or his two weeks off, and so am accustomed to the men, but when I see these women I think something went wrong, to send all those dressed-up people out on the road when the dew hasn't dried yet. Maybe it's because I so dislike getting up early, but am also doing what I choose to do, while they have no choice. At heart I am lazy, yet I find such peace and delight in it that I believe it is a natural state, and in what looks like my laziest periods I am closest to my center. The ride to St. John's is fifteen minutes. The horses and I do it in all weather; the road is well plowed in winter, and there are only a few days a year when ice makes me drive the pickup. People always look at someone on horseback, and for a moment their faces change and many drivers and I wave to each other. Then at St. John's, Father Paul and five or six regulars and I celebrate the Mass.

Do not think of me as a spiritual man whose every thought during those twenty-five minutes is at one with the words of the Mass. Each morning I try, each morning I fail, and know that always I will be a creature who, looking at Father Paul and the altar, and uttering prayers, will be distracted by scrambled eggs, horses, the weather, and memories and daydreams that have nothing to do with the sacrament I am about to receive. I can receive, though: the Eucharist. and also, at Mass and at other times, moments and even minutes of contemplation. But I cannot achieve contemplation, as some can; and so, having to face and forgive my own failures, I have learned from them both the necessity and wonder of ritual. For ritual allows those who cannot will themselves out of the secular to perform the spiritual, as dancing allows the tongue-tied man a ceremony of love. And, while my mind dwells on breakfast, or Major or Duchess tethered under the church eave, there is, as I take the Host from Father Paul and place it on my tongue and return to the pew, a feeling that I am thankful I have not lost in the forty-eight years since my first Communion. At its center is excitement; spreading out from it is the peace of certainty. Or the certainty of peace. One night Father Paul and I talked about faith. It was long ago, and all I remember is him saying: Belief is believing in God; faith is believing that God believes in you. That is the excitement, and the peace; then the Mass is over, and I go into the sacristy and we have a cigarette and chat, the mystery ends, we are two men talking like any two men on a morning in America, about baseball, plane crashes, presidents, governors, murders, the sun, the clouds. Then I go to the horse and ride back to the life people see, the one in which I move and talk, and most days I enjoy it.

It is late summer now, the time between fishing and hunting, but a good time for baseball. It has been two weeks since Jennifer left, to drive home to Gloria's after her summer visit. She is the only one who still visits; the boys are married and have children, and sometimes fly up for a holiday, or I fly down or west to visit one of them. Jennifer is twenty, and I worry about her the way fathers worry about daughters but not sons. I want to know what she's up to, and at the same time I don't. She looks athletic, and she is: she swims and runs and of course rides. All my children do. When she comes for six weeks in summer, the house is loud with girls, friends of hers since childhood, and new ones. I am glad she kept the girl friends. They have been young company for me and, being with them, I have been able to gauge her growth between summers. On their riding days, I'd take them back to the house when their lessons were over and they had walked the horses and put them back in the stalls, and we'd have lemonade or Coke, and cookies if I had some, and talk until their parents came to drive them home. One year their breasts grew, so I wasn't startled when I saw Jennifer in July. Then they were driving cars to the stable, and beginning to look like young women, and I was passing out beer and ashtrays and they were talking about college.

When Jennifer was here in summer, they were at the house most days. I would say generally that as they got older they became quieter, and though I enjoyed both, I sometimes missed the giggles and shouts. The quiet voices, just low enough for me not to hear from wherever I was, rising and falling in proportion to my distance from them, frightened me. Not that I believed they were planning or recounting anything really wicked, but there was a female seriousness about them, and it was secretive, and of course I thought: love, sex. But it was more than that: it was woman-hood they were entering, the deep forest of it, and no matter how many women and men too are saying these days that there is little difference between us, the truth is that men find their way into that forest only on clearly marked trails, while women move about in it like birds. So hearing Jennifer and her friends talking so quietly, yet intensely, I wanted very much to have a wife.

But not as much as in the old days, when Gloria had left but her presence was still in the house as strongly as if she had only gone to visit her folks for a week. There were no clothes or cosmetics, but potted plants endured my neglect-ful care as long as they could, and slowly died; I did not kill them on purpose, to exorcise the house of her, but I could not remember to water them. For weeks, because I did not use it much, the house was as neat as she had kept it, though dust layered the order she had made. The kitchen went first: I got the dishes in and out of the dishwasher and wiped the top of the stove, but did not return cooking spoons and pot holders to their hooks on the wall, and soon the burners and oven were caked with spillings, the refrigerator had more space and was spotted with juices. The living room and my bedroom went next; I did not go into the children's rooms except on bad nights when I went from room to room and looked and touched and smelled, so they did not lose their order until a year later when the kids came for six weeks. It was three months before I ate the last of the food Gloria had cooked and frozen: I remember it was a beef stew, and very good. By then I had four cookbooks, and was boasting a bit, and talking about recipes with the women at the stables, and looking forward to cooking for Father Paul. But I never looked forward to cooking at night only for myself, though I made myself do it; on some nights I gave in to my daily temptation, and took a newspaper or detective novel to a restaurant. By the end of the second year, though, I had stopped turning on the radio as soon as I woke in the morning, and was able to be silent and alone in the evening too, and then I enjoyed my dinners.

It is not hard to live through a day, if you can live through a moment. What creates despair is the imagination, which pretends there is a future, and insists on predicting millions of moments, thousands of days, and so drains you that you cannot live the moment at hand. That is what Father Paul told me in those first two years, on some of the bad nights when I believed I could not bear what I had to: the most painful loss was my children, then the loss of Gloria, whom I still loved despite or maybe because of our long periods of sadness that rendered us helpless, so neither of us could break out of it to give a hand to the other. Twelve years later I believe ritual would have healed us more quickly than the repetitious talks we had, perhaps even kept us healed. Marriages have lost that, and I wish I had known then what I know now, and we had performed certain acts together every day, no matter how we felt, and perhaps then we could have subordinated feeling to action, for surely that is the essence of love. I know this from my distractions during Mass, and during everything else I do, so that my actions and feelings are seldom one. It does happen every day, but in proportion to everything else in a day, it is rare, like joy. The third most painful loss, which became second and sometimes first as months passed, was the knowledge that I could never marry again, and so dared not even keep company with a woman.

On some of the bad nights I was bitter about this with Father Paul, and I so pitied myself that I cried, or nearly did, speaking with damp eyes and breaking voice. I believe that celibacy is for him the same trial it is for me, not of the flesh, but the spirit; the heart longing to love. But the difference is he chose it, and did not wake one day to a life with thirty horses. In my anger I said I had done my service to love and chastity, and I told him of the actual physical and spiritual pain of practicing rhythm: nights of striking the mattress with a fist, two young animals lying side by side in heat, leaving the bed to pace, to smoke, to curse, and too passionate to question, for we were so angered and oppressed by our passion that we could see no further than our loins. So now I understand how people can be enslaved for generations before they throw down their tools or use them as weapons, the form of their slavery—the cotton fields, the shacks and puny cupboards and untended illnesses—absorbing their emotions and thoughts until finally they have little or none at all to direct with clarity and energy at the owners and legislators. And I told him of the trick of passion and its slaking: how during what we had to believe were safe periods, though all four children were conceived at those times, we were able with some coherence to question the tradition and reason and justice of the law against birth control, but not with enough conviction to soberly act against it, as though regular satisfaction in bed tempered our revolutionary as well as our erotic desires. Only when abstinence drove us hotly away from each other did we receive an urge so strong it lasted all the way to the drugstore and back; but always, after release, we threw away the remaining condoms; and after going through this a few times, we knew what would happen, and from then on we submitted to the calendar she so precisely marked on the bedroom wall. I told him that living two lives each month, one as celibates, one as lovers, made us tense and short-tempered, so we snapped at each other like dogs.

To have endured that, to have reached a time when we burned slowly and could gain from bed the comfort of lying down at night with one who loves you and whom you love, could for weeks on end go to bed tired and peacefully sleep after a kiss, a touch of the hands, and then to be thrown out of the marriage like a bundle from a moving freight car, was unjust, was intolerable, and I could not or would not muster the strength to endure it. But I did, a moment at a time, a day, a night, except twice, each time with a different woman and more than a year apart, and this was so long ago that I clearly see their faces in my memory, can hear the pitch of their voices, and the way they pronounced words, one with a Massachusetts accent, one midwestern, but I feel as though I only heard about them from someone else. Each rode at the stables and was with me for part of an evening; one was badly married, one divorced, so none of us was free. They did not understand this Catholic view, but they were understanding about my having it, and I remained friends with both of them until the married one left her husband and went to Boston, and the divorced one moved to Maine. After both those evenings, those good women, I went to Mass early while Father Paul was still in the confessional, and received his absolution. I did not tell him who I was, but of course he knew, though I never saw it in his eyes. Now my longing for a wife comes only once in a while, like a cold: on some late afternoons when I am alone in the barn, then I lock up and walk to the house, daydreaming, then suddenly look at it and see it empty, as though for the first time, and all at once I'm weary and feel I do not have the energy to broil meat, and I think of driving to a restaurant, then shake my head and go on to the house, the refrigerator, the oven; and some mornings when I wake in the dark and listen to the silence and run my hand over the cold sheet beside me; and some days in summer when Jennifer is here.

Gloria left first me, then the Church, and that was the end of religion for the children, though on visits they went to Sunday Mass with me, and still do, out of respect for my life that they manage to keep free of patronage. Jennifer is an agnostic, though I doubt she would call herself that, any more than she would call herself any other name that implied she had made a decision, a choice, about existence, death, and God. In truth she tends to pantheism, a good sign, I think; but not wanting to be a father who tells his children what they ought to believe, I do not say to her that Catholicism includes pantheism, like onions in a stew. Besides, I have no missionary instincts and do not believe everyone should or even could live with the Catholic faith. It is Jennifer's womanhood that renders me awkward. And womanhood now is frank, not like when Gloria was twenty and there were symbols: high heels and cosmetics and dresses, a cigarette, a cocktail. I am glad that women are free now of false modesty and all its attention paid the flesh; but, still, it is difficult to see so much of your daughter, to hear her talk as only men and bawdy women used to, and most of all to see in her face the deep and unabashed sensuality of women, with no tricks of the eyes and mouth to hide the pleasure she feels at having a strong young body. I am certain, with the way things are now, that she has very happily not been a virgin for years. That does not bother me. What bothers me is my certainty about it, just from watching her walk across a room or light a cigarette or pour milk on cereal.

She told me all of it, waking me that night when I had gone to sleep listening to the wind in the trees and against the house, a wind so strong that I had to shut all but the lee windows, and still the house cooled; told it to me in such detail and so clearly that now, when she has driven the car to Florida, I remember it all as though I had been a passenger in the front seat, or even at the wheel. It started with a movie, then beer and driving to the sea to look at the waves in the night and the wind, Jennifer and Betsy and Liz. They drank a beer on the beach and wanted to go in naked but were afraid they would drown in the high surf. They bought another six-pack at a grocery store in New Hampshire, and drove home. I can see it now, feel it: the three girls and the beer and the ride on country roads where pines curved in the wind and the big deciduous trees swayed and shook as if they might leap from the earth. They would have some windows partly open so they could feel the wind; Jennifer would be playing a cassette, the music stirring them, as it does the young, to memories of another time, other people and places in what is for them the past.

She took Betsy home, then Liz, and sang with her cassette as she left the town west of us and started home, a twenty-minute drive on the road that passes my house. They had each had four beers, but now there were twelve empty bottles in the bag on the floor at the passenger seat, and I keep focusing on their sound against each other when the car shifted speeds or changed directions. For I want to understand that one moment out of all her heart's time on earth, and whether her history had any bearing on it, or whether her heart was then isolated from all it had known, and the sound of those bottles urged it. She was just leaving the town, accelerating past a night club on the right, gaining speed to climb a long, gradual hill, then she went up it, singing, patting the beat on the steering wheel, the wind loud through her few inches of open window, blowing her hair as it did the high branches alongside the road, and she looked up at them and watched the top of the hill for someone drunk or heedless coming over it in part of her lane. She crested to an open black road, and there he was: a bulk, a blur, a thing running across her headlights, and she swerved left and her foot went for the brake and was stomping air above its pedal when she hit him, saw his legs and body in the air, flying out of her light, into the dark. Her brakes were screaming into the wind, bottles clinking in the fallen bag, and with the music and wind inside the car was his sound, already a memory but as real as an echo, that car-shuddering thump as though she had struck a tree. Her foot was back on the accelerator. Then she shifted gears and pushed it. She ejected the cassette and closed the window. She did not start to cry until she knocked on my bedroom door, then called: 'Dad?'

Her voice, her tears, broke through my dream and the wind I heard in my sleep, and I stepped into jeans and hurried to the door, thinking harm, rape, death. All were in her face, and I hugged her and pressed her cheek to my chest and smoothed her blown hair, then led her, weeping, to the kitchen and set her at the table where still she could not speak, nor look at me; when she raised her face it fell forward again, as of its own weight, into her palms. I offered tea and she shook her head, so I offered beer twice, then she shook her head, so I offered whiskey and she nodded. I had some rye that Father Paul and I had not finished last hunting season, and I poured some over ice and set it in front of her and was putting away the ice but stopped and got another glass and poured one for myself too, and brought the ice and bottle to the table where she was trying to get one of her long menthols out of the pack, but her fingers jerked like severed snakes, and I took the pack and lit one for her and took one for myself. I watched her shudder with her first swallow of rye, and push hair back from her face, it is auburn and gleamed in the overhead light, and I remembered how beautiful she looked riding a sorrel; she was smoking fast, then the sobs in her throat stopped, and she looked at me and said it, the words coming out with smoke: 'I hit somebody. With the *car* '

Then she was crying and I was on my feet, moving back and forth, looking down at her, asking *Who? Where? Where?*

She was pointing at the wall over the stove, jabbing her fingers and cigarette at it, her other hand at her eyes, and twice in horror I actually looked at the wall. She finished the whiskey in a swallow and I stopped pacing and asking and poured another, and either the drink or the exhaustion of tears quieted her, even the dry sobs, and she told me; not as I tell it now, for that was later as again and again we relived it in the kitchen or living room, and, if in daylight, fled it on horseback out on the trails through the woods and, if at night, walked quietly around in the moonlit pasture, walked around and around it, sweating through our clothes. She told it in bursts, like she was a child again, running to me, injured from play. I put on boots and a shirt and left her with the bottle and her streaked face and a cigarette twitching between her fingers, pushed the door open against the wind, and eased it shut. The wind squinted and watered my eyes as I leaned into it and went to the pickup.

When I passed St. John's I looked at it, and Father Paul's little white rectory in the rear, and wanted to stop, wished I could as I could if he were simply a friend who sold hardware or something. I had forgotten my watch but I always know the time within minutes, even when a sound or dream or my bladder wakes me in the night. It was nearly two; we had been in the kitchen about twenty minutes; she had hit him around one-fifteen. Or her. The road was empty and I drove between blowing trees; caught for an instant in my lights, they seemed to be in panic. I smoked and let hope play its tricks on me: it was neither man nor woman but an animal, a goat or calf or deer on the road; it was a man who had jumped away in time, the collision of metal and body glancing not direct, and he had limped home to nurse bruises and cuts. Then I threw the cigarette and hope both out the window and prayed that he was alive, while beneath that prayer, a reserve deeper in my heart, another one stirred: that if he were dead, they would not get Jennifer.

From our direction, east and a bit south, the road to that

hill and the night club beyond it and finally the town, is for its last four or five miles, straight through farming country. When I reached that stretch I slowed the truck and opened my window for the fierce air; on both sides were scattered farmhouses and barns and sometimes a silo, looking not like shelters but like unsheltered things the wind would flatten. Corn bent toward the road from a field on my right, and always something blew in front of me: paper, leaves, dried weeds, branches. I slowed approaching the hill, and went up it in second, staring through my open window at the ditch on the left side of the road, its weeds alive, whipping, a mad dance with the trees above them. I went over the hill and down and, opposite the club, turned right onto a side street of houses, and parked there, in the leaping shadows of trees. I walked back across the road to the club's parking lot, the wind behind me, lifting me as I strode, and I could not hear my boots on pavement. I walked up the hill, on the shoulder, watching the branches above me, hearing their leaves and the creaking trunks and the wind. Then I was at the top, looking down the road and at the farms and fields; the night was clear, and I could see a long way; clouds scudded past the half-moon and stars, blown out to sea.

I started down, watching the tall grass under the trees to my right, glancing into the dark of the ditch, listening for cars behind me; but as soon as I cleared one tree, its sound was gone, its flapping leaves and rattling branches far behind me, as though the greatest distance I had at my back was a matter of feet, while ahead of me I could see a barn two miles off. Then I saw her skid marks: short, and going left and downhill, into the other lane. I stood at the ditch, its weeds blowing; across it were trees and their moving shadows, like the clouds. I stepped onto its slope, and it took me sliding on my feet, then rump, to the bottom, where I sat still, my body gathered to itself, lest a part of me should touch him. But there was only tall grass, and I stood, my shoulders reaching the sides of the ditch, and I walked uphill, wishing for the flashlight in the pickup, walking slowly, and down in the ditch I could hear my feet in the grass and on the earth, and kicking cans and bottles. At the top of the hill I turned and went down, watching the ground above the ditch on my right, praying my prayer from the truck again, the first one, the one I would admit, that he was not dead, was in fact home, and began to hope again, memory telling me of lost pheasants and grouse I had shot, but they were small and the colors of their home, while a man was either there or not; and from that memory I left where I was and while walking in the ditch under the wind was in the deceit of imagination with Jennifer in the kitchen, telling her she had hit no one, or at least had not badly hurt anyone, when I realized he could be in the hospital now and I would have to think of a way to check there, something to say on the phone. I see now that, once hope returned, I should have been certain what it prepared me for: ahead of me, in high grass and the shadows of trees, I saw his shirt. Or that is all my mind would allow itself: a shirt, and I stood looking at it for the moments it took my mind to admit the arm and head and the dark length covered by pants. He lay face down, the arm I could see near his side, his head turned from me, on its cheek.

'Fella?' I said. I had meant to call, but it came out quiet and high, lost inches from my face in the wind. Then I said, 'Oh God,' and felt Him in the wind and the sky moving past the stars and moon and the fields around me, but only watching me as He might have watched Cain or Job, I did not know which, and I said it again, and wanted to sink to the earth and weep till I slept there in the weeds. I climbed, scrambling up the side of the ditch, pulling at clutched grass, gained the top on hands and knees, and went to him like that, panting, moving through the grass as high and higher than my face, crawling under that sky, making sounds too, like some animal, there being no words to let him know I was here with him now. He was long; that is the word that came to me, not tall. I kneeled beside him, my hands on my legs. His right arm was by his side, his left arm straight out

from the shoulder, but turned, so his palm was open to the
tree above us. His left cheek was cleanshaven, his eye closed,
and there was no blood. I leaned forward to look at his
open mouth and saw the blood on it, going down into the
grass. I straightened and looked ahead at the wind blowing
past me through grass and trees to a distant light, and I
stared at the light, imagining someone awake out there,
wanting someone to be, a gathering of old friends, or someone alone listening to music or painting a picture, then I
figured it was a night light at a farmyard whose house I
couldn't see. *Going,* I thought. *Still going.* I leaned over
again and looked at dripping blood.

So I had to touch his wrist, a thick one with a watch and
expansion band that I pushed up his arm, thinking *he's
left-handed,* my three fingers pressing his wrist, and all I felt
was my tough fingertips on that smooth underside flesh and
small bones, then relief, then certainty. But against my will,
or only because of it, I still don't know, I touched his neck,
ran my fingers down it as if petting, then pressed, and my
hand sprang back as from fire. I lowered it again, held it
there until it felt that faint beating that I could not believe.
There was too much wind. Nothing could make a sound in
it. A pulse could not be felt in it, nor could mere fingers in
that wind feel the absolute silence of a dead man's artery. I
was making sounds again; I grabbed his left arm and his
waist, and pulled him toward me, and that side of him rose,
turned, and I lowered him to his back, his face tilted up
toward the tree that was groaning, the tree and I the only
sounds in the wind. Turning my face from his, looking down
the length of him at his sneakers, I placed my ear on his
heart, and heard not that but something else, and I clamped
a hand over my exposed ear, heard something liquid and
alive, like when you pump a well and after a few strokes you
hear air and water moving in the pipe, and I knew I must
raise his legs and cover him and run to a phone, while still I
listened to his chest, thinking *raise with what? cover with
what?* and amid the liquid sound I heard the heart, then lost

it, and pressed my ear against bone, but his chest was quiet, and I did not know when the liquid had stopped, and do not know now when I heard air, a faint rush of it, and whether under my ear or at his mouth or whether I heard it at all. I straightened and looked at the light, dim and yellow. Then I touched his throat, looking him full in the face. He was blond and young. He could have been sleeping in the shade of a tree, but for the smear of blood from his mouth to his hair, and the night sky, and the weeds blowing against his head, and the leaves shaking in the dark above us.

I stood. Then I kneeled again and prayed for his soul to join in peace and joy all the dead and living; and, doing so, confronted my first sin against him, not stopping for Father Paul, who could have given him the last rites, and immediately then my second one, or, I saw then, my first, not calling an ambulance to meet me there, and I stood and turned into the wind, slid down the ditch and crawled out of it, and went up the hill and down it, across the road to the street of houses whose people I had left behind forever, so that I moved with stealth in the shadows to my truck.

When I came around the bend near my house, I saw the kitchen light at the rear. She sat as I had left her, the ashtray filled, and I looked at the bottle, felt her eyes on me, felt what she was seeing too: the dirt from my crawling. She had not drunk much of the rye. I poured some in my glass, with the water from melted ice, and sat down and swallowed some and looked at her and swallowed some more, and said: 'He's dead.'

She rubbed her eyes with the heels of her hands, rubbed the cheeks under them, but she was dry now.

'He was probably dead when he hit the ground. I mean, that's probably what killed—'

'Where was he?'

'Across the ditch, under a tree.'

'Was he—did you see his face?'

'No. Not really. I just felt. For life, pulse. I'm going out to the car.'

'What for? Oh.'

I finished the rye, and pushed back the chair, then she was standing too.

'I'll go with you.'

'There's no need.'

'I'll go.'

I took a flashlight from a drawer and pushed open the door and held it while she went out. We turned our faces from the wind. It was like on the hill, when I was walking, and the wind closed the distance behind me: after three or four steps I felt there was no house back there. She took my hand, as I was reaching for hers. In the garage we let go, and squeezed between the pickup and her little car, to the front of it, where we had more room, and we stepped back from the grill and I shone the light on the fender, the smashed headlight turned into it, the concave chrome staring to the right, at the garage wall.

'We ought to get the bottles,' I said.

She moved between the garage and the car, on the passenger side, and had room to open the door and lift the bag. I reached out, and she gave me the bag and backed up and shut the door and came around the car. We sidled to the doorway, and she put her arm around my waist and I hugged her shoulders.

'I thought you'd call the police,' she said.

We crossed the yard, faces bowed from the wind, her hair blowing away from her neck, and in the kitchen I put the bag of bottles in the garbage basket. She was working at the table: capping the rye and putting it away, filling the ice tray, washing the glasses, emptying the ashtray, sponging the table.

'Try to sleep now,' I said.

She nodded at the sponge circling under her hand, gathering ashes. Then she dropped it in the sink and, looking me full in the face, as I had never seen her look, as perhaps she never had, being for so long a daughter on visits (or so it seemed to me and still does: that until then our eyes had never seriously met), she crossed to me from the sink and kissed my lips, then held me so tightly I lost balance, and would have stumbled forward had she not held me so hard.

I sat in the living room, the house darkened, and watched the maple and hemlock. When I believed she was asleep I put on *La Boheme*, and kept it at the same volume as the wind so it would not wake her. Then I listened to *Madame Butterfly*, and in the third act had to rise quickly to lower the sound: the wind was gone. I looked at the still maple near the window, and thought of the wind leaving farms and towns and the coast, going out over the sea to die on the waves. I smoked and gazed out the window. The sky was darker, and at daybreak the rain came. I listened to *Tosca*, and at six-fifteen went to the kitchen where Jennifer's purse lay on the table, a leather shoulder purse crammed with the things of an adult woman, things she had begun accumulating only a few years back, and I nearly wept, thinking of what sandy foundations they were: driver's license, credit card, disposable lighter, cigarettes, checkbook, ballpoint pen, cash, cosmetics, comb, brush, Kleenex, these the rite of passage from childhood, and I took one of them—her keys— and went out, remembering a jacket and hat when the rain struck me, but I kept going to the car, and squeezed and lowered myself into it, pulled the seat belt over my shoulder and fastened it and backed out, turning in the drive, going forward into the road, toward St. John's and Father Paul.

Cars were on the road, the workers, and I did not worry about any of them noticing the fender and light. Only a horse distracted them from what they drove to. In front of St. John's is a parking lot; at its far side, past the church and at the edge of the lawn, is an old pine, taller than the steeple now. I shifted to third, left the road, and, aiming the right headlight at the tree, accelerated past the white blur of church, into the black trunk growing bigger till it was all I could see, then I rocked in that resonant thump she had heard, had felt, and when I turned off the ignition it was still in my ears, my blood, and I saw the boy flying in the wind. I lowered my forehead to the wheel. Father Paul opened the door, his face white in the rain.

'I'm all right.'

'What happened?'

'I don't know. I fainted.'

I got out and went around to the front of the car, looked at the smashed light, the crumpled and torn fender.

'Come to the house and lie down.'

'I'm all right.'

'When was your last physical?'

'I'm due for one. Let's get out of this rain.'

'You'd better lie down.'

'No. I want to receive.'

That was the time to say I want to confess, but I have not and will not. Though I could now, for Jennifer is in Florida, and weeks have passed, and perhaps now Father Paul would not feel that he must tell me to go to the police. And, for that very reason, to confess now would be unfair. It is a world of secrets, and now I have one from my best, in truth my only, friend. I have one from Jennifer too, but that is the nature of fatherhood.

Most of that day it rained, so it was only in early evening, when the sky cleared, with a setting sun, that two little boys, leaving their confinement for some play before dinner. found him. Jennifer and I got that on the local news, which we listened to every hour, meeting at the radio, standing with cigarettes, until the one at eight o'clock; when she stopped crying, we went out and walked on the wet grass, around the pasture, the last of sunlight still in the air and trees His name was Patrick Mitchell, he was nineteen years old, was employed by CETA, lived at home with his parents and brother and sister. The paper next day said he had been at a friend's house and was walking home, and I thought of that light I had seen, then knew it was not for him; he lived on one of the streets behind the club. The paper did not say then, or in the next few days, anything to make Jennifer think he was alive while she was with me in the kitchen. Nor do I know if we—I—could have saved him.

In keeping her secret from her friends, Jennifer had to perform so often, as I did with Father Paul and at the stables, that I believe the acting, which took more of her than our daylight trail rides and our night walks in the pasture, was her healing. Her friends teased me about wrecking her car. When I carried her luggage out to the car on that last morning, we spoke only of the weather for her trip—the day was clear, with a dry cool breeze—and hugged and kissed, and I stood watching as she started the car and turned it around. But then she shifted to neutral and put on the parking brake and unclasped the belt, looking at me all the while, then she was coming to me, as she had that night in the kitchen, and I opened my arms.

I have said I talk with God in the mornings, as I start my day, and sometimes as I sit with coffee, looking at the birds, and the woods. Of course He has never spoken to me, but that is not something I require. Nor does He need to. I know Him, as I know the part of myself that knows Him, that felt Him watching from the wind and the night as I knelt over the dying boy. Lately I have taken to arguing with Him, as I can't with Father Paul, who, when he hears my monthly confession, has not heard and will not hear anything of failure to do all that one can to save an anonymous life, of injustice to a family in their grief, of deepening their pain at the chance and mystery of death by giving them nothing—no one—to hate. With Father Paul I feel lonely about this, but not with God. When I received the Eucharist while Jennifer's car sat twice-damaged, so redeemed, in the rain, I felt neither loneliness nor shame, but as though He were watching me, even from my tongue, intestines, blood, as I have watched my sons at times in their young lives when I was able to judge but without anger, and so keep silent while they, in the agony of their youth, decided how they must act; or found reasons, after their actions, for what they had done. Their reasons were never as good or as bad as their actions, but they needed to find them, to believe they were living by them, instead of the awful solitude of the heart.

I do not feel the peace I once did: not with God, nor the earth, or anyone on it. I have begun to prefer this state, to remember with fondness the other one as a period of peace I neither earned nor deserved. Now in the mornings while I watch purple finches driving larger titmice from the feeder, I say to Him: I would do it again. For when she knocked on my door, then called me, she woke what had flowed dormant in my blood since her birth, so that what rose from the bed was not a stable owner or a Catholic or any other Luke Ripley I had lived with for a long time, but the father of a girl.

And he says: I am a Father too.

Yes, I say, as You are a Son Whom this morning I will receive; unless You kill me on the way to church, then I trust You will receive me. And as a Son You made Your plea.

Yes, He says, but I would not lift the cup.

True, and I don't want You to lift it from me either. And if one of my sons had come to me that night, I would have phoned the police and told them to meet us with an ambulance at the top of the hill.

Why? Do you love them less?

I tell Him no, it is not that I love them less, but that I could bear the pain of watching and knowing my sons' pain, could bear it with pride as they took the whip and nails. But You never had a daughter and, if You had, You could not have borne her passion.

So, He says, you love her more than you love Me.

I love her more than I love truth.

Then you love in weakness, He says.

As You love me, I say, and I go with an apple or carrot out to the barn.

ALICE ADAMS

◇ ◇ ◇

Snow

On a trail high up in the California Sierra, between heavy smooth white snowbanks, four people on cross-country skis form a straggling line. A man and three women: Graham, dark and good-looking, a San Francisco architect, who is originally from Georgia; Carol, his girlfriend, a gray-eyed blonde, a florist; Susannah, daughter of Graham, dark and fat and now living in Venice, California; and, quite a way behind Susannah, tall thin Rose, Susannah's friend and lover. Susannah and Rose both have film-related jobs—Graham has never been quite sure what they do.

Graham and Carol both wear smart cross-country outfits: knickers and Norwegian wool stockings. The younger women are in jeans and heavy sweaters. And actually, despite the bright cold look of so much snow, this April day is warm, and the sky is a lovely spring blue, reflected in distant small lakes, just visible, at intervals.

Graham is by far the best skier of the four, a natural; he does anything athletic easily. He strides and glides along, hardly aware of what he is doing, except for a sense of physical well-being. However, just now he is cursing himself for having dreamed up this weekend, renting an unknown

house in Alpine Meadows, near Lake Tahoe, even for bringing these women together. He had hoped for a diversion
from a situation that could be tricky, difficult: a visit from
Susannah, who was bringing Rose, whom he had previously
been told about but had not met. Well, skiing was a diversion, but what in God's name would they all do tonight? Or
talk about? And why had he wanted to get them together
anyway? He wasn't all that serious about Carol (was he?);
why introduce her to his daughter? And why did he have to
meet Rose?

Carol is a fair skier, although she doesn't like it much: it
takes all her breath. At the moment, with the part of her
mind that is not concentrated on skiing, she is thinking that
although Graham is smarter than most of the men she
knows, talented and successful, and really nice as well, she
is tired of going out with men who don't *see* her, don't know
who she is. That's partly her fault, she knows; she lies about
her age and dyes her hair, and she *never* mentions the
daughter in Vallejo, put out for adoption when Carol was
fifteen (she would be almost twenty now, almost as old as
Graham's girl, this unfriendly fat Susannah). But sometimes
Carol would like to say to the men she knows, Look, I'm
thirty-five, and in some ways my life has been terrible—
being blond and pretty doesn't save you from anything.

But, being more fair-minded than given to self-pity, next
Carol thinks, Well, as far as that goes Graham didn't tell me
much about his girl, either, and for all I know mine is that
way, too. So many of them are, these days.

How can he possibly be so dumb, Susannah is passionately thinking, of her father. And the fact that she has
asked that question hundreds of times in her life does not
diminish its intensity or the accompanying pain. He doesn't
understand anything, she wildly, silently screams. Stupid,
straight blondes: a *florist. Skiing.* How could he think that I
. . . that Rose. . . ?

Then, thinking of Rose in a more immediate way, she
remembers that Rose has hardly skied before—just a couple

of times in Vermont, where she comes from. In the almost noon sun Susannah stops to wait for Rose, halfheartedly aware of the lakes, just now in view, and the smell of pines, as sweat collects under her heavy breasts, slides down her ribs.

Far behind them all, and terrified of everything, Rose moves along with stiffened desperation. Her ankles, her calves, her thighs, her lower back are all tight with dread. Snow is stuck to the bottoms of her skis, she knows—she can hardly move them—but she doesn't dare stop. She will fall, break something, get lost. And everyone will hate her, even Susannah.

Suddenly, like a gift to a man in his time of need, just ahead of Graham there appears a lovely open glade, to one side of the trail. Two huge heavy trees have fallen there, at right angles to each other; at the far side of the open space runs a brook, darkly glistening over small smooth rocks. High overhead a wind sings through the pines, in the brilliant sunlight.

It is perfect, a perfect picnic place, and it is just now time for lunch. Graham is hungry; he decides that hunger is what has been unsettling him. He gets out of his skis in an instant, and he has just found a smooth, level stump for the knapsack, a natural table, when Carol skis up—out of breath, not looking happy.

But at the sight of that place she instantly smiles. She says, "Oh, how perfect! Graham, it's beautiful." Her gray eyes praise him, and the warmth of her voice. "Even benches to sit on. Graham, what a perfect Southern host you are." She laughs in a pleased, cheered-up way, and bends to unclip her skis. But something is wrong, and they stick. Graham comes over to help. He gets her out easily; he takes her hand and lightly he kisses her mouth, and then they both go over and start removing food from the knapsack, spreading it out.

"Two bottles of wine. Lord, we'll all get plastered." Carol

laughs again, as she sets up the tall green bottles in a deep patch of snow.

Graham laughs, too, just then very happy with her, although he is also feeling the familiar apprehension that any approach of his daughter brings on: *will* Susannah like what he has done, will she approve of him, ever? He looks at his watch and he says to Carol, "I wonder if they're okay. Rose is pretty new on skis. I wonder . . ."

But there they are, Susannah and Rose. They have both taken off their skis and are walking along the side of the trail, carrying the skis on their shoulders. Susannah's neatly together, Rose's at a clumsy, difficult angle. There are snowflakes in Susannah's dark-brown hair—hair like Graham's. Rose's hair is light, dirty blond; she is not even pretty, Graham has unkindly thought. At the moment they both look exhausted and miserable.

In a slow, tired way, not speaking, the two girls lean their skis and poles against a tree; they turn toward Graham and Carol, and then, seemingly on a single impulse, they stop and look around. And with a wide smile Susannah says, "Christ, Dad, it's just beautiful. It's great."

Rose looks toward the spread of food. "Oh, roast chicken. That's my favorite thing." These are the first nice words she has said to Graham. (Good manners are not a strong suit of Rose's, he has observed, in an interior, Southern voice.)

He has indeed provided a superior lunch, as well as the lovely place—his discovery. Besides the chicken, there are cherry tomatoes (called love apples where Graham comes from, in Georgia), cheese (Jack and cheddar), Triscuits and oranges and chocolate. And the nice cold dry white wine. They all eat and drink a lot, and they talk eagerly about how good it all is, how beautiful the place where they are. The sky, the trees, the running brook.

Susannah even asks Carol about her work, in a polite, interested way that Graham has not heard from her for years. "Do you have to get up early and go to the flower mart every morning?" Susannah asks.

"No, but I used to, and really that was more fun—getting out so early, all those nice fresh smells. Now there's a boy I hire to do all that, and I'm pretty busy making arrangements."

"Oh, arrangements," says Rose, disparagingly.

Carol laughs, "Me, too, I hate them. I just try to make them as nice as I can, and the money I get is really good."

Both Rose and Susannah regard Carol in an agreeing, respectful way. For a moment Graham is surprised: these kids respecting money? Then he remembers that this is the Seventies: women are supposed to earn money, it's good for them.

The main thing, though, is what a good time they all have together. Graham even finds Rose looking at him with a small, shy smile. He offers her more wine, which she accepts— another smile as he pours it out for her. And he thinks, Well, of course it's tough on her, too, meeting me. Poor girl, I'm sure she's doing the best she can.

"You all really like it down there in Hollywood?" he asks the two girls, and he notes that his voice is much more Southern than usual; maybe the wine.

"Universal City," Susannah corrects him, but she gives a serious answer. "I love it. There's this neat woman in the cutting room, and she knows I'm interested, so she lets me come in and look at the rushes, and hear them talk about what has to go. I'm really learning. It's great."

And Rose: "There's so many really exciting people around."

At that moment they both look so young, so enviably involved in their work, so happy, that Graham thinks, Well, really, why not?

Occasionally the wind will move a branch from a nearby tree and some snow will sift down, through sunlight. The sky seems a deeper blue than when they first came to this glade, a pure azure. The brook gurgles more loudly, and the sun is very hot.

And then they are all through with lunch; they have finished off the wine, and it is time to go.

They put on their skis, and they set off again, in the same order in which they began the day.

For no good reason, as he glides along, striding through snow in the early California afternoon, the heat, Graham is suddenly, sharply visited by a painful memory of the childhood of Susannah. He remembers a ferociously hot summer night in Atlanta, when he and his former wife, mother of Susannah, had quarreled all through suppertime, and had finally got Susannah off to bed; she must have been about two. But she kept getting up again, screaming for her bottle, her Teddy bear, a sandwich. Her mother and Graham took turns going to her, and then finally, about three in the morning, Graham picked her up and smacked her bottom, very hard; he can remember the sting on his hand—and good Christ, what a thing to do to a little baby. No wonder she is as she is; he probably frightened her right then, for good. Not to mention all the other times he got mad and just yelled at her—or his love affairs, the move to San Francisco, the divorce, more love affairs.

If only she were two right now, he desperately thinks, he could change everything; he could give her a stable, loving father. Now he has a nice house on Russian Hill; he is a successful man; he could give her—anything.

Then his mind painfully reverses itself and he thinks. But I was a loving father, most of the time. Susannah's got no real cause to be the way she is. Lots of girls—most girls—come out all right. At that overheated moment he feels that his heart will truly break. It is more than I can stand, he thinks; why do I have to?

Carol's problem is simply a physical one: a headache. But she never has headaches, and this one is especially severe; for the first time she knows exactly what her mother meant by "splitting headache." Is she going to get more and more like her mother as she herself ages? Could she be having an early menopause, beginning with migraines? She could die, the pain is so sharp. She could die, and would anyone care much, really? She's *lonely*.

Susannah is absorbed in the problem of Rose, who keeps falling down. Almost every time Susannah looks back, there is Rose, fallen in the snow. Susannah smiles at her encouragingly, and sometimes she calls back, "You're okay?" She knows that Rose would not like it if she actually skied back to her and helped her up; Rose has that ferocious Vermont Yankee pride, difficult in a fragile frightened woman.

It is breezier now than earlier in the morning, and somewhat cooler. Whenever Susannah stops, stands still and waits for Rose, she is aware of her own wind-chilled sweat, and she worries, thinking of Rose, of wet and cold. Last winter Rose had a terrible, prolonged bout of flu, a racking cough.

Talking over their "relationship," at times Susannah and Rose have (somewhat jokingly) concluded that there certainly are elements of mothering within it; in many ways Susannah takes care of Rose. She is stronger—that is simply true. Now for the first time it occurs to Susannah (wryly, her style is wry) that she is somewhat fatherly with Rose, too: the sometimes stern guardian, the protector. And she thinks, Actually, Graham wasn't all that bad with me; I've been rough on him. Look at the example he set me: I work hard, and I care about my work, the way he does. And he taught me to ski, come to think of it. I should thank him, sometime, somehow, for some of it.

Rose is falling, falling, again and again, and oh Christ, how much she hates it—hates her helplessness, hates the horrible snow, the cold wet. Drinking all that wine at lunchtime, in the pretty glade, the sunlight, she had thought that wine would make her brave; she knows her main problem to be fear—no confidence and hence no balance. But the wine, and the sun, and sheer fatigue have destroyed whatever equilibrium she had, so that all she can do is fall, fall miserably, and each time the snow is colder and it is harder for her to get up.

*   *   *

Therefore, they are all extremely glad when, finally, they are out of their skis and off the trail and at last back in their house, in Alpine Meadows. It is small—two tiny, juxtaposed bedrooms—but the living room is pleasant: it looks out to steeply wooded, snowy slopes. Even more pleasant at the moment is the fact that the hot-water supply is vast; there is enough for deep baths for everyone, and then they will all have much-needed before-dinner naps.

Carol gets the first bath, and then, in turn, the two younger women. Graham last. All three women have left a tidy room, a clean tub, he happily notices, and the steamy air smells vaguely sweet, of something perfumed, feminine. Luxuriating in his own full, hot tub, he thinks tenderly, in a general way, of women, how warm and sexual they are, more often than not, how frequently intelligent and kind. And then he wonders what he has not quite, ever, put into words before: what is it that women do, women together? What ever could they do that they couldn't do with men, and *why*?

However, these questions are much less urgent and less painful than most of his musings along those lines; he simply wonders.

In their bedroom, disappointingly, Carol is already fast asleep. He has not seen her actually sleeping before; she is always first awake when he stays over at her place. Now she looks so drained, so entirely exhausted, with one hand protectively across her eyes, that he is touched. Carefully, so as not to wake her, he slips in beside her, and in minutes he, too, is sound asleep.

Graham has planned and shopped for their dinner, which he intends to cook. He likes to cook, and does it well, but in his bachelor life he has done it less and less, perhaps because he and most of the women he meets tend to shy off from such domestic encounters. Somehow the implication of cooking *for* someone has become alarming, more so than making love to them. But tonight Graham happily prepares to make pork chops with milk gravy and mashed potatoes, green peas, an apple-and-nut salad and cherry pie (from a bakery, to be heated). A down-home meal, for his girlfriend, and his daughter, and her friend.

From the kitchen, which is at one end of the living room, he can hear the pleasant sounds of the three women's voices, in amiable conversation, as he blends butter and flour in the pan in which he has browned the chops, and begins to add hot milk. And then he notices a change in the tone of those voices: what was gentle and soft has gone shrill, strident—the sounds of a quarrel. He hates the thought of women fighting; it is almost frightening, and, of course, he is anxious for this particular group to get along, if only for the weekend.

He had meant, at just that moment, to go in and see if anyone wanted another glass of wine; dinner is almost ready. And so, reluctantly he does; he gets into the living room just in time to hear Rose say, in a shakily loud voice, "No one who hasn't actually experienced rape can have the least idea what it's like."

Such a desperately serious sentence could have sounded ludicrous, but it does not. Graham is horrified; he thinks, Ah, poor girl, poor Rose. Jesus, *raped.* It is a crime that he absolutely cannot imagine.

In a calm, conciliatory way, Susannah says to Carol, "You see, Rose actually was raped, when she was very young, and it was terrible for her—"

Surprisingly, Carol reacts almost with anger. "Of course it's terrible, but you kids think you're the only ones things happen to. I got pregnant when I was fifteen, and I had it, a girl, and I put her out for adoption." Seeming to have just now noticed Graham, she addresses him in a low, defiant, scolding voice. "And I'm not thirty. I'm thirty-five."

Graham has no idea, really, of what to do, but he is aware of strong feelings that lead him to Carol. He goes over and puts his arms around her. Behind him he hears the gentle voice of Susannah, who is saying, "Oh Carol, that's terrible. God, that's *awful.*"

Carol's large eyes are teary but in a friendly way she disengages herself from Graham; she even smiles as she says, "Well, I'm sorry, I didn't mean to say that. But you see? You really can't tell what's happened to anyone.'

And Susannah: "Oh, you're right, of course you are. . . ."

And Rose: "It's true, we do get arrogant. . . ."

Graham says that he thinks they should eat. The food is hot; they must be hungry. He brings the dinner to them at the table, and he serves out hot food onto the heated plates.

Carol and Rose are talking about the towns they came from: Vallejo, California, and Manchester, Vermont.

"It's thirty miles from San Francisco," Carol says. ' And that's all we talked about. The City. How to get there. and what was going on there. Vallejo was just a place we ignored, dirt under our feet."

"All the kids in Manchester wanted to make it to New York," Rose says. "All but me, and I was fixated on Cambridge. Not getting into Radcliffe was terrible for me—it's why I never went to college at all."

"I didn't either," Carol says, with a slight irony that Graham thinks may have been lost on Rose: Carol would not have expected to go to college, probably—it wasn't what high-school kids from Vallejo did. But how does he know this?

"I went to work instead," says Rose, a little priggishly (thinks Graham).

"Me too," Carol says, with a small laugh.

Susannah breaks in. "Dad, this is absolutely the greatest dinner. You're still the best cook I know. It's good I don't have your dinners more often."

"I'm glad you like it. I haven't cooked a lot lately."

And Rose, and Carol: "It's super. It's great."

Warmed by praise, and just then wanting to be nice to Rose (partly because he has to admit to himself that he doesn't much like her), Graham says to her, "Cambridge was where I wanted to go to school, too. The Harvard School of Design. Chicago seemed second-best. But I guess it's all worked out."

"I guess." Rose smiles.

She looks almost pretty at that moment, but not quite; looking at her, Graham thinks again, If it had to be another girl, why her? But he knows this to be unfair, and, as far as that goes, why anyone for anyone, when you come to think of it? Any pairing is basically mysterious.

Partly as a diversion from such unsettling thoughts, and also from real curiosity, he asks Carol, "But was it worth it when you got to the city?"

She laughs, in her low, self-deprecating way. "Oh, I thought so. I really liked it. My first job was with a florist on Union Street. It was nice there then, before it got all junked up with body shops and stuff. I had a good time."

Some memory of that era has put a younger, musing look on Carol's face, and Graham wonders if she is thinking of a love affair; jealously he wonders, Who? Who did you know, back then?

"I was working for this really nice older man," says Carol, in a higher than usual voice (as Graham thinks, *Ah*). "He taught me all he could. I was pretty dumb, at first. About marketing, arranging, keeping stuff fresh, all that. He lived by himself. A lonely person, I guess. He was—uh—gay, and then he died, and it turned out he'd left the store to me." For the second time that night tears have come to her eyes. "I was so touched, and it was too late to thank him, or anything." Then, the tears gone, her voice returns to its usual depth as she sums it up, "Well, that's how I got my start in the business world."

These sudden shifts in mood, along with her absolute refusal to see herself as an object of pity, are strongly, newly attractive to Graham; he has the sense of being with an unknown, exciting woman.

And then, in a quick, clairvoyant way, he gets a picture of Carol as a twenty-year-old girl, new in town: tall and a little awkward, working in the florist shop and worrying about her hands, her fingers scratched up from stems and wires; worrying about her darkening blond hair and then, deciding, what the hell, better dye it; worrying about money, and men, and her parents back in Vallejo—and *should* she have put the baby out for adoption? He feels an unfamiliar tenderness for this new Carol.

"You guys are making me feel very boring," says Susannah. "I always wanted to go to Berkeley, and I did, and I wanted to go to L.A. and work in films."

"I think you're just more direct," amends Rose, affectionate admiration in her voice, and in her eyes. "You just know what you're doing. I fall into things."

Susannah laughs. "Well, you do all right, you've got to admit." And, to Graham and Carol: "She's only moved up twice since January. At this rate she'll be casting something in August."

What Graham had earlier named discomfort he now recognizes as envy: Susannah is closer to Rose than she is to him; they are closer to each other than he is to anyone. He says, "Well, Rose, that's really swell. That's *swell*."

Carol glances at Graham for an instant before she says, "Well, I'll bet your father didn't even tell you about his most recent prize." And she tells them about an award from the A.I.A., which Graham had indeed not mentioned to Susannah, but which had pleased him at the time of its announcement (immoderately, he told himself).

And now Susannah and Rose join Carol in congratulations, saying how terrific, really great.

Dinner is over, and in a rather disorganized way they all clear the table and load the dishwasher.

They go into the living room, where Graham lights the fire, and the three women sit down—or, rather, sprawl—Rose and Susannah at either end of the sofa, Carol in an easy chair. For dinner Carol put on velvet pants and a red silk shirt. In the bright hot firelight her gray eyes shine, and the fine line under her chin, that first age line, is just barely visible. She is very beautiful at that moment—probably more so now than she was fifteen years ago, Graham decides.

Susannah, in clean, faded, too tight Levi's, stretches her legs out stiffly before her. "Oh, I'm really going to feel that skiing in the morning!"

And Carol: "Me too. I haven't had that much exercise forever."

Rose says, "If I could just not fall."

"Oh, you won't; tomorrow you'll see. Tomorrow . . ." says everyone.

They are all exhausted. Silly to stay up late. And so as the fire dies down, Graham covers it and they all four go off to bed, in the two separate rooms.

Outside a strong wind has come up, creaking the walls and rattling windowpanes.

In the middle of the night, in what has become a storm— lashing snow and violent wind—Rose wakes up, terrified. From the depths of bad dreams, she has no idea where she is, what time it is, what day. With whom she is. She struggles for clues, her wide eyes scouring the dark, her tentative hands reaching out, encountering Susannah's familiar, fleshy back. Everything comes into focus for her; she knows where she is. She breathes out softly, "Oh, thank God it's you," moving closer to her friend.

JOHN O'HARA

◇ ◇ ◇

Appearances

Howard Ambrie stopped the car at the porte-cochere to let his wife out, then proceeded to the garage. The M-G was already there, the left-hand door was open, and the overhead lamp was burning, indicating that their daughter was home. Ambrie put the sedan in its customary place, snapped out the light, rang down the door, and walked slowly toward the house. He stopped midway and looked at the sky. The moon was high and plain, the stars were abundant.

In the kitchen his wife had poured him a glass of milk, which rested on the table with a piece of sponge cake. "I'll be able to play tomorrow after all," said Howard Ambrie. "There's hardly a cloud in the sky."

"Oh, then you've thought it over," said Lois Ambrie.

"Thought what over?"

"Jack Hill's funeral. You're not going."

"Was I thinking it over?"

"You said at dinner that you hadn't decided whether to go or not," said Lois Ambrie.

"That was only because I knew the McIvers planned to go."

"I don't understand your reasoning," she said.

"Well, then I'll explain it to you. Peter and Cathy *want* to go to the funeral. I don't. No reason why I should. But I didn't want to inflict my *not* wanting to go on their *wanting* to go. Impose, I guess, would be a better word. Influence them. Or for that matter, take away their pleasure in going to the service. I said I hadn't made up my mind, and so there was no discussion about it. If I'd said I definitely wasn't going, or if I'd definitely said I wasn't going, they would have wanted to know why."

"What would you have told them?"

"What would I have told them? I'd have told them that I'd much rather play golf tomorrow."

"Well, that would have started a discussion, all right," she said.

"I know it would," he said. "And I know what the discussion would have been. Wasn't Jack Hill one of my best friends? Couldn't I play golf after the service? And so forth. But I disposed of all that by simply saying I hadn't made up my mind."

"You disposed of it as far as the McIvers were concerned, but will you tell *me* why you're not going?"

"I don't mind telling you. In the first place, I've never considered Jack Hill one of my best friends. He wasn't. He was a lifelong acquaintance, a contemporary, our families were always friends, or friendly. And if you wanted to stretch a point, we were related. All of which you know. But in a town this size, at least until just before the War, damn near everybody is related in some way or other."

"Yes, and damn near everybody will be at that funeral tomorrow," she said. "Therefore your absence will be noticed."

"Maybe it will. I thought of that. But the fact is, I never liked Jack and he never liked me. If the circumstances were reversed, I'm sure he'd be playing golf tomorrow. There won't be many more days we can play this year. I noticed driving by this afternoon, they've taken the pins out of the cups, and I wouldn't be surprised if they filled in the holes. The golf shop is boarded up for the winter. In fact, Charley closed up a week ago and went to Florida. I hope there's enough hot water for a shower. I hate to come in after playing golf in this weather and find no hot water."

"You're playing in the morning," she said.

"Playing in the morning. We're meeting at ten o'clock, playing eighteen holes. Having something to eat. Probably the usual club sandwiches. And then playing bridge. I'll be home around five, I should think."

"Who are you playing with?"

"Same three I play with every Saturday, and they won't be missed at Jack's funeral."

"No, they certainly won't be. None of Jack's old friends, and none of your old friends, either, not in that foursome."

"Lois, you talk as though the whole of Suffolk County were going to be at the church tomorrow, checking to see who stayed away. Are *you* going to the funeral?"

"Yes, I'm going. Or I was. I don't know whether I want to go without you."

"Oh, hell, call up somebody and go with *them*."

"No, if you're not going, I won't. That would make your not going so much more noticeable. 'Where's Howard?' 'Playing golf.' "

"Listen, I'm not going, so don't try to persuade me."

"I think you ought to go," she said.

"No."

"I'll make one more try. I'm *asking* you to go," she said.

"And my answer is I think you're being God damn unreasonable about this. Jack Hill and I have known each other over fifty years, we were thrown together by age and financial circumstances. His family and my family had about the same amount of dough. But when we got older and could choose our friends, he never chose me and I never chose him. We were never enemies, but maybe if we had been we'd have found out why we didn't like each other. Then maybe we could have been friends. But we never had any serious quarrel. We never had a God damn thing."

"He was an usher at our wedding."

"I *knew* you'd bring that up. That was twenty-five years ago, and I had to have him and he had to have me because our parents were friends. It was one of those automatic things in a small town. I couldn't ask one of the clammers, and he couldn't ask one of the potato farmers, but that's *all* it was. And since you bring that up, about being ushers, Celia didn't ask me to be a pallbearer or whatever the hell she's having. Celia has more sense about this than you have."

"There aren't going to be any pallbearers, and you know it."

"All right, I do know it. And she's very sensible, Celia."

"I'm asking you again, Howard, please. Put off your golf till after lunch, and go to this funeral with me. It isn't much to ask."

"Why do you care so much whether I go or not?"

"Because I don't want Celia knowing that you stayed away."

"Oh, Christ. All right. Although why you care what Celia knows or doesn't know—you and Celia were never that good friends."

"But you will go?"

"Yes, I said I would, and I will. But you certainly screwed up my weekend."

"You can play in the afternoon and Sunday."

"Father O'Sullivan can't play Saturday afternoon, he has to hear confessions, and he can't play Sunday at all. And Joe Bushmill is going skeet-shooting this Sunday. It's not only my schedule you loused up."

"I'm sorry about that, Howard, but I do appreciate it."

"Oh, sure. You have no idea how you complicate things. We had to get a fourth for bridge, because O'Sullivan has to be in church at three o'clock. And now they'll have to get someone to take my place at golf *and* bridge."

"I'll do something for you sometime."

"Why didn't you make your big pitch before tonight?"

"Because I took for granted that you'd be going to the funeral. I just took it for granted."

"I suppose the same way that people took for granted that Jack Hill was a friend of mine. Well, he wasn't. I'm going to bed. Oh, Amy's home. The M-G's in the garage."

"I know. Goodnight, dear."

"Goodnight," he said. He bent down and kissed her cheek.

Light showed on the floor beneath Amy's bedroom door, and he knocked gently. "Amy? You awake?" he said softly.

"Father? Come in."

She was sitting up in bed, and when he entered she took off her reading glasses. "Hi," she said.

"What are you reading?" he said.

"Detective story. Who won?"

"Oh, your mother and I took them. We always do, at their house, and they usually win when they come here." He sat on the chaise-longue. "As Mr. McCaffery says, what kind of a day's it been today?"

"Fridays are always easier than other days. The children seem to behave better on Friday. That is, their behavior is better, probably because they're in a better mood. Their schoolwork isn't as good, but you can't have everything."

"Do you like teaching?"

"Not very much, but I like the children."

"Well, it's nice having you home for a year."

"Thank you, Father. It's nice being home."

"Is it?" he said.

"Have a cigarette?" She held up a package.

"No thanks. You didn't answer my question."

"I know I didn't. Yes, it's nice being home."

"But that's as far as you'll commit yourself?" he said.

"That's as far as I want to commit myself."

"You mean you don't want to think more deeply than that?"

"Yes, I guess that's what I mean. I'm comfortable here, I have my job, my car to run around in, and I had no idea we had so many detective stories. This one was copyrighted 1924."

"There are some older than that, early Mary Roberts Rinehart," he said. "Believe I will have one of your cigarettes." He caught the pack she tossed him and lit a cigarette. "Are you making any plans for next year?"

"Not exactly. I may get married again. I may not."

"This time you ought to have children right away."

"It wouldn't be so good if I had a child now, would it?"

"It might have kept you together, Amy, a child. We had you the first year, your mother and I."

"Father, you're practically implying that if you hadn't had me—"

"I know what I'm implying," he said. "And I know you're no fool. You know it's often been touch and go with your mother and I. You've seen that."

"I guess it is with everybody. But a child wouldn't have kept Dave and me together. Nothing would."

"Well, what really separated you?"

"Well, it wasn't his fault. I fell in love with someone else."

"The man you're thinking of marrying?"

"No."

"The man you're thinking of marrying is that doctor in Greenport?"

"Yes."

"But the man you left Dave for was someone else?"

"Yes."

"And what's happened to him? He's gone out of your life?"

She looked at him sharply. "Yes."

"Why? Was he married?"

"Yes."

"Where did you know him? At Cornell?"

"No, Father. And don't ask me any more questions, please. You voluntarily said you wouldn't ask me any questions, you promised that when I came home after my divorce."

"I did, but with the understanding that when you were ready to tell us, you would. It isn't just idle curiosity, Amy. Your mother and I have a right to know those things, if only to keep you from making the same mistakes all over again."

"I won't make that mistake over again. And I'm not ready to tell you what happened to me with Dave."

"As far as I know, Dave was a hell of a nice boy."

"He was, and is, but I wasn't a hell of a nice girl. No father likes to face that fact about his daughter, but there it is."

"You're not a tart, you're not a chippy."

"No. But that's not all there is besides virgins, Father."

"Oh, I know that."

"Well, when does a girl get to be a tart in your estimation? Is it a question of how many men she sleeps with?"

"It most certainly is, yes."

"How many?"

"Yes, I walked into that one, didn't I? Well, a girl who sleeps with more than two men before she gets married, she's on her way. I can see a girl having an affair the first time she thinks she's in love. And then the second time, when she's more apt to be really in love. But the next time she'd better be damned sure, or she's going to be a push-over for everybody."

"Well—that's more or less my record. The second time was also the man I left Dave for."

"Oh, you had an affair and married Dave and continued to have this other affair?"

"Yes."

"What's going to prevent your having an affair with this same guy after you marry your doctor? . . . You had an affair with a married man before you married Dave. He sounds like a real son of a bitch."

"I guess maybe he was, although I didn't think so. I guess he was, though."

"You're not still seeing him?"

"No. I did after I divorced Dave, but not after I began dating the doctor."

"You're—to use an old-fashioned word—faithful to the doctor?"

"Oh, you're so smart, Father. You've tricked me into admitting I'm having an affair with the doctor. The answer is yes."

"Hell, I knew you were probably having an affair with the doctor. I'm no fool, either, you know. Well, it's been a very interesting conversation between father and daughter. It's a good thing I'm not *my* father, or you'd be—well, you wouldn't be here."

"No, but we wouldn't have had this conversation, either."

"You have a point. Goodnight, dear." He kissed her cheek and she squeezed his hand. "There *is* that," he said. "We wouldn't have had this conversation. Goodnight again."

"Goodnight, Father," she said.

The girl sat in her bed, holding her glasses loosely with her right hand, her book with her left, both hands lying on the pink comforter. Her mother came in. "What was that all about?" said Lois Ambrie.

"Our conversation? Oh, mostly above Dave and me."

"He didn't say anything about Jack Hill?"

"No."

"I'll be glad when Jack is buried and out of the way."

"I know," said Amy.

"Your father is getting closer to the truth, Amy."

"I guess he is."

"I had a very difficult time persuading him to go to the funeral tomorrow."

"Why did you bother?"

"Appearances. 'Why didn't Howard Ambrie go to Jack Hill's funeral?' They'd be talking about that for a month, and somebody'd be sure to say something to Celia. And then Celia'd start asking herself questions."

"I wonder. I think Mrs. Hill stopped asking questions a long time ago. She should have. I wasn't the only one he played around with."

"You can be so casual about it. 'Played around with.'

And you haven't shown the slightest feeling about him, his dying."

"I didn't show any because I haven't got any. Other than relief. I'm not grief-stricken that he died, Mother. As long as he was alive I was afraid to marry Joe. Now I think I can marry Joe and settle down in Greenport and be what I always wanted to be. But not while Jack was alive. That's the effect he had on me."

"He was no good," said Lois Ambrie. "Strange how your father knew that without knowing why."

"I know why," said Amy. "Jack was the kind of man that husbands are naturally suspicious of. Father was afraid Jack would make a play for you. Instead he made a play for me, but Father never gave that a thought."

"I suppose so. And in your father's eyes it would be just as bad for me to cover up for you as it would have been for me to have had an affair with Jack. I'll be glad when he's out of the way. Really glad when you can marry Joe."

"Did you go over and call on Mrs. Hill?"

"I went over this afternoon, but she wasn't seeing anyone. Fortunately."

"She *is* grief-stricken?"

"I don't think it's that. No, I don't think it's that. As you said a moment ago, Celia probably stopped asking questions a long time ago. I'd put it another way. That she's known for years about Jack. Now she doesn't want to see anybody because whatever she's feeling, she doesn't want anybody to see *her*. Grief, or relief. Maybe she doesn't even know yet what she feels. Fear, maybe. Whatever he was, she stuck with him all those years, and suddenly he's gone and she's fifty-two or -three. I don't know what's in Celia's mind, but I'm glad I'm not her. Did you see Joe tonight?"

"Yes, I had dinner with him. We had dinner at his sister's house in Southold. Spaghetti. She's a very good cook."

"That will be quite something, an Ambrie marrying an Italian boy. Will you have to turn Catholic?"

"I will if he wants me to. If it means that much to him.

I'm not sure it does, but it would probably make a difference to his family."

"Can he marry a divorced woman? I have no idea what the Catholic church says on that."

"We haven't discussed it, so I don't know either."

"Your father's great friends with the new Catholic priest, O'Sullivan. They play golf and bridge together every Saturday."

"So I gather. When the time comes, whatever they say I'll do."

"It would be quite a feather in their cap, an Ambrie turning Catholic."

"They may not see it that way. I understand they can be very tough about some things."

"Well, I suppose it's their turn. Goodness knows I still can't get used to the idea of having one in the White House. Can I get you a glass of milk or anything?"

"No thanks, Mother."

"Then I guess I'll be off to bed."

"Mother?"

"What?"

"I'm sorry I caused you and Father so much trouble. You especially. All those lies you had to tell."

"Oh, that's all right. It's over now. And it was really harder on your father. He never knew why he didn't like that man."

"And *you* couldn't tell him, *could* you, Mother?"

"What?"

"Oh, Mother."

Lois Ambrie looked at her daughter. "Is that another detective story you're reading? You mustn't get carried away, Amy." She smiled. "Goodnight, dear," she said, and closed the door.

STEPHEN MINOT

◇ ◇ ◇

The Tide and Isaac Bates

He'd wrecked her. No doubt about that. He'd been careless and his luck had run out. Finally, and what was a man to do then?

He was standing high on the bluff they had just climbed. Below him his *Diana* lay broadside to the wind and to the fist of the sea. Each breaker drove her hard against the black raw edge of the ledge. Her cockpit was flooded, her decks awash. There was no saving her now. It was enough to make an old man sick.

"Rest here," he said to Cory, his daughter. "Catch your breath."

He started to reach out, to reassure her. But, hell, she was all of twenty-five and still a tomboy—she could take whatever came along. Besides, how can you offer an encouraging hand to someone done up in lobstermen's rubber pants and hooded jacket? Almost his height, she could have been some fisherman's adolescent boy, tall, lean, and undernourished. Her thin lips were tight and a little blue with cold, but her expression was blank. She wasn't complaining. Hell, she could shrug off anything.

A wave of exhaustion swept over him without warning

and he sat down in the coarse brown grass, his muscles trembling. Carefully he reached under his torn yellow slicker, under his leather jacket, down to the wool shirt where he kept his cigarettes and matches. They were in a plastic case. He took out one cigarette and the box of wooden matches and tried to strike a light, his hands cupped against the November wind. The head of the first match came off like putty. The second merely smeared the striking edge of the box. It hardly seemed fair. Silent, drained of profanity, he put the case back into his inner pocket and chewed on the end of the cigarette.

All this time his eyes never left his boat. Four, five, six breakers had come and washed back. Turning his head, he spat tobacco juice downwind. Then a leviathan wave lifted his *Diana* up on her side, cracked her on the solid face of the ledge, sucked back and let the hull jounce after it. This time the shock shattered everything above deck, canopy, cabin and all scattering into bits of flotsam, the glass of the windshield exploding noiselessly into an instant of glittering spray. Isaac Bates heard himself utter a startled "Aaa!"

And then, embarrassed, he said to Cory, "Well, it's just a matter of time now."

He tried to make it sound offhand. The two of them never talked much about their inner feelings. They got along best just sharing chores—repairs around the house, chopping wood, or sometimes going over the books down at the cannery. The rest of the time she helped her mother. If anything bothered her, she didn't feel obliged to tell him, and in return he didn't burden her with his own worries. Of the eight children, she was the only one who would stay home, and he wasn't about to drive her away.

So there were times—like on early-morning crow hunts or off fishing somewhere—when her eyes would fill with tears for no reason and he wouldn't ask why. And right now he had cried out and she had said nothing.

Because it *was* nothing, really. The *Diana* wasn't his livelihood, nothing fundamental had been shattered, there was insurance and he wasn't poor anyway; they had not been injured, and they were lucky to have ended up on the mainland rather than on some tide-scoured ledge. Cory knew all that. She had a level head, she did.

Again the dark November water slithered back, and this time he saw that her hull had been stove in. There was no longer any hope of salvage. Isaac squeezed his eyes shut, wincing from the sting of salt. He would not look at her in that November way. He would see her as she had been twenty-two years ago, newly built and still unpainted, red oak planking pink as a baby's rump, the admiration even of strangers.

Maine craftsmen had built her, some of them using the hand tools their fathers had given them. The oak itself came from Isaac's own woodland, a section so rough that only oxen could get the logs out to the truck on the highway.

"What's a man like you messin' around with a *lobster* boat for?" That's what Elias Skolfield had asked when the *Diana* first took shape on his ways. He wasn't being critical; he wasn't even asking a question. He was simply approving the design, nodding because she was to be the solid, high and dry design of the Maine coast lobster boat. He was also noting the fact that Isaac Bates was no simple fisherman, that the slogan "You Can't Beat Bates for Frozen Fishcakes" had done more than pay off the mortgage. A man in Isaac's position—at his crest then at only thirty-six—might easily have invested in one of those factory-built speedsters. But he hadn't.

"Well, it's got honest lines," Isaac said, his trumpet muted as it had been for the birth of all eight children.

"*Proud* lines," Skolfield said. There was just a bit more sheer to her than the average lobsterman, but only a builder would have noticed it. "And power enough for three boats."

"Good to be on the safe side," he said, but he was thinking about the feel of the throttle and the lurch forward at his command.

As they talked there in the yard, the shifting May breezes

brought to Isaac odors of cedar planking, mahogany shavings, tar and pine pitch. The sun was warm in his face and anticipation radiated in him like a good rum.

"Let's go," someone was saying.

He watched a shipbuilder on *Diana*'s deck take wood plugs from a keg and hammer them into drilled holes, setting each with the first blow and driving it home with two more. With his left hand he caressed the surface before setting the next, checking the level of each plug, a regular motion, rhythmical. . . .

"Let's go now."

Rhythmical as waves, breakers pounding. . . .

"Come on now," Cory was saying. "We'd better get moving."

The November gale suddenly tore at his face again. His cheeks felt raw. He looked down at the ledge below them and then quickly up at Cory. She had taken off her bulky foul weather pants and stood there in wet, clinging Levi's. The hood of her jacket was thrown back now. Her hair, sand-colored and stringy, was soaked. He felt a rush of concern for her. She was a strong girl, but still. . . .

Pulling his sleeve up, he tried to read his watch. The crystal was clouded with droplets on the inside.

"Your watch working?" he asked her.

She reached up under her jacket and pulled out her wrist watch from some dry pocket. She looked at it and put it to her ear.

"It's working," she said.

"What time is it?"

"Five fifteen."

"Well, it's turned now. It's on the ebb. Might as well go."

He had planned to wait until the tide had passed its peak at five. There had been a slim chance that some boat might have passed and with the tide still on the flood they might have tried to get her off. The odds of that were hard against him, of course. The tourists were all gone by Labor Day and half the lobstermen quit for the winter by the first of November. What few remained wouldn't tour the traps on an afternoon like this. Still, a man had to be an optimist if he was going to get a thing out of life.

Like coming through the gut in the first place. He and Cory had navigated that channel between Black Island and the mainland a number of times. It was risky, of course, but there was always enough water so long as they were twenty minutes before or after the peak of the tide—always until today. Still, for all this, he didn't regret the other times. Summer folks used to shake their heads, seeing them run through a channel that was naked ledge at half-tide. A man had to take chances just for the sake of living.

Like having women friends. It was no mean trick for a married man in a small town like that to have his pleasures on the side. His old Mercury sedan was familiar all over that part of Maine. Even school children knew that he was the one that owned the cannery. And the risk of hurting his wife was a real one since his love for her was honest and full. Ella was a good woman. But any man worth his salt had to run risks just to keep himself alive.

"There was still a chance to save her," he said, "until her side was stove in . . . if only someone had come along before the tide changed."

"It won't change for another hour," she said flatly. "It won't be high until 6:00."

He looked up at her sharply, squinting. It wasn't like her to contradict. "Not that it makes any difference now," she added.

"It was high at five," he said. "Just fifteen minutes ago."

That settled, he heaved himself up and with a grunt set the duffle bag on his shoulder. It held all they were able to salvage from the *Diana*—her personal effects, so to speak.

"Got to get to the highway before dark," he said. Then he set off with his back to the sea, assuming that Cory would follow close behind.

The grass bluff gave way to a tangle of spruce and hemlock with clumps of briar between which waved like whips in the wind. As they moved inland, the sound of the surf died behind them, but always there was the moan from the treetops. It was growing dark much more suddenly than he had expected. He wanted to stop and try looking at his watch again—perhaps the condensation had cleared. It was an uneasy feeling to have the crystal clouded like that. He hated having to depend on Cory's. Still, what time *was* it? And when was sunset?

They walked for what must have been an hour—or was it only half that long?—all the time expecting to come out on the highway. Somehow it retreated darkly before them. His luck was still bad.

Suddenly he heard his wife Ella cry out from her hospital bed. He stopped dead. Time hung motionless in the twilight.

"An owl," Cory said flatly. "Did you hear it?"

So they continued without a word. An owl. Yes. Of course. He had taught her to identify the cry of birds and she had been a good student. So much for that.

But the picture of Ella lingered there in the gloom. Poor Ella in a strange city in the miserable hospital bed, alone and wondering what would become of her next month. She was strong—she was strength itself—but she'd never had to face anything like this.

"First trip to a hospital in eighteen years," she had said with that taut smile of hers. That was only three days ago. Eighteen years previous she had given birth to the last of their eight children. It was, he remembered, quickly done, neat and on time. Just like her. And in those days the nurses and friends always commented on how strong she was, how healthy. But this time the swelling in her uterus was not a new life. It was a lump which at best was bad. The doctors in Portland had consulted, tested, and talked more. So Isaac made some long distance calls, told Cory to pack, and drove the three of them down to Phillips House, the expensive wing of the Massachusetts General Hospital in Boston.

The first thing he did there was to tell the doctor in

charge that in any event he was to "talk straight." Then, sitting awkwardly on the edge of the easy chair in Ella's private room, he made plans for the family:

"This may take time," he told them. "And I don't intend to do much commuting. So as soon as we get the place closed up and the *Diana* over to the yard for the winter, Cory and me will find a hotel room nearby."

"Don't go to all that trouble," Ella said. "I'll be all right."

"No trouble. Never did think much of a Maine winter anyway," he said, echoing his own annual refrain.

"Been suffering in silence?" she said with a hint of a smile.

A wave of affection caught him off balance.

"Only thing that makes me suffer," he said, "is having you in this goddamned nunnery instead of where you should be."

"Never you mind about that," she said. Then she began with a long list of things which would have to be done at the house: kitchen cleaned, refrigerator emptied, linen packed away.

"I sure hate leaving all this to you two," she said, shaking her head. "But I guess I've got no choice."

That struck him hard. She was right, he supposed. But it was a terrible thing to hear someone utter the words "no choice." Worse than dying. Perhaps the same.

And now, in this miserable, darkening forest, did he have any choice? He was heading for the highway with his head down, driving one foot before the other, mindless.

When they finally broke through onto the tar road they almost fell, stumbling giddily. The rhythm of effort had been interrupted. Legs tingling, they turned this way and that in the middle of the road, surprised and without plan. What had been a gray, fast-moving overcast was now a dark, blood-tinted haze. Looking up he saw three gulls flying hard and into the wind. It was a bad sign—only during the worst of gales did they risk crossing straight through the center rather than riding it out.

"Rest yourself," he said. "Someone's bound to come by."

They waited, sitting silently in the winter-killed grass next to the road, leaning against the duffle. He tried to take a look at his watch again, but even when he turned it so as to catch the last dull glow from the sky, he could not see the hands.

After a time—more or less—a pickup truck came by and stopped without Isaac having to make a gesture. He slung the duffle in back and got in the cab. Cory climbed in after him.

"Mr. Bates?" the driver asked. His voice was adolescent. He sounded like one of the Skolfield grandsons, but Isaac could never tell them apart.

"Right," Isaac said. "You're one of the Skolfields?"

"Pete."

They drove in silence. As they passed a cluster of three houses by the general store, Isaac noticed a kerosene lamp in the window of one. The electric line was down again. But there was no need to comment.

Finally the boy gave in to his curiosity. "Been hunting?" he asked.

"Lost my boat," Isaac said. "Had to beach her."

That wasn't really honest, of course. He had driven her hard on the ledge. An incredible miscalculation. Baffling. No, he hadn't beached her; he'd wrecked her. But how could you say that aloud?

"It's a bad night," the boy said.

When they came to Isaac's mailbox the boy turned in without a word. It was a five-minute drive in over that rutted dirt road and another five out, but the boy was offering his time as condolences.

When they came out on the hillside where Isaac's house and barn were, they were hit with the gale again. The truck shuddered with a gust before they drew into the lee of the house itself.

"Can we get her off at dawn?" the boy asked as they got out. "Tide's high again at six-thirty."

"*Five*-thirty," Isaac said sharply. "Besides, it's too late. She's broke up."

A wave of despair broke over him. He opened his mouth to say thanks, but he couldn't utter a word to the boy. What did *he* know about such things?

"You're lucky to be alive," the boy said.

"You think so?"

But Isaac's answer never reached the boy; it was lost in the wind and in the decades that lay between them. The headlights swung sharply and soon were only a winking flicker through the forest on the other side of the pasture, streaking back to town, leaving the night blacker than ever.

They entered the kitchen like two blind strangers. It hardly seemed possible: for more than twenty years the house had been filled with children—eight of them in the peak years. They had gone, one by one. Scattered. And was there, finally, only this blackness? Was that all?

The power must have been off for hours, for without the oil furnace going the place had picked up the dank, tomb-like chill of a house long deserted. Isaac flipped the light switch from habit and the blackness became more intense. He shivered, groping for matches.

When in doubt, Isaac gave orders. "Find a flashlight," he said to Cory. "And get the kitchen matches." It didn't pay to speak softly if you wanted action. "We need about four lamps going. Start with the ones in the pantry." They hadn't had electricity in the place until 1935 and a part of him had always resented all that too-easy glare. "Then get some spills for the range."

He groped about for a flashlight, but before he could locate one there was a flicker of orange behind him. She was lighting the lamp. The room appeared and the storm outside was forced back hissing.

"Now some kindling," he said. She lit a second lamp for her own use and tossed to him the matches and a fresh pack of cigarettes. When she was safely out in the woodshed, he began to study the tide chart which was hanging on the wall. His hands ripped carelessly at the cigarette package as he squinted to make out the blur of fine print. "November . . . November . . . November 10, High. . . ." He lit a cigarette and inhaled deeply. "November . . . 10 . . . High *5:05.*"

"Ha!" He whooped and called to Cory.

But the black wave which had sucked back for an instant thundered down on him once again: November 10th they had driven Ella to Boston. And the 11th they were still there. This was the *12th.* He put his hands to his temples. Gears had slipped.

"Was that you?" Cory asked. She was standing there at the door with a coal hod half-filled with the spills—wood chips and bark.

"Me? No," he muttered, taking the hod from her. "Just the wind." He started laying the fire.

She didn't question it. He could hear her behind him, bustling about like a young Ella, lighting lamps, stuffing wads of paper in the windows that rattled, mopping the front hall where the rain had driven under the door, filling jugs of water from the last remaining trickle from the faucet. When his fire was roaring with pine slabs he converted to oak and she put the kettle on the hottest section of the stove.

"You'll be needing a hot whiskey, I suppose," she said in an offhand, affectionate way. The echo of Ella was startling.

"We both will tonight."

"Now don't get me all giddy," she said, setting the kitchen table for two with quick motions. "I've a lot to do tonight."

He didn't press it, seeing her set out two white mugs. That was something his wife would never have done—not once over the course of decades. And there had been times— like this one—when it would have been good to have shared a drink.

She brought him the bottle of King's Whiskey and he measured by eye a double shot for them both, the slosh in each mug as quick and accurate as a bartender's. Then she filled each with steaming water from the kettle.

"Sugar and lemon for yours," he said. "Nothing for mine."

He watched her as she went to the pantry and sliced lemons. It seemed senseless to him to have pants cut like that. All the young folks were wearing them. He sniffed the steam from his drink and felt sweat come to his forehead.

"You should get out of those wet things," he said abruptly.

"They're drying out."

"Women shouldn't wear pants anyhow."

"First I've heard you complain," she said lightly. She was holding her mug in both hands, warming them, and taking quick sips.

"Just change them."

The smile went from her face. He thought he saw a flicker of fear there and cursed himself for speaking roughly to her. Still, why not? She hadn't been raised to be just another fair-weather girl. Not like the other two—fooling around with men too old for them and stumbling into marriage and moving away. No, Cory had her feet squarely on the ground.

And as if to prove it she obeyed him by heading up the stairs to her room. She was back down only half a mug later with sweater and skirt over her arm.

"It's winter up there," she said. "Turn around so I can change without freezing."

He faced the stove, his mug in hand, and listened as her wet Levi's hit the floor with a splot and her dressing filled the room with a charged silence. The heat from the range prickled his face.

"Stove heat makes sense," he said, speaking only to hear his own voice. "You know just where it comes from. Keeps people together. As soon as you put in a furnace, the family scatters all over the house, each to his own damn room. Good feeling to have the heat at your face and cold at your back."

"So who put the furnace in?" she asked, hanging her wet clothes up on the pegs behind the range.

"Ella did," he said. It was meant as a kind of easy joke, but strangely the name of Ella cast a pall on the place. Cory paused, hand on peg, and took in a deep breath. Isaac took a scalding slug of his drink. He wished he hadn't brought her name into that kitchen. She was gone. He and Cory had the place to themselves.

"Will she live?" Cory asked very quietly.

"Live?" It was a rotten question to ask about a dying woman. "Of course she'll live. Good God, don't you know that *all* wives outlive their men? What's the matter with you, d'you want to wish her right into her grave?"

She was looking at him now, her mouth open, her eyes squinting, and face pale.

"Oh, come on, now," he said, jovial again, "don't take everything so serious."

"Sorry."

"Nothing to be *sorry* about. You sound like your Uncle Will." She grinned. His older brother, William, was a perpetual victim. The very mention of his name brought smiles in Isaac's home. "Like when he was trying to teach your cousin Tina how to drive. . . ."

"And was standing in the garage?"

"So as to direct her in backing out. . . ."

"But she wasn't in reverse?"

"In first. That's right." They were both laughing now. "So Uncle Will gets pinned to the wall. . . ."

"Between the studs?"

"That's all that saved him. And she gets flustered and shouts at him. . . ."

" 'Why do you have to stand right in front of me?' "

"And he says," Isaac could hardly finish. " '*Sorry.*' "

Isaac wiped the tears from his eyes and poured more whiskey in each mug. It was the first time he had told the story without Ella shaking her head and saying "Poor Will." Cory added the hot water to his drink from the kettle. She hesitated over her own mug, then shrugged and added the water.

"You won't tell on me?" she said with a grin.

"I wouldn't tell on my Cory," he said.

"You may just have to do without supper."

"There's more in this world than a goddamned series of homecooked suppers."

"Let's drink to that," she said. They clinked mugs. "No more meals, no more brooms."

" '. . . No more teacher's dirty looks,' " he chanted.

"Doesn't rhyme."

"Say, did I ever tell you about your Uncle Will and the mop salesman?"

"Never," she said. He knew she was lying, but neither of them cared. He loved the telling and she loved the listening so he started right in. The pieces of the story fitted together, link by link, building. Then, finally, at precisely the right moment they exploded into laughter.

After a lull he said, "You know, we're goddamned lucky to be alive."

"Sure are," she said. "You've got a genius for picking the right ledge to land on."

He snorted a laugh right in the middle of a gulp. Whiskey sprayed the air. They broke into laughter again. The sound sent him back years to a rooming house in town and some Latvian woman named . . . what *was* her name? But by heaven she could laugh. From the gut. Free and open. God she loved life. And everyone else. Danced until you were out of your pants and then brought you down with a whoop.

"No one really loves a cook," he said to Cory, sloshing a careless round into their mugs. "A man who hauls himself off a black ledge doesn't cry out for a meal. No sir!"

"And what *does* he cry for?" She was heading for the kettle.

"Celebration. Thanksgiving."

"So you shall have it," she said, kettle in hand. "Today is a holiday."

"Celebration for being alive."

"We'll have one every day. This place *needs* a celebration every day. Forever."

She was pouring the water with a flourish, kettle a foot above the mugs. It splashed over the table, steaming. Some ran from the table onto his pants and he jumped up, laughing.

"God but you're sloppy," he said, delighted with her. The room turned on its mooring; the deck rose and fell under him. The kettle went somewhere and she was laughing, her head back, and he was holding her, dancing about the room singing "O Sole Mio!" and feeling her close against him and laughing and his hand drove itself down between the fabric of her skirt onto the round of a buttock firm as youth itself and the other hand wrenched at the cloth, ripping it.

Her fingers were suddenly at his face, ripping like winter spray. He threw her back from him and with a crack of timbers she went down hard.

He staggered back, sober. She was lying there on the floor, broadside to the black cookstove, rocking. Her hands were over her face; she began sobbing like the winds, lost.

Later that night, the electric lights glared back on. That was when she stood again, solemn, dry-eyed, white, and unreal. Ghostlike.

"We'd better eat something," she said.

She heated some tasteless spaghetti. Silently they ate, knowing that it would be the first of many like that—just the two of them there like figures in a waiting room, afraid to touch each other even with words.

WILLIAM TREVOR

◇ ◇ ◇

Autumn Sunshine

The rectory was in County Wexford, eight miles from Enniscorthy. It was a handsome eighteenth-century house, with Virginia creeper covering three sides and a tangled garden full of buddleia and struggling japonica which had always been too much for its incumbents. It stood alone, seeming lonely even, approximately at the centre of the country parish it served. Its church—St. Michael's Church of Ireland—was two miles away, in the village of Boharbawn.

For twenty-six years the Morans had lived there, not wishing to live anywhere else. Canon Moran had never been an ambitious man; his wife, Frances, had found contentment easy to attain in her lifetime. Their four girls had been born in the rectory, and had become a happy family there. They were grown up now, Frances's death was still recent: like the rectory itself, its remaining occupant was alone in the countryside. The death had occurred in the spring of the year, and the summer had somehow been bearable. The clergyman's eldest daughter had spent May and part of June at the rectory with her children. Another one had brought her family for most of August, and a third was to bring her newly married husband in the winter. At Christmas nearly

239

all of them would gather at the rectory and some would come at Easter. But that September, as the days drew in, the season was melancholy.

Then, one Tuesday morning, Slattery brought a letter from Canon Moran's youngest daughter. There were two other letters as well, in unsealed buff envelopes which meant that they were either bills or receipts. Frail and grey-haired in his elderliness, Canon Moran had been wondering if he should give the lawn in front of the house a last cut when he heard the approach of Slattery's van. The lawn-mower was the kind that had to be pushed, and in the spring the job was always easier if the grass had been cropped close at the end of the previous summer.

"Isn't that a great bit of weather, Canon?" Slattery remarked, winding down the window of the van and passing out the three envelopes. "We're set for a while, would you say?"

"I hope so, certainly."

"Ah, we surely are, sir."

The conversation continued for a few moments longer, as it did whenever Slattery came to the rectory. The postman was young and easy-going, not long the successor to old Mr. O'Brien, who'd been making the round on a bicycle when the Morans first came to the rectory in 1952. Mr. O'Brien used to talk about his garden; Slattery talked about fishing, and often brought a share of his catch to the rectory.

"It's a great time of year for it," he said now, "except for the darkness coming in."

Canon Moran smiled and nodded; the van turned round on the gravel, dust rising behind it as it moved swiftly down the avenue to the road. Everyone said Slattery drove too fast.

He carried the letters to a wooden seat on the edge of the lawn he'd been wondering about cutting. Deirdre's handwriting hadn't changed since she'd been a child; it was round and neat, not at all a reflection of the girl she was.

The blue English stamp, the Queen in profile blotched a bit by the London postmark, wasn't on its side or half upside down, as you might possibly expect with Deirdre. Of all the Moran children, she'd grown up to be the only difficult one. She hadn't come to the funeral and hadn't written about her mother's death. She hadn't been to the rectory for three years.

"I'm sorry," she wrote now. "I couldn't stop crying actually. I've never known anyone as nice or as generous as she was. For ages I didn't even want to believe she was dead. I went on imagining her in the rectory and doing the flowers in church and shopping in Enniscorthy."

Deirdre was twenty-one now. He and Frances had hoped she'd go to Trinity and settle down, but although at school she'd seemed to be the cleverest of their children she'd had no desire to become a student. She'd taken the Rosslare boat to Fishguard one night, having said she was going to spend a week with her friend Maeve Coles in Cork. They hadn't known she'd gone to England until they received a picture postcard from London telling them not to worry, saying she'd found work in an egg-packing factory.

"Well, I'm coming back for a little while now," she wrote, "if you could put up with me and if you wouldn't find it too much. I'll cross over to Rosslare on the twenty-ninth, the morning crossing, and then I'll come on to Enniscorthy on the bus. I don't know what time it will be but there's a pub just by where the bus drops you so could we meet in the small bar there at six o'clock and then I won't have to lug my cases too far? I hope you won't mind going into such a place. If you can't make it, or don't want to see me, it's understandable, so if you don't turn up by half six I'll see if I can get a bus on up to Dublin. Only I need to get back to Ireland for a while."

It was, as he and Slattery had agreed, a lovely autumn. Gentle sunshine mellowed the old garden, casting an extra sheen of gold on leaves that were gold already. Roses that had been ebullient in June and July bloomed modestly now. Michaelmas daisies were just beginning to bud. Already the crab-apples were falling, hydrangeas had a forgotten look. Canon Moran carried the letter from his daughter into the walled vegetable-garden and leaned against the side of the greenhouse, half sitting on a protruding ledge, reading the letter again. Panes of glass were broken in the greenhouse, white paint and putty needed to be renewed, but inside a vine still thrived, and was heavy now with black ripe fruit. Later that morning he would pick some and drive into Enniscorthy, to sell the grapes to Mrs. Roche in Slaney Street.

"Love, Deirdre": the letter was marvelous. Beyond the rectory the fields of wheat had been harvested, and the remaining stubble had the same tinge of gold in the autumn light; the beech-trees and the chestnuts were triumphantly magnificent. But decay and rotting were only weeks away, and the letter from Deirdre was full of life. *"Love, Deirdre"* were words more beautiful than all the season's glories. He prayed as he leaned against the sunny greenhouse, thanking God for this salvation.

For all the years of their marriage Frances had been a help. As a younger man, Canon Moran hadn't known quite what to do. He'd been at a loss among his parishioners, hesitating in the face of this weakness or that: the pregnancy of Alice Pratt in 1954, the argument about grazing rights between Mr. Willoughby and Eugene Ryan in 1960, the theft of an altar cloth from St. Michael's and reports that Mrs. Tobin had been seen wearing it as a skirt. Alice Pratt had been going out with a Catholic boy, one of Father Hayes's flock, which made the matter more difficult than ever. Eugene Ryan was one of Father Hayes's also, and so was Mrs. Tobin.

"Father Hayes and I had a chat," Frances had said, and she'd had a chat as well with Alice Pratt's mother. A month later Alice Pratt married the Catholic boy, but to this day

attended St. Michael's every Sunday, the children going to
Father Hayes. Mrs. Tobin was given Hail Marys to say by
the priest; Mr. Willoughby agreed that his father had years
ago granted Eugene Ryan the grazing rights. Everything, in
these cases and in many others, had come out all right in the
end: order emerged from the confusion that Canon Moran
so disliked, and it was Frances who had always begun the
process, though no one ever said in the rectory that she
understood the mystery of people as well as he understood
the teachings of the New Testament. She'd been a freckle-
faced girl when he'd married her, pretty in her way. He was
the one with the brains.

Frances had seen human frailty everywhere: it was weakness in people, she said, that made them what they were as
much as strength did. And she herself had her own share of
such frailty, falling short in all sorts of ways of the God's
image her husband preached about. With the small amount
of housekeeping money she could be allowed she was a
spendthrift, and she said she was lazy. She loved clothes and
often overreached herself on visits to Dublin; she sat in the
sun while the rectory gathered dust and the garden became
rank; it was only where people were concerned that she was
practical. But for what she was her husband had loved her
with unobtrusive passion for fifty years, appreciating her
conversation and the help she'd given him because she could
so easily sense the truth. When he'd found her dead in the
garden one morning he'd felt he had lost some part of
himself.

Though many months had passed since then, the trouble
was that Frances hadn't yet become a ghost. Her being alive
was still too recent, the shock of her death too raw. He
couldn't distance himself; the past refused to be the past.
Often he thought that her fingerprints were still in the
rectory, and when he picked the grapes or cut the grass of
the lawn it was impossible not to pause and remember other
years. Autumn had been her favorite time.

*   *   *

"Of course I'd come," he said. "Of course, dear. Of course."

"I haven't treated you very well."

"It's over and done with, Deirdre."

She smiled, and it was nice to see her smile again, although it was strange to be sitting in the back bar of a public house in Enniscorthy. He saw her looking at him, her eyes passing over his clerical collar and black clothes, and his thin quiet face. He could feel her thinking that he had aged, and putting it down to the death of the wife he'd been so fond of.

"I'm sorry I didn't write," she said.

"You explained in your letter, Deirdre."

"It was ages before I knew about it. That was an old address you wrote to."

"I guessed."

In turn he examined her. Years ago she'd had her long hair cut. It was short now, like a neat black cap on her head. And her face had lost its chubbiness; hollows where her cheeks had been made her eyes more dominant, pools of seaweed green. He remembered her child's stocky body, and the uneasy adolescence that had spoilt the family's serenity. Her voice had lost its Irish intonation.

"I'd have met you off the boat, you know."

"I didn't want to bother you with that."

"Oh, now, it isn't far, Deirdre."

She drank Irish whiskey, and smoked a brand of cigarettes called Three Castles. He'd asked for a mineral himself, and the woman serving them had brought him a bottle of something that looked like water but which fizzed up when she'd poured it. A kind of lemonade he imagined it was, and didn't much care for it.

"I have grapes for Mrs. Roche," he said.

"Who's that?"

"She has a shop in Slaney Street. We always sold her the grapes. You remember?"

She didn't, and he reminded her of the vine in the greenhouse. A shop surely wouldn't be open at this hour of the evening, she said, forgetting that in a country town of course it would be. She asked if the cinema was still the same in Enniscorthy, a cement building halfway up a hill. She said she remembered bicycling home from it at night with her sisters, not being able to keep up with them. She asked after her sisters and he told her about the two marriages that had taken place since she'd left: she had in-laws she'd never met, and nephews and a niece.

They left the bar, and he drove his dusty black Vauxhall straight to the small shop he'd spoken of. She remained in the car while he carried into the shop two large chip-baskets full of grapes. Afterwards Mrs. Roche came to the door with him.

"Well, is that Deirdre?" she said as Deirdre wound down the window of the car. "I'd never know you, Deirdre."

"She's come back for a little while," Canon Moran explained, raising his voice a little because he was walking round the car to the driver's seat as he spoke.

"Well, isn't that grand?" said Mrs. Roche.

Everyone in Enniscorthy knew Deirdre had just gone off, but it didn't matter now. Mrs. Roche's husband, who was a red-cheeked man with a cap, much smaller than his wife, appeared beside her in the shop doorway. He inclined his head in greeting, and Deirdre smiled and waved at both of them. Canon Moran thought it was pleasant when she went on waving while he drove off.

In the rectory he lay wakeful that night, his mind excited by Deirdre's presence. He would have loved Frances to know, and guessed that she probably did. He fell asleep at half past two and dreamed that he and Frances were young again, that Deirdre was still a baby. The freckles on Frances's face were out in profusion, for they were sitting in the sunshine in the garden, tea things spread about them, the children playing some game among the shrubs. It was au-

tumn then also, the last of the September heat. But because
he was younger in his dream he didn't feel part of the
season himself, or sense its melancholy.

A week went by. The time passed slowly because a lot
was happening, or so it seemed. Deirdre insisted on cooking
all the meals and on doing the shopping in Boharbawn's
single shop or in Enniscorthy. She still smoked her endless
cigarettes, but the peakiness there had been in her face
when she'd first arrived wasn't quite so pronounced—or
perhaps, he thought, he'd become used to it. She told him
about the different jobs she'd had in London and the different places she'd lived in, because on the postcards she'd
occasionally sent there hadn't been room to go into detail.
In the rectory they had always hoped she'd managed to get
a training of some sort, though guessing she hadn't. In fact,
her jobs had been of the most rudimentary kind: as well as
her spell in the egg-packing factory, there'd been a factory
that made plastic earphones, a cleaning job in a hotel near
Euston, and a year working for the Use-Us Office Cleansing
Service. "But you can't have liked any of that work, Deirdre?" he suggested, and she agreed she hadn't.
From the way she spoke he felt that that period of her life
was over: adolescence was done with, she had steadied and
taken stock. He didn't suggest to her that any of this might
be so, not wishing to seem either too anxious or too pleased,
but he felt she had returned to the rectory in a very different
frame of mind from the one in which she'd left it. He
imagined she would remain for quite a while, still taking
stock, and in a sense occupying her mother's place. He
thought he recognized in her a loneliness that matched his
own, and he wondered if it was a feeling that their loneliness might be shared which had brought her back at this
particular time. Sitting in the drawing-room while she cooked
or washed up, or gathering grapes in the greenhouse while
she did the shopping, he warmed delightedly to this theme.
It seemed like an act of God that their circumstances should

interlace this autumn. By Christmas she would know what she wanted to do with her life, and in the spring that followed she would perhaps be ready to set forth again. A year would have passed since the death of Frances.

"I have a friend," Deirdre said when they were having a cup of coffee together in the middle of one morning. "Someone who's been good to me."

She had carried a tray to where he was composing next week's sermon, sitting on the wooden seat by the lawn at the front of the house. He laid aside his exercise book, and a pencil and a rubber. "Who's that?" he inquired.

"Someone called Harold."

He nodded, stirring sugar into his coffee.

"I want to tell you about Harold, Father. I want you to meet him."

"Yes, of course."

She lit a cigarette. She said, "We have a lot in common. I mean, he's the only person . . ."

She faltered and then hesitated. She lifted her cigarette to her lips and drew on it.

He said, "Are you fond of him, Deirdre?"

"Yes, I am."

Another silence gathered. She smoked and drank her coffee. He added more sugar to his.

"Of course I'd like to meet him," he said.

"Could he come to stay with us, Father? Would you mind? Would it be all right?"

"Of course I wouldn't mind. I'd be delighted."

Harold was summoned, and arrived at Rosslare a few days later. In the meantime Deirdre had explained to her father that her friend was an electrician by trade and had let it fall that he was an intellectual kind of person. She borrowed the old Vauxhall and drove it to Rosslare to meet him, returning to the rectory in the early evening.

"How d'you do?" Canon Moran said, stretching out a hand in the direction of an excessively thin youth with a birthmark on his face. His dark hair was cut very short, cropped almost. He was wearing a black leather jacket.

"I'm fine," Harold said.

"You've had a good journey?"

"Lousy, 'smatter of fact, Mr. Moran."

Harold's voice was strongly Cockney, and Canon Moran wondered if Deirdre had perhaps picked up some of her English vowel sounds from it. But then he realized that most people in London would speak like that, as people did on the television and the wireless. It was just a little surprising that Harold and Deirdre should have so much in common, as they clearly had from the affectionate way they held one another's hand. None of the other Moran girls had gone in so much for holding hands in front of the family.

He was to sit in the drawing-room, they insisted, while they made supper in the kitchen, so he picked up the *Irish Times* and did as he was bidden. Half an hour later Harold appeared and said that the meal was ready: fried eggs and sausages and bacon, and some tinned beans. Canon Moran said grace.

Having stated that Co. Wexford looked great, Harold didn't say much else. He didn't smile much, either. His afflicted face bore an edgy look, as if he'd never become wholly reconciled to his birthmark. It was like a scarlet map on his left cheek, a shape that reminded Canon Moran of the toe of Italy. Poor fellow, he thought. And yet a birthmark was so much less to bear than other afflictions there could be.

"Harold's fascinated actually," Deirdre said, "by Ireland."

Her friend didn't add anything to that remark for a moment, even though Canon Moran smiled and nodded interestedly. Eventually Harold said, "The struggle of the Irish people."

"I didn't know a thing about Irish history," Deirdre said. "I mean, not anything that made sense."

The conversation lapsed at this point, leaving Canon Moran

greatly puzzled. He began to say that Irish history had always been of considerable interest to him also, that it had a good story to it, its tragedy uncomplicated. But the other two didn't appear to understand what he was talking about and so he changed the subject. It was a particularly splendid autumn, he pointed out.

"Harold doesn't go in for anything like that," Deirdre replied.

During the days that followed Harold began to talk more, surprising Canon Moran with almost everything he said. Deirdre had been right to say he was fascinated by Ireland, and it wasn't just a tourist's fascination. Harold had read widely: he spoke of ancient battles, and of the plantations of James I and Elizabeth, of Robert Emmet and the Mitchelstown martyrs, of Pearse and De Valera. "The struggle of the Irish people" was the expression he most regularly employed. It seemed to Canon Moran that the relationship between Harold and Deirdre had a lot to do with Harold's fascination, as though his interest in Deirdre's native land had somehow caused him to become interested in Deirdre herself.

There was something else as well. Fascinated by Ireland, Harold hated his own country. A sneer whispered through his voice when he spoke of England: a degenerate place, he called it, destroyed by class-consciousness and the unjust distribution of wealth. He described in detail the city of Nottingham, to which he appeared to have a particular aversion. He spoke of unnecessary motorways and the stupidity of bureaucracy, the stifling presence of a Royal family. "You could keep an Indian village," he claimed, "on what those corgis eat. You could house five hundred homeless in Buckingham Palace." There was brainwashing by television and the newspaper barons. No ordinary person had a chance because pap was fed to the ordinary person, a deliberate policy going back into Victorian times when education and religion had been geared to the enslavement of minds. The English people had brought it on themselves, having lost their spunk, settling instead for consumer durables. "What better can you expect," Harold demanded, "after the hyprocrisy of that empire the bosses ran?"

Deirdre didn't appear to find anything specious in this line of talk, which surprised her father. "Oh, I wonder about that," he said himself from time to time, but he said it mildly, not wishing to cause an argument, and in any case his interjections were not acknowledged. Quite a few of the criticisms Harold leveled at his own country could be leveled at Ireland also and, Canon Moran guessed, at many countries throughout the world. It was strange that the two neighboring islands had been so picked out, although once Germany was mentioned and the point made that developments beneath the surface there were a hopeful sign, that a big upset was on the way.

"We're taking a walk," Harold said one afternoon. "She's going to show me Kinsella's Barn."

Canon Moran nodded, saying to himself that he disliked Harold. It was the first time he had admitted it, but the feeling was familiar. The less generous side of his nature had always emerged when his daughters brought to the rectory the men they'd become friendly with or even proposed to marry. Emma, the eldest girl, had brought several before settling in the end for Thomas. Linda had brought only John, already engaged to him. Una had married Carley not long after the death, and Carley had not yet visited the rectory: Canon Moran had met him in Dublin, where the wedding had taken place, for in the circumstances Una had not been married from home. Carley was an older man, an importer of tea and wine, stout and flushed, certainly not someone Canon Moran would have chosen for his second-youngest daughter. But, then, he had thought the same about Emma's Thomas and about Linda's John.

Thomas was a farmer, sharing a sizeable acreage with his father in Co. Meath. He always brought to mind the sarcasm of an old schoolmaster who in Canon Moran's distant schooldays used to refer to a gang of boys at the back of the classroom as "farmers' sons," meaning that not much could be expected of them. It was an inaccurate assumption but even now, whenever Canon Moran found himself in the company of Thomas, he couldn't help recalling it. Thomas was mostly silent, with a good-natured smile that came slowly and lingered too long. According to his father, and there was no reason to doubt the claim, he was a good judge of beef cattle.

Linda's John was the oppostie. Wiry and suave, he was making his way in the Bank of Ireland, at present stationed in Waterford. He had a tiny orange-colored moustache and was good at golf. Linda's ambition for him was that he should become the Bank of Ireland's manager in Limerick or Galway, where the insurances that went with the position were particularly lucrative. Unlike Thomas, John talked all the time, telling jokes and stories about the Bank of Ireland's customers.

"Nothing is perfect," Frances used to say, chiding her husband for an uncharitableness he did his best to combat. He disliked being so particular about the men his daughters chose, and he was aware that other people saw them differently: Thomas would do anything for you, John was fun, the middle-aged Carley laid his success at Una's feet. But whoever the husbands of his daughters had been, Canon Moran knew he'd have felt the same. He was jealous of the husbands because ever since his daughters had been born he had loved them unstintingly. When he had prayed after Frances's death he'd felt jealous of God, who had taken her from him.

"There's nothing much to see," he pointed out when Harold announced that Deirdre was going to show him Kinsella's Barn. "Just the ruin of a wall is all that's left."

"Harold's interested, Father."

They set off on their walk, leaving the old clergyman ashamed that he could not like Harold more. It wasn't just his griminess: there was something sinister about Harold, something furtive about the way he looked at you, peering at you cruelly out of his afflicted face, not meeting your eye. Why was he so fascinated about a country that wasn't his own? Why did he refer so often to "Ireland's struggle" as if that struggle particularly concerned him? He hated walking, he had said, yet he'd just set out to walk six miles through woods and fields to examine a ruined wall.

Canon Moran had wondered as suspiciously about Thomas and John and Carley, privately questioning every statement they made, finding hidden motives everywhere. He'd hated the thought of his daughters being embraced or even touched, and had forced himself not to think about that. He'd prayed, ashamed of himself then, too. "It's just a frailty in you," Frances had said, her favorite way of cutting things down to size.

He sat for a while in the afternoon sunshine, letting all of it hang in his mind. It would be nice if they quarrelled on their walk. It would be nice if they didn't speak when they returned, if Harold simply went away. But that wouldn't happen, because they had come to the rectory with a purpose. He didn't know why he thought that, but he knew it was true: they had come for a reason, something that was all tied up with Harold's fascination and with the kind of person Harold was, with his cold eyes and his afflicted face.

In March 1798 an incident had taken place in Kinsella's Barn, which at that time had just been a barn. Twelve men and women, accused of harboring insurgents, had been tied together with ropes at the command of a Sergeant James. They had been led through the village of Boharbawn, the Sergeant's soldiers on horseback on either side of the procession, the Sergeant himself bringing up the rear. Designed as an act of education, an example to the inhabitants of Boharbawn and the country people around, the twelve had been herded into a barn owned by a farmer called Kinsella and there burned to death. Kinsella, who had played no part either in the harboring of insurgents or in the execution of the twelve, was afterwards murdered by his own farm laborers.

"Sergeant James was a Nottingham man," Harold said that evening at supper. "A soldier of fortune who didn't care what he did. Did you know he acquired great wealth, Mr. Moran?"

"No, I wasn't at all aware of that," Canon Moran replied.

"Harold found out about him," Deirdre said.

"He used to boast he was responsible for the death of a thousand Irish people. It was in Boharbawn he reached the thousand. They rewarded him well for that."

"Not much is known about Sergeant James locally. Just the legend of Kinsella's Barn."

"No way it's a legend."

Deirdre nodded; Canon Moran did not say anything. They were eating cooked ham and salad. On the table there was a cake which Deirdre had bought in Murphy Flood's in Enniscorthy, and a pot of tea. There were several bunches of grapes from the greenhouse, and a plate of wafer biscuits. Harold was fond of salad cream, Canon Moran had noticed; he had a way of hitting the base of the jar with his hand, causing large dollops to spurt all over his ham. He didn't place his knife and fork together on the plate when he'd finished, but just left them anyhow. His fingernails were edged with black.

"You'd feel sick," he was saying now, working the salad cream again. "You'd stand there looking at that wall and you'd feel a revulsion in your stomach."

"What I meant," Canon Moran said, "is that it has passed into local legend. No one doubts it took place; there's no question about that. But two centures have almost passed."

"And nothing has changed," Harold interjected. "The Irish people still share their bondage with the twelve in Kinsella's Barn."

"Round here of course—"

"It's not round here that matters, Mr. Moran. The struggle's world-wide; the sickness is everywhere actually."

Again Deirdre nodded. She was like a zombie, her father thought. She was being used because she was an Irish girl; she was Harold's Irish connection, and in some almost frightening way she believed herself in love with him. Frances had once said they'd made a mistake with her. She had wondered if Deirdre had perhaps found all the love they'd offered her too much to bear. They were quite old when Deirdre was a child, the last expression of their own love. She was special because of that.

"At least Kinsella got his chips," Harold pursued, his voice relentless. "At least that's something."

Canon Moran protested. The owner of the barn had been an innocent man, he pointed out. The barn had simply been a convenient one, large enough for the purpose, with heavy stones near it that could be pileld up against the door before the conflagration. Kinsella, that day, had been miles away, ditching a field.

"It's too long ago to say where he was," Harold retorted swiftly. "And if he was keeping a low profile in a ditch it would have been by arrangement with the imperial forces."

When Harold said that, there occurred in Canon Moran's mind a flash of what appeared to be the simple truth. Harold was an Englishman who had espoused a cause because it was one through which the status quo in his own country might be damaged. Similar such Englishmen, read about in newspapers, stirred in the clergyman's mind: men from Ealing and Liverpool and Wolverhampton who had changed their names to Irish names, who had even learned the Irish language, in order to ingratiate themselves with the new Irish revolutionaries. Such men dealt out death and chaos, announcing that their conscience insisted on it.

"Well, we'd better wash the dishes," Deirdre said, and Harold rose obediently to help her.

*   *   *

The walk to Kinsella's Barn had taken place on a Saturday afternoon. The following morning Canon Moran conducted his services in St. Michael's, addressing his small Protestant congregation, twelve at Holy Communion, eighteen at morning service. He had prepared a sermon about repentance, taking as his text St. Luke, 15:32: ". . . *for this thy brother was dead, and is alive again; and was lost, and is found.*" But at the last moment he changed his mind and spoke instead of the incident in Kinsella's Barn nearly two centuries ago. He tried to make the point that one horror should not fuel another, that passing time contained its own forgiveness. Deirdre and Harold were naturally not in the church, but they'd been present at breakfast, Harold frying eggs on the kitchen stove, Deirdre pouring tea. He had looked at them and tried to think of them as two young people on holiday. He had tried to tell himself they'd come to the rectory for a rest and for his blessing, that he should be grateful instead of fanciful. It was for his blessing that Emma had brought Thomas to the rectory, that Linda had brought John. Una would bring Carley in November. "Now, don't be silly," Frances would have said.

"The man Kinsella was innocent of everything," he heard his voice insisting in his church. "He should never have been murdered also."

Harold would have delighted in the vengeance exacted on an innocent man. Harold wanted to inflict pain, to cause suffering and destruction. The end justified the means for Harold, even if the end was an artificial one, a pettiness grandly dressed up. In his sermon Canon Moran spoke of such matters without mentioning Harold's name. He spoke of how evil drained people of their humor and compassion, how people pretended even to themselves. It was worse than Frances's death, he thought as his voice continued in the church: it was worse that Deirdre should be part of wickedness.

He could tell that his parishioners found his sermon odd, and he didn't blame them. He was confused, and naturally distressed. In the rectory Deirdre and Harold would be waiting for him. They would all sit down to Sunday lunch while plans for atrocities filled Harold's mind, while Deirdre loved him.

"Are you well again, Mrs. Davis?" he inquired at the church door of a woman who suffered from asthma.

"Not too bad, Canon. Not too bad, thank you."

He spoke to all the others, inquiring about health, remarking on the beautiful autumn. They were farmers mostly and displayed a farmer's gratitude for the satisfactory season. He wondered suddenly who'd replace him among them when he retired or died. Father Hayes had had to give up a year ago. The young man, Father White, was always in a hurry.

"Goodbye so, Canon," Mr. Willoughby said, shaking hands as he always did, every Sunday. It was a long time since there'd been the trouble about Eugene Ryan's grazing rights; three years ago Mr. Willoughby had been left a widower himself. "You're managing all right, Canon?" he asked, as he also always did.

"Yes, I'm all right, thank you, Mr. Willoughby."

Someone else inquired if Deirdre was still at the rectory, and he said she was. Heads nodded, the unspoken thought being that that was nice for him, his youngest daughter at home again after all these years. There was forgiveness in several faces, forgiveness of Deirdre, who had been thoughtless to go off to an egg-packing factory. There was the feeling, also unexpressed, that the young were a bit like that.

"Goodbye," he said in a general way. Car doors banged, engines started. In the vestry he removed his surplice and his cassock and hung them in a cupboard.

"We'll probably go tomorrow," Deirdre said during lunch.

"Go?"

"We'll probably take the Dublin bus."

"I'd like to see Dublin," Harold said.

"And then you're returning to London?"

"We're easy about that," Harold interjected before Deirdre could reply. "I'm a tradesman, Mr. Moran, an electrician."

"I know you're an electrician, Harold."

"What I mean is, I'm on my own; I'm not answerable to the bosses. There's always a bob or two waiting in London."

For some reason Canon Moran felt that Harold was lying. There was a quickness about the way he'd said they were easy about their plans, and it didn't seem quite to make sense, the logic of not being answerable to bosses and a bob or two always waiting for him. Harold was being evasive about their movements, hiding the fact that they would probably remain in Dublin for longer than he implied, meeting other people like himself.

"It was good of you to have us," Deirdre said that evening, all three of them sitting around the fire in the drawing-room because the evenings had just begun to get chilly. Harold was reading a book about Che Guevera and hadn't spoken for several hours. "We've enjoyed it, Father."

"It's been nice having you, Deirdre."

"I'll write to you from London."

It was safe to say that: he knew she wouldn't because she hadn't before, until she'd wanted something. She wouldn't write to thank him for the rectory's hospitality, and that would be quite in keeping. Harold was the same kind of man as Sergeant James had been: it didn't matter that they were on different sides. Sergeant James had maybe borne an affliction also, a humped back or a withered arm. He had ravaged a country that existed then for its spoils, and his most celebrated crime was neatly at hand so that another Englishman could make matters worse by attempting to make amends. In Harold's view the trouble had always been that these acts of war and murder died beneath the weight of print in history books, and were forgotten. But history could be rewritten, and for that Kinsella's Barn was an inspiration: Harold had journeyed to it as people make journeys to holy places.

"Yes?" Deirdre said, for while these reflections had passed through his mind he had spoken her name, wanting to ask her to tell him the truth about her friend.

He shook his head. "I wish you could have seen your mother again," he said instead. "I wish she were here now."

The faces of his three sons-in-law irrelevantly appeared in his mind: Carley's flushed cheeks, Thomas's slow good-natured smile, John's little moustache. It astonished him that he'd ever felt suspicious of their natures, for they would never let his daughters down. But Deirdre had turned her back on the rectory, and what could be expected when she came back with a man? She had never been like Emma or Linda or Una, none of whom smoked Three Castles cigarettes and wore clothes that didn't seem quite clean. It was impossible to imagine any of them becoming involved with a revolutionary, a man who wanted to commit atrocities.

"He was just a farmer, you know," he heard himself saying. "Kinsella."

Surprise showed in Deirdre's face. "It was Mother we were talking about," she reminded him, and he could see her trying to connect her mother with a farmer who had died two hundred years ago, and not being able to. Elderliness, he could see her thinking. "Only time he wandered," she would probably say to her friend.

"It was good of you to come, Deirdre."

He looked at her, far into her eyes, admitting to himself that she had always been his favorite. When the other girls were busily growing up she had still wanted to sit on his knee. She'd had a way of interrupting him no matter what he was doing, arriving beside him with a book she wanted him to read to her.

"Goodbye, Father," she said the next morning while they waited in Enniscorthy for the Dublin bus. "Thank you for everything."

"Yeah, thanks a ton, Mr. Moran," Harold said.

"Goodbye, Harold. Goodbye, my dear."

He watched them finding their seats when the bus arrived and then he drove the old Vauxhall back to Boharbawn, meeting Slattery in his postman's van and returning his salute. There was shopping he should have done, meat and potatoes, and tins of things to keep him going. But his mind was full of Harold's afflicted face and his black-rimmed fingernails, and Deirdre's hand in his. And then flames burst from the straw that had been packed around living people in Kinsella's Barn. They burned through the wood of the barn itself, revealing the writhing bodies. On his horse the man called Sergeant James laughed.

Canon Moran drove the car into the rectory's ramshackle garage, and walked around the house to the wooden seat on the front lawn. Frances should come now with two cups of coffee, appearing at the front door with the tray and then crossing the gravel and the lawn. He saw her as she had been when first they came to the rectory, when only Emma had been born; but the grey-haired Frances was somehow there as well, shadowing her youth. "Funny little Deirdre," she said, placing the tray on the seat between them.

It seemed to him that everything that had just happened in the rectory had to do with Frances, with meeting her for the first time when she was eighteen, with loving her and marrying her. He knew it was a trick of the autumn sunshine that again she crossed the gravel and the lawn, no more than pretence that she handed him a cup and saucer. "Harold's just a talker," she said. "Not at all like Sergeant James."

He sat for a while longer on the wooden seat, clinging to these words, knowing they were true. Of course it was cowardice that ran through Harold, inspiring the whisper of his sneer when he spoke of the England he hated so. In the presence of a befuddled girl and an old Irish clergyman England was an easy target, and Ireland's troubles a kind of target also.

Frances laughed, and for the first time her death seemed

far away, as her life did too. In the rectory the visitors had blurred her fingerprints to nothing, and had made of her a ghost that could come back. The sunshine warmed him as he sat there, the garden was less melancholy than it had been.

MAVIS GALLANT

◇ ◇ ◇

The Prodigal Parent

We sat on the screened porch of Rhoda's new house, which was close to a beach on the ocean side of Vancouver Island. I had come here in a straight line, from the East, and now that I could not go any farther without running my car into the sea, any consideration of wreckage and loss, or elegance of behavior, or debts owed (not of money, of my person) came to a halt. A conqueror in a worn blazer and a regimental tie, I sat facing my daughter, listening to her voice—now describing, now complaining—as if I had all the time in the world. Her glance drifted round the porch, which still contained packing cases. She could not do, or take in, a great deal at once. I have light eyes, like Rhoda's, but mine have been used for summing up.

Rhoda had bought this house and the cabins round it and a strip of maimed landscape with her divorce settlement. She hoped to make something out of the cabins, renting them weekends to respectable people who wanted a quiet place to drink. "Dune Vista" said a sign, waiting for someone to nail it to a tree. I wondered how I would fit in here—what she expected me to do. She still hadn't said. After the first formal Martinis she had made to mark my

261

arrival, she began drinking rye, which she preferred. It was sweeter, less biting than the whiskey I remembered in my youth, and I wondered if my palate or its composition had changed. I started to say so, and my daughter said, "Oh, God, your accent again! You know what I thought you said now? 'Oxbow was a Cheswick charmer.' "

"No, no. Nothing like that."

"Try not sounding so British," she said.

"I don't, you know."

"Well, you don't sound Canadian."

The day ended suddenly, as if there had been a partial eclipse. In the new light I could see my daughter's face and hands.

"I guess I'm different from all my female relatives," she said. She had been comparing herself with her mother, and with half sisters she hardly knew. "I don't despise men, like Joanne does. There's always somebody. There's one now, in fact. I'll tell you about him. I'll tell you the whole thing, and you say what you think. It's a real mess. He's Irish, he's married, and he's got no money. Four children. He doesn't sleep with his wife."

"Surely there's an age limit for this?" I said. "By my count, you must be twenty-eight or -nine now."

"Don't I know it." She looked into the dark trees, darkened still more by the screens, and said without rancor, "It's not my fault. I wouldn't keep on falling for lushes and phonies if you hadn't been that way."

I put my glass down on the packing case she had pushed before me, and said, "I am not, I never was, and I never could be an alcoholic."

Rhoda seemed genuinely shocked. "I never said *that*. I never heard you had to be put in a hospital or anything, like my stepdaddy. But you used to stand me on a table when you had parties, Mother told me, and I used to dance to 'Piccolo Pete.' What happened to that record, I wonder? One of your wives most likely got it in lieu of alimony. But may God strike us both dead here and now if I ever said you were alcoholic." It must have been to her a harsh, clinical word, associated with straitjackets. "I'd like you to meet him," she said. "But I never know when he'll turn up. He's Harry Pay. The writer," she said, rather primly. "Somebody said he was a new-type Renaissance Man—I mean, he doesn't just sit around, he's a judo expert. He could throw *you* down in a second."

"Is he Japanese?"

"God, no. What makes you say that? I already told you what he is. He's white. Quite white, *entirely* white I mean."

"Well—I could hardly have guessed."

"You shouldn't have to guess," she said. "The name should be enough. He's famous. Round here, anyway."

"I'm sorry," I said. "I've been away so many years. Would you write the name down for me? So I can see how it's spelled?"

"I'll do better than that." It touched me to see the large girl she was suddenly moving so lightly. I heard her slamming doors in the living room behind me. She had been clumsy as a child, in every gesture like a wild creature caught. She came back to me with a dun folder out of which spilled loose pages, yellow and smudged. She thrust it at me and, as I groped for my spectacles, turned on an overhead light. "You read this," she said, "and I'll go make us some sandwiches, while I still can. Otherwise we'll break into another bottle and never eat anything. This is something he never shows *anyone*."

"It is my own life exactly," I said when she returned with the sandwiches, which she set awkwardly down. "At least, so far as school in England is concerned. Cold beds, cold food, cold lavatories. Odd that anyone still finds it interesting. There must be twenty written like it every year. The revolting school, the homosexual master, then a girl—saved!"

"Homo *what*?" said Rhoda, clawing the pages. "It's possible. He has a dirty mind, actually."

"Really? Has he ever asked you to do anything unpleasant, such as type his manuscripts?"

"Certainly not. He's got a perfectly good wife for that."

When I laughed, she looked indignant. She had given a serious answer to what she thought was a serious question. Our conversations were always like this—collisions.

"Well?" she said.

"Get rid of him."

She looked at me and sank down on the arm of my chair. I felt her breath on my face, light as a child's. She said, "I was waiting for something. I was waiting all day for you to say something personal, but I didn't think it would be that. Get rid of him? He's all I've got."

"All the more reason. You can do better."

"Who, for instance?" she said. "You? You're no use to me."

She had sent for me. I had come to Rhoda from her half sister Joanne, in Montreal. Joanne had repatriated me from Europe, with an air passage to back the claim. In a new bare apartment, she played severe sad music that was like herself. We ate at a scrubbed table the sort of food that can be picked up with the hand. She was the richest of my children, through her mother, but I recognized in her guarded, slanting looks the sort of avarice and fear I think of as a specific of women. One look seemed meant to tell me, "You waltzed off, old boy, but look at me now," though I could not believe she had wanted me only for that. "I'll never get married" was a remark that might have given me a lead. "I won't have anyone to lie to me, or make a fool of me, or spend my money for me." She waited to see what I would say. She had just come into this money.

"Feeling as you do, you probably shouldn't marry," I said. She looked at me as Rhoda was looking now. "Don't expect too much from men," I said.

"Oh, I don't!" she cried, so eagerly I knew she always would. The cheap sweet Ontario wine she favored and the smell of paint in her new rooms and the raw meals and incessant music combined to give me a violent attack of claustrophobia. It was probably the most important conversation we had.

"We can't have any more conversation now," said Rhoda. "Not after that. It's the end. You've queered it. I should have known. Well, eat your sandwiches now that I've made them."

"Would it seem petulant if, at this point, I did not eat a tomato sandwich?" I said.

"Don't be funny. I can't understand what you're saying anyway."

"If you don't mind, my dear," I said, "I'd rather be on my way."

"What do you mean, on your way? For one thing, you're in no condition to drive. Where d'you think you're going?"

"I can't very well go that way," I said, indicating the ocean I could not see. "I can't go back as I've come."

"It was a nutty thing, to come by car," she said. "It's not even all that cheap."

"As I can't go any farther," I said, "I shall stay. Not here, but perhaps not far."

"Doing what? What *can* you do? We've never been sure."

"I can get a white cane and walk the streets of towns. I can ask people to help me over busy intersections and then beg for money."

"You're kidding."

"I'm not. I shall say—let me think—I shall say I've had a mishap, lost my wallet, pension check not due for another week, postal strike delaying it even more . . ."

"That won't work. They'll send you to the welfare. You should see how we hand out welfare around here."

"I'm counting on seeing it," I said.

"You can't. It would look—" She narrowed her eyes and said, "If you're trying to shame me, forget it. Someone

comes and says, 'That poor old blind bum says he's your
father,' I'll just answer, 'Yes, what about it?' "

"My sight *is* failing, actually."

"There's welfare for that, too."

"We're at cross-purposes," I said. "I'm not looking for
money."

"Then waja come here for?"

"Because Regan sent me on to Goneril, I suppose."

"That's a lie. Don't try to make yourself big. Nothing's
ever happened to you."

"Well, in my uneventful life," I began, but my mind
answered for me, "No, nothing." There are substitutes for
incest but none whatever for love. What I needed now was
someone who knew nothing about me and would never
measure me against a promise or a past. I blamed myself,
not for anything I had said but for having remembered too
late what Rhoda was like. She was positively savage as an
infant, though her school tamed her later on. I remember
sitting opposite her when she was nine—she in an unbecom-
ing tartan coat—while she slowly and seriously ate a large
plate of ice cream. She was in London on a holiday with her
mother, and as I happened to be there with my new family I
gave her a day.

"Every Monday we have Thinking Day," she had said, of
her school. "We think about the Brownies and the Baden-
Powells and sometimes Jesus and all."

"Do you, really?"

"I can't *really,*" Rhoda had said. "I never met any of
them."

"Are you happy, at least?" I said, to justify my belief that
no one was ever needed. But the savage little girl had
become an extremely careful one.

That afternoon, at a matinée performance of "Peter Pan,"
I went to sleep. The slaughter of the pirates woke me, and
as I turned, confident, expecting her to be rapt, I encoun-
tered a face of refusal. She tucked her lips in, folded her
hands, and shrugged away when I helped her into a taxi.

"I'm sorry, I should not have slept in your company," I said. "It was impolite."

"It wasn't that," she burst out. "It was 'Peter Pan.' I hated it. It wasn't what I expected. You could see the wires. Mrs. Darling didn't look right. She didn't have a lovely dress on—only an old pink thing like a nightgown Nana wasn't a real dog, it was a lady. I couldn't understand anything they said. Peter Pan wasn't a boy, he had bosoms."

"I noticed that, too," I said. "There must be a sound traditional reason for it. Perhaps Peter is really a mother figure."

"No, he's a *boy*."

I intercepted, again, a glance of stony denial—of me? We had scarcely met.

"I couldn't understand. They all had English accents," she complained.

For some reason that irritated me. "What the hell did you expect them to have?" I said.

"When I was little," said the nine-year-old, close to tears now, "I thought they were all Canadian."

The old car Joanne had given me was down on the beach, on the hard sand, with ribbons of tire racks behind it as a sign of life, and my luggage locked inside. It had been there a few hours and already it looked abandoned—an old heap someone had left to rust among the lava rock. The sky was lighter than it had seemed from the porch. I picked up a sand dollar, chalky and white, with the tree of life on its underside, and as I slid it in my pocket, for luck, I felt between my fingers a rush of sand. I had spoken the truth, in part; the landscape through which I had recently travelled still shuddered before my eyes and I would not go back. I heard, then saw, Rhoda running down to where I stood. Her hair, which she wore gathered up in a bun, was half down, and she breathed, running, with her lips apart. For the first time I remembered something of the way she had seemed as a child, something more than an anecdote. She clutched my arm and said, "Why did you say I should ditch him? *Why?*"

I disengaged my arm, because she was hurting me, and said, "He can only give you bad habits."

"At my age?"

"Any age. Dissimulation. Voluntary barrenness—someone else has had his children. Playing house, a Peter-and-Wendy game, a life he would never dare try at home. There's the real meaning of Peter, by the way." But she had forgotten.

She clutched me again, to steady herself, and said. "I'm old enough to know everything. I'll soon be in my thirties. That's all I care to say."

It seemed to me I had only recently begun making grave mistakes. I had until now accepted all my children, regardless of who their mothers were. The immortality I had imagined had not been in them but on the faces of women in love. I saw, on the dark beach, Rhoda's mother, the soft hysterical girl whose fatal "I am pregnant" might have enmeshed me for life.

I said, "I wish they would find a substitute for immortality."

"I'm working on it," said Rhoda, grimly, seeming herself again. She let go my arm and watched me unlock the car door. "You'd have hated it here," she said, then, pleading, "You wouldn't want to live here like some charity case—have me support you?"

"I'd be enchanted," I said.

"No, no, you'd hate it," she said. "I couldn't look after you. I haven't got time. And you'd keep thinking I should do better than *him*, and the truth is I can't. You wouldn't want to end up like some old relation, fed in the kitchen and all."

"I don't know," I said. "It would be new."

"Oh," she cried, with what seemed unnecessary despair, "what did you come for? All right," she said. "I give up. You asked for it. You can stay. I mean, I'm inviting you. You can sit around and say, 'Oxbow was a Cheswick charmer,' all day and when someone says to me, 'Where jer

father get his accent?' I'll say, 'It was a whole way of life.'
But remember, you're not a prisoner or anything, around
here. You can go whenever you don't like the food. I mean,
if you don't like it, don't come to me and say, 'I don't like
the food.' You're not my prisoner," she yelled, though her
face was only a few inches from mine. "You're only my
father. That's all you are."

E. M. FORSTER

◇ ◇ ◇

The Road from Colonus

For no very intelligible reason, Mr. Lucas had hurried ahead of his party. He was perhaps reaching the age at which independence becomes valuable, because it is so soon to be lost. Tired of attention and consideration, he liked breaking away from the younger members, to ride by himself, and to dismount unassisted. Perhaps he also relished that more subtle pleasure of being kept waiting for lunch, and of telling the others on their arrival that it was of no consequence.

So, with childish impatience, he battered the animal's sides with his heels, and made the muleteer bang it with a thick stick and prick it with a sharp one, and jolted down the hill sides through clumps of flowering shrubs and stretches of anemones and asphodel, till he heard the sound of running water, and came in sight of the group of plane trees where they were to have their meal.

Even in England those trees would have been remarkable, so huge were they, so interlaced, so magnificently clothed in quivering green. And here in Greece they were unique, the one cool spot in that hard brilliant landscape, already scorched by the heat of an April sun. In their midst was hidden a tiny Khan or country inn, a frail mud building with a broad wooden balcony in which sat an old woman spinning, while a small brown pig, eating orange peel, stood beside her. On the wet earth below squatted two children, playing some primeval game with their fingers; and their mother, none too clean either, was messing with some rice inside. As Mrs. Forman would have said, it was all very Greek, and the fastidious Mr. Lucas felt thankful that they were bringing their own food with them, and should eat it in the open air.

Still, he was glad to be there—the muleteer had helped him off—and glad that Mrs. Forman was not there to forestall his opinions—glad even that he should not see Ethel for quite half an hour. Ethel was his youngest daughter, still unmarried. She was unselfish and affectionate, and it was generally understood that she was to devote her life to her father, and be the comfort of his old age. Mrs. Forman always referred to her as Antigone, and Mr. Lucas tried to settle down to the role of Oedipus, which seemed the only one that public opinion allowed him.

He had this in common with Oedipus, that he was growing old. Even to himself it had become obvious. He had lost interest in other people's affairs, and seldom attended when they spoke to him. He was fond of talking himself but often forgot what he was going to say, and even when he succeeded, it seldom seemed worth the effort. His phrases and gestures had become stiff and set, his anecdotes, once so successful, fell flat, his silence was as meaningless as his speech. Yet he had led a healthy, active life, had worked steadily, made money, educated his children. There was nothing and no one to blame: he was simply growing old.

At the present moment, here he was in Greece, and one of the dreams of his life was realized. Forty years ago he had caught the fever of Hellenism, and all his life he had felt that could he but visit that land, he would not have lived in vain. But Athens had been dusty, Delphi wet, Thermopylae flat, and he had listened with amazement and cynicism to the rapturous exclamations of his companions. Greece was like England: it was a man who was growing old, and it made no difference whether that man looked at the Thames or the Eurotas. It was his last hope of contradicting that logic of experience, and it was failing.

Yet Greece had done something for him, though he did not know it. It had made him discontented, and there are stirrings of life in discontent. He knew that he was not the victim of continual ill-luck. Something great was wrong, and he was pitted against no mediocre or accidental enemy. For the last month a strange desire had possessed him to die fighting.

"Greece is the land for young people," he said to himself as he stood under the plane trees, "but I will enter into it, I will possess it. Leaves shall be green again, water shall be sweet, the sky shall be blue. They were so forty years ago, and I will win them back. I do mind being old, and I will pretend no longer."

He took two steps forward, and immediately cold waters were gurgling over his ankle.

"Where does the water come from?" he asked himself. "I do not even know that." He remembered that all the hill sides were dry; yet here the road was suddenly covered with flowing streams.

He stopped still in amazement, saying: "Water out of a tree—out of a hollow tree? I never saw nor thought of that before."

For the enormous plane that leant towards the Khan was hollow—it had been burnt out for charcoal—and from its living trunk there gushed an impetuous spring, coating the bark with fern and moss, and flowing over the mule track to create fertile meadows beyond. The simple country folk had paid to beauty and mystery such tribute as they could, for in the rind of the tree a shrine was cut, holding a lamp and a little picture of the Virgin, inheritor of the Naiad's and Dryad's joint abode.

"I never saw anything so marvelous before," said Mr.

Lucas. "I could even step inside the trunk and see where the water comes from."

For a moment he hesitated to violate the shrine. Then he remembered with a smile his own thought—"the place shall be mine; I will enter it and possess it"—and leapt almost aggressively on to a stone within.

The water pressed up steadily and noiselessly from the hollow roots and hidden crevices of the plane, forming a wonderful amber pool ere it spilt over the lip of bark on to the earth outside. Mr. Lucas tasted it and it was sweet, and when he looked up the black funnel of the trunk he saw sky which was blue, and some leaves which were green; and he remembered, without smiling, another of his thoughts.

Others had been before him—indeed he had a curious sense of companionship. Little votive offerings to the presiding Power were fastened on to the bark—tiny arms and legs and eyes in tin, grotesque models of the brain or the heart—all tokens of some recovery of strength or wisdom or love. There was no such thing as the solitude of nature, for the sorrows and joys of humanity had pressed even into the bosom of a tree. He spread out his arms and steadied himself against the soft charred wood, and then slowly leant back, till his body was resting on the trunk behind. His eyes closed, and he had the strange feeling of one who is moving, yet at peace—the feeling of the swimmer, who, after long struggling with chopping seas, finds that after all the tide will sweep him to his goal.

So he lay motionless, conscious only of the stream below his feet, and that all things were a stream, in which he was moving.

He was aroused at last by a shock—the shock of an arrival perhaps, for when he opened his eyes, something unimagined, indefinable, had passed over all things, and made them intelligible and good.

There was meaning in the stoop of the old woman over her work, and in the quick motions of the little pig, and in her diminishing globe of wool. A young man came singing over the streams on a mule, and there was beauty in his pose and sincerity in his greeting. The sun made no accidental patterns upon the spreading roots of the trees, and there was intention in the nodding clumps of asphodel, and in the music of the water. To Mr. Lucas, who, in a brief space of time, had discovered not only Greece, but England and all the world and life, there seemed nothing ludicrous in the desire to hang within the tree another votive offering—a little model of an entire man.

"Why, here's papa, playing at being Merlin."

All unnoticed they had arrived—Ethel, Mrs. Forman, Mr. Graham, and the English-speaking dragoman. Mr. Lucas peered out at them suspiciously. They had suddenly become unfamiliar, and all that they did seemed strained and coarse.

"Allow me to give you a hand," said Mr. Graham, a young man who was always polite to his elders.

Mr. Lucas felt annoyed. "Thank you, I can manage perfectly well by myself," he replied. His foot slipped as he stepped out of the tree, and went into the spring.

"Oh papa, my papa!" said Ethel, "what are you doing? Thank goodness I have got a change for you on the mule."

She tended him carefully, giving him clean socks and dry boots, and then sat him down on the rug beside the lunch basket, while she went with the others to explore the grove.

They came back in ecstasies, in which Mr. Lucas tried to join. But he found them intolerable. Their enthusiasm was superficial, commonplace, and spasmodic. They had no perception of the coherent beauty that was flowering around them. He tried at least to explain his feelings, and what he said was:

"I am altogether pleased with the appearance of this place. It impresses me very favorably. The trees are fine, remarkably fine for Greece, and there is something very poetic in the spring of clear running water. The people too seem kindly and civil. It is decidedly an attractive place."

Mrs. Forman upbraided him for his tepid praise.

"Oh, it is a place in a thousand!" she cried. "I could live

and die here! I really would stop if I had not to be back at Athens! It reminds me of the Colonus of Sophocles."

"Well, *I* must stop," said Ethel. "I positively must."

"Yes, do! You and your father! Antigone and Oedipus. Of course you must stop at Colonus!"

Mr. Lucas was almost breathless with excitement. When he stood within the tree, he had believed that his happiness would be independent of locality. But these few minutes' conversation had undeceived him. He no longer trusted himself to journey through the world, for old thoughts, old wearinesses might be waiting to rejoin him as soon as he left the shade of the planes, and the music of the virgin water. To sleep in the Khan with the gracious, kind-eyed country people, to watch the bats flit about within the globe of shade, and see the moon turn the golden patterns into silver—one such night would place him beyond relapse, and confirm him for ever in the kingdom he had regained. But all his lips could say was: "I should be willing to put in a night here."

"You mean a week, papa! It would be sacrilege to put in less."

"A week then, a week," said his lips, irritated at being corrected, while his heart was leaping with joy. All through lunch he spoke to them no more, but watched the place he should know so well, and the people who would so soon be his companions and friends. The inmates of the Khan only consisted of an old woman, a middle-aged woman, a young man and two children, and to none of them had he spoken, yet he loved them as he loved everything that moved or breathed or existed beneath the benedictory shade of the planes.

"*En route!*" said the shrill voice of Mrs. Forman. "Ethel! Mr. Graham! The best of things must end."

"Tonight," thought Mr. Lucas, "they will light the little lamp by the shrine. And when we all sit together on the balcony, perhaps they will tell me which offerings they put up."

"I beg your pardon, Mr. Lucas," said Graham, "but they want to fold up the rug you are sitting on."

Mr. Lucas got up, saying to himself: "Ethel shall go to bed first, and then I will try to tell them about my offering too—for it is a thing I must do. I think they will understand if I am left with them alone."

Ethel touched him on the cheek. "Papa! I've called you three times. All the mules are here."

"Mules? What mules?"

"Our mules. We're all waiting. Oh, Mr. Graham, do help my father on."

"I don't know what you're talking about, Ethel."

"My dearest papa, we must start. You know we have to get to Olympia tonight."

Mr. Lucas in pompous, confident tones replied: "I always did wish, Ethel, that you had a better head for plans. You know perfectly well that we are putting in a week here. It is your own suggestion."

Ethel was startled into impoliteness. "What a perfectly ridiculous idea. You must have known I was joking. Of course I meant I wished we could."

"Ah! If we could only do what we wished!" sighed Mrs. Forman, already seated on her mule.

"Surely," Ethel continued in calmer tones, "you didn't think I meant it."

"Most certainly I did. I have made all my plans on the supposition that we are stopping here, and it will be extremely inconvenient, indeed, impossible for me to start."

He delivered this remark with an air of great conviction, and Mrs. Forman and Mr. Graham had to turn away to hide their smiles.

"I am sorry I spoke so carelessly; it was wrong of me. But, you know, we can't break up our party, and even one night here would make us miss the boat at Patras."

Mrs. Forman, in an aside, called Mr. Graham's attention to the excellent way in which Ethel managed her father.

"I don't mind about the Patras boat. You said that we should stop here, and we are stopping."

It seemed as if the inhabitants of the Khan had divined in some mysterious way that the altercation touched them. The old woman stopped her spinning, while the young man and the two children stood behind Mr. Lucas, as if supporting him.

Neither arguments nor entreaties moved him. He said little, but he was absolutely determined, because for the first time he saw his daily life aright. What need had he to return to England? Who would miss him? His friends were dead or cold. Ethel loved him in a way, but, as was right, she had other interests. His other children he seldom saw. He had only one other relative, his sister Julia, whom he both feared and hated. It was no effort to struggle. He would be a fool as well as a coward if he stirred from the place which brought him happiness and peace.

At last Ethel, to humor him, and not disinclined to air her modern Greek, went into the Khan with the astonished dragoman to look at the rooms. The woman inside received them with loud welcomes, and the young man, when no one was looking, began to lead Mr. Lucas' mule to the stable.

"Drop it, you brigand!" shouted Graham, who always declared that foreigners could understand English if they chose. He was right, for the man obeyed, and they all stood waiting for Ethel's return.

She emerged at last, with close-gathered skirts, followed by the dragoman bearing the little pig, which he had bought at a bargain.

"My dear papa, I will do all I can for you, but stop in that Khan—no."

"Are there—*fleas*?" asked Mrs. Forman.

Ethel intimated that "fleas" was not the word.

"Well, I am afraid that settles it," said Mrs. Forman, "I know how particular Mr. Lucas is."

"It does not settle it," said Mr. Lucas. "Ethel, you go on. I do not want you. I don't know why I ever consulted you. I shall stop here alone."

"That is absolute nonsense," said Ethel, losing her temper. "How can you be left alone at your age? How would you get your meals or your bath? All your letters are waiting for you at Patras. You'll miss the boat. That means missing the London operas, and upsetting all your engagements for the month. And as if you could travel by yourself!"

"They might knife you," was Mr. Graham's contribution.

The Greeks said nothing; but whenever Mr. Lucas looked their way, they beckoned him towards the Khan. The children would even have drawn him by the coat, and the old woman on the balcony stopped her almost completed spinning, and fixed him with mysterious appealing eyes. As he fought, the issue assumed gigantic proportions, and he believed that he was not merely stopping because he had regained youth or seen beauty or found happiness, but because in that place and with those people a supreme event was awaiting him which would transfigure the face of the world. The moment was so tremendous that he abandoned words and arguments as useless, and rested on the strength of his mighty unrevealed allies: silent men, murmuring water, and whispering trees. For the whole place called with one voice, articulate to him, and his garrulous opponents became every minute more meaningless and absurd. Soon they would be tired and go chattering away into the sun, leaving him to the cool grove and the moonlight and the destiny he foresaw.

Mrs. Forman and the dragoman had indeed already started, amid the piercing screams of the little pig, and the struggle might have gone on indefinitely if Ethel had not called in Mr. Graham.

"Can you help me?" she whispered. "He is absolutely unmanageable."

"I'm no good at arguing—but if I could help you in any other way—" and he looked down complacently at his well-made figure.

Ethel hesitated. Then she said: "Help me in any way you can. After all, it is for his good that we do it."

"Then have his mule led up behind him."

So when Mr. Lucas thought he had gained the day, he suddenly felt himself lifted off the ground, and sat sideways on the saddle, and at the same time the mule started off at a trot. He said nothing, for he had nothing to say, and even his face showed little emotion as he felt the shade pass and heard the sound of the water cease. Mr. Graham was running at his side, hat in hand, apologizing.

"I know I had no business to do it, and I do beg your pardon awfully. But I do hope that some day you too will feel that I was—damn!"

A stone had caught him in the middle of the back. It was thrown by the little boy, who was pursuing them along the mule track. He was followed by his sister, also throwing stones.

Ethel screamed to the dragoman, who was some way ahead with Mrs. Forman, but before he could rejoin them, another adversary appeared. It was the young Greek, who had cut them off in front, and now dashed down at Mr. Lucas' bridle. Fortunately Graham was an expert boxer, and it did not take him a moment to beat down the youth's feeble defence, and to send him sprawling with a bleeding mouth into the asphodel. By this time the dragoman had arrived, the children, alarmed at the fate of their brother, had desisted, and the rescue party, if such it is to be considered, retired in disorder to the trees.

"Little devils!" said Graham, laughing with triumph. "That's the modern Greek all over. Your father meant money if he stopped, and they consider we were taking it out of their pocket."

"Oh, they are terrible—simple savages! I don't know how I shall ever thank you. You've saved my father."

"I only hope you didn't think me brutal."

"No," replied Ethel with a little sigh. "I admire strength."

Meanwhile the cavalcade reformed, and Mr. Lucas, who, as Mrs. Forman said, bore his disappointment wonderfully well, was put comfortably on to his mule. They hurried up the opposite hillside, fearful of another attack, and it was not until they had left the eventful place far behind that Ethel found an opportunity to speak to her father and ask his pardon for the way she had treated him.

"You seemed so different, dear father, and you quite frightened me. Now I feel that you are your old self again."

He did not answer, and she concluded that he was not unnaturally offended at her behavior.

By one of those curious tricks of mountain scenery, the place they had left an hour before suddenly reappeared far below them. The Khan was hidden under the green dome, but in the open there still stood three figures, and through the pure air rose up a faint cry of defiance or farewell.

Mr. Lucas stopped irresolutely, and let the reins fall from his hand.

"Come, father dear," said Ethel gently.

He obeyed, and in another moment a spur of the hill hid the dangerous scene forever.

II

It was breakfast time, but the gas was alight, owing to the fog. Mr. Lucas was in the middle of an account of a bad night he had spent. Ethel, who was to be married in a few weeks, had her arms on the table, listening.

"First the doorbell rang, then you came back from the theater. Then the dog started, and after the dog the cat. And at three in the morning a young hooligan passed by singing. Oh yes: then there was the water gurgling in the pipe above my head."

"I think that was only the bath water running away," said Ethel, looking rather worn.

"Well, there's nothing I dislike more than running water. It's perfectly impossible to sleep in the house. I shall give it up. I shall give notice next quarter. I shall tell the landlord plainly, 'The reason I am giving up the house is this: it is perfectly impossible to sleep in it.' If he says—says—well, what has he got to say?"

"Some more toast, father?"

"Thank you, my dear." He took it, and there was an interval of peace.

But he soon recommenced. "I'm not going to submit to the practicing next door as tamely as they think. I wrote and told them so—didn't I?"

"Yes," said Ethel, who had taken care that the letter should not reach. "I have seen the governess, and she has promised to arrange it differently. And Aunt Julia hates noise. It will sure to be all right."

Her aunt, being the only unattached member of the family, was coming to keep house for her father when she left him. The reference was not a happy one, and Mr. Lucas commenced a series of half articulate sighs, which was only stopped by the arrival of the post.

"Oh, what a parcel!" cried Ethel. "For me! What can it be! Greek stamps. This is most exciting!"

It proved to be some asphodel bulbs, sent by Mrs. Forman from Athens for planting in the conservatory.

"Doesn't it bring it all back! You remember the asphodels, father. And all wrapped up in Greek newspapers. I wonder if I can read them still. I used to be able to, you know."

She rattled on, hoping to conceal the laughter of the children next door—a favorite source of querulousness at breakfast time.

"Listen to me! 'A rural disaster.' Oh, I've hit on something sad. But never mind. 'Last Tuesday at Plataniste, in the province of Messenia, a shocking tragedy occurred. A large tree'—aren't I getting on well?—'blew down in the night and'—wait a minute—oh, dear! 'crushed to death the five occupants of the little Khan there, who had apparently been sitting in the balcony. The bodies of Maria Rhomaides, the aged proprietress, and of her daughter, aged forty-six, were easily recognizable, whereas that of her grandson'—oh, the rest is really too horrid; I wish I had never tried it, and what's more I feel to have heard the name Plataniste before. We didn't stop there, did we, in the spring?"

"We had lunch," said Mr. Lucas, with a faint expression of trouble on his vacant face. "Perhaps it was where the dragoman bought the pig."

"Of course," said Ethel in a nervous voice. "Where the dragoman bought the little pig. How terrible!"

"Very terrible!" said her father, whose attention was wandering to the noisy children next door. Ethel suddenly started to her feet with genuine interest.

"Good gracious!" she exclaimed. "This is an old paper. It happened not lately but in April—the night of Tuesday the eighteenth—and we—we must have been there in the afternoon."

"So we were," said Mr. Lucas. She put her hand to her heart, scarcely able to speak.

"Father, dear father, I must say it: you wanted to stop there. All those people, those poor half-savage people, tried to keep you, and they're dead. The whole place, it says, is in ruins, and even the stream has changed its course. Father, dear, if it had not been for me, and if Arthur had not helped me, you must have been killed."

Mr. Lucas waved his hand irritably. "It is not a bit of good speaking to the governess, I shall write to the landlord and say, 'The reason I am giving up the house is this: the dog barks, the children next door are intolerable, and I cannot stand the noise of running water.' "

Ethel did not check his babbling. She was aghast at the narrowness of the escape, and for a long time kept silence. At last she said: "Such a marvelous deliverance does make one believe in Providence."

Mr. Lucas, who was still composing his letter to the landlord, did not reply.

MURIEL SPARK

◇ ◇ ◇

The Fathers' Daughters

She left the old man in his deck-chair on the front, having first adjusted the umbrella awning with her own hand, and with her own hand, put his panama hat at a comfortable angle. The beach attendant had been sulky, but she didn't see why one should lay out tips only for adjusting an umbrella and a panama hat. Since the introduction of the new franc it was impossible to tip less than a franc. There seemed to be a conspiracy all along the coast to hide the lesser coins from the visitors, and one could only find franc pieces in one's purse, and one had to be careful not to embarrass Father, and one . . .

She hurried along the Rue Paradis, keeping in the hot shade, among all the old, old smells of Nice, not only garlic wafting from the cafés, and of the hot invisible air itself, but the smells from her memory, from thirty-five summers at Nice in apartments of long ago, Father's summer salon, Father's friends' children, Father's friends, writers, young artists dating back five years at Nice, six, nine years; and then, before the war, twenty years ago—when we were at Nice, do you remember, Father? Do you remember the pension on the Boulevard Victor Hugo when we were rather poor? Do you remember the Americans at the Negresco in 1937—how changed, how demure they are now! Do you remember, Father, how in the old days we disliked the thick carpets—at least, you disliked them, and what you dislike, I dislike, isn't it so, Father?

Yes, Dora, we don't care for luxury. Comfort, yes, but luxury, no.

I doubt if we can afford to stay at a hotel on the front this year, Father.

What's that? What's that you say?

I said I doubt if we ought to stay on the front this year, Father; the Promenade des Anglais is becoming very trippery. Remember you disliked the thick carpets. . . .

Yes, yes, of course.

Of course, and so we'll go, I suggest, to a little place I've found on the Boulevard Gambetta, and if we don't like that there's a very good place on the Boulevard Victor Hugo. Within our means, Father, modest and . . .

What's that you say?

I said it wasn't a vulgar place, Father.

Ah. No.

And so I'll just drop them a note and book a couple of bedrooms. They may be small, but the food . . .

Facing the sea, Dora.

They are all very vulgar places facing the sea, Father. Very distracting. No peace at all. Times have changed, you know.

Ah. Well, I leave it to you, dear. Tell them I desire a large room, suitable for entertaining. Spare no expense, Dora.

Oh, of course not, Father.

And I hope to God we've won the lottery, she thought, as she hurried up the little street to the lottery kiosk. Someone's got to win it out of the whole of France. The dark-skinned blonde at the lottery kiosk took an interest in Dora, who came so regularly each morning rather than buy a newspaper to see the results. She leaned over the ticket, holding her card of numbers, comparing it with Dora's ticket, with an expression of earnest sympathy.

"No luck," Dora said.

"Try again tomorrow," said the woman. "One never knows. Life is a lottery . . ."

Dora smiled as one who must either smile or weep. On her way back to the sea front she thought, tomorrow I will buy five hundred francs' worth. Then she thought, no, no, I'd better not, I may run short of francs and have to take Father home before time. Dora, the food here is inferior.—I know, Father, but it's the same everywhere in France now, times have changed.—I think we should move to another hotel, Dora.—The others are all very expensive, Father. —What's that? What's that you say?—There are no other rooms available. Father, because of the tourists, these days.

The brown legs of lovely young men and girls passed her as she approached the sea. I ought to appreciate every minute of this, she thought, it may be the last time. This thoroughly blue sea, these brown limbs, these white teeth and innocent inane tongues, these palm trees—all this is what we are paying for.

"Everything all right, Father?"

"Where have you been, dear?"

"Only for a walk round the back streets to smell the savors."

"Dora, you are a chip off the old block. What did you see?"

"Brown limbs, white teeth, men in shirt sleeves behind café windows, playing cards with green bottles in front of them."

"Good—you see everything with my eyes, Dora."

"Heat, smell, brown legs—it's what we are paying for, Father."

"Dora, you are becoming vulgar, if you don't mind my saying so. The eye of the true artist doesn't see life in the way of goods paid for. The world is ours. It is our birthright. We take it without payment."

"I'm not an artist like you, Father. Let me move the umbrella—you mustn't get too much sun."

"Times have changed," he said, glancing along the pebble beach, "the young men today have no interest in life."

She knew what her father meant. All along the beach, the young men playing with the air, girls, the sun; they were coming in from the sea, shaking the water from their heads; they were walking over the pebbles, then splashing into the water; they were taking an interest in their environment with every pore of their skin, as Father would have said in younger days when he was writing his books. What he meant, now, when he said, "the young men today have no interest in life" was that his young disciples, his admirers, had all gone, they were grown old and preoccupied, and had not been replaced. The last young man to seek out Father had been a bloodless-looking youth—not that one judged by appearances—who had called about seven years ago at their house in Essex. Father had made the most of him, giving up many of his mornings to sitting in the library talking about books with the young man, about life and the old days. But this, the last of Father's disciples, had left after two weeks with a promise to send them the article he was going to write about Father and his works. Indeed he had sent a letter: "Dear Henry Castlemaine,—Words cannot express my admiration . . ." After that they had heard no more. Dora was not really sorry. He was a poor specimen compared with the men who, in earlier days, used to visit Father. Dora in her late teens could have married one of three or four vigorous members of the Henry Castlemaine set, but she had not done so because of her widowed father and his needs as a public figure; and now she sometimes felt it would have served Father better if she had married, because of Father—one could have contributed from a husband's income, perhaps, to his declining years.

Dora said, "We must be going back to the hotel for lunch."

"Let us lunch somewhere else. The food there is . . ."

She helped her father from the deck-chair and, turning to the sea, took a grateful breath of the warm blue breeze. A young man, coming up from the sea, shook his head blindly and splashed her with water; then noticing what he done he said—turning and catching her by the arm—"Oh, I'm so sorry." He spoke in English, was an Englishman, and she knew already how unmistakably she was an Englishwoman. "All right," she said, with a quick little laugh. The father was fumbling with his stick, the incident had passed, was immediately forgotten by Dora as she took his arm and propelled him across the wide hot boulevard where the white-suited policemen held up the impetuous traffic. "How would you like to be arrested by one of those, Dora?" He gave his deep short laugh and looked down at her. "I'd love it, Father." Perhaps he wouldn't insist on lunching elsewhere. If only they could reach the hotel, it would be all right; Father would be too exhausted to insist. But already he was saying, "Let's find somewhere for lunch."

"Well, we've paid for it at the hotel, Father."

"Don't be vulgar, my love."

In the following March, when Dora met Ben Donadieu for the first time, she had the feeling she had seen him somewhere before, she knew not where. Later, she told him of this, but he could not recall having seen her. But this sense of having seen him somewhere remained with Dora all her life. She came to believe she had met him in a former existence. In fact, it was on the beach at Nice that she had seen him, when he came up among the pebbles from the sea, and shook his hair, wetting her, and took her arm, apologizing.

"Don't be vulgar, my love. The hotel food is appalling. Not French at all."

"It's the same all over France, Father, these days."

"There used to be a restaurant—what was its name?—in one of those little streets behind the Casino. Let's go there. All the writers go there."

"Not any more, Father."

"Well, so much the better. Let's go there in any case. What's the name of the place?—Anyway, come on, I could go there blindfold. All the writers used to go . . ."

She laughed, because, after all, he was sweet. As she walked with him towards the Casino she did not say—Not any more, Father, do the writers go there. The writers don't come to Nice, not those of moderate means. But there's one writer here this year, Father, called Kenneth Hope, whom you haven't heard about. He uses our beach, and I've seen him once—a shy, thin, middle-aged man. But he won't speak to anyone. He writes wonderfully, Father. I've read his novels, they open windows in the mind that have been bricked-up for a hundred years. I have read *The Inventors,* which made great fame and fortune for him. it is about the inventors of patent gadgets, what lives they lead, how their minds apply themselves to invention and to love, and you would think, while you were reading *The Inventors,* that the place they live in was dominated by inventors. He has that magic, Father—he can make you believe anything. Dora did not say this, for her father had done great work too, and deserved a revival. His name was revered, his books were not greatly spoken of, they were not read. He would not understand the fame of Kenneth Hope. Father's novels were about the individual consciences of men and women, no one could do the individual conscience like Father. "Here we are, Father—this is the place, isn't it?"

"No, Dora, it's further along."

"Oh, but that's the Trumbril; it's wildly expensive."

"Really, darling!"

She decided to plead the heat, and to order only a slice of melon for lunch with a glass of her father's wine. Both tall and slim, they entered the restaurant. Her hair was drawn back, the bones of her face were good, her eyes were small and fixed ready for humor, for she had decided to be a spinster and do it properly; she looked forty-six and she did not look forty-six; her skin was dry; her mouth was thin, and was growing thinner with the worry about money. The father looked eighty years old, as he was. Thirty years ago people used to turn round and say, as he passed, "That's Henry Castlemaine."

Ben lay on his stomach on his mattress on the beach enclosure. Carmelita Hope lay on her mattress, next to him. They were eating rolls and cheese and drinking white wine which the beach attendant had brought to them from the café. Carmelita's tan was like a perfect garment, drawn skintight over her body. Since leaving school she had been in numerous jobs behind the scenes of film and television studios. Now she was out of a job again. She thought of marrying Ben, he was so entirely different from all the other men of her acquaintance, he was joyful and he was serious. He was also good-looking: he was half-French, brought up in England. And an interesting age, thirty-one. He was a school teacher, but Father could probably get him a job in advertising or publishing. Father could do a lot of things for them both if only he would exert himself. Perhaps if she got married he would exert himself.

"Did you see your father at all yesterday, Carmelita?"

"No; as a matter of fact he's driven up the coast. I think he's gone to stay at some villa on the Italian border."

"I should like to see more of him," said Ben. "And have a talk with him. I've never really had a chance to have a talk with him."

"He's awfully shy," said Carmelita, "with my friends."

Sometimes she felt a stab of dissatisfaction when Ben talked about her father. Ben had read all his books through and through—that seemed rather obsessive to Carmelita, reading books a second time and a third, as if one's memory was defective. It seemed to her that Ben loved her only because she was Kenneth Hope's daughter, and then, again, it seemed to her that this couldn't be so, for Ben wasn't attracted by money and success. Carmelita knew lots of daughters of famous men, and they were beset by suitors who were keen on their fathers' money and success. But it was the books that Ben liked about her father.

"He never interferes with me," she said. "He's rather good that way."

"I would like to have a long talk with him," Ben said.

"What about?—He doesn't like talking about his work."

"No, but a man like that. I would like to know his mind."

"What about my mind?"

"You've got a lovely mind. Full of pleasant laziness. No guile." He drew his forefinger from her knee to her ankle. She was wearing a pink bikini. She was very pretty and had hoped to become a starlet before her eighteenth birthday. Now she was very close to twenty-one and was thinking of marrying Ben instead, and was relieved that she no longer wanted to be an actress. He had lasted longer than any other boy-friend. She had often found a boy exciting at first but usually went off him quite soon. Ben was an intellectual, and intellectuals, say what you like, seemed to last longer than anyone else. There was more in them to find out about. One was always discovering new things—she supposed it was Father's blood in her that drew her towards the cultivated type, like Ben.

He was staying at a tiny hotel in a back street near the old quay. The entrance was dark, but the room itself was right at the top of the house, with a little balcony. Carmelita was staying with friends at a villa. She spent a lot of time in Ben's room, and sometimes slept there. It was turning out to be a remarkably happy summer.

"You won't see much of Father," she said, "if we get married. He works and sees nobody. When he doesn't write he goes away. Perhaps he'll get married again and—"

"That's all right," he said, "I don't want to marry your father."

Dora Castlemaine had several diplomas for elocution which she had never put to use. She got a part-time job, after the Christmas holidays that year, in Basil Street Grammar School in London, and her job was to try to reform the more pronounced Cockney accents of the more promising boys into a near-standard English. Her father was amazed.

"Money, money, you are always talking about money. Let us run up debts. One is nobody without debts."

"One's credit is limited, Father. Don't be an old goose."

"Have you consulted Waite?" Waite was the publisher's young man who looked after the Castlemaine royalties, diminishing year by year.

"We've drawn more than our due for the present."

"Well, it's a bore, you going out to teach."

"It may be a bore for you," she said at last, "but it isn't for me."

"Dora, do you really mean you want to go to this job in London?"

"Yes, I want to. I'm looking forward to it."

He didn't believe her. But he said, "I suppose I'm a bit of a burden on you, Dora, these days. Perhaps I ought to go off and die."

"Like Oates at the South Pole," Dora commented.

He looked at her and she looked at him. They were shrewd in their love for each other.

She was the only woman teacher in the school, with hardly the status of a teacher. She had her own corner of the common room and, anxious to reassure the men that she had no intention of intruding upon them, would, during free periods, spread out on the table one of the weekly journals and study it intently, only looking up to say good morning or good afternoon to the masters who came in with piles of exercise books under their arms. Dora had no exercise books to correct, she was something apart, a reformer of vowel sounds. One of the masters, and then another, made conversation with her during morning break, when she passed round the sugar for the coffee. Some were in their early thirties. The ginger-moustached science master was not long graduated from Cambridge. Nobody said to her, as intelligent young men had done as late as fifteen years ago, "Are you any relation, Miss Castlemaine, to Henry Castlemaine the writer?"

Ben walked with Carmelita under the trees of Lincoln's Inn Fields in the spring of the year, after school, and watched the children at their games. They were a beautiful couple. Carmelita was doing secretarial work in the City. Her father was in Morocco, having first taken them out to dinner to celebrate their engagement.

Ben said, "There's a woman at the school, teaching elocution."

"Oh?" said Carmelita. She was jumpy, because since her father's departure for Morocco Ben had given a new turn to their relationship. He would not let her stay overnight in his flat in Bayswater, not even at the week-ends. He said it would be nice, perhaps, to practice restraint until they were married in the summer, and that would give them something to look forward to. "And I'm interested to see," said Ben, "what we mean to each other without sex."

This made her understand how greatly she had become obsessed with him. She thought perhaps he was practicing a form of cruelty to intensify her obsession. In fact, he did want to see what they meant to each other without sex.

She called at his flat unexpectedly and found him reading, with piles of other books set out on the table as if waiting to be read.

She accused him: You only want to get rid of me so that you can read your books.

"The fourth form is reading Trollope," he explained, pointing to a novel of Trollope's among the pile.

"But you aren't studying Trollope just now."

He had been reading a life of James Joyce. He banged it down and said, "I've been reading all my life, and you won't stop me, Carmelita."

She sat down. "I don't want to stop you," she said.

"I know," he said.

"We aren't getting on at all well without sex," she said, and on that occasion stayed the night.

He was writing an essay on her father. She wished that her father had taken more interest in it. Father had taken them out to dinner with his party face, smiling and boyish. Carmelita had seen him otherwise—in his acute dejection, when he seemed hardly able to endure the light of day.

"What's the matter, Father?"

"There's a comedy of errors going on inside me, Carmelita." He sat at his desk most of the day while he was in these moods, doing nothing. Then, during the night, he would perhaps start writing, and sleep all the next morning, and gradually in the following days the weight would pass.

"There's a man on the phone wants you, Father—an interview."

"Tell him I'm in the Middle East."

"What did you think of Ben, Father?"

"A terribly nice man, Carmelita. You've made the right choice, I think."

"An intellectual—I do like them best, you know."

"I'd say he was the student type. Always will be."

"He wants to write an essay about you, Father. He's absolutely mad about your books."

"Yes."

"I mean, couldn't you help him, Father? Couldn't you talk to him about your work, you know?"

"Oh, God, Carmelita. It would be easier to write the bloody essay myself."

"All right, all right. I was only asking."

"I don't want any disciples, Carmelita. They give me the creeps."

"Yes, yes, all right. I know you're an artist, Father, there's no need to show off your temperament. I only wanted you to help Ben. I only . . ."

I only, she thought as she walked in Lincoln's Inn Fields with Ben, wanted him to help me. I should have said, "I want you to talk more to Ben, to help me." And Father would have said, "How do you mean?" And I would have said, "I don't know, quite." And he would have said, "Well, if you don't know what you mean, how the hell do I?"

Ben was saying, "There's a woman at the school, teaching elocution."

"Oh?" said Carmelita jumpily.

"A Miss Castlemaine. She's been there four months, and I only found out today that she's the daughter of Henry Castlemaine."

"But he's dead!" said Carmelita.

"Well, I thought so too. But apparently he isn't dead, he's very much alive in a house in Essex."

"How old is Miss Castlemaine?" said Carmelita.

"Middle-aged. Middle forties. Perhaps late forties. She's a nice woman, a classic English spinster. She teaches the boys to say 'How now brown cow.' You could imagine her doing wood-engravings in the Cotswolds. I only found out today—"

"You might manage to get invited to meet him, with any luck," Carmelita said.

"Yes, she said I must come and see him, perhaps for a week-end. Miss Castlemaine is going to arrange it. She was awfully friendly when she found I was a Castlemaine admirer. A lot of people must think he's dead. Of course, his work belongs to a past world, but it's wonderful. Do you know *The Pebbled Shore?*—that's an early one."

"No, but I've read *Sin of Substance,* I think. It—"

"You mean *The Sinner and the Substance.* Oh, it has fine things in it. Castlemaine's due for a revival."

Carmelita felt a sharp stab of anger with her father, and then a kind of despair which was not as yet entirely familiar to her, although already she wondered if this was how Father felt in his great depressions when he sat all day, staring and enduring, and all night miraculously wrote the ache out of his system in prose of harsh merriment.

Helplessly, she said, "Castlemaine's novels aren't as good as Father's, are they?"

"Oh, there's no comparison. Castlemaine is quite different. You can't say one type is *better* than another—goodness me!" He was looking academically towards the chimney stacks of Lincoln's Inn. This was the look in which she loved him most. After all, she thought, the Castlemaines might make everything easier for both of us.

"Father, it's really absurd. A difference of sixteen years. . . . People will say—"

"Don't be vulgar, Dora dear. What does it matter what people say? Mere age makes no difference when there's a true affinity, a marriage of true minds."

"Ben and I have a lot in common."

"I know it," he said, and sat a little higher in his chair.

"I shall be able to give up my job, Father, and spend my time here with you again. I never really wanted that job. And you are so much better in health now . . ."

"I know."

"And Ben will be here in the evenings and the weekends. You get on well with Ben, don't you?"

"A remarkably fine man, Dora. He'll go far. He's perceptive."

"He's keen to revive your work."

"I know. He should give up that job, as I told him, and devote himself entirely to literary studies. A born essayist."

"Oh, Father, he'll have to keep his job for the meantime, anyhow. We'll need the money. It will help us all; we—"

"What's that? What's that you say?"

"I said he finds work in the grammar school stimulating, Father."

"Do you love the man?"

"It's a little difficult to say, at my age, Father."

"To me, you both seem children. Do you love him?"

"I feel," she said, "that I have known him much longer than I have. Sometimes I think I've known him all my life.

I'm sure we have met before, perhaps even in a former existence. That's the decisive factor. There's something of *destiny* about my marrying Ben; do you know what I mean?"

"Yes, I think I do."

"He was engaged, last year for a short time, to marry quite a young girl," she said. "The daughter of a novelist called Kenneth Hope. Have you heard of him, Father?"

"Vaguely," he said. "Ben," he said, "is a born disciple."

She looked at him and he looked at her, shrewd in their love for each other.

◇ ◇ ◇

About the Authors

The stories of **Alice Adams** (b. 1926) have appeared in the *Atlantic Monthly, The New Yorker,* and *The Paris Review,* and many of them have been selected for O. Henry Awards. She has published five collections of stories, *Beautiful Girl* (1979), *To See You Again* (1982), *You Can't Keep a Good Woman Down* (1981), *Return Trips* (1985), and *After You're Gone* (1989) as well as six novels, including, most recently, *Superior Women* (1984) and *Second Chances* (1988).

S. Y. Agnon (1888–1970), Israeli novelist and short-story writer, won the Nobel prize for Literature in 1966. Some of his stories have been collected in *Twenty-One Stories* (1970). *The Bridal Canopy* (1930), his first major work, is an account of the travels and travails of a poor, pious father in quest of dowries for his three daughters. His other fiction includes *Agunot* (1909), *A Guest for the Night* (1937), and *Only Yesterday* (1945).

Max Apple (b. 1941) is Professor of English at Rice University. His fiction includes *The Oranging of America and Other Stories* (1976), *Zip: A Novel of the Left and the Right* (1978), and *Free Agents* (1984).

The stories of **Harold Brodkey** (b. 1930) have appeared regularly over the years in *The New Yorker*. They have recently been collected in *Stories in an Almost Classical Mode* (1988). He is also the author of *First Love and Other Sorrows* (1957) and *Women and Angels* (1985). His story "Verona: A Young Woman Speaks" also touches on the theme of fathers and daughters who are traveling in Italy.

Raymond Carver (1938–1988) is the author of several short-story collections, including *Put Yourself in My Shoes* (1974), *Will You Please Be Quiet, Please?* (1976), *The Furious Seasons* (1977), *What We Talk About When We Talk About Love* (1981), *Cathedral* (1983), and *Where I'm Calling From: New and Selected Stories* (1988). *Fires* (1983) is a collection of his stories, essays, and poems. He also wrote seven volumes of poetry, including *A New Path to the Waterfall* (1989), which appeared posthumously. He published another version of "Distance" under the title "Everything Stuck to Him."

Joyce Cary (1888–1957), English novelist and writer of short stories, settled in Oxford after working for six years in the Nigerian colonial administration. *Mister Johnson* (1939) is the most celebrated of his African novels. He also wrote *A Fearful Joy* (1949); and two trilogies, one of them comprised of *Herself Surprised* (1941), *To Be a Pilgrim* (1942), and *The Horse's Mouth* (1944); and the other comprised of *Prisoner at Grace* (1952), *Except the Lord* (1953), and *Not Honor More* (1955).

The stories of **Andre Dubus** (b. 1936) are collected in *Adultery* (1977); *The Last Worthless Evening: Four Novellas and Two Stories* (1986); and *Finding a Girl in America* (1981). His novels include *Separate Flights* (1975) and *Voices From the Moon* (1984). Dubus is a recent winner of a five-year MacArthur Fellowship. His story "Bless Me, Father" is about a philandering father and his daughter. It appears in

The Times Are Never So Bad: A Novella and Eight Short Stories (1983).

F. Scott Fitzgerald (1896–1940) is best-known for his novels of the twenties and thirties, including *This Side of Paradise* (1920), *The Beautiful and the Damned* (1922), *The Great Gatsby* (1925), and *Tender Is the Night* (1934). His short stories have been brought together in numerous collections. Besides "The Baby Party," Fitzgerald wrote two other stories about fathers of daughters, "Outside the Cabinet Maker's" and "Babylon Revisited." Together with his letters to his daughter, Frances, these stories form a sort of coherent treatise on aspects of the life of a father of a daughter.

The stories of **E. M. Forster** (1879–1970) are gathered in *The Collected Short Stories of E. M. Forster.* He is best-known for his novels, including *A Passage to India* (1924), *Howard's End* (1910), *A Room With a View* (1908), and for a book of literary criticism, *Aspects of the Novel* (1927).

The stories of **Mavis Gallant** (b. 1922), Canadian writer and expatriate, have been collected in *The Other Paris* (1956), *The Pegnitz Junction* (1973), *The End of the World and Other Stories* (1974), *Home Truths* (1981), *Overhead in a Balloon* (1985), and *In Transit* (1988).

Herbert Gold (b. 1924) has published several collections of his stories, including *Love and Like* (1960), *The Magic Will* (1971), *Stories of Misbegotten Love* (1985), and *Lovers and Cohorts* (1986). His novels include *Fathers* (1967) and *He/ She* (1980). His story "Love and Like" takes still another look at fathers of daughters.

The two stories in this collection by **Stephen Minot** (b. 1927) are from *Crossings* (1975). He has also written *Chill of Dusk* (1964), *Ghost Images* (1979), and *Surviving the Flood* (1981). His stories have appeared in *Atlantic Monthly, Harper's, Kenyon Review, Paris Review, Antaeus, North American*

Review, and other literary quarterlies and several have been selected for O. Henry Awards.

R. K. Narayan (b. 1907), Indian writer of short stories, novels, travel literature, and memoirs, is the author of more than two dozen books, including *Malgudi Days* (1943), *Mysore* (1944), *The Printer of Malgudi* (1949), *My Dateless Diary* (1960), *The Painter of Signs* (1976), and *Under the Banyan Tree and Other Stories* (1985).

Joyce Carol Oates (b. 1938) is the prolific author of novels, stories, plays, poems, and essays. Among her numerous collections of short stories are *The Wheel of Love* (1970), *Marriages and Infidelities* (1972), *Where Have You Been* (1974), *All the Good People I've Left Behind* (1979); and *The Assignation* (1988). Her recent novels include *Bellefleur* (1980), *A Bloodsmoor Romance* (1982), *Mysteries of Winterhurn* (1984) and *Raven's Wing* (1986). Her novel *Them* (1970) won the National Book Award.

John O'Hara (1905–1970) published scores of his short stories in *The New Yorker*. They were collected in several volumes, including *The Doctor's Son* (1935), *Pipe Night* (1945), *Hellbox* (1947), *Sermons and Soda Water* (1960) and *The Cape Code Lighter* (1962). His novels include *Appointment in Samarra* (1934), *Butterfield 8* (1935), *A Rage to Live* (1949), *From the Terrace* (1958), and *Elizabeth Appleton* (1963). His story "The Lesson" also recounts an aspect of the relationship between a father and his adult daughter.

Budd Schulberg (b. 1914) is perhaps best-known as the author of the screenplay for the Academy Award-winning film *On the Waterfront* (1954). He also collaborated with F. Scott Fitzgerald on the screenplay of *Winter Carnival* (1939). He began his career as a novelist with the publication of *What Makes Sammy Run?* and has gone on to publish a number of other books, including *The Harder They Fall*

(1947), *The Disenchanted* (1950), and a volume of short stories, *Some Faces in the Crowd* (1953).

Scottish-born **Muriel Spark** (b. 1918) is the author of several novels, including *The Prime of Miss Jean Brodie* (1961) and *The Mandelbaum Gate* (1965); several volumes of poetry; and edited volumes of the letters of Mary Shelley, the Brontës, and John Henry Newman. Her short stories are collected in *The Stories of Muriel Spark* (1986).

Peter Taylor (b. 1919), who teaches at the University of Virginia, has published seven collections of short stories, including *The Collected Stories of Peter Taylor* (1969) and *The Old Forest and Other Stories* (1985). His novel *A Summons to Memphis* (1986) was awarded the Pulitzer prize. Another of his stories, "The Wall," is a twist on Hawthorne's "Rappacini's Daughter," the template for much fiction about fathers and daughters. "Je Suis Perdu" was originally published under the title "A Pair of Bright Blue Eyes."

William Trevor (b. 1928), an Irishman, has written novels, plays, and several volumes of short stories, many of which are collected in *The Stories of William Trevor* (1983). Since that collection was published, he has written *A Writer's Ireland: Landscape in Literature* (1984), *The News From Ireland and Other Stories* (1986), and *Nights at the Alexandra* (1987).

The stories, poems, and essays of **John Updike** (b. 1932) have found their usual home in *The New Yorker*. His collections of short stories include, among others, *The Music School* (1966), *Museums and Women and Other Stories* (1972), and *Trust Me* (1986). He is the author of eleven novels, including *Rabbit, Run* (1960), *Couples* (1968), *A Month of Sundays* (1975), *Marry Me* (1976), *The Coup* (1978), and *Roger's Version* (1986); five volumes of verse; and *Hugging the*

Shore: Essays and Criticism (1983). Updike takes up the theme of fathers and daughters in his stories "Nevada," "Daughter, Last Glimpse Of," and "The Lovely Troubled Daughters of Our Old Crowd."

The stories of **Larry Woiwode** (b. 1941) have appeared in *The New Yorker* and literary quarterlies. He has written the novels *What I'm to Do, I Think* (1969), *Beyond the Bedroom Wall* (1975), and *Poppa John* (1981), and a volume of poetry, *Even Tide* (1977).

◇ ◇ ◇

Plume

GREAT MODERN CLASSICS

(0452)

☐ **CRAMPTON HODNET by Barbara Pym.** This wryly elegant comedy of manners is a journey into quintessential Pym country. Written during the novelist's years at Oxford, *Crampton Hodnet* is a wickedly funny farce starring her famous clergymen, excellent women, dotty dons, ingenuous students, assorted academic hangers-on—and a hilariously romantic plot revolving around a pair of eminently unsuitable attachments. . . .   (264928—$8.95)*

☐ **THE WATERFALL by Margaret Drabble.** Jane Grey believed in abandoning herself to fate. Even if she were falling in love with the wrong man. First her husband left her, just as she was about to give birth to their second child. Then she met James. James was reckless, unsuccessful . . . and married. Jane had two choices. She could rationalize. Or she could face the truth. . . .   (261929—$9.95)

☐ **THREE NIGHTS IN THE HEART OF THE EARTH by Brett Laidlaw.** Bryce Fraser is the precocious younger son of a college professor/poet and his wife. He is about to experience three days in his family's history that will transform his world and theirs. As in Arthur Miller's *Death of a Salesman,* the characters in the Fraser family are both ordinary and heroic . . . and headed toward tragedy. This powerful and moving, exquisitely written family novel reveals an extraordinary fictional talent. "Admirable . . . narrative that achieves considerable intensity and grace." —*The New York Times Book Review*   (262208—$7.95)

☐ **MONTGOMERY'S CHILDREN by Richard Perry.** "Perry shares Toni Morrison's gifts for psychological as well as pathological insights. The male bonding between Gerald and Iceman is reminiscent of Milkman and Guitar's in *Song of Solomon.* Perry's gift makes him a writer to be savored and watched."—*The Village Voice*   (256747—$7.95)

*Prices slightly higher in Canada.

Buy them at your local bookstore or use this convenient coupon for ordering.

NEW AMERICAN LIBRARY
P.O. Box 999, Bergenfield, New Jersey 07621

Please send me the books I have checked above. I am enclosing $_____ (please add $1.50 to this order to cover postage and handling). Send check or money order—no cash or C.O.D.'s. Prices and numbers are subject to change without notice.

Name _____

Address _____

City _____ State _____ Zip Code _____

Allow 4-6 weeks for delivery.
This offer is subject to withdrawal without notice.

Plume

THE FINEST IN SHORT FICTION